THE
MOONCALF
MURDERS

THE
MOONCALF
MURDERS

Noël Vreeland Carter

WALKER AND COMPANY
New York

First published in the United States of America in 1989 by Walker Publishing Company, Inc.

Published simultaneously in Canada by Thomas Allen & Son Canada, Limited, Markham, Ontario

Library of Congress Cataloging-in-Publication Data
Carter, Noël Vreeland.
The mooncalf murders / Noël Vreeland Carter.
p.   cm.
ISBN 0-8027-5744-8
I. Title.
PS3553.A7827M66   1989
813'.54—dc20   89-14636
CIP

Printed in the United States of America

2   4   6   8   10   9   7   5   3   1

This book is in memory of my aunt, Ann Claire Vreeland Sims, who, by the gift of thirteen pages of typescript, has set me on a quest through time that may never end and taught me that "there is history in all men's lives,"
and for
Deborah S. Kogan, the value of whose friendship and encouragement is beyond measure. "All shall be well."

Moon-calf. (Cf. G. *Mondkalb* (Luther); also *mondkind,* MLG. *mannenkind (kind* = child). +1. An abortive shapeless fleshy mass in the womb; a false conception. *Obs.* Regarded as being produced by the influence of the moon.

. . . 1658 tr. *Porta's Nat. Magic* 11.ii.29 A certain woman . . . brought forth instead of a child, four creatures like to frogs . . . But this was a kind of a Moon-calf.

b. A misshapen birth, a monstrosity. *Obs.* or *arch.* 1610 SHAKS. *Temp.* 11.ii. 139 How now Moone-Calfe.

Oxford English Dictionary

$\triangledown$

1

ENTER CALIBAN

THERE is no light like the light on a clear, clean, crisp October day and no smell like the smell of earth and dry leaves baked by a low, yellow sun on such a day. It is a gift of the gods and it is to be savored.

Molly Brown felt it too. She took a joyous leap of freedom as I loosened her leash, and made a dash for the underbrush. I gave a contented sigh and flopped down into several inches of leaves that had blown into a thick carpet on a tiny grassy patch above the path. All I wanted to do was relax and contemplate the beauty of early-morning light sparkling on the Hudson.

Across the river, if I ignored the ugliness of the GM plant at Tarrytown to the south and the darker implications of the low, high-walled red brick compound to the north at Ossining, I could contemplate the ineffably beautiful patchwork of color that nature was painting across the western edge of Westchester. How good it felt to be alive that morning, to be full of enthusiasm for the new book on which I was working—my third and my most important—and to be lying on the grass, smelling dry earth, leaves, and the sparkling, slightly salt-sour pungence of the river.

A sound intruded: the light scrape of a measured footfall upon the packed cinders of the path. I opened one eye just in time to see a tall, slender black man, elderly, by the amount of grizzled hair showing under the brim of his hat, disappear around the bend in the track. I lay back down and let my mind drift where it would.

Some time later, with Molly Brown sniffing my closed eyes interestedly and clawing at my arm with one not-so-gentle paw, I woke up, amazed that I had actually fallen asleep. I looked at my watch. I had dozed for nearly half an hour.

It was then I heard the black man coming back around the bend in the path. I watched with interest as he approached. He was dressed strangely for Nyack in early autumn, in a grim black suit and heavy black overcoat that hung open. He must have been warm, for it was an exceedingly mild morning and gave promise of being a hot afternoon. He wore a clean, starched white shirt that had begun to look yellow around the collar and a wide maroon tie that no amount of cleaning could have rid of the greasy look around the knot. There was a small gold pin in his lapel. He had an air of refinement about him that made the indignity of yellowed collars and foxed shoes rather poignant.

As he passed, I caught his eye and smiled.

"Ma'am," he acknowledged me with a start, as if I had pulled him out of a reverie. He lifted his hat slightly, which was polite enough, but walked on with a quickened step.

He had been nearly a dozen feet away when he passed by, but even at that distance, the fear in his eyes was unmistakable. It was a fear tinged with deep sadness and something else less definable—a sort of sick-at-heart perplexity, perhaps. That was a great deal to read into one human face in a matter of seconds, yet I saw it all at a glance. After he had passed, I scrambled to my feet and brushed leaves off my fanny. "Come on! Home and breakfast, Molly."

We passed the black man at the top of the road leading from the parking lot onto North Broadway in Upper Nyack. He evidently had no car and it was a long hike to town, if that was where he was going, but I decided not to slow down and offer him a lift. I didn't think he'd take it in the first place, and somehow I didn't want my impression of him spoiled by closer association.

That had been on the first Tuesday in October. We didn't go

back to the path at the foot of Hook Mountain until Friday afternoon because the rain that had started Tuesday night stayed until early Friday morning. By afternoon, the sky was still steel gray, but the rain had blown past Rockland County and could be seen in sheets of mist and blown spume on the far bank of the river in Westchester.

The wind and rain of the previous three days had washed every tree of dust, so that the leaves gleamed like polished gold and copper. Some looked as if they had been daubed with fresh blood. Bittersweet vines along the trail hung in looped masses of orange and scarlet berries, their leaves lime green and looking more like spring than autumn. Everything dripped and glowed luminously against the brightening gray sky and I could not help but think what a feast it all was for the eyes and for the healing soul. The past few months since I had left Max had certainly been balm for my healing soul, I reflected. Now I hardly thought of him at all except when he phoned to annoy me.

Yes, life was beginning to be sweet again. The air smelled of wet rich earth, a pair of mallards rode the lapping swells of the river, gossiping idly, a few gulls wheeled against the sky, and there was a royalty check newly deposited in my bank to insure against a bleak Christmas and a cold New Year. What more could I want than that, except possibly an unlikely week or two on the bestseller list for my current work-in-progress, a biography of Charlotte Hungerford, the minor Regency novelist who had been a contemporary of Jane Austen.

Molly and I came to our usual turn-around spot: a picnic table under a tree where I relaxed while Molly continued her rummaging where she would. The rain had packed the bare earth all around and under the table, washing loose pebbles of dust and exposing each grain of gravel and shard of broken glass in perfect outline. Amongst all this detritus were scattered three pennies and a safety pin, each of which I carefully picked up and pocketed. Quite a haul, I smiled as I climbed up onto the wet picnic table and sat

cross-legged, looking south toward the Tappan Zee. The bridge
was vaguely outlined in mist.

I hadn't found a coin or a pin or anything at all in over a week,
so three cents in one shot was going far to make up—and another
reason to be glad Max wasn't here. He hated my little habit of
finding things, though I don't suppose he'd have minded my
finding a diamond solitaire or a wallet full of hundred-dollar bills.
It was the pennies, dimes, and pins that got to him. Max had no
sense of humor or eye for the ridiculous, which was one of the
reasons our marriage was over. One needs to laugh, after all.

Now, M. Brown Doggish was far better at finding things than
I. If my specialty was small change, pins, and broken jewelry
interspersed with the occasional wadded-up dollar bill, she dabbled
in small dead birds and mice. Once she had even taken a quick,
sybaritic roll on the putrid remains of a raccoon. For days after that
adventure, despite a bath in Pine-Sol, she had been socially acceptable only when we kept upwind of her. Like Polonius, she could
be nosed in the closet.

Now something told me she was at it again. She had stopped
questing after rodents and persistently scratched at something she
had found under an overhang of rock about ten or fifteen feet up a
steep incline above the path. She was still scratching at whatever it
was she found as I scrambled up the slope toward her.

"You wicked little mutt," I yelled as I reached her. I hauled her
bodily off her prize and looked. She squatted beside me, her tail
wagging in the wet leaves, quite pleased with herself and eager to
show me her find.

At first I saw only a sodden grocery bag with the words "Met
Foods" printed on the crumpled side in a large blue semicircle. The
rain had turned it to a pulpy mass that Molly had been able to claw
open easily, rending the bag into two ragged pieces and exposing
thereby a second, slightly less sodden bag within. She had had to
work harder on the inner bag and it had torn less easily, leaving
stiff, fibrous edges that resembled nothing so much as a deep gash

across human flesh. It was an unpleasant simile as it occurred to me but then it was nothing to the unpleasant reality yet to come.

Only slowly did I make out the dark, ugly mass inside the bundle, and even then it took a few seconds to recognize it for the placenta that it was, a large, dark, ring-shaped mass of membrane.

Molly made a move to investigate. Pushing her back behind me, I squatted down and looked again at the bundle. It had been wedged in against the base of an outcropping of red shale, where, while being protected from the recent rain, it had been in the direct path of a rivulet of runoff, the natural drainage of which led it around the base of the rocks from above. Eons of such runoff were probably responsible for undermining the rocks in the first place and for the formation of the cavity into which the thing had been pushed.

I reached around me and groped in the sopping underbrush on the slope to my right until I found a small, sturdy stick with which to probe. I was far too curious not to investigate further. After all, how often, I remember thinking at the time, does one find a grocery bag full of afterbirth? What I found as I turned back the ragged edges of the bag and pushed aside the placenta, was too sobering for further levity.

I supposed at first that it was the head of an animal—some large unborn thing like a calf or even a deer. Something in the dry, shiny look of the brownish skin reminded me unpleasantly of veal that had been left in the air too long. The eyes were bulbous and starting from the sockets, obviously open, though a red-gray film had covered the pupils, taking all semblance of life from them. The jaws were long and misshapen, by which I mean that they were asymmetrical, the one side to the other. The nose was a flat, splayed mass with oddly shaped holes rather than chiseled nostrils, and it was placed far too low on the facial structure, too close to the long, curving, lipless slit of the mouth to be even remotely normal. The ears were well up and back on the long skull and the forehead was flat like a horse's rather than bulbous like that of a human or a monkey.

At first, all I saw was the head, dark and vealy and awfully large—perhaps six inches from jaw to the top of the skull. Squatting over it with my stick poised like some Aborigine digging for roots, I frowned and began to ruminate on what the devil it could be. It wasn't a dog's head, which I'd have been apt to recognize readily, nor, I thought, that of a calf or a pony. A goat, I speculated briefly, and then finally gave up. After all, it was too unformed to have been born yet, and since it was in company with a placenta, I could only suppose that it had been removed from the mother before its time. That raised quite another question: What sort of mother was it that carried anything with a head like this?

Then, I turned the thing over. There was more to it than just that hideous skull and vealy hide. The thing had a body: tiny, malformed, and slighty bloated looking, like an old rubber doll, with smooth, nakedly glossy, almost translucent skin of a darkish, café au lait color. It was tiny by comparison to the head, which was why I had not seen it at first, with gangly, oddly bent legs and arms at the ends of which were crudely molded little hands and feet that would have been recognizably human if it were not for the dainty, perfect blackish little claws that took the place of nails.

I sat back on my hunkers, feeling slightly queasy. Whatever the head might appear to be, the body was, for all its deformity, a human one. I didn't like to think of what it would have looked like had it lived to term; still less the thought of it toddling off to kindergarten.

The Moll, attracted by the ghastly odor, was beginning to be too persistent in her attempts to get back at her find. I pulled her leash out of my jacket pocket and attached it to her collar. Scrambling to my knees, I dragged her away, stretched my cramped muscles, and pulled her down the slope toward the path, where I tethered her to a tree. She yelped and whimpered as I left her and scrambled back up the incline toward the outcropping. I stood there lost in contemplation, my eyes fixed on the distant bank of the Hudson. It had stopped raining and the late afternoon sun was peeping cheerfully through sheets of silver mist.

I began to think of the old black man I had seen on Tuesday. He had been dressed in somber black, like an undertaker, but it occurred to me that he might just as well have been a doctor. That gold pin in his lapel might as easily have been the insignia of a medical fraternity as of the Masons or Shriners. And then there was the look of fear in his eyes. It would seem that there had been damned good reason for that look. I'd be afraid too, if I'd just delivered a monster into this breathing world, scarce half made-up.

So, he most likely was a doctor—and an abortionist. I frowned at the thought even as it occurred to me. After all, it wasn't illegal any more and damned well should never have been so in the first place. No woman should ever have been denied the right of her own body and its uses as if she were a brood mare or a cow, but that was another issue. The question I could not help but ask myself as I stood gazing blindly out over the river was why, since abortion isn't illegal, had he got rid of this—this thing in such a manner? Could he have thought it would go undetected? Granted, he could hardly have anticipated Molly Brown and her questing nose, but surely he must have realized that it would be found eventually?

"Eventually" was probably the operative word. It was October already and the park was far less used by this time of year. In another month or so the snow would begin to fly. He must have figured that by spring there would be little or nothing left to be found but bones, and if anyone chanced to find them, they'd probably assume that they belonged to some animal or other. On the whole, the old man hadn't chosen a bad spot. His luck just ran out when he invaded M. Brown's bailiwick.

I took a deep breath, steeled myself for one last look, and dropped onto my knees, probing carefully at the head with the stick. What I saw confirmed a sudden suspicion that had formed in my mind as I had asked myself why the old man had left the thing here in the first place. I also ended for good and all any debate I had entertained on whether or not I should inform the police.

The umbilical cord, which was still attached to the placenta at one end and the creature's belly at the other, had been wrapped twice around the neck, which of course might have occurred naturally during the thing's time in the womb. Babies can be born strangled by their own umbilicals, after all, but in this case I thought not. The cord had been pulled so tight that it had been stretched wire-thin and was quite taut for several inches to either side of the neck. Closer to both the belly and the placenta itself, the cord was still thick and rubbery and pliable to the probing end of my stick.

I backed out from under the outcropping and stood up, painfully, thoughtfully, and gasping for the breath that I had held so long. I was suddenly quite somber of mood. Whatever it was—whoever it might have become—there was no doubt in my mind that it had been deliberately murdered.

I slid down the incline, untethered Molly, and walked back to the car. In another ten minutes I had stuck a quarter in the meter in front of Nyack Village Hall and was standing at the Plexiglas-enclosed counter in the nook given over to the uses of the police department, trying to explain to a smirking policeman that it was a human baby and not someone's pet monkey lying in that Met Foods bag up the river in Nyack Beach State Park.

∇

2

PROCEDURAL

"For Chrissake, what'd you have to tell anyone for? That goddamn mutt—always in the garbage or something. Do you remember that day at Rockl—?"

"I remember. I remember. How could I forget? You have just never understood the nature of the puppy dog. Their noses . . ." I broke off. It was no use trying to explain. I rolled over on the bed and flicked open the curtains. It was sunny and glorious out and I had slept far too late, even if I had been up half the night with police, the deputy medical examiner, reporters, and my landlady, telling everything over and over again, first for posterity and then for catharsis.

"She stank for a week." Max's voice, sour and annoyed as ever, came across the wire like the small angry buzz of a fly caught between a window and a screen. "For shit's sake," he went on elegantly, "your name's in the paper. The *Post* and the *News*. How the hell do you think I like seeing that over my morning coffee? Everyone in that office Monday'll—"

That was Max. It was always what someone had done to him. My find, my reporting it, my name in the paper was all a plot against him. How such an experience might have affected me, how I felt, mattered not at all. It was all the world doing a job on poor egocentric little Max.

"*My* name, remember, dear," I broke in sweetly. "Miranda. Miranda Fay. Not Mrs. Max Lindquist, but my very own name— the one I was born with. Besides, Monday's Columbus Day. All this will have blown over by Tuesday when you go back, so quit bitching. What about the *Times?* I suppose it only rated a sentence in the second section."

"I don't know. I didn't get it."

"Did they at least mention that I'm a biographer?"

"The *News* did." He sounded sulky.

"Great! Good ole *News,* but screw the *Post.* It's bad enough to have my name in Murdoch's rag at all, but at least they could give me a little publicity out of it. Since they've become the sleazemerchants of the local tabloids, they must lie awake nights praying for lurid stuff like this. What's the headline?"

Max sounded strangled and distant, as if he spoke both unwillingly and away from the phone. " 'Thing Found Dead in River' in caps."

"How accurate," I broke in, "and how typical of the quality of their reporting."

"Below, in smaller caps, 'Is It Human? Search for mother— Story page three.' " He paused and I heard the rustle of paper. "There's a picture of the sign at the entrance to the state park. None of you, thank God."

"Amen to that," I agreed cheerfully. "I'm delighted to be so obscure a writer that they can't even pull an old photo out of their files. Saves husbands, both ex and not-so-ex, just heaps of embarrassment." There was silence on the other end of the phone, a silence that I didn't know any more how to fill. He hated my breezy humor. "Sorry you disapprove," I said at last, feeling suddenly deflated and itching to end the conversation.

"For someone who's supposed to be so goddamn smart, you sure can be stupid."

"It was the only moral thing to do. I couldn't just walk away. Look, Max, thanks for calling. I'm okay, really, and I have a lot to do today. I want to get up to town and pick up the papers myself."

"You writing?" he challenged.

"Yes, I am, and loving it. But, really, I've gotta go, okay?"

"Yeah, so long."

"Bye-bye." I hung up with a sigh. That was the man I had married, happily believing us to be a pair and a great match. Instead we were two strangers growling between the silences. How bloody, bloody sad.

There was really no time to be reflective, however. I took one last glance at the bright morning light coming through my newly run-up white lace curtains and bounced out of bed. I dressed, fed Moll her breakfast and put on the kettle for my tea. I set the table in my usual careful morning ritual, setting my treasured early Wedgewood stoneware teapot on my Jubilee teapot stand—known with great affection as "the world's ugliest teapot stand," since it sports a glum-looking Queen Victoria dressed in all the jewels and jowls she had accrued over the first sixty years of her reign. I dropped in a generous scoop of Constant Comment and toyed with the idea of eggs and toast as opposed to toast and jelly.

Coddled eggs won the day. As I buttered the coddler, I began to plot further the course I had decided on before Max's call. I was a writer and working on a book, but my latest royalties and Max's grudging checks—which I hated to accept—were not going to keep me in tea and dog food forever. It had occurred to me that I might be able to establish a small side income with some occasional newspaper articles, and now, finding myself involved in a lurid little murder, I had revived that thought. The water began to boil, the phone rang, and there came a rapping at my chamber door. It was one of those mornings.

I took the kettle off, got rid of the *Journal-News* man on the phone with a cheery "No comment," and scampered across the room to open the door before Molly clawed her way through it. The subtleties of the current situation made me think of Sherlock Holmes and Baker Street. Now if only Meta's name was Mrs. Hudson instead of Mrs. Sullivan, I thought to myself as I unlocked the door. At least her Irish accent was somewhat in character and lent a touch of verisimilitude to the atmosphere. The late Victorian walnut, hunter green and burgundy of my living room and writing alcove did the rest. All I needed was a Turkey carpet and a "patriotic V.R. done in bullet pocks," though I was doubtful that Meta would view the latter with the same delight as would some of my Baker Street Irregular friends.

"Good morning, Mrs. Hudson. Do I look like Sherlock Holmes to you?" I stood aside and let my landlady pass.

"No, dear, I can't say that you do. Oh, the good Lord, I've disturbed your breakfast."

"No, you haven't," I insisted cheerfully. "The tea water's ready, I've brushed off the *Journal-News* for the second time since seven-thirty and I'm about to coddle us some eggs. Max called and he's furious, of course. It's all over the New York papers, which he takes as a personal affront. He thinks I'm a fool for opening my mouth."

"You had to, dear. Think of that poor little soul lying out in the wild. How could you have just left it there?!"

"Yes," I agreed, "and believe me, Meta, it was a poor soul; nothing that bears the light of day. Now at least it will be buried eventually, I suppose." I scooped the eggs out of the coddler and onto my toast. "Sure you won't have something?" I asked again, coming to the table with my plate.

"Nothing, luv. I ate at seven. I'll have some tea, though, and a bit of a chin-wag."

"The man from the medical examiner's office wasn't too pleased with me, you know. He'd rather I hadn't mucked the thing about with my little stick, but until I'd poked at it I didn't even know what it was, least of all that it was human and a police matter," I exclaimed, waving a forkful of dripping egg. Meta cozily poured the tea for us and slipped Molly a piece of toast from the rack between us. "It didn't take the IQ of an artichoke to see that the thing had been strangled, but the SOB waffled on that, insisting that my deduction 'might' be right, 'seemed' logical on the face of it, but that to 'assume' manual strangulation with the cord before the autopsy was 'premature.' 'Like the baby,' I suggested, and he gave me such a look, but then, amazingly, he actually cracked up. That broke the ice and he's promised to let me know what the findings are. They'll do the autopsy late this morning."

Meta gave a little shudder and sipped her tea. "Why do you want to know, luv?"

I couldn't help but smile at her delicacy. Meta was an odd, endearing combination of practical strength with an overlay of old fashioned, ladylike modesty. She had come from Belfast by way of London, where she had married a "Yank" after the war. They had bought this house, raised a small family, and been quite happy until her Jimmy had had his first heart attack. There had been three others in as many years, which had strapped finances, strained the family's nerves, and resulted in Jimmy Sullivan's death at the age of fifty-six. Now Meta herself was sixty or so, her two daughters were married and living half a continent away, her son was in Alaska doing something on an oil rig in the Beaufort Sea, and she was making ends meet by converting first the second floor and eventually the attic of her big old house into two very cheerful and pleasant apartments. I was her first tenant and the attic was soon to be renovated for a second. The last five years since her husband's death had not been easy. I had come to know her well enough in the past few months to be aware of it, just as she had been sympathetic to the rupture my impending divorce had caused in my own life.

"That's a good question," I said, after giving it some thought. "I have a hard time thinking of it as human—and if you'd seen it, you'd know what I mean—but I *am* the one who found it and I just don't think I can let go of it. The investigation is in the hands of the Bear Mountain police—the Nyack cops don't have jurisdiction over state park property, it seems—and the medical examiner's office has the body, but beyond that, who actually cares? I mean *cares* in the sense of the story behind whatever happened—who the mother is, why the thing was left like that."

"Oh, luv, babies are left in all sorts of awful places. I remember

one was found in an incinerator, and another—" Meta read the
Post.

"You are right, I suppose. This sort of thing is all too common,
but—" I broke off, unable to articulate quite what I meant. "Maybe
I'm just feeling guilty," I said at last, finishing up the last of my
egg and polishing off my orange juice at a gulp, "and that's why I
don't want to forget it."

"Guilty? Why on God's green earth should you feel guilty,
child? You've done all you could, after all."

"Not quite," I grinned sheepishly and poured another cup of
tea. I rose, pushed in my chair, and carried my cup to the couch.
Meta perched comfortably in my pillow-strewn oak throne chair
with her feet on a low stool in front of the empty fireplace.

"I know how the thing got there. I think I know when it was
put in that cavity under the rocks, and I think I can describe the
person who put it there." I paused and let the words sink in. Not
for Meta's benefit—she was, in this instance, just an admirable
sounding board—but rather for my own. I had not told the police
about the old man on the path, nor was I quite sure why I had
withheld what might be information vital to the investigation. I
think it was simply that I couldn't believe it of him—could not
believe that that sad-faced and haunted old man could have strangled a baby with its own umbilical cord. Even that baby.

"I can still rectify matters by going to the police and telling
them that I have remembered something that might be a clue.
They'll probably think I'm a crank, but they may follow through
and get somewhere with it. The other alternative is to say nothing
and let them do their professional thing without my amateur aid,
which they'd sneer at anyway."

Meta had silently sipped her tea during my ruminations. Now
she set down her cup on the nearest uncluttered surface and asked
pointedly, "You have an idea, luv, don't you?"

I frowned. "Yes, damn it, I do. It may be the writer in me, or
the romantic, or even the true-crime buff, but whatever it is, yes,
I've got an itch to put this thing on paper. I've got an appointment

with Peter Polhemus at the *Stop-Press* at eleven. When he called this morning for an interview, I told him I'd be in for a chat. I'm going to ask him to give me a byline and let me follow the case. If I'm smart, I just might parlay this little tragedy into a nice investigative series that one of the bigger newspapers will pick up for syndication. That, dear landlady mine, would mean something to stash away toward my divorce. There might even be a true-crime book in it eventually, if the case is ever solved and goes to trial and has some human interest, which I suspect it might. That whole wall of books over there," I said, waving toward a tall, narrow section of bookshelves in my writing alcove, "is all true crime and criminology. I've thought for years of writing something in that vein. I always figured I'd do a rehash of a good old case some day, but a contemporary case, and one with human interest and close personal involvement, is like being handed a subject on a silver platter." I could see Meta eyeing me with a jaundiced glint.

"What? What?" I asked. "You don't like the idea? Look at what Diana Trilling did with Mrs. Harris. That book is fascinating."

"Oh," she said quietly, "I like the idea of the book just fine and the newspapers articles as well, but you are fooling yourself if you don't see that that's why you don't tell the police all you know about this person you saw. You want to play detective yourself. Don't you think that'd be a bit foolish and rather dangerous into the bargain?"

I frowned, but she was right on all counts, and suddenly I realized it. In fact, what she said relieved me of my doubts, and I resolved to stop at the police station and tell them that I'd thought of something new. They'd get the Bear Mountain police back down by the time I'd finished my interview at the offices of the *Nyack Stop-Press* and I'd tell them all I knew of the old black man in the somber suit and heavy overcoat. My conscience would be clear and I'd still be free to play cub reporter like Roz Russell in an early forties comedy.

"Bless you, luv," I cried and leapt to my feet decisively. "I do believe you are right." I planted an airy kiss on the top of her gray-streaked red hair and went to the kitchen for Molly's leash.

"Hasn't she been out to spend a penny yet?" Meta asked as she saw Moll leaping and yelping at my feet.

"She has not. This has been a crazy morning, remember?"

"Then you get ready, luv, and I'll walk her. I've got to go post a letter anyway, and Duchess has had her time out this morning. I'll take Molly."

"What a landlady! Mrs. Hudson has nothing on you," I cried, and began to think that I just might risk the bullet pocks yet.

The *Nyack Stop-Press* is a fledgling weekly run by a retired state university journalism professor, Peter Polhemus, whose son, Pete Jr., practices law in town. I had known him, in passing, for years and had dealt with his son professionally. Pete Jr. was advising me on my legal rights in my separation from Max and would, I supposed, eventually handle my divorce, but about that there was no hurry. Being legally separated was just fine for now. It gave me time to breathe and prepare for my future.

The original *Stop-Press* had been founded by Peter Sr.'s great-grandfather before the Civil War, when politics and emanicipation issues were hot reading. The paper had not survived the Depression nor his father the end of the paper. Most locals thought that Polhemus was a sentimental fool for throwing what was left of the family money into reviving it, but Pete Jr. was well-fixed in a successful practice, his daughter had married a wealthy Westchester politician, and, if the old man wanted to dabble in the fourth estate, who had the right to say him nay? Pete Jr. had put it all in prospective quite simply: "If it keeps him off the streets, out of the whorehouses and away from old-age homes, I'm all for it. He's bound to live longer and be healthier running a newspaper in Nyack than playing golf and making ceramic planters with Red Buttons down in Florida. That way lies early senility."

The *Stop-Press* office was a small, untidy closet with an old cylinder-top desk that any antique dealer in town would have coveted, a battered swivel chair and the din of a press going in the large back room. The whole building was probably only fifty by seventy-five, if that, and was a relic of the days when Nyack had been a steamboat stop along the river. It had once been a warehouse for cargo bound to and from Albany and New York, and had been empty for years before Polhemus had leased it for the *Press*. Now it shook and throbbed with life again in a way that did my heart good. I was one of the paper's biggest fans and first subscribers and wanted badly to see it make a success, though I realized along with everyone else in town that it would most likely fold with Peter Polhemus himself, unless Peter outlasted his bank account. He looked, as he entered his tiny office from the pressroom, as if he'd live to be ninety. He was tall and spare and gray, with a friendly, rawboned face that was both uglier than his son's and more beautiful, full of warmth and character of the sort that had made Raymond Massey a star in the old days. They didn't make faces like that anymore, I reflected, as he came in and shook my hand. It was a big hand, bony and firm of grip.

"Well, which is it, Mrs. Lindquist or Mrs. Fay?" he asked genially, recalling the inevitable confusion of a woman with a professional name and a married name. Only my lawyer, who knew I was Mrs. Lindquist, and my agent, who knew I was Miranda Fay, were sure.

"Miranda to you," I returned, "but if I get what I came here for, Miranda Fay will do nicely." He motioned me to be seated, which was not easy since it involved keeping my elbows in, lest I knock over one of his great piles of debris. They hemmed us both in on all sides, threatening to collapse and bury us in an avalanche of pulp and old news clippings.

"I'd like to interview you about this find you made yesterday. I was hoping you'd be more frank with me about it than you seem to have been with the city papers and the *Journal-News*. We could use a good lead on this for next week's edition. I'm having a helluva time getting the circulation up to where I can turn biweekly, and a good lead on a lurid story is, I'm sorry to say, the kind of thing that helps."

"All the *Journal-News* has gotten out of me is a 'no comment' and a smile. I've got nothing against them, mind, but they've got the Gannett organization behind them, and all you've got is the ghost of Joris Polhemus and a few loyal subscribers. But I won't give you an interview."

Peter Polhemus started to protest, but I held up my hand and he fell silent.

"I want a byline. I want to write the article and any follow-up myself. I've gotten chummy with the deputy medical examiner assigned to the case. His name is Galveston. I don't know if he'll do the autopsy himself or if he just assists, but he's promised to call me with the results. I think he'll give me a bit more than they're likely to release to the press. For one thing, I know more than the press does already about the cause of death. It was murder. Now, knowing that, and with the aid of the deputy medical examiner, I may be able to keep a step or two ahead of other reporters. I'm also about to have another conference with the police. What I plan to tell them will most likely be kept under wraps for a while since it may bear on how the body got where it was found. They won't tell the papers more than they want the guilty parties to know, but I don't think they can stop me from writing from my own knowledge under my own byline."

Peter Polhemus scratched his long jaw thoughtfully and grinned at me. "Clever, and you've got your byline of course. Only one thing. I can't pay you a cent right now."

My spirits fell, but only slightly. I hadn't been sure he could pay me in the first place. He and his son wrote most of the paper themselves and got the rest of their copy from small syndications and local contributors for whom it was enough to see their names and words in print.

"Suppose I click and the articles are picked up for syndication?"

He grinned at my optimism, or else he had some insight that I wouldn't be going to all this trouble unless I thought I had something. "That's when we both make money, Miranda. You thinking to get a book out of this?"

"I had it in mind," I admitted. "I can't be sure, of course, until more happens. If there is a case, if it's murder, as I'm sure it is, and if there is a trial, why then, maybe I will get a book out of it. My landlady said this morning that babies are being found in incinerators and garbage cans all the time, but she didn't see this baby. It— wasn't a baby. It was a *thing*."

Peter Sr. frowned. "It was a fetus, as I understand it."

"Oh, it was a fetus, all right, but before I saw its body, I had no idea from the head that it was human. My guess is that no matter what they say to the papers after the autopsy this morning, they won't say much about just how strange that creature is. I've got an eerie feeling about it, you know. I'd dearly like to see the mother that carried that thing. I'll bet she's thanking her lucky stars she doesn't have to carry it to term. I got the man from the medical examiner's office to estimate how far along it had been. He thinks about five months or a little more."

"Do you think it's a case of drug addiction? Drugs can produce some pretty terrible deformities."

"I honestly don't know, Mr. Polhemus."

"How do I rate a 'Mr.' and my son, 'Pete'? You make me feel as old as I look and til now I'd thought I'd avoided that. Please call me Peter."

"I'd rather call you boss." I smiled at him like a wily child. "Peter."

"Call me that, too. Handshake enough? Your deadline's Sunday night for the Tuesday edition. I'll leave the length to you. Just don't write a book." He rose and so did I. We shook hands on our little deal and I turned toward the door.

"I've got to get up to Pomona to the Health Complex for the autopsy press conference in about an hour. Want to come?"

I would have loved to drive up with him, but I knew I had to get my secret off my chest to the police first. "I can't, Peter, but will you call me with the official word? Then I can be prepared to pump my friend for the unofficial word. It'll help to be able to read between the lines."

"Yes, ma'am," he returned.

We smiled at each other like two happy conspirators and I turned to leave. On the doorstep outside the *Stop-Press* building I picked up a dime. It was old and tarnished and apparently had been wedged into a split in the wooden steps for ages. I was torn between looking upon the finding of it as a tribute to my sharp eyes or as an omen of luck to come. Maybe it was a bit of both.

I pressed on to the village hall, stopping at the deli only long enough to buy a copy of every paper lying on the wire rack in front of the refrigerated counter. It was nearly a quarter of an hour before the Bear Mountain police arrived, so I had plenty of time to glance at the sketchy but sensational treatment the city papers had given to the story. The *Journal-News* covered the find in greater detail, with restraint and reasonable accuracy. Clearly they didn't know much about what sells papers. I'd be damned if I'd enlighten them.

There were two things in the mailbox when I got back home that afternoon: a dunning notice from the History Book Club and a fat, unstamped business envelope with "Miranda" scrawled across it in a huge round hand.

Molly greeted me at the door in a fit of thumping tails and squeezed-up eyes that denoted mischief had been afoot. She had spent the afternoon stripping the sweaty linings from my old deck shoes and now grimaced at me with bits of foam rubber still caught between her teeth.

I swatted her lightly, picked up the shoes, and threw them, along with the book club bill, into the kitchen wastebasket, after which I returned to the living room to see what was in the envelope.

It contained a brief note from Peter Polhemus, a press card with my name on it, and a copy of the medical examiner's statement on the preliminary autopsy report, along with a page of his own notes on the press conference, which, he indicated, had been brief. It had also been unenlightening.

The statement informed the reader that the body in question was the fetus of a male child in approximately its fifth month, that it was severely deformed, and appeared to have either been born prematurely or aborted alive. It had died of asphyxia accomplished by ligature and the asphyxial agent had been the fetus's own umbilical cord—and that was that!

On a separate sheet, Peter Sr. had copied out a statement by the Bear Mountain police chief to the effect that an investigation was being made at area hospitals, abortion clinics, and so on in hopes of finding the mother.

All very predictable. I threw the papers on the coffee table, made us each a quick dinner, took the Moll for her evening walk, and came back to the typewriter to bang out my article on the finding of the body and the sparse results of the autopsy report. I was finding out to my chagrin that there wasn't much I could say when the phone rang.

Dr. Guy Galveston was a deputy medical examiner of the county and it was he who had made the in situ examination of the body late on Friday afternoon. He was in his late thirties and seemed to me a trifle on the defensive about his position in the official pecking order at the M. E.'s office. I'd picked up on that rather quickly and set about buttering him up in what I hoped was subtle fashion. It had worked. Now, with his phone call, I'd hit a jackpot in the form of the story behind the autopsy report.

"It has to be one of the most deformed bodies that I've ever had on the table." His tone had me envisioning the solemn shake of the head that must accompany the remark. He sounded older than his years and frowningly thoughtful.

"What could possibly cause such monstrous deformity? Drugs?"

"Drugs?" he mused. "Yes, I suppose so. I haven't got the tox reports yet, but I'd venture to guess the mother's an addict. Some of the deformities are definitely genetic, however, as opposed to being mutations. Would you like a rundown? Might sound good in that article you say you're writing, and I wouldn't be telling tales out of school since it'll all go on record at the inquest."

"Would I? I'm all set, but slowly, please. I don't take shorthand."

"Some reporter," he teased, and I could imagine the boyish grin on his ruddy, freckled face. "Here goes," and he began to itemize the various deformities for me, explaining them in layman's terms with the utmost patience.

"The formation of the nail plates—they are thickened and curved into that clawlike conformation you noticed as a result of abnormal keratinization." He paused to spell the word for me. "I must stress that not only is the process pathological but also extremely precocious. The nails should not yet be to the tips of the fingers at five months, let alone have begun to curve over them in that way. As I say, the condition is pathological."

"Is it common?" I asked, though I hardly thought it could be.

"On the contrary. Most uncommon—in such an extreme form, at least." He paused and I could hear the rattling of the pages of his report come crisply over the wire. In the living room, my mantel clock gave a single warning click followed by a melodious declaration that it was seven o'clock.

"Mrs. Fay," he began, but I cut him off before he could say another word.

"Please, call me Miranda. Mrs. Fay was my mother and I am in no mood to be called Mrs. Lindquist right now."

I heard what I took to be a cynical snort come through the receiver. "Divorced?"

"No, but close. I'm separated."

"You're not the only one." He sounded suddenly gloomy and on the verge of being sorry for himself. A bad sign. When I felt like that, I usually hid from people, so I wouldn't inflict myself on them.

"You too, I gather?"

"Nearly a year and I'm still not used to it. The whole world's divorced or separated it seems." Glummer and glummer.

"Well, cheer up. Better days ahead and what better distraction than a good murder, eh?" My own pain was too close to the surface to bear thinking about. It was better to avoid it.

"Murder," he echoed. "It *was* a murder, of course, and not just simply an abortion. That, I think, is what has me spinning over this case, Miranda. Why the hell was it necessary to kill it? By rights it shouldn't have been alive to begin with. The abortion process alone should have done the trick—I think a saline solution was used—but there's no doubt that this thing was born alive and went on breathing air on its own for some time after. Someone actually had to strangle it."

He paused again and then went on in a different, less agitated tone, as if he was assessing the import of his own words as he said them.

"Can you picture that thing, small and massive of head, lying on its back, say, or it side, wet and slick from the birthing, still breathing, struggling in spite of all odds, to stay alive, and then someone wrapping the umbilical cord around that tiny throat—"

"Of course I can picture it. I saw the cord. I knew before the police or you ever saw it that it had been strangled. It isn't very pleasant to contemplate, but in fairness, would you have wanted that thing alive?"

"Hell no, but please, listen to this scenario. Imagine the cord tightening around the throat and that little thing writhing and kicking and raking the hands of its killer with those tiny, mal-formed claws, digging into the wrists and lower arms with its deformed little feet and hands like a wild kitten or a ferret, leaving long, fine gashes in its murderer's flesh—gashes by which that murderer may yet be identified and brought to justice."

I had read enough criminology to understand the import of what he was telling me. I pulled my pad closer to me and began to scribble furiously.

"Now listen," he said earnestly, "it's my hide in this cockama-mie office if you write too much. 'Unspecified physical evidence from an unnamed source,' remember, but the particulars are strictly off the record or it's my ass, and since my wife's already got one cheek of it in a sling already . . . You hear me?"

"Guy, I hear and obey. I'll keep it circumspect, I promise. These are just a few newspaper articles I'm writing—I'm saving up for my divorce—but one day I may find I've got enough for a book, so please, every bit of info you can provide."

"Saving up for a divorce? Why should it cost you? It's the guy who pays through the nose."

I snickered. "Maybe in your neck of the woods, perhaps, but chivalry died just before Max Lindquist was born, I think. He doesn't want the separation. He keeps calling up and telling me that being unhappy together is no excuse for a divorce and that I'm weak for not being able to stand a little heartache. After all, what's five years of gloom and brooding and fighting in a lifetime. Anyway, I've decided I'd rather be a scared and struggling middle-aged divorcée than go through the rest of my life in the *Inferno* with Max."

"Are you scared?" His voice had lost the humorous edge.

I almost didn't answer. "Hell, yes, but I whistle a lot of happy tunes and I find I'm more scared of being trapped in a miserable marriage than I am of being alone or financially insecure. I'll walk out before I'm carried out, thank you. Now, please, no more on this subject. I prefer the cheery details of an autopsy report to a postmortem on Max and me."

"I understand. Getting back to what I'm about to tell you"—he cleared his throat in a small grating sound that came over the wire like a thin cough—"the physical evidence is this: I was able to take samples of skin tissue from under those claws. From the thickness of the hyaline layer in the samples, I can be reasonably sure that the cells come from the backs of the hands and perhaps the forearms as well, of a person either in late middle age or perhaps even elderly. The cells do not have the elasticity one finds in youthful skin. You can see, I think, how the picture of the struggle forms when given that information?"

"I certainly can. It's remarkable what can be told from so little. Is it black skin—?" I was thinking of the old man on the path.

"I can't be sure. The melanocytes in the tissue were not present in great enough quantities to indicate the degree of melanin production going on. The blood type is A Rh + and constitutes proof that there was a third party in the room with the mother and child."

"How do you figure that?"

"The blood type of the fetus is O +. The presence of blood group antigen FY (a − b −) indicates that it was black."

"Black. I thought so. The skin color—"

"Slow down, Miranda. You can't go by the pigmentation of a five-month fetus, and especially one that's been lying out for several days. The asphyxiation and the lividity both contribute to the dark color that you saw. In fact, if I were rash enough to hazard a guess, I'd say that had it lived, it would have had a rather light complexion—but that's only a guess."

"But it was a black child?"

"Yes. The blood group antigens are the best racial indicators. I can also be sure that the mother was a black woman. She was of blood A Rh −, the same antigens were present in her blood, and she was a carrier of the gene for abnormal hemoglobin S."

"Sickle-cell anemia," I exclaimed. "That I know about. So that poor creature would have had sickle-cell anemia too?" I was making notes at a furious pace and wishing with all my heart that I had a decent tape recorder. I was, however, cursed with a mania for antiques rather than gadgets.

"Not actually. The sickle-cell trait was passed on as a recessive gene. The Rh − blood of the mother, however, was bound to cause trouble for the thing had it survived to term. It was Rh + and there is every indication that it would have been born brain-damaged because of the incompatibility. This fact also infers that this woman—the mother—has had other children or, at least, a child. Usually the first Rh + child of an Rh − mother has no trouble, but the mother generally develops antibodies that are damaging to any subsequent Rh+ children. On that basis, I'd say this is not a first child."

"You amaze me. How much information from so little evidence. Forensic detection is mind-blowing."

"That's why I love my work so much and put up with the internecine politics up in Pomona. My wife thinks I'd be better off in private practice making a bundle catering to anxious old ladies with the pip. I probably would be from a financial standpoint, but if you don't love your work and wake up every morning raring to go, what the hell good is it? I love scraping the nails of corpses and rooting around in a skull looking for cranial fractures, and I'll be damned if I'll go back to med school so she can move back to Westchester and join some Junior League."

"Oh, she's one of those."

"Scarsdale."

"Now it's my turn to get the picture. The best antidote, however, is a good corpse. What else have you detected, Shoilock?"

"Let's see, what's calculated to impress a gullible amateur sleuth? Ah, yes. The Met Foods bags. They came from a store in the metropolitan New York area and were used to carry a sack of rice and a bag of kitty litter. Bits of litter and grains of rice were found in the inner flaps of the inner bag. They must have been doubled to accommodate a heavy or bulky bundle. Somebody who owns a cat, wouldn't you say?"

"I would imagine. What else have you got? That skull . . ."

"You're insatiable, aren't you?" he laughed. "Let's see," he drawled and began rattling off various items of the pathology. "Carpal fusion, brachydactyly of the digits of the feet, cleft palate, harelip, encephalocoele—"

"Whoa, you're going too fast for me. Slow down and explain."

"Carpal fusion is fusion of some of the small bones of the wrist—a fairly common minor abnormality and another indication of African ancestry. By brachydactyly I mean shortened toes in this case, but it can be present in fingers as well. It, too, is a common birth anomaly." He spelled encephalocoele for me and went on to explain it. "It's a condition in which part of the brain actually occurs outside the cranium."

"That reddish black veined lump at the back of the head?" I asked.

"That's it," he agreed enthusiastically. "Boy, but you're sharp. That lump was part of the brain protruding through the skull."

"Is that why the skull was so long?"

"No. That's caused by another condition entirely. You're asking about acrocephaly or 'dome-shaped skull.' It occurs with harelip and other malformation in a variety of syndromes. I've never seen one quite like this, though. By rights, this creature should never have survived to five months, let alone lived through an abortion."

"And put up a fight for its life into the bargain." I shuddered at the image of that hideous little imp actually moving and struggling with its killer, bent on its own survival.

"By the way," he asked, "If I Xerox this report, want a copy for your files?"

"God, yes."

"Your eyes only," he cautioned.

"I promise."

"Well, I guess that's it." He sounded reluctant to hang up. "I suppose I should let you write your article?" I grunted noncommittally. "I'll probably hit the local pub. Maybe I'll get lucky."

Hint? Hint? I wondered.

"Sounds swell," I countered lamely. "Hope you do."

"Do what?"

"Get lucky. You're a brick and you deserve it. I do thank you so much, Guy. Toodle-oo. I'll call tomorrow." On that cheery note I hung up and began to digest the mad scrawl that comprised my notes. Hallelujah.

It was just short of nine on the following evening when Meta knocked on the door.

"C'mon in, Mrs. Hudson, and sit down. Read that stuff I put on the coffee table. I won't be long." I kept up a clatter at the typewriter as Meta crossed the room, put on the TV, and sat down with my article. After another minute or two, I pulled the last sheet from the roller with a cry of triumph and straightened the shaggy pile of papers with which my desk was littered. The floor of my tiny writing alcove was strewn with books that I returned to their places on the shelves of my criminology bookcase.

"What are you doin', luv?" Meta asked, looking up briefly from my article.

"Putting away my books on blood types and pathology. I really should have been a forensic pathologist, I think. I find this sort of thing so fascinating." I flipped open one of the volumes to a nice gory photo of a corpse on a slab in an advanced state of dissection. Meta took one look, shuddered, and went back to her reading. "You know," I continued with a leer, "jars of stomach contents. The action of various poisons on the major organs. That sort of stuff." I was in high spirits and feeling mischievous.

Meta shook her head, grinned, and then nodded at the set. Alistair Cooke popped onto the screen. I turned up the sound and for the next fifty minutes we were lost in a new Masterpiece Theater series. After that, Meta finished the article and glanced over it once more before putting it down. "Will it do?" I asked.

"Oh, yes, luv. It's a smasher—and it sounds just like a real newspaper article. But how on earth did you get so much information? And 'reliable sources'! It sounds so official."

"It is official," and I told her all about Guy Galveston and what a help he'd been. "I read it back to him this afternoon. I took it down to Peter Polhemus ten minutes later and he'd okayed it by four with only minor changes. I suppose Peter is responsible for the editorial polish you mention. I'm no reporter yet, you know. He thinks that it should be picked up by one of the wire services." I held up my hand, crossed my fingers for luck, and taking a new manila file folder out of my desk, I bundled my notes, copies of my article, and all the newspaper clippings on the case into it. I sat down to fill out a label. "How shall I file this mess, Mrs. H.? Under abortion or murder of fetus or—" I stopped short, feeling the full impact of inspiration coming unbidden to a tired but receptive mind.

"Or what, luv?" she asked absently, her eyes fixed on Basil Fawlty's frantic, boneless antics.

"—or under mooncalf."

"Mooncalf?"

"Yes, that's perfect and it's accurate, by God. It's an old, obsolete word for an abortion or a misshapen, monstrous birth. Shakespeare calls Caliban a mooncalf, so what could be fitter? The mooncalf it shall be! In fact, Meta, I'm going to call Peter in the morning and have him use *mooncalf* in the header on my article. It will be a real attention grabber." I crowed in delight at my own inspiration as I printed the word in red across the label and affixed it to my folder: MOONCALF.

And with that, the game surely was afoot.

$\triangledown$

3

NOSED IN THE LOBBY

"JESUS H. Christ!"

It was with that, under the circumstances, quite forgivable exclamation that Officer Anthony Capiello of the Fortieth Precinct in the Bronx reacted to the sight of a particular object in a particular room in a building on Hawthorne Terrace in the Mott Haven section of the borough. It was a warm Thursday in the second week of October.

Less than three hours later, I stood in that room myself and heard a reiteration of those words and that discovery from the young officer himself. Words and phrases like "poipetrata" and "my partner and myself entered the premises," so humorously trite and smacking of the worst New Yorkese when heard on the nightly news, tumbled from his lips like a litany of terror. He was no more than twenty-two or -three and still in his salad days. What he had seen had shaken him in a way that any number of strung-out junkies wielding their Saturday-night specials could never have done.

I was back working on my Charlotte Hungerford biography after enjoying several days of praise for my article in the *Stop-Press*. Circulation had gone up on account of our little local murder and

Peter was quite happy; an abbreviated form of my article had gone
out over one of the wire services.

Now, I sat at my small walnut roll-top desk, surrounded by
copies of Charlotte Hungerford's marvelous old potboiler ro-
mances and my biographical notes, when the phone rang.

"Miranda?"

"Yes."

"This is Guy Galveston. Are you game for a ride down to the
city?"

"New York? Why? What's up?" I had diverted a request for a
date once already on the grounds of my separation being so recent.
Was he trying again?

"They think they've found the mother."

I sat up like a shot. "You're kidding!"

"Nope. Nothing's certain but it looks like it could be. They
want someone from our office to see the scene before anything is
moved. Since this has been my baby, no pun intended, from the
beginning, I'm going to witness the postmortem tomorrow. I'm
bringing along all our workups on the mother's blood type, the
fetus's, and my profile on the blood and skin samples from the
probable murderer." He sounded eager.

"Wait. It's just sinking in. Postmortem. Then she's—"

" 'Nor a door nail.' They say she's such a mess that the cop who
found her barfed all over the evidence, so be warned. If you'd
rather not—"

"I'm no ninny, Guy, for God's sake. When should I be ready?"

"Now! As fast as I can get down from Pomona. I'll honk and
you come out. Oh, and bring a barf bag just in case." With that he
chuckled richly and hung up.

"Funny," I smirked into the dead phone.

But it wasn't so funny after all.

It is hard to describe the combination of aged decrepitude, desolate
housing-project slum, and just plain filth and destruction through

which we rode once we pulled off the Bruckner Expressway and onto Southern Boulevard, where vistas of soulless brick towers—"the projects"—loom over narrow streets and where forlorn churches like St. Anselm's and St. Ann's have kept watch over the death of neighborhoods and birth of ghettos. For every recently built day-care center or row of rehabilitated tenements, there were streets of continued decay. The devastation around St. Mary's Park, haven for junkies and all manner of detritus, made me sick.

Hawthorne Terrace, when we found it at last, turned out to be a short, desolate single block that was squeezed in between Conway and Dykeman Avenues to the east and west and Willow and Cypress Terraces to the north and south. The tall, branchless stumps of half a dozen plane trees testified to the fact that once green life had flourished where now only a rubble of brick, concrete, glass, and old bedsprings served for inspiration.

A clutter of blue and white police cruisers, a police emergency vehicle, a medical examiner's van, and desultory clusters of idle policemen marked the scene of the crime. At the far end of the block, kept back more by the litter in the street than by the police, several TV camera crews and newspaper reporters were setting up their equipment and nosing about among the bystanders. It appeared to be a thankless task.

The cops all looked alike in their black leather jackets and peaked caps, their hips wide with guns and walkie-talkies and all the other paraphernalia of keeping the peace in New York's own version of the Gaza Strip.

We both sat for a moment, drawing in our breath and girding up our loins.

"Ready, Miranda?" Guy asked at last.

"Yes," I answered resolutely. "I'm for the penny *and* the pound. This is all material for a future book and I've got to see it through, capture the whole ambience or else it won't work." I looked at him with my Fay jaw stuck out in determination.

"Brave girl, but remember, take your time and nobody'll think you're chicken if you back out. Really, now, promise."

"Promise," I agreed, but only to placate him. He didn't yet know the implication of the Fay jaw. My father wasn't alive to tell him and Uncle Jeremiah was probably still in London. He patted my hand, gave me the beginning of a thoughtful look, checked himself, and got out of the car. Three of New York's finest converged upon us with the agile waddle of a trio of penguins, and, talking police-ese in various versions of Brooklyn and Bronx dialect, swept us toward the middle of the block where loomed, in solitary misery, the partially burned-out wreck of what had once been 13 Hawthorne Terrace, The Bronx, 54, New York.

The first stench was of cat pee with its unmistakable pungence. The wave of human urine that came after was, if anything, even more offensive. It mingled with the dusty smell of wood rot and the limy tang of deteriorating plaster, carrying those lesser odors before it with the overpowering headiness of a bad cologne.

We held our breath for as long as we could, climbing the filthy stairs past a welter of garbage composed of dead cats, beer cans, pint bottles of vile liquors, hypodermic syringes, small plastic bags, human waste, used condoms and heaps of less readily identifiable garbage. It was hard to believe that human beings could create such squalor, let alone survive in it, yet several blank and hooded faces peered warily from behind the few doors that remained upright and on their hinges. The doors were hastily closed as we passed.

"People live here?" I exclaimed in disbelief.

"There's no runnin' water, no heat, no plumbin' an' half the roof's burned out but there's three families squattin' in here. At night, this place is as full of junkies as it is of rats." The officer who preceded us up the stairs was talking, shaking his head, moving his lumbering, wide bottom slowly up the filthy steps at an almost stately pace. I noticed with detached fascination as his handcuffs, hooked to the back of his belt, swung from side to side in rhythmic accompaniment. It was one of those tiny details that remain indelibly in the mind. "Better take a deep breath. You ain't gonna want to smell what's lyin' in that room up there, lady," he warned with brutal concern. He had been against my coming up in the first place, his sensibilities having been formed in the old-fashioned, pre-feminist dark ages when chivalrous men protected their women from all bad smells except those of boiling cabbage, diapers, and soiled but manly underwear.

We climbed to a landing, stepped past the remnants of Officer Capiello's breakfast, and entered a flat the likes of which I could never have imagined in my most hideous flights of literary fancy.

The old peeling walls that smelled of rotten plaster had at some point in the relatively recent past been painted with a single coat of cheap Chinese red enamel. It had run in sheets of watery drippings before it had dried, leaving patches of translucent color here, curtains of thick, blood-red dribbles there. The old-fashioned wall sconces and ceiling fixture that must once have lit the place had long since been torn out for the copper wiring behind them. Only a few draggled, fraying ends of ancient cloth-covered wires hung from gaping holes that exposed the rough wood of the laths beneath.

The floor had been cleared of debris by the ineffectual device of shoving it to the far corners of the small room, where it lay in heaps. In the squalor of this hellish place, it was what passed for housekeeping. Here and there on a windowsill, or on the several crates that served as tables or seats, were candle ends, some merely set in a waxen puddle on the bare wood, others mounted on the aluminum lids of beer or soda cans.

The stench was impossible: sickly and overpoweringly sweet. It was accompanied by the constant and suggestive drone of a hundred million flies. Someone had opened what few windows still retained their panes, but since it was a warm, still day, no air moved and the sense of humid oppression in that dreadful room was palpable.

Across from the door, against the farthest wall, were a queen-size mattress and box spring. They were covered by a large black plastic sheet that hid the thing that lay upon them without conceal-

ing the suggestiveness of its spread-eagled contours. A deputy New
York City medical examiner, a police photographer, and two
plainclothes detectives stood near the wall at the head of the bed,
deep in a conversation made inaudible by the wadded handkerchiefs
that they held discreetly to their noses. On his knees near them, a
fingerprint expert used black powder and a small brush on the
runny red-enamel wall behind the body. He looked slightly tense
from the effort of holding his breath.

"We think it's your mother, Galveston," one of the detectives
said solemnly, unconscious of his faux pas. Once introductions
were made, he went on in the same flat monotone. "There's no
sign of a fetus, she's been here at least a week, so the time tallies,
and she's black."

"How far along, do you guess?" I heard Guy ask the deputy M.
E., a big man who dwarfed Guy and most of the other men in the
room.

He frowned and shrugged a pair of wide, stooping shoulders.
"Five months, maybe. Too far along for this kind of witch-doctor
setup. Look," and he motioned to one of the cops hovering near
the door to the hall. The man leaned across the floor in a sort of
half-crouch, as if he did not want to move his feet any closer to the
mattress than he had to, and flipped a corner of the black plastic
from off the end of the bed, laying bare a length of rubber tubing,
a red rubber douche, and an old gray enamel basin from which
some liquid had long since evaporated, leaving only a rusty brown
residue behind. It was evocative of ugly things.

A blue cardboard container of salt lay on its side against the base
of the box spring, its silvery spout wide open. A triangular cascade
of salt crystals had flowed from it and now glistened whitely in a
shaft of afternoon sun.

I watched Guy's face as he squatted over the things, a slender,
dapper figure in a pristine sport jacket and slacks. He shook his
head. "Christ," he said at last and with such feeling that, though
his voice was deep and low, it sounded shattering against the
monotonous litany of the flies. "Why, in God's name? This shit

went out with the Dark Ages. There's no reason for it. There are clinics—"

The deputy M. E. shook his great head helplessly. "Time was we used to see a lot of this, but not in years. Even before they changed the abortion laws, things had got past this." He turned to one of the detectives. "You ought to run down the old-timers on this one—any elderly women in the area who might have been nurses or midwives. It stinks of old time, to me." He paused. "But still, why?"

"Any idea who she is?" Guy asked.

"None." the younger detective answered. "She's black, in her twenties . . ."

"And probably has had children before this. At least that's what I deduce from my gross examination," the deputy broke in, shrugging those stooped shoulders again. He wore a rumpled black suit and a great gray, rumpled face to coordinate with it. It gave him the look of a mortician. His gray eyes were weary rather than sad, the eyes of a man who's just one step away from having seen too much.

"Got any idea of what caused her death?" Guy asked in the same flat tone.

"Could have bled to death," the deputy M. E. shrugged again. "There was enough blood lost from the look of her, but I'm inclined to think it was a combination of things—blood loss, shock, and very possibly cardiac arrest. The pain must have been—well, you see when you take a look at the face. Lift the corner of the sheet a bit more and look at that foot."

She had been light-skinned, but from midcalf to her ankle the skin was bloated and obscene, darkly discolored in a line that followed the contour of the back of her leg down to the heel. This, I learned later, was the pattern of lividity caused by the action of the blood settling at the lowest parts of the body soon after death. But that was not the worst of it. A length of light cord had been bound round the ankle and because of the swelling, now appeared to cut deeply into the flesh.

Guy whistled. "Jesus Christ. What in hell went on here?" He stood up and surveyed the rest of the room. "Candles? For light or magic, I wonder? Anything to indicate a ritual killing?"

The smaller, Irish detective shook his head. "Unless tyin' her to the mattress was ritual enough. We think she must have been drugged. Doc here says she was a junkie—needle tracks like a road map." The great solemn head nodded its agreement. "She was probably so high she didn't know what the hell was going on."

"Well, for Chrissake let's hope so! I'd better take a look. Everything been printed?" The fingrprint man, busy over his equipment, nodded. He was about to confiscate the candles.

"And photographed. I've got it all," the police photographer added. "After you've taken a gander, turn her over, gentlemen, and I'll do the back."

Guy looked over his shoulder at me thoughtfully. "You ready?" he asked softly. The others looked at me with ill-disguised curiosity, but made no attempt to question my presence. It paid to be a quiet little mouse. I grinned what must have been the sickliest of grins and nodded gamely. Officer Capiello stuck a face of paper-white dough through the door to the bathroom, saw what was about to happen, and quickly retreated. It was hard to blame him.

She had been tied hand and foot to the mattress, the cord from one ankle being drawn around the mattress between it and the box spring and then tied to the other ankle. The same arrangement had been used to hold her arms, now as terribly swollen as her legs, wide apart and over her head. The settling of her blood had caused the same discolorations along their length.

It was impossible to tell from the swelling of her face if she had ever been pretty. All color seemed to have drained from those bloated features, giving her the stark look of an albino. Her mouth gaped in a wide, soundless scream, made even more horrible to contemplate by the end of filthy rag, rusty with dried blood, that protruded from it in a crumpled wad. Her eyes stared vacantly at the ceiling, all semblance of life lost to the thick gray film that glazed the dark pupils.

However bearable I had found this wreckage so far, nothing could have prepared me for the gaping pit that had once been her belly—black as rotten meat and roiling with maggots. I turned back to the window and gulped in lungfuls of the outside air, closing my eyes and trying to translate the image of that dark cavern into something endurable. I knew I had to master myself and look at her one last time. I had to see it all and comprehend it in its totality, perhaps for no other reason than because it was the price I must pay for whatever benefit might one day come my way from this experience. Turning, I leaned closer to Guy, looking past the brown houndstooth check of his jacket and down into the gaping hole that lay between her two sharp hipbones.

My mind began to work again. "Guy," I whispered over his shoulder as he continued his examination, "they don't do abortions like that, do they? This looks like it might have been a cesarean."

"Precisely, and under the most deplorable conditions imaginable." He didn't take his eyes from his task. "I think I've got a scenario worked out. I'll be finished here soon." I took his last words as a kind of dismissal and withdrew to the window again.

He stood up, stretched momentarily, and began to inch along the side of the bed toward her right arm, trying as best he could under the circumstances to move the hand back and forth. The cords and the swelling made it difficult. He murmured something to the deputy M. E. and the other man nodded with customary solemnity. "Carpal fusion" was the only phrase I caught, but I knew instantly what he was driving at. He looked across to where I stood and gave me the ghost of a smile.

We had indeed found the mother.

By the time they had finished, it was dark, and one could see from the windows the glow of yellow streetlights and glaring swaths of neon beyond the immediate devastation and darkness of Hawthorne Terrace itself. Out there, wretched taverns, liquor stores, and bodegas flickered with desultory life, cars honked and shrill voices carried on the chilling night air—an alien cityscape that I watched with curiosity. The evening news programs were long over, the camera crews had dispersed, most of the police cars had gone, and those that remained squawked and crackled with the raucous sound of police radio calls. The raw white glare of trouble lights and flash lamps illuminated the body for a few more minutes and then went out with deathlike finality. The flies, cold now, and in the darkness of night, settled where they could and grew mercifully silent. A black body bag was put into the M. E.'s van and one by one we all departed, save the men who would secure the crime scene and keep vigil.

"You must be starved. I know I am," Guy said as he opened the car door for me.

"I haven't even thought of food, but since my skull is splitting, I suppose I must be hungry."

We pulled away from Hawthorne Terrace and found our way back onto the Bruckner Expressway. I breathed a sigh of relief. It was good to return to civilization from the violent savagery of that nightmare apartment on that dreadful street. Guy glanced at me briefly and then back to the road.

"Tired?" he asked.

"No more than you, I suppose."

He smiled. "Then you must be tired, 'cause I'm beat."

By that time we were turning into the parking lot at the Red Coach Grill. "No more pathology," he said. "You've seen my work from the inside today—which is more, incidentally, then my wife would ever do. Now, over dinner, you tell me all about writing biographies."

"You're going to regret that," I laughed. "I'll chew your ear off." I did, but he didn't seem to mind. It proved a catharsis for both of us and helped to exorcise the demons of the day.

That, however, had been over a long, leisurely, and very late supper, warmed by Bloody Marys and brandy with our coffee. Now it was three-thirty in the morning and I was wide awake, pursued by vivid images of roiling maggots and gouts of dried blood smeared across a vile and filthy mattress.

Who was she? Whoever she was, no human being should have to endure such agony and degradation. I got up and began to pace, listening to the refrigerator click on and off in the utter soundlessness of the early morning. I felt my way into the kitchen and, closing my eyes against the sudden glare, turned on the light.

There is something eerie and lonely about being in the one solitary lighted room in a world of darkness. In a sense, it isolated me even more than I felt already, to stand in that chilly kitchen with its raw yellow light. The darkness had been a comfort, of sorts, and now I found myself feeling that in all the world I alone was awake.

It was at that point that I knew I really cared—not just about the solution to the murder of the mooncalf and now its mother, but about who she was. I was still thinking of the book, of course, but by now it had become something more than just a way to make a buck and get out from under Max's reluctant separation agreement. It was a chance to learn about her life and how that life had led, step by step, to her horrible death.

The horror of the crime and its eventual solution would be the hook on which to catch the reader's attention, but could I bring her, whoever she was, back to life and make her cry out her terrible, sad story in such a way that a world grown deaf and callous with indifference to the suffering of an individual human woman— a sister—would read and listen and care?

It was a scary question to try and answer, but in the early, blue-green light of that dawning day, I made up my mind that I would try.

$\triangledown$

4

VALDALENE PEARSALL

B Y Friday they knew who she was. She'd been fingerprinted far too often to remain a Jane Doe for long. She was twenty-five and had been picked up routinely for prostitution, shoplifting, and drug possession since she was fourteen. She lived on welfare, had four children all under the age of eight, and had never been married. She had been living for the past few months with her younger sister in the Widdecomb Housing Projects on Eagle Avenue in the northern Mott Haven section, just a few blocks from where she had died, and only a few miles from Morrisania Hospital, where she had been born. She had never lived anywhere but the Bronx, never been any farther away from the Bronx than Philadelphia. Her name was Valdalene Pearsall.

Those, of course, were the bare facts, which Guy phoned to tell me from the city morgue at eight that morning. He was about to witness the autopsy and seemed enviably wide awake and alert, despite the hour and the fatigue both physical and mental of the previous day.

"You sound out of it, kid," he said. "Bad night?"

"I couldn't sleep. I kept thinking of her."

He grunted. "I shouldn't have let you come along. You should never have seen—"

"No, no," I interrupted impatiently. "It wasn't the body. It was *her.* Who she is, why it happened . . ." I trailed off, at a loss to explain my feelings adequately. Perhaps if we had been face to face I could have, but it is hard to pour out one's heart to a telephone.

"You really care, don't you?" he said quietly. I could hear a hollow commotion of voices behind him. "Yeah, in a minute, be right there," he muttered away from the receiver, returning to me before I could answer him. "Listen, Miranda, don't think I don't understand. I may be approaching this thing from a more academic point of view myself, but there have been times when I've torn myself to pieces caring. You get some beautiful kid on a slab in front of you and you want to kill the bastard who's raped her and killed her—or a little boy who's been smashed by some drunk driver. You can become obsessed, I know. Now listen to me, relax a little today. Try to let go, and I promise when I'm through here I'll come by and tell you the whole story. Okay?"

"Okay." I could hear a chorus of insistent voices behind him. "Guy, you had better go."

"If they knew how pretty you are, they'd understand," he said softly. "And how smart and gutsy, too. See you around four-thirty or five." He hung up and I listened like a sleepwalker to the click and buzz of the disconnected line for a full five seconds before I finally put the phone down.

"Damn," I thought. "Don't let this happen. I'm not even rid of Max yet. I need time—lots of time."

I ate breakfast at the Skylark, had enough cups of bitter, strong coffee to blast my brain out of the past night's sleepies, and went over the *News* article on the discovery in the South Bronx. Since it was the early edition, which is trucked to Rockland County in the wee hours, there was very little information beyond the bare facts of the discovery itself and speculation that this was the mother of the fetus found in Nyack Beach State Park. They hadn't even managed to get her name before going to press. The *Post,* on the other hand, had put out a later edition that not only named the victim as Valdalene Pearsall, but gave the name and address of her sister as well. The headline, in screaming thirty-point type, was enough to give Peter Polhemus apoplexy:

FIND MOTHER OF NYACK THING?
ABORTION HORROR REVEALED

The story was on page three—a lurid three hundred words of fluff with hardly an accurate fact to the paragraph, but laced with plenty of grue and accompanied by a large, grainy picture— obviously a family snapshot—of Valdalene Pearsall and her children.

Well, one question had been answered at least. She had been pretty—very pretty—once.

It was just after eleven in the morning when I collected Molly, revved up the old Mustang, which idled away most of its days in my landlady's garage, and set off on a safari to the wilds of the South Bronx in quest of one Ismeralda Jackson. It seemed to me at the moment that the only way to lay the image of Valdalene Pearsall's dead, gray-filmed, pleading eyes to rest was to see her sister.

She lived on the tenth floor of Building Number Eight in the Widdecomb Housing Project, a dreary, red-brick tower that could not have been more penitentiary-like had it sported machine-gun turrets and lookout towers. I rode up in a dank, urine-smelling elevator with only one working neon bar and several buttons missing from the panel. It was the kind of place where children, playing on the tops of elevator cars, so often seem to slip and die horribly, providing, with their brief lives, more grist for the nightly news mill; sad incidents and careless accidents blown up and turned into the stuff of tragedy. No one remembered any more the classical definition of tragedy. Now it simply meant, for the moments it was given on videotape, a kid hit by a car or a jogger killed by a drugged-out mugger in Prospect Park. Sophocles would have retched.

Ismeralda Jackson wasn't any more than twenty—plump, dark-skinned, and alert. She was prettier in person than she would appear later that night on the ten o'clock news, but she couldn't compare with her older sister. Once she had lifted the mask of dumb indifference with which she greeted me, she had a liveliness and mobility of feature that was quite attractive. It had taken me five minutes of selling to get her to listen to me, and then I think it was only because I was a lone white woman, not backed up by a camera crew or slew of newspaper photographers, that she finally relented.

"You alone? Really?" She had asked from the cracked door.

"Yes. I—I must speak to you. I'm the lady who found the baby. They think now it's your sister's baby."

It was as if she hadn't heard me. She peered beyond me at two black teenagers in shabby imitation-leather jackets idling in the hall. "Shit, honey, this ain't no place for you." With that she closed the door, rattled the safety chain out of its socket, and opened the door to admit me. "Get in here, girl," she urged with the same scolding tone she might use to a child. She locked the door behind us, turned, and preceded me down a tiny stretch of hall, shaking her head with the manner of an older soul than I, though I must have had twenty years on her.

I followed her into a living room lit by the typical metal-framed casement windows of a fifties city housing project. The room itself was painted in a raw pink latex, decorated with sheer white ruffled curtains, cheap pink plush drapes that hung as stiff as cardboard, and a living-room set of antique white "French Provincial," picked out with lots of gold-painted highlights. The pink plush upholstery was as immaculate as custom plastic slipcovers could keep it. Above the couch, a nude in dayglow colors arched sinuously against the texture of her black velvet "canvas." The lamps were large and ornate "Greek goddesses," their plaster forms painted ivory and gold. The wall-to-wall carpeting was a blinding hot pink.

On the coffee table were a pink marble ball on a gilt stand and a huge pink-glass ashtray. A color television blared with a snap, crackle, and whomp of kiddie cartoons before the mesmerized gaze of a gaggle of avid little faces. My entrance distracted them not at all.

On top of the TV stood a framed photograph, a professional portrait of a cool-looking girl of about nineteen or twenty. It was Valdalene. Someone had draped a dime-store black crepe head scarf around the frame and placed a votive candle before it. The flame was out, but earlier it had burned for a short time. I suspected the fine hand of some network sob sister. That evening, Channel Seven's six o'clock report proved me right.

"Are these her children?" I asked lamely, turning away from Valdalene Pearsall's picture and pulling myself into the here and now.

"That's right. All four of 'em. I ain't such a fool, m'self. I ain't got no use for a man, honey, 'less I someday find one got brains and money and pride in himself, and that ain't likely." She grinned, chuckling richly at what was obviously a frequent comment of hers. "I got me a job over to Lincoln Hospital and I sleep alone, honey, a-lone. Valda's the one had all the truck with the dudes."

"What was she like?" I asked, siting on the slippery plastic of the sofa. It made a rude noise as I settled down, and the oldest child, a scrawny boy with gray eyes, snickered and nudged his sister before turning back to the Smurfs.

Miss Jackson sat down more carefully on a pink plush side chair and looked at me oddly.

"What you care for?" she asked me suspiciously, but not with any obvious malice. "You say you ain't from the TV or the papers, so what you want?"

"As I told you, I'm the woman who found the baby up in Nyack. I was allowed to see your sister after they found her. Miss Jackson, I saw what they had done to her."

Ismeralda Jackson frowned and grunted. "I seen her at the morgue this mornin' damn near seven o'clock. She didn't hardly look like Valda, but it was her all right. She had her ring on, what

Momma give her." She grew silent and reflective, her dark, fleshy face drawn up in thick creases.

"It was a terrible sight," I said, trying not to remember just how terrible. "Can you understand, Miss Jackson, woman to woman—" She looked up at me, an odd expression on her face. "Truly, I mean it, woman to woman, that I find myself caring about what happened to her. I—I'm a writer. Not, strictly speaking, a reporter," I added hastily, "but I write books . . ."

"Books? You write books?"

I smiled. "Yes, I write books. Biographies, mostly, but now I think perhaps I'd like to write about your sister."

"Valda?" she repeated in amazement. "What for?"

"Because I—I'm involved somehow. Because I found her child and because I saw her. She died horribly, and I think that she has been much mistreated in her life, and I find myself caring about her. Why it happened—how—"

"Why it happen!" she said with sudden vehemence. "Shit, I can tell you why it happen, girl. She was a nympho! She be fuckin' around since she be thirteen, fourteen and she smoke weed and she drink wine an'—an' then she gets above her li'l black self and she be shootin' up and drinkin' Chivas and be goin' downtown to turn tricks in them ho-tels. That's why it happen—"

"But why? Why her? You don't do any of those things, obviously."

"I sure don't. My momma whip the skin off my butt in stripes if'n I do like Valda. Ain't no whippin' ever did Valda no good."

"Yet you were sisters. You grew up in the same house—"

"Valda an' me wasn't no full sisters, chile. We was half sisters. Her pa was some no-account white trash—pardon—"

"No offense, really." I smiled. We all have our prejudices, after all. Who was I to take exception to hers?

"Valda's pa was all the time drunk. He run out on them when Valda be two. Now, my father was a black man, an' he work for the city. He try beatin' some sense into Valda, but it be too late. She trash like her pa and too damn proud of being so light. OOO-eeh, you think that she be the onliest high-yalla gal in the whole Bronx. My, but what she be proud o' that hide o' hers."

If Ismeralda Jackson was jealous of her sister's light skin, it was hard to tell, but she clearly wanted no part of the life her sister had led. She spoke at great length, once she had warmed to me and to the subject, of their childhood, two such disparate lives lived under one tenement roof. To her, the projects into which they had moved several years earlier had marked a way up and out. To Valda they had been a trap from which she had to escape, hoping to use her light-skinned body as a key to some better future, perhaps as a model or an actress. And she had wanted a white man.

"Was the father of this last child of hers white?"

"He was," Ismeralda nodded vigorously, "an' he be one scary dude. She so scart o' him she got to hide from him—that why she move in here with me last August."

I sat up sharply. Here it comes, I thought. "She came here to hide from him?"

"She did. An'—she move out o' here near a month ago afta he find she livin' with me. I don't hear nothin' from her since."

"Weren't you worried?" I asked.

"Some. I figured she was gonna hide til she could get rid o' that baby."

"So she wanted an abortion?"

"Hell, no, she don't want no abortion. Not at first she don't. He want a baby so bad he promise her five thousand dollars and she glad she gonna have it, but shit, she be in nothin' but pain for months. She tells him she need money for an abortion and he curse her out, girl. He beat her face black an' blue an' tell her he kill her if she don't have that baby. He be like a crazy man, she tell me."

"Kill her?"

"That's right," she insisted with a firm nod. "He say she must have that baby and she don't get no five thousand dollar til she do. He got no use fo' her high-yaller ass, chile. He just want that baby. She tells him somethin' wrong, that the baby don't act right and there be too much pain, but he don't care. He say that baby his and he don't care nothin' for her pain. She be gettin' paid for her pain."

She's been paid, all right, I thought to myself. The more I heard, the more horrible things became. "Tell me," I said at last, "have you heard from him since?"

"Not since the day before the papers say about that baby. Not since then. He call lots after she leave here, an', oooo-eeh, girl, if he ain't one mad mother. He curse me out. Shit, I dint know no white man know all them words, but my, do he say 'em fancy! He don't bother me none. I tell him where ta get off, yes sir. He ain't fuckin' around with this here nigga. I tell him I don't know where she at an that's that." She looked at me almost gleefully, her full, round face impish as a child's. She had a lovely, flashing light in her eyes.

"And he hasn't called since?" I repeated thoughtfully, more to myself than to Ismeralda Jackson.

"He has not—an', shit, he better not, honey, 'cause afta what happen to Valda, I take a ax to that dude, he come around here."

My mind was trying to work. I felt sluggish and tired after my long night, and finally, though I fought it, I began to yawn.

"Honey, you don't look so good. You okay?"

"Miss Jackson, I am just plain tired. I hardly slept last night and I've been up since before eight."

"Would you like a cup o' tea? Shit, we be better off in the kitchen anyways, with these kids an' them cartoon shows. I should of make them do they lessons, but what with Valda and them TV people, I just dint have the heart, ya know."

I followed Ismeralda Jackson into her small, immaculate kitchen. It too was pink, save for the conventional white sink, refrigerator, and stove, about which little could be done, save for the pink-flowered contact paper that had been pasted over the freezer door.

I sat down at the formica-topped kitchen table and watched as Ismeralda made us tea. She put out a bowl of sugar and a green bottle of Realemon and filled the cream pitcher with milk, all without saying a word. She put a cup in front of me—thin, inexpensive white china with a spray of pink carnations curving around the cup and matching saucer. The lip and handle were rimmed with silver luster. It was not a good set, but it matched well the kitchen with its pink walls and pink formica and pink plastic-upholstered chrome chairs. This was a young woman who tried. She was striving and I liked her for it. She saw me examining the cup and grinned.

"That china be my momma's. She start it at the A & P and we get pritty near the whole set before they stops givin' it. When my father die, she get the in-surance and we decide ta get all new furniture. They was always talkin' they get a new sofa an' bed, so we decide that my pa would want us to get the best. We don't never regret it, neither."

"And why should you?"

"Valda say we selfish. She think we should of give it to her for modellin' lessons, but that's all foolishness. She never be no model. She a hooker."

"Where is your mother now?"

"She be down Baltimore with my sister Jovonelle. She be expectin', herself. Her husband be in the po-lice force down there."

"Does she know yet about Valda?"

"She know, but she can't come now. This be Jovonelle's first, an' she have some female trouble, so my mother say I got to do everythin' til she see Jo through the birth. I can handle the kids an' the po-lice. They ain't release the body for days yet, they tell me, so Momma be back for the funeral, I espects."

We sat together over the teacups, ate Nabisco wafers, and munched silently for a while. The tea helped. I began to get my thoughts into some order.

"Tell me, how did they meet, Valda and this man?"

"That always strike me funny, you know," Ismeralda answered with a thoughtful frown. "He pick her up on the street along her apartment. She be waitin' on the stoop for her welfare check an' he be sittin' in his car—one of them limousines with the driver in a fancy cap. Well, the driver, he gets out an' open the door for this

rich white man. He come out an' cross over to where Valda sittin'
an' he starts to sweet-talk her and git around her. He say he lookin'
for a gal just as pretty as her. He ax her name and he treat her real
good for a while."

"So he actually found her—almost as if he had been looking just
for her. Interesting."

"He don't do no messin' around with her for a while. He takes
her to a doctor to see she be clean—which she is, hard as that be to
believe—and that she ain't pregnant already. He tell her he want a
baby and he pay her to have it for him."

"What did Valdalene say to that?"

"OOOh girl, she be in heaven. Shit, she ain't neva had no
trouble carrying them babies out there—not even the twins—and
shit, no dude never paid her no five thousand dollars to have 'em,
so she figured it be a easy way to get rich quick. She gonna take
acting lessons and modellin' and maybe she get on the TV. And he
was good ta her—he takes Valda out to eat in them fancy places
donwtown, Mamma Leone's and that Cooky's Steak Place you
always see on the TV. He buy her clothes and say he buy her a
rabbit-fur coat come winter and he takes her to his house—"

"His house!? Where does he live?"

"That's right," she nodded emphatically. "After he find she
okay from the doctor, he takes her to his house. It some place in
Long Island or New Jersey, maybe. They goes over a bridge, she
say. She say it be big and real fancy. That night he get her drunk
on champagne and shit, chile, he damn near rape her, he go so
crazy ta have her high-yalla ass." She pursed her lips, wrinkled her
coarse-skinned brow, and fell into a head-shaking reverie at the
thought.

This tale that was unfolding—the sick seduction of a strangely
guileless though streetwise young woman, so easily taken in, so
cheaply bought, so violently dealt with—made me queasy with
disgust and pity. It was all so sordid and dreadful and sad.

Ismeralda Jackson shook her head as if to clear her mind and pushed the printed foil package of wafers toward me across the pink formica surface of the table.

"Valda, she scared of him after that. He be so re-fined and all and talk so pretty and he treat her so good—then he gets inta her, he be like a animal." She shook her head again, obviously disapproving.

"She say he hurt her. She be drunk on champagne and pills—he wouldn't let her shoot up at first, 'cause of the baby—so, shit, if she be hurting, he must be one mean dude," she said, looking at me thoughtfully.

"Well, he hurts her, sure enough, but shit, it only be but once a night, so she figga for five thousand dollars she can stand it. After the first night, he let her shoot up just enough so she don't know what happening no more and don't scream or nothin'. Every night for a week he gets her high and he takes her. She say he sweat, honey, and stink something awful when he be messin' with her, but she say she so high she don't even be conscious when he at her. He like it that way. And in the morning, when she go down for breakfast, there he be, up and at his breakfast—'brunch,' he calls it—reading his newspaper, just like nothin' happen, an he ain't never been at her at all—cool as you please."

Somehow I wanted to get this recitation over with and back on track. "Miss Jackson, what happened when the week was up?"

"Oh, he take her back to her apartment. They stops here first to pick up the kids. I be workin', but my momma was here. Then he drives her and the kids to the market so she shop."

"What market?"

"The Met Foods over on the Avenue," she answered, eyeing me strangely. It was an odd question on the face of it. "He make her git vitamins and vegetables and stuff. After that, he call every day and make sure she be there and don't do no fucking around. He sent his driver with groceries every week, and when she miss her next period, he take her to the doctors. Sure, she be pregnant, easy, and he be pleased—he so happy he take her out to a fancy dinner and he tell her he give her money every month.

"After that, he don't see her again but once a month, when he takes her to the doctor. After a while, she tell the doctor she don't like the way things be going, but he say it be okay and not to worry. Valda be in pain, though, and finally even doing drugs don't do no good—she can't stand the pain and she run away. Now she dead."

"I'm so sorry," I muttered. I was such a bundle of unsorted feelings that I couldn't articulate very well. "It was a terrible thing to have happened. I really am sorry." I was thinking of those four children watching cartoons in the living room. Perhaps, out of all this, they'd be better off. Ismeralda and her motherly fierceness might do them more good than Valda ever could have with her empty dreams and drugs and oft-turned tricks.

Ismeralda shook her head again. "Ain't no white dude never done her no good—not her pa or her white johns in they three-piece suits, scared shit that they gonna catch somethin' from her and bring it home to they wives, or Mr. Highfalutin Smith with his fancy talk and his five thousand dollars. Honest, Mizz Fay, I ain't kiddin' you. Valdalene be better off dead and that's the truth. She be my sister an' I care for her an' all—and I love her kids—but the way she die, chile, she be headed all her life."

Was that all there was to it? Was that to be Valdalene Pearsall's epitaph?

The autopsy had taken most of Friday morning. The preliminary reports were in, her medical records had been checked, and Guy Galveston, true to his word, was waiting for me when I got back to Nyack.

"Where were you? I said five-ish," he called across the lawn from Meta's front porch. "Your landlady took pity on me," he said, waving a highball glass. "She's absolutely super and she's making dinner—"

"Dinner! How'd you manage to wangle that?" Molly scooted out of the car and across the lawn to do her thing in Meta's hydrangeas.

"Faith, and how did I manage it? It's me Nugent and O'Neill blood, I expect, dearie, or perhaps me way with the whiskey bottle. She's daft about autopsies, too." His attempt at an Irish brogue was so endearingly execrable that I even managed a battle-weary smile as I herded the Moll up the steps and into the house.

"Aren't we all," I grinned as I stepped past him into Meta's cheery living room and flopped down on her green paisley sofa. "Hi, Mrs. Hudson, Shoilock's back," I called out toward the kitchen, "and Christ, is she beat!"

"Where the hell were you?" Guy asked again. "And what'll you have to drink?"

"A screwdriver," I said, but before Guy could reply, Meta appeared, bearing a tall, frosted glass of orange juice on the rocks. "She only drinks this damned orange muck 'cause she's a bloody Prot," she explained to Guy with a twinkle as she added a fearful slug of vodka from the Smirnoff bottle on her server, stirred it well, and handed it to me with a cocktail napkin.

"God bless, luv, you look all done in," she clucked.

"And God bless you, Meta, my blessed St. Margaret of the Screwdrivers." I let out a long sigh, kicked off my shoes, and lay my head back against the soft cushions.

"Where were you?" Guy asked again for the third time.

"Well, for most of the past hour and fifty-five minutes, stuck in traffic on the Bruckner Expressway behind an overturned tractor-trailer. Despite WINS reporter Carol D'Auria, who kept telling me not to go near it, I had but little choice. Molly had a barky-fight with a German shepherd in a station wagon in the next lane. It's been charming." I took another sip of the golden fluid and let the vodka do its job.

"What were you doing on the Bruckner Expressway?" Guy asked.

"What else?" I shrugged. "Coming back from visiting Ismeralda Jackson."

"The sister?" Meta asked softly, her glance straying to the *Post* and the *Journal-News* lying on the coffee table. "Did you go there alone? You shouldn't have." She got up then and went into the kitchen, leaving me alone with Guy.

"No, you shouldn't have," Guy agreed severely. "That's no place for a woman alone."

For the next few minutes I endured his lecture on the dangers of a woman alone in the South Bronx. I kept silent, but as I listened, I realized I was not ready for this stifling male overprotectiveness of his. It smacked too much of what I had found unbearable in Max.

Later, with the dishes in Meta's dishwasher and Meta on the phone with her daughter in California, Guy and I gave Molly and Duchess their last run of the evening.

We strolled along in silence for a while as the two dogs roamed the grassy verges ahead of us, sniffing and piddling as they went. At last Guy spoke, hesitantly, I could tell, and after much rumination.

"You're very nice to me, very pleasant most of the time, but you can also be a bit testy. Are you angry with me?"

"No, of course not." I hesitated. "No, not really—at least not at you. Guy, I'm just coming off a very bad time in my life, the end of a disaster of a marriage."

"I know that. You told me the other night."

"Well, this evening, when you began lecturing me about how unwise I had been to go down to the South Bronx . . ."

"Yes?"

"Guy, I don't need lectures, I don't need any protection or possessiveness. It's stifling and demeaning. I had it all the time with Max. If I wasn't home at five o'clock when he got home from his office, it was, 'Where were you? What were you doing? Who were you with?' He hated my writing. He hated my hours of research. He hated my friends. I felt strangled—do you understand?"

"I get the picture," Guy said dryly. "So I pushed the wrong buttons when I asked you where you were and when I lectured you. Mea culpa. I won't do it again."

"Good," I said curtly. His tone was so nonchalant that it sounded too patronizing. We walked on in silence for another minute.

"So now I know. You're an independent lady and I mustn't curb that independence."

"Right. Now you know." I began to cry for no discernable reason.

"It's okay, kid," Guy whispered. He put an arm around me and held me as we walked back toward the house. "I do understand, you know. After all, it was I who took you to see Valdalene, wasn't it? Was that overprotective?"

"No," I murmured.

"Good. Now believe me, I do understand. And I won't strangle you."

Of course he wouldn't. I'd never let him.

The next morning, I invited Meta to have breakfast with me. As we ate and chatted, I sorted through the two or three days of mail that I had neglected. Bills lay in one pile, and in the other were notes from friends and even one or two old acquaintances whose memories had been jogged by my recent appearance in print.

Most noticeable was an elegant-looking letter postmarked Staten Island. That one I opened at once.

"A letter from my Uncle Jeremiah—of the Irish Fays, of course," I explained as I used a butter knife to slit the envelope.

"I didn't realize you had an uncle, luv," Meta said absently as she stuck a fork into her eggs Benedict.

I laughed. "Neither do I, hardly. We speak on the phone occasionally, usually at birthdays and Christmas, but I haven't seen him since my father's funeral and that was nearly nine years ago. The Fay clan are notorious for not seeing each other save at weddings and funerals. We're a bunch of rugged individualists who love each other when in sight, but who get on with other things when we're not.

"Now, let's see what Mr. J. P. Fay of Fay Hall, Stapleton, Staten

Island has to say," I said, reading the engraved lettering on the flap
of the envelope. It was heavy, cream-colored bond, wonderful to
the touch. The note within was brief and very Uncle Jeremiah:

Dear Miranda,

I have just come across your name on the byline of a very
impressive article about the unfortunate infant found murdered in Rockland County. Does this mean that you have
given up biography for journalism, or are you merely
diversifying?

Do please call or write when you get the chance. I should
love to have you visit. It is far too long since we've had a chat.

You loving uncle,

Jeremiah Pearsall Fay

I got to the signature and blinked.

"Meta! Valdalene *Pearsall!* Pearsall. Don't you see? I had forgotten, but it's a family name of mine. I knew that it sounded familiar,
but I couldn't place it. Actually, there's no reason why I should
have. He's called Pearsall after his mother's mother, I think. Yes," I
mused, playing with the butter knife while the eggs Benedict grew
cold on my plate, "that's it. My father was the older of the two
brothers. They named him Luke after his father and Van Voorst for
his mother's family name. Uncle Jeremiah was named after his
mother's father Jeremiah Merrick Van Voorst along with his mother's mother's family name. They broke the chain when they named
me plain old Miranda. Anyway, it is odd, don't you think? The
name Pearsall, I mean." I laughed a short, sharp cackle. "Do you
suppose we were cousins, Valdalene and I?"

"Oh, luv, I don't think so. She was black." Meta sounded a
trifle scandalized. Certain old southern traditions were unknown in
the British Isles evidently.

She pursed her lips, as she always did when she was thoughtful
or about to say something that she thought might be taken amiss,
and poured another cup of coffee. Her small blues eyes lost their

color and light for a moment. "You've become so involved in this thing—finding the poor baby, you couldn't help that, of course— but going to that place where they found the mother, and now going back there alone to see the sister. It's becoming an obsession."

"I know, Meta, but I can't seem to help it. I keep rationalizing about money and a book and writing these articles for Peter Polhemus, but there is something more to it. Last night, it wasn't Guy's description of the autopsy and their findings that kept me awake, it was something—someone—else. Valda had four children. The youngest is a small, plump-faced darling of a girl about three, three and a half. She's a beauty."

We had made friends at once, after a brief peek-a-boo game played behind the jamb of the door leading into the hall. I had taken her up on my lap and learned her name, Valentine. She had been born on February fourteenth and would soon be four, but Halloween was the next big day in her young life. "I'm going to be a Smurf," she had said in a loud, satisfied boast. She had slipped off my lap and, after running into another room, had come back to show me a dime-store costume in a cardboard box. The blue-and-white plastic face of a Smurf mask grinned at me from the cellophane window. "See, I going to be Smurf for Halloween."

"You lucky girl," I grinned at her as she tried on the mask for me. She was so adorable and so alive with her innocent pride and pleasure. Her older brother and sisters watched with the solemn wariness of wisdom from the kitchen door. They knew that their mother was dead, knew that she was gone and would not come back—ever—and they knew that I was white and that there was a barrier between us because I was. Valentine was still too small to know about either death or race. She was going to be a Smurf and that was quite enough for her.

Ismeralda had come back from the living room and seen the little girl on my lap. "Child, what you doin'? You don't bother the lady like that."

"She's no bother. She's a love. She's so pretty," I said, all the time flirting with Valentine.

Ismeralda had liked that. "She is pretty, ain't she? Valda always be sayin' she too black." She shook her head as if to wipe away the image.

"How awful." How could a mother have said such a thing about such a dear child as this? A stab of dislike for Valda went through me. I could forgive or overlook so much about her ugly life-style, but how does one forgive cruelty meted out to her own baby? I stroked Valentine's smooth chocolate skin. "You are a beauty, honey." She grinned at me and hid her face behind the costume box.

I returned from my tale with a shake of my head. "Too black, indeed!" I exclaimed. "You know, Meta, I've never known anyone like Valdalene Pearsall—or Ismeralda, for that matter, though I think she is a far nicer person than Valda must have been. Who was she? How little must she have loved herself to have lead such a life. She actually prized in herself the very whiteness of a man who could father her and then not be a reasonable human being toward her or her mother. She might have rejected all things white, but it was her blackness she rejected, and that of her little child. Damn it, she was worth more than that, and what is so sad, she never knew it."

Meta looked at me thoughtfully, pursing her lips again. "And what can you do about it, luv? Valda's dead."

"That's just it. There are so many Valdas in this world, and they're not all black either. She may be dead, but the others are still alive. Little Valentine is still alive, and unless someone says that she's worth something—that she's not too black or too something else—why, what's to stop her from becoming another Valdalene Pearsall in her day? Somehow, Ismeralda Jackson has escaped the curse. She has pride in herself and a sense of her own person and value. She has it—why didn't Valda?" Then, hit by a sudden impulse, I got up from the table and made a dash for the front door.

"Where are you off to, luv?"

"Upstairs to make a call. Ismeralda said her sister had an apartment up near the projects. If the police haven't sealed it for evidence, I want to have a look."

Over my shoulder, I could see my landlady shake her head. She was right—I was obsessed. I knew it and I knew that there was no help for it. Now if only I knew *why* I was so obsessed. . . .

$\triangledown$

5

THE EIGHTEENTH-CENTURY GENTLEMAN

ISMERALDA Jackson had made no objection to showing me her sister's apartment as long as I met her at once and didn't take too long. She had to be at work at Lincoln Hospital by eleven. I pulled up in front of the address she had given me at 9:45, cracked the window slightly for Molly Brown, and climbed out of the car. She was anxiously waiting for me on the stoop of a fairly neat graystone rowhouse whose first-floor windows were rendered blank by dusty, old-fashioned wide-slatted venetian blinds. The second-floor windows were clean and revealed masses of indoor plants, green and well-tended between panels of machine-made white lace curtains.

Ismeralda greeted me with an informality that I found comfortable and reassuring. "Come on, honey, we ain't got much time an' I don't want to run into the landlord." She saw me looking up. "She live on the top floor—" I looked up and saw the third set of windows, hung with red drapes, dirty-looking and faded to pinkish yellow along the folds as if they were rarely opened and never cleaned.

"Have the police been here yet?" I asked as I followed Ismeralda into the vestibule.

"Uh-uh, girl. I ain't never even told them about this place. If they know, why, honey, you an' me'd be locked out already. I don't want them ta know. I ain't payin' no rent on this here place so no po-lice can poke in her stuff, uh-uh."

We climbed the stairs. There was a smell of garbage coming from the back of the lower hall, but otherwise it was a fairly decent place to live, old but reasonably clean and free from the depredations of junkies and winos.

Valda's flat was stale from weeks of being unoccupied. The formica wood-grained furniture, as seen in the translucence of her dark, dusty drapes, looked cheap and shabby and hardly serviceable, with its slender screw-in wooden legs. Even the nondescript "Danish Modern" sofa had a disillusioned dentist's-office look to it. There were no pictures, no books, no personal items save a scattering of brightly colored plastic toys, a vase of plastic roses that looked filthy and forlorn, and two framed photos of Valda herself.

I didn't know precisely what it was that I was looking for, but whatever it was, that sparse, dusty living room didn't seem to hold any secrets. I walked slowly across the thin carpet and down a short stretch of hall into the bathroom. The paint was green and peeling away in blistered flakes. The tile was cracked in places. The sink, toilet, and old-fashioned claw-footed bathtub were all worn, discolored, and rust-red around the chipped drains, but, other than that, kept quite clean. There was the usual complement of toothbrushes, soap, sponges, washcloths, and aspirin around and in a small straw hamper under the sink, a host of female-hygiene products, and birth-control supplies of various sorts. I dropped the lid with distaste and moved on to the bedroom that had been Valda's.

The morning sun was streaming in through a chink in imperfectly closed pink drapes. Ismeralda moved across the room with clucking tongue and opened them wide. The walls were pink and the furniture, like Ismeralda's living room suite, was white, but there the similarity ended. This was the room of a teenage girl—all pink and white ruffles, a flimsy white four-poster that hardly looked like the place to entertain a john, and a frilly dressing table tarted up with all the cheap gaudiness of schlock-shop eyelet and velveteen drapery. On the fussy pink-and-white bedspread lay a garish hot-pink-and-white plush panda—a huge thing with plastic eyes, a big red tongue, and a satin bow around its neck. It had obviously come from an amusement arcade. Coney Island, perhaps? Atlantic City?

I could picture her, laughing, her blue eyes alight, as some fellow threw soft balls or shot an air rifle or tossed rings to win it for her. She must have carried it home with pride and happiness— not for her children, but rather for the child that was Valda.

"She always did want nice things, Valda, an' she do her best to get them," Ismeralda said softly, looking past my shoulder into the hall, across which the children's room lay, a tiny room stacked with two sets of bunk beds and a shabby end table. There was a slide bolt on the door so she could lock them in. Shades of Alice Crimmins, I thought.

I looked back at the frilly bed and its ludicrous teddy bear, wondering about Valda and touched by her vulnerability. She had lived by her body—a woman old beyond her twenty-five years— yet inside she had been a frightened little girl who slept with a pink teddy bear—when she wasn't sleeping with a man whose strange desire for a child had led to her death. It was all so bizarre, so remote from my own life.

"Was Valda's father's name Pearsall or was that your mother's maiden name?" I asked suddenly.

Ismeralda looked at me with a furrowed brow. "My momma, she ain't no tramp like Valda," she said emphatically. For me, that answer came completely out of left field. Then I saw the inference of my question.

"Oh, Ismeralda, I—I didn't . . ."

She looked at me with hurt in her eyes, a hurt that I shrank from seeing because I liked her and the last thing I could have wanted was to cause her pain. "You be askin', Mizz Fay, if my momma an' Ned Pearsall have Valdalene out o' wedlock. Well, Valda weren't no bastard an' I ain't neither. My grandma Doris, she did cleanin' for Ned Pearsall's mother in Bay Ridge, Brooklyn, and sometime my momma help. Ned, he come back from Korea and he laid up for years with his leg, on disability. He sweet-talk my momma sure enough," she said defensively, "but when momma tell him Valda on the way, he marry her proper. Shit, girl, he be nothin' but trash. He always talkin' on about his leg an' gettin' disability an' he don't work hardly at all, but he drink more an' more til finally he walk out an' don't come back. Valda be two, maybe a bit older. My momma divorce Ned Pearsall legal an' she marry my father. My father was a fine man."

"I don't doubt it, Ismeralda, really I don't. I was only asking about the name Pearsall because I happened to remember that my great-grandmother's name was Pearsall, too. We might have been cousins, Valda and I." I wanted so badly to tell her I was sorry, yet I didn't know how, but Ismeralda surprised me by shaking off her momentary hurt and bouncing back to her usual pragmatic self.

She laughed out loud. "Cousins! Ooo-eeh, honey, but you have got it bad. She be hauntin' you, that crazy sister o' mine."

"You think I'm a fool, don't you?" I asked, looking at her plump, merry face doubtfully.

She responded by crossing the room and putting one short, chubby arm around my shoulder gently. "Shit, no, honey. I just think you one funny white gal, that's all. But you no fool. You too nice for a fool. I know that from the way you treat my little Valentine. She be so sweet an' so alive, that chile—an' Valdalene got no use for her little black self. She be the darkest one, you see. I told you yesterday her pa be a black pimp, but the other kids, they all got white pas, so Valdalene always favor them. I tries ta be fair to them all—I loves them all—but Valentine, she special. You understand."

"Yes, I do," I whispered, returning her hug. After that brief moment of self-conscious affection and understanding, we grew embarrassed and pulled abruptly away, she to the dressing table to collect a few of Valda's things and I to the kitchen, in my aimless

quest for impressions of the child-woman who had been Valdalene
Pearsall.

When Ismeralda found me, I was leaning against the kitchen sink,
breathing shallow breaths and fighting a feeling of nausea that had
come over me in a succession of waves. I motioned her away. "It's
all right. I'm okay," I croaked. "I won't be sick." I turned on the
tap and watched the water run rusty into the sink before it finally
began to clear. Ismeralda came up to me with a glass, rinsed it, and
gave it to me filled with cold water. I drank slowly, seeing my own
paper-white face like a mask in the mirror over the sink.

"Ismeralda," I said at last, emptying the glass and rinsing it
under the tap, "what the hell is that jar on the table there?" I turned
and pointed to a large mayonnaise jar. The label was gone, but two
long, flat smears of glue on one side of the glass indicated where it
had once been attached. The jar itself was filled to overflowing
with a tangled mess of assorted junk—pennies and slugs, loose
change, safety pins both old and new, some rusty and some bent,
broken bits of jewelry, small lengths of chains, broken earrings,
plastic charms, marbles, even a rabbit's foot.

She laughed. "Valdalene an' her junk. She always be findin'
things, that girl. Her pockets, her purse, she always got them full
o' trash she find. Finally, Momma, she give her a jar once an' she
say 'here, girl, you find what you want, but you puts it all in one
place an' don't be clutterin' up my house with your trash.' That's
years ago, honey, when I was just a little thing, but ever since,
when Valda come home, she drop what she find in a jar on the
kitchen table. She'd find a gold ring now and then or a nice bracelet
once or a five-dollar bill, but mostly it be junk: safety pins an'
pennies." She chuckled and shook her head. "That gal, she just
never can resist."

As she spoke, I felt uneasily for a chair and sat down, staring
sickly at the jar before me in the center of the table. It was flanked
by a plastic napkin holder and a nondescript pair of chrome-topped
glass salt and pepper shakers that might have been swiped from a

Nedick's or a diner somewhere. But despite the innocuousness of the surroundings, that jar and its contents were absolutely evil in their implications—the last link in the chain that bound me to the woman on the slab in the city morgue.

"Thank you so much, Ismeralda. I—I've been here long enough and I know that you have to get to work. I won't keep you any longer." I spoke through a buzzing in my head so loud that I remember wondering vaguely how it could be that she didn't hear it too.

Down on the street, she looked at me curiously. "Are you all right?" she asked, with that characteristic frown.

"Yes, yes, really, I'm fine. I—I'm on my way to the ferry. I have to go to Staten Island."

There are few things so salubrious to my troubled spirits as a ride on the Staten Island Ferry. Even the grim green paint and grime of the terminal at South Ferry cannot take much away from the glories of what is still the cheapest and best thrill left in what was once a city of clean fun, family outings, free museums, and safe streets. One of the things that keeps this disillusioned New Yorker still loving New York is the ferry, with its incomparable views of the Battery, the Manhattan skyline, and the Lady in the Harbor. And its ultimate destination, that low-hilled old island that is the seat of so many of my early ancestors—the seafaring Dutchmen and English sea captains, the Huguenot refugees and Irish businessmen who settled there and whose daughters married and intermarried into the vast melting pot that is America.

Standing as far forward as the flexible iron gates permit, with my arms resting on the wooden railing of the upper deck, I brave, in rain, fog, or even sleet, the raw wind that comes up the Narrows from the Great South Bay with what I hope is some of the stoic endurance of my great-grandfather, Captain Jeremiah Merrick Van Voorst. He piloted old Commodore Vanderbilt's steam ferries through these waters for several decades beginning in the 1840s, surviving the disastrous *Westfield* explosion at the Battery in 1871, though 104 others lost their lives. Had he died then, at the age of forty-six, I would not now exist, for his oldest daughter, my grandmother, Marion Van Voorst Fay, was not born until 1874. Upon such small accidents of fate hang all our lives and those of our posterity. On such an accident as Molly Brown and I finding Valdalene's dead mooncalf hung—what? What thread was now being spun, and where, in what remote future, would that thread ravel and break?

Fortunately, Uncle Jeremiah's phone was listed, so when I called from the ferry terminal at St. George, it took only a minute or two of sparring with a very superior-sounding general factotum before he came on the wire himself. His voice was amiable and his manner such that I felt immediately at my ease with him.

"Splendid, splendid. You're in St. George, you say? Marvelous. I dine at one so you are just in time to join me. Stay near the taxi rank, and I shall send Rogers down to fetch you."

When Rogers arrived, it was in the 1937 Rolls Royce Phantom III limousine that, rumor had it, my uncle had purchased in London in order to attend the coronation of King George VI and Queen Elizabeth in proper style. It had been one of my father's favorite gripes against his younger, richer brother. The Rolls passed through the shabby streets of ancient St. George like an aging grande dame, sniffing delicately as she pretends not to notice the derelict snoozing on the park bench. I hailed Rogers, completely perfect in his livery of maroon and gray, and followed in my little red Mustang like a cur with her tail between her legs.

"Well, Moll," I said, speaking to my own cur, "you get to pee on the lawn of a house that owns a Rolls. What do you think of that, you little mutt? Is that the high life or is that the high life?"

She looked at me, sniffed as if to say she considered it no less than her due, and went back to contemplating the decaying grandeur of some of Tomkinsville's finest old houses. There were plane trees with their mottled, peeling trunks, and maples and chestnuts in abundance on Dissoway Drive as we rode up the hill from Van Duzer Street. Dissoway, which climbed and wound for a while, ended abruptly at the ridge of the hill in a rusted iron railing, beyond which a steep incline covered with a thick copse of untended trees and undergrowth led down the other side to Howard Avenue nearly a quarter of a mile off.

On either side of the drive stood two large houses, virtually identical save for the various additions made over the last century. Each was set well back from old uneven slate slab sidewalks and each was surrounded by an identical high, crumbling, and mossy brick wall, ornamented with massive iron gates that looked as if they had not been painted in decades. As in the less noble, but not inconsequential houses on the winding road leading to these grand edifices, there was an air of shabby gentility, of grandeur past its prime and lost in the mists of another century.

Ahead of me, beneath the great shade trees, glowing orange and gold with bright unshed leaves, Rogers slowed the Rolls to a crawl, honked once, and guided it into the wide laurel-bordered driveway of the mansion to the left—huge, high, and middle Victorian. It sat on the largest and highest plot of ground on Dissoway Drive, actually looking down on its near twin, which stood on the lower side of the road. Leave it to Uncle Jeremiah.

As I pulled in after the Rolls feeling exactly like the poor relation that I was, a tall old man in the slightly rusty black kit of a movie butler came scuttling like a crab from under the porte cochere at the side of the house to drag the iron gates closed behind us. He padlocked them with care and turned to help me out of the car. Molly scrambled across my lap with a series of hysterical yelps, projecting herself onto the lawn while using my thighs as a launching pad. She had spotted a squirrel.

"It's all right, Miss. She can't get off the property. She'll be quite safe." His accent was decidedly British, with the culture and reserve of a proper, old-fashioned English butler.

"Yes, but the garden? She's no respecter of other people's lawns, I'm afraid." Even as I spoke, she gave up on the squirrels and squatted to piddle. The old man smiled.

"It hardly matters," he said. "We only have a man in to rake leaves at this time of year, and your uncle won't mind. He loves dogs, though we haven't had one since Sir Dennis died three years ago."

We walked up the front steps. Rogers and the Rolls had disappeared into a long, two-storied garage at the back of the property. It looked as if it had once been a stable and coach house. The windows above were curtained, suggesting that Rogers' quarters were there, which, I learned later was indeed the case.

"Your uncle was quite delighted with your call. He has read your article on that unfortunate infant with great interest. We all have, in fact."

"Really? How flattering," I answered, blinking at the reference to the "unfortunate infant." He sounded just like my uncle—or maybe after years of a master-servant relationship, it was the other way around.

"I am Lynch, by the way, Miss. You won't remem—"

"Lynch!" I exclaimed. "But of course I remember. You were wonderful. It was the time of Grandpa Fay's funeral—that monstrous snowstorm, the Blizzard of forty-seven, in fact—and you kept me and the other children out of everyone's hair. You played games with us, carried me piggyback in the snow—" I stopped, blushing at the thought. "I was a great deal smaller then, wasn't I, Lynch?"

He smiled. "And I was a great deal younger, Miss. That was too, too long ago. And you are a writer now, Miss. Most impressive, that. Your uncle was delighted when you chose the name Fay rather than your married name. . . ."

"Lynch, married names come and go these days. What name one was born with is one's only sure identity."

"That is well spoken, child, and Lynch is right. I was indeed happy that you stuck with Fay. It's a fine old name—our name. Now, man, do stop monopolizing this girl of mine and see to luncheon." With that, I found myself enfolded in Uncle Jeremiah's arms, squeezed against the rough English tweed of his hand-tailored lapels and then pushed to the length of his arms so that he could survey me from head to toe. "Miranda, how exceptionally well you look."

"Separation agrees with me. Wait till I get the divorce, Uncle Jeremiah. I shall positively bloom."

"You *sound* like your father, but you're your mother all over again. Claire was such a pretty woman—the same smile, the same nose and eyes. But that Fay jaw of yours, poor girl," he winced, shaking his head and giving me a wry smile. "You've got the same stubborn jaw that your father and I inherited from our grand-mother, Lydia Pearsall Fay." He pulled me to him again, hugged me once more, and guided me, with one arm firmly around my shoulder, through the front door and into a spacious, oak-panelled hall. To the right was his library, a great long room with tall, narrow windows set in groups of two or three.

"Welcome to my sanctum sanctorum, Miranda. You've never been here, have you?"

I gasped audibly at the room that lay before me. It was all that I could have dreamed of in the world, had fortune ever smiled upon me. "Not since I was three," I answered breathily, not tearing my eyes from the beauty and serenity of what I saw. "Back then, eight-foot snowdrifts and a young handsome manservant named Lynch held more attractions for me than fine walnut bookcases packed with all the books in the world. I've changed a bit since then," I added with a grin as I stepped reverently onto an eigh-teenth-century Kashan carpet of lovely mellow golds and greens and reds.

"Uncle Jeremiah, this room is absolutely magnificent."

I turned toward him. He was leaning against his desk, a huge, broad mahogany pedestal desk piled with stacks of books, some neat and carefully studded with bookmarks, others spread open for immediate use, their pages weighted with paperweights of bronze and glass and malachite. He had several stacks of leather-bound ring binders both on and around the desk at his feet. As I observed him I saw that he had the extremely contented and self-satisfied air of an accomplished scholar about him. How I envied that air and how, I realized, I aspired to just such a contentment. With his arms folded across his deep chest, he watched me quite cannily, as if assessing me with those glittering dark eyes of his. They sparkled knowingly from beneath his thick, tufted white eyesbrows.

"This is the most wonderful room I have ever been in." I must have sounded terribly ingenuous, but I could not help myself. Parian busts of Shakespeare, Byron, Napoleon, Caesar, Gordon, Burns, and any number of others alternated with a valuable collection of eighteenth- and early nineteenth-century creamware ale pitchers and tankards along the tops of the bookcases. The walls behind them were hunter green to the beginning of the vaulted ceiling, which was of creamy white strapworked plaster studded with Tudor roses.

"There are nearly thirty thousand books in this room alone. Above is the rest of the collection." He pointed an elfish finger upward.

I looked beyond him to a spiral staircase, a perfect but stationary replica of the movable library steps near which I stood. It rose into the fifteen-foot ceiling in the left front corner of the room near a heavily draped bow of windows. Cocking my head to one side, I could just see the beginnings of more shelves and more books at the top of the stairway.

"Down here are kept art, archaeology, anthropology, biography, history, first editions, and genealogy. Above are languages, literature, medicine, the natural sciences, general fiction, and in my bedroom, my two great weaknesses: detective fiction and criminology." He paused, grinning apologetically. "I also have a penchant for supernatural literature, something that I do not admit to everyone."

"Poe, M. R. James, William Hope Hodgson . . . I have the same weaknesses, you see."

"And Lovecraft! From the description of that infant that you found, Nyack may yet rank as another Arkham."

I laughed at that. "I'm afraid not, Uncle Jeremiah. That babe was strictly a product of the South Bronx. Criminology is an even greater passion with me, though," I added.

"So I gather," he answered dryly, "or else why write so forcefully about that unpleasant find of yours? Your article shows just how caught up you have become. It is very good, by the way."

"Thank you. I am caught up—more and more, in fact, though I must admit that filthy lucre had something to do with it at first. As for these articles, you haven't heard the half of it. It's getting deeper, and something happened today that put the wind up my sails—I suppose that that's why I've turned up on your doorstep so suddenly."

"Does it have to do with this woman that they've found—this Valdalene Pearsall?" He placed, I noticed, a very heavy emphasis on the name Pearsall. I nodded weakly. "She is the mother, then?" he asked with a frown. "The papers suggested she might be."

"She is, but I think that there's more to it than that. I've just come from her flat, and it's not just the name. She—*finds things* too. Like I do. It made me so sick. I actually shook when I saw the jar— I mean the name is funny enough. A coincidence, one could say, but not the finding things—not that too. I—I know that I'm not making sense, but I actually came here as if by instinct. I left that kitchen with that jar on the table and I knew that I had to come here—to see you. Oh, damn, I must sound crazy."

I was suddenly talking too much and too fast, growing dizzy and faint. Uncle Jeremiah was eighteenth century enough to produce from a drawer somewhere a tiny cut-glass vial of smelling salts. He sat me down in a great leather wing chair by the empty fireplace and waved them under my nose. I could hardly believe what was happening, it was a gesture so out of time, but they did revive me, or perhaps it was just that they annoyed me enough to make me pull myself together. In any case, he soon removed the vial and replaced it with a tot of brandy.

"Drink this. You look quite ill, my dear."

"Oh, Uncle Jeremiah, how trying for you to have a long-lost

niece pop out of nowhere and nearly faint onto your carpet." I slung the brandy down my throat like a whiskey neat.

"It's quite a good brandy, actually," he drawled good-naturedly. "You really ought to try tasting it first."

I knew at once that he was teasing me. "I will if you give me another," I retorted, holding up the delicate glass for a refill. It was good, as he suggested, and so I nursed the second glass, savoring it and letting it warm my innards and settle my nerves. He distracted me for a time with a discourse on the various treasures with which the room was filled and then, with a glance at his watch, he announced. "Now we shall lunch. When you are ready, you will tell me all about this 'mooncalf'—very apt term, that—and of course, all about our Cousin Valdalene who finds things."

"Our cousin?"

"Of course, our cousin," he repeated and led me across the hall into an elegant, gracefully proportioned, sunny dining room. "You must have have half-suspected the relationship, or the name would not have upset you so." He raised his tufted eyebrows expressively as he saw me to the chair that Lynch had pulled out for me.

"It wasn't the name that upset me. I even joked about our possible relationship with my landlady over breakfast this morning. But when I saw that jar—"

"Yes, yes, of course," Uncle Jeremiah said hurriedly, perhaps trying to head off another fit of the vapors. "You say Pearsall was her father's name?" he asked as he took his seat and shook out his damask napkin. Lynch poured our wine.

I nodded, looking into the ruby depths of my glass.

"And that her father was white—or is?"

"Or is," I concurred. "He may be living still for all I know. She herself was only twenty-five, not quite twenty-six."

"So," he mused, tilting back slightly as Lynch served our first course, "this was a legitimate surname given to her by her white father and not, as in so many cases, merely a name that was long ago passed on to a black slave by a white master who may or may not have had a blood tie to him. That is most interesting, and makes it virtually certain that she was indeed a collateral relation of ours. A cousin, if you will, however distant. You see, almost every person in America with Pearsall blood descends from one man, Thomas Pearsall, through one of his five sons: Thomas the younger, Henry, Nicholas, George, and Samuel. We descend in two separate lines from his second son, Henry Pearsall of Hempstead, Long Island, who married Ann Valentine . . ."

And so, over a delicious luncheon and a prodigal amount of wine, I learned all about my Pearsall forebears—all I wanted to know and perhaps a good deal more. In turn, Uncle Jeremiah learned all there was to know as yet about Valdalene Pearsall, which was a good deal more than he might have wished to know. We were a pair of enthusiasts, my uncle and I. It seemed to be a family trait.

After that day, I never thought of him as just Uncle Jeremiah. For me he became the perfect eighteenth-century gentleman, raising the heavy, simply cut lead crystal decanter at his elbow and saying most casually, "More port, my dear?" A man out of another, lovelier age.

I loved to hear him speak, for though his voice was high and thinned by age, his speech was impeccable and more than slightly tempered by all the years he spent in England between the wars and after World War II. He had the polished, immaculate look that some well-groomed elderly men are blessed with: rosy cheeks against pink scrubbed skin, a fringe of neat silver hair circling a smooth, well-shaped bald pate, and eyes of an unimaginably bright, clear amber-brown, untouched by rheum, broken blood vessels, or the clouding of incipient cataracts. His hands were slender, graceful, steady, and elegantly manicured. He had been a lawyer until his retirement in the early sixties, as at ease with the weight of the law books as he was now with the weight of *Burke's Peerage* and *Debrett's*.

"Your grandmother found things too, you know," he said quite casually as he rested the decanter in its silver coaster.

"Did she?" I asked eagerly. The combination of Uncle Jeremiah and his wine had done much to bring me back to myself. I was eager to find the answer to what seemed at the moment to be simply a strange sort of mystery. "But wait, I—I think I knew that. I remember now that Mother said she had spent her childhood being embarrassed by her mama always finding pennies and buttons and pins and now had spawned a daughter who did the same. It *is* an awful habit, I suppose, to someone who does not have it, but it's really second nature with me. For instance, I found forty-seven cents and a subway token today, between the newspaper stand in Nyack and the ferry terminal in St. George, and that was without even trying. Max finds it quite offensive."

He regarded me quietly for a long moment. "That is most interesting, Miranda. I was not, however, referring to your mother's mother, whom I never knew, of course. I was referring to my own mother, Marion Pearsall Van Voorst."

"Were you?" I sounded cool and calm, but I set down my glass abruptly. The wine had become vinegar in my mouth.

"Interesting," he repeated, raising a tufted silver eyebrow.

"Yes," I agreed with constraint.

"You say that you have always found things and that this unfortunate young Negress—she too had a similar penchant. And now you have been linked by the bizarre fact of your finding the infant that she lost—that quite literally was taken from her. Curious but hardly indicative of any more than another of those peculiar coincidences that life offers up now and then." He paused to challenge me. "Wouldn't you say?"

"I—it's a feeling I have," I insisted stubbornly. "And the coincidence of the name. You say that we are related?"

"More than likely," he agreed.

"Well, then, doesn't that set you to thinking? It does me."

"Yes, it has," he admitted with a shrug, "but it is not always the wisest course, is it?" He smiled tolerantly, making me feel very young indeed.

"If you had seen—"

"Quite so, but I haven't. Perhaps I should. Tomorrow I shall visit the morgue. The body has not been released yet, has it?"

"No, no it hasn't. Would you go?" I asked eagerly, though in retrospect I cannot imagine what good I thought it would do.

"But of course. It is a long time since I was in a dissecting room, but I'm sure I shall manage. Your grandfather intended me to be a doctor, you see, but I preferred law and switched eventually. I was more obedient for a longer time than your father. It took more effort for me to defy the old man."

He smiled and began to reminisce about my father and the family.

After our leisurely luncheon, Uncle Jeremiah took me on a tour of the rest of the house, ending with his second-floor library, which he called the "lounge" since it had a pair of well-sprung and mellow leather chesterfield sofas and matching hassocks set before the fireplace. It was a less awesome and formal room than the main library below and had an air of solidly masculine mid-Victorian comfort.

I had been kneeling on the velvet cushion of the seat in the bow window, watching Molly root about in the underbrush, happily questing after field mice. "Moll in Boots," I said, turning back to my uncle, who was engaged in pulling books off the shelves to show me. "I've always thought she should wear high boots, a cavalier's cape and hat, and come back home each day with her catch of mice strung by their tails to her belt—you know, just like Puss in Boots."

Uncle Jeremiah put an arm around my shoulder affectionately. "Seeing her makes me realize how much I miss old Dennis. I've become a rather insular old fellow since I don't have a dog to walk."

I snickered. "When you are not being uncommonly peripatetic, I expect you are, Uncle Jeremiah, but these annual trips to England and France and the side trips to Boston and Washington and goodness knows where else hardly smack of insularity. In fact, it's actually quite a marvel that I found you in today when I called."

"Yes, it *is*, come to that!" He smiled. "In fact, if it were not for my neighbor over there, I doubt I should have been home this afternoon at all. I am having him and his mother to dinner this evening and so thought I'd better spend the day quietly." Uncle Jeremiah nodded toward the driveway of the twin house opposite us across Dissoway Drive. We could look down from our height into the walled garden and see a long black Cadillac Seville that had just pulled up under the porte cochere. A manservant stepped forward and opened the passenger door for an imposing-looking man who stepped ponderously out onto the driveway and turned to offer a hand to his companions.

"Gilbert St. Mauger." He pronounced the Gilbert in the French manner. "That's his mother, Isabelle," he explained as a small, frail-looking elderly lady climbed from the car. The son passed her along to the butler and turned to help another woman.

"Well now, this is a surprise," Uncle Jeremiah said with his eyebrows raised and his eyes wide. "Hillary St. Mauger herself— and as beautiful as ever. It hardly seems possible. Remarkable."

He did not explain then who she was or why her presence should be so remarkable, but to say that she was beautiful was something of an understatement. Like my uncle himself, she had an air of having stepped out of time, albeit another time than that which seemed to suit him. She was a stunning ash blonde, very tall and slender though her frame was rather on the large side. Her hair was coiffed in an exaggeratedly marcelled style reminiscent of the thirties, which gave one an impression, further heightened by her clinging black crepe dress, small-veiled hat, and huge black fox wrap, that she belonged in that era more than in our own.

"What a smart-looking woman."

"Shall I make a wager with you, Miranda, my dear? My friend St. Mauger will call within the next ten minutes to say that he regrets he and his mama shan't be able to dine this evening because his sister has arrived suddenly from Paris or Cannes or wherever and is too fatigued to join us—the Concorde is so tiring, you know—and of course they, in good conscience, cannot leave her alone on her first night in his home, and I will understand, surely."

"But why?" I asked, puzzled by his suggestion. The trio had disappeared into the house by now and a vast quantity of luggage was being taken from the front seat and trunk of the car by servants. Miss St. Mauger did not travel light.

"Because, Miranda—" Before he could finish, the phone did indeed begin to ring. "Because," he said jauntily as he reached across his desk for the extension, "Hillary St. Mauger hates your poor old uncle with a passion. Yes, yes, St. Mauger, Fay here." He winked at me merrily as he listened to the voice at the other end of the line. "How are you, old man? Splendid, splendid. No? I didn't know. Oh, I see. She's rather fagged, I should imagine, after the flight. Yes, yes, of course I understand. Think nothing of it. What a pity though. My niece Miranda is here unexpectedly. I'd just prevailed upon her to stay and join us. Miranda Fay. She's my older brother's only child. Yes, of course I have a niece. I suppose I've just never mentioned her. No, I haven't seen her in nine years as a matter of fact. Well, never mind, another time. Do send my regards to Hillary, and your mother, of course."

Uncle Jeremiah put down the phone chuckling. "Sorry, my dear, but I just couldn't help using you as bait. He's such an old busybody. If it were up to him, he'd be over here alone tonight just to see what my niece looks like. Shame on me for putting a flea in his ear like that."

We had just settled down on the couch nearest the windows to look over some first editions that my uncle had taken down when the phone rang again. I went on browsing while he spoke briefly, first to the caller and then to Lynch on the house line. He came back to the couch shaking his head quizzically.

"We shall have company for dinner after all, it seems. St. Mauger has changed his mind—or rather, his sister feels it would be rude to cancel, especially when another lady is invited to dine. We are honored, niece, we are truly honored," he said solemnly before giving me the sort of wink I might have expected from my father.

Gilbert St. Hilaire St. Mauger arrived a few steps ahead of his mother and sister and was introduced forthwith. "My sister's son died last winter, you understand," he explained in a hushed, confidential whisper, busily arranging his white silk scarf before handing it to Lynch. "She and Mama have been just crushed as you will see. Such a promising lad, but shhh for now," he said fussily with one finger against his pursed lips. He turned from us and oversaw the removal of his mother's coat and his sister's furs and their delivery into the arms of the efficient and infinitely patient Lynch.

I could see why my uncle had referred to St. Mauger as a gossip. He had an air about him from time to time that, together with his imposing height and solid bulk, created the impression of a fussy court chamberlain out of *The Arabian Nights*. That, I perceived quickly, was but one aspect of the man. When sure of his ground and on a subject of his own choosing, he spoke with a warmth and authority that far more matched his imposing size than did the busybody side of his nature that so amused my uncle. On the whole, I found him rather more likable than comic and my respect for his intellect, despite his occasional lapses in behavior, grew as the evening lengthened.

If her son impressed one as both large and imposing, Madame St. Mauger appeared both in size and manner to be a virtual nonentity. A tiny sharp-featured woman, she seemed like a twittering linnet caught between a slow, intelligent owl on the one hand and a sleek, predatory falcon on the other—unlikely nestlings for such a dame.

Besides her mother, tremulous and frail, Hillary St. Mauger was indeed a falcon; aloof, stately, and hawklike even to the finely chiseled, faintly beaky features of her pale face with its creamy, flawless skin, tinted ever so slightly with rouge, her lips with pale peach lipstick. Her age I could not place with any greater accuracy than somewhere between thirty-five and forty-eight, for while her hair and skin and svelte figure bespoke youth, her languid manner and somber movements seemed those of an older woman.

Whatever the reason, it became obvious that she did truly detest my uncle and had only made a showing at the behest of her far more gregarious brother. I doubted that she had come out of deference to my presence, though she did, after one withering glance of appraisal at my shoulder-length auburn hair, simple suit, and plain walking shoes, endeavor to make polite conversation, first in the library over cocktails and then, briefly at dinner—before her brother and my uncle had swung the conversation onto the lively topic of criminology.

"Your uncle, Jeremiah Pearsall here," St. Mauger said, "tells me that you are a writer and that it is your article about the aborted child that I have read in the local paper. They seemed to have found the mother, haven't they?"

"Yes, they have. I shall be handing in my next column on the latest findings to my editor tomorrow afternoon." I glanced uneasily across the table toward Hillary St. Mauger. This hardly seemed the sort of conversation for a woman in mourning for a child.

"May we have a preview, so to speak? Won't you tell us all about it?" he coaxed. "Your uncle tells me you were a witness to the autopsy in the morgue. I find that utterly fascinating." He stared at me owlishly.

I felt profoundly uncomfortable. His sister had shifted in her seat and taken a mouthful of food. Clearly, she didn't like the subject under discussion. "It is hardly dinner conversation," I suggested politely and nodded toward his sister, hoping he would take my point.

"Twaddle, twaddle, twaddle. Hillary is not so fragile as all that. She loves a good murder as much as I do." He might have been a spoiled child instead of a grown man of about forty-five or fifty. I almost expected him to end his exclamation with a rude face at his sister.

"Gilbert, that will be enough. Can you not see that you are

upsetting your poor sister needlessly, and that you are embarrassing your host's niece? Jeremiah Fay is used to your behavior and is kind enough to tolerate it, but I will not." Madame St. Mauger had laid down her fork decisively and with it, all illusion that she was but a poor linnet to her unlikely chicks. Her black eyes flashed wickedly and her mouth closed like a trap.

"Miranda and I were discussing Roughead and Pearson this afternoon, St. Mauger," Uncle Jeremiah said affably in what proved to be a successful attempt to get the conversational ball rolling again. "I showed her all my material on the murders at Smutty Nose. She prefers Edmund Pearson to Tennyson-Jesse and Lizzie Borden to Mrs. Bravo."

"Does she now?" St. Mauger asked brightly, forgetting his mother's scolding at once and getting down to cases just as gory as Valdalene Pearsall's but less controversial for not being so immediate. Murder done one hundred years ago is somehow more acceptable then the grue in one's daily headlines, and can even be elevated to the level of high-flown philosophical discussion when in the proper hands.

By the time I had rolled my car into Meta's garage in South Nyack and taken Molly for her last walk of the evening, the world seemed in better perspective than it had when I had fled from the Bronx that morning, headed for Staten Island.

My Uncle Jermiah, with his elegant manner and warm good sense, had calmed and charmed me. Gilbert St. Mauger had delighted and intrigued me, for he had, in spite of his quaintness, a wit and mischief that was engaging. He was as charming to me as Guy was not, and in spite of myself I found I was thinking for the first time in a long time with warmth about a member of the opposite sex.

But that aside, I felt that somehow my obsession with Valdalene Pearsall was exorcised and that she, poor woman, was simply what the screaming headlines in the New York tabloids said she was:

another dead prostitute, one among many casualties of drugs and violence on the underside of life.

The fact that both of us "found things" was merely coincidence—an accidental and irrelevant coincidence.

$\triangledown$

6

BRENDA SOLDANO

I had my article ready for Peter Polhemus well before the three o'clock deadline. He was on the phone in his crowded little office. "Here, read this and see what you think," I whispered, tossing the envelope onto his desk. "If it needs a rewrite I'll be at the tearoom having lunch."

The Hudson Street Tearoom was one of Nyack's most charming secrets, a perfect little oasis of charm and serenity in which to lunch. I picked my way down the narrow steps and into a large, long basement room made clean and cool by sparkling white-washed walls into which were set dark wood beams and deep shelves brightened with rows of old teapots and leather-bound books. There was a rack of magazines through which to browse and as always a vase or two of seasonal flowers and plants. Something by Handel was playing softly on the stereo as a background to the quiet conversations taking place at several of the tables.

I stopped at the counter and ordered my usual: the house salad with tahini dressing and a pot of black raspberry tea. Outside, beyond the pair of six-over-six windows at the far end of the room, the thin autumn sun shone down on a few tables still set out on the mossy brick patio. I crossed the room and strode out through the old-fashioned screen door that led to the garden. There was a clutch of rusty mums in a bud vase on each table and only two other couples enjoying a late meal, so I felt more or less as if the whole place were mine alone. I sat down and stretched expansively, so glad to be alive and to have Peter's article finished.

I had hardly settled in when something in the dirt of the flowerbed that bordered the old bricks of the patio caught my eye: a round black object, flat and unmistakably milled along its edge.

It was a silver sixpence, blackened by years in the earth but still quite legible: a sixpence of King George V dated 1930. As I tried to polish it the waitress came out with my tea. "What have you got there?" she asked as she set down the pot and cup.

"A sixpence," I told her in slight wonderment.

"Oh, but that's good luck."

"What's good luck?" Peter Polhemus asked, striding up behind us on his long, loose-jointed legs.

"Miranda just found a sixpence," she answered.

Peter humphed grumpily and made a face. "Miranda doesn't need good luck. She's got talent. Miranda, you've got the makings of a damned good feature writer." He slapped my latest article down on the table and ordered more tea and a plate of cookies. He straddled the chair across from me awkwardly and sat down. I looked at the sixpence, continuing to polish it absently with my napkin.

"There seems to be more to this than you bargained for, I take it," he said softly. I looked up. He was glaring at me thoughtfully and with such kindness in those deep-set brown eyes of his, peering intently from beneath shaggy, iron-gray brows. It occurred to me just then as I watched him that there was something about that face of his that I found very appealing.

"There is, Peter, there is."

When he saw that I wouldn't speak, he went on himself. "You've put real pathos—genuine human interest, to be trite—into this article on the mother. It's a grisly subject but you've handled it well. This will definitely go out over the wires."

"Thank you," I murmured, feeling that damned sixpence grow hot in my hand. I slipped it into the pocket of my jacket.

My salad arrived—freshly cut and crisp and inviting. I stabbed into a slice of yellow squash, suddenly feeling very testy and agitated. The release I had felt after finishing the article for the *Stop-Press* was evaporating rapidly and my telling myself that "finding things" was a coincidence was rot! Finding that blasted sixpence had plunged me right back to where I had been the day before. "Sorry, Peter. I'm a wreck these days but I shouldn't take it out on you. You've been just super." I braced my arms on the edge of the table and bowed my head onto them wearily.

"I understand," he said quietly, reaching his long arm over to put his big knobby hand on top of my head like a benediction.

"No, Peter, actually you don't," I contradicted, shifting and sitting up to face him.

"There's an aspect of this whole thing that has me sort of spooked—something so crazy that I wouldn't dare put it on paper," and with that, between bites of salad and sips of tea, I told him the story of my finding things, of the blue and white onion-patterned salt box in my kitchen, full to overflowing with junk and coins and bits of broken jewelry, and of Valdalene's mayonnaise jar and of the Pearsall name and my two grandmothers who also found things.

"To top it all off, I called Ismeralda Jackson this morning and it seems that Valdalene's grandmother, Doris, used to find things too and so did her older sister, Willie Mae Debbins, who died when Doris was still a child. So it's a family trait for her too. I tried to get my Uncle Jeremiah to let him know, but he had already left for the city."

"It all sounds so silly, kid. You can't take it seriously," he asked, "can you?"

"Oh, Peter, you're no help at all," I groaned, getting the last bit of salad onto my fork. At that we both laughed and he called for the check.

Monday morning dawned splendidly bright and crisp although WINS predicted afternoon temperatures in the midseventies, still an abnormally warm temperature range for the middle of October.

I staggered sleepily into the kitchen to give Moll her Alpo, took one look at the salt box full of junk and found objects sitting benignly on the counter, and suddenly lost my yen to make breakfast. Instead, I dressed slowly, gave M. Brown her walk, waved to Meta through her porch window, and strolled up Piermont Avenue to town. I carried my notebook with me, hoping somewhat unrealistically to read over the last couple of chapters of my book and get back to work on something healthier than autopsy reports.

My favorite waitress at the Skylark had just put a plate of French toast and bacon down before me when Peter came tearing in and sat down across the booth from me. He ordered coffee and began to talk excitedly.

"This is getting to be a habit, boss man," I commented dryly. I am never at my best before eleven, and Peter was positively vibrating with energy.

"I phoned you and you didn't answer. I called your landlady and she said you might be here. Have you seen the *Post?*"

"No. I abhor that rag," I grumped.

"As do I," he agreed cheerfully, "but look." He held up the paper that he had had tucked under his arm. The headline read:

MONSTER BORN ON LONG ISLAND
Rape Victim Gives Birth Prematurely

"Really, Peter, do you expect me to read that over breakfast? It doesn't exactly go with French toast, you know."

"Why not? Millions of New Yorkers are," he shrugged, that big ugly face of his splitting into a grin.

"We are not amused," I huffed, "and we are not millions of New Yorkers. We are *this* New Yorker."

Peter ran his hands through his iron-gray locks in exasperation. "Miranda, be serious. After that article you gave me yesterday and the stuff about the Pearsall woman being promised money for that baby—my God, what an exclusive that's going to be come tomorrow morning," he added parenthetically, lowering his voice suddenly and looking around us like a Bolshevik conspirator. "The idea of another, what do you call it, mooncalf, being born in this area and under circumstances that are peculiar, to say the least . . . Hell, maybe we ought to look into it. Read the article at least, for Chrissake."

"Okay, okay, I will, but not over breakfast, thanks. I've been trying to shake the image of Valdalene Pearsall since last Thursday and to figure out what the hell has been going on with that stuff about finding things and being related. . . . I've just about got myself convinced that it is all just coincidence, so let me eat in peace and start this week off right, okay?"

"Well, read it if you want to. If not, just forget about it. I'm probably barking up the wrong tree anyway." He rose and started to leave.

"Peter," I called after him, "don't mind me. I just feel bitchy this morning, that's all. I'll read it and call you later." I grinned at him, a grotesque parody of my normal wide smile.

He grinned back just as grotesquely and blew me a kiss. Just as he left, the waitress came with his coffee. "Don't worry," I assured her, "I'll drink it. I have the feeling that this is going to be a four-cup Monday."

Trying to get back on the Hungerford biography was useless. My brains seemed to have turned to sludge and the coffee just gave me the shakes, so I browsed among the shelves at the Ben Franklin Bookshop in Upper Nyack for a while and then trudged home through the sunlit noon hour like a sleepwalker, wishing I could blink myself out of my foul mood.

I banged the notebook down on the coffee table and threw myself onto the sofa to brood. The notebook tipped and slid off onto the floor, carrying with it Peter's copy of the *Post*, which I still hadn't read.

"Actually, M. Brown, there are probably a lot of monsters born on Long Island." Molly, who had curled up on the sofa at my feet, offered no comment. The headline, less discreet than the Moll, blared at me. "Oh, hell," I groaned resignedly, picked up the paper and began to read:

> An unidentified nineteen-year-old Valley Stream woman, the victim of rape last March, gave birth yesterday afternoon to a premature baby so grossly malformed that reliable sources in attendance termed it a monster.
>
> It has been reported to the *Post* on good authority that the child, a female born six weeks premature, is bicephalic or two-headed, and that a third, partially formed arm grows out of the trunk near the left breast.
>
> Officials at Franklin General Hospital in Franklin Square refused to comment on the birth.

A second article recapped the original report of the kidnapping, which had occurred on the night of March 15 in the parking lot of a shopping mall on the Sunrise Highway in Valley Stream. The victim, who had just gotten off work in one of the stores in the mall, had been forced into her own car by a heavyset white man in his late thirties or early forties who then drove to a secluded area of Jamaica Bay where he proceeded to rape and sodomize her. The victim claimed to have lost consciousness for some time during the ordeal and awoke about midnight to find herself alone in her vehicle. She drove to her parents' home in Valley Stream and her father reported the incident to the police.

The assailant had been described as being a heavyset man with dark hair, dark clothes, and a three-day growth of beard. He was sweating profusely despite the cold night air and had an offensive body odor.

I tossed the paper halfway across the room. I was just considering calling Peter to tell him he was out of his mind when the phone rang. It was Guy.

"Miranda," he began without any preliminaries, "do you have an Uncle Jeremiah Fay?"

"Yes, yes, I do." I stammered. "How—"

"Relax, I don't have him on a table, if that's what you're

thinking. He called yesterday and asked me a whole bunch of questions about the fetus and Valdalene's autopsy results, all without a word of explanation. Oh, he did say he was calling from the city morgue. Is he a doctor, by the way? He sure sounded like one."

"No, he's a lawyer, but he studied medicine for a while."

"That explains it. Anyway, he thanked me and hung up. That was yesterday. He called back just now and asked if I can get him a peep at some baby out on Long Island. It's not expected to live, he says, and wants to know if I can get him in to observe the autopsy when it's held. Is he nuts?" Guy had a nice voice. I could hear the brisk good humor in it even over the wire.

"Far from it, Guy," I assured him happily. "He may even be a bloody genius. He's helping me with the mooncalf and Valdalene. I tried to get you last evening but you were out and I forgot to try again this morning."

"And I tried to get you all day Saturday. Then the shit hit and I've been busy ever since with the bodies from that big fire in Haverstraw. There'll be insurance claims and lawsuits all over the place. Right now, we're swimming in cadavers and tox reports. Look, I've got to run now, Miranda, but I'l be finished here in a couple of hours. How about dinner?"

"Okay. We've got lots to catch up on. I've been busy too."

"Fine, I'll pick you up at seven. And invite your landlady. I owe her a dinner and she's nice company."

"Fine. See you at seven." I was relieved that he was including Meta. Evidently my words the other evening had sunk in and he was backing off a bit.

Ten minutes later, Uncle Jeremiah called. "Miranda, now it's my turn to pop up out of the blue. Would you mind meeting me in Valley Stream, Long Island? Rogers informs me that you should be there in a little over an hour at most, if you leave now."

I didn't have to consider for a minute. "Yes, yes, I'll meet you wherever you like." He gave me an address: 27 Peach Tree Lane, repeating it to make sure I had it down correctly.

"You cannot imagine what I've found out in a few hours of research over this weekend," he chortled.

"About Valdalene?"

"About Cousin Valdalene, of course, but now it's on to Brenda Soldano." There was a pinging on the line. Uncle Jeremiah cursed midlly and dropped in a coin. The operator broke in to ask for more.

"Who? Uncle Jermiah—"

"Sorry, Miranda," he shouted over a buzz of interference on the wire, "I have no more change. I'll see you soon."

Peach Tree Lane in Valley Stream was a modest street of neat post-war colonials: square brick boxes with gabled half stories above. Here and there some had been enlarged and "improved" with varying degrees of success.

Uncle Jeremiah was parked at the first turning. I pulled up behind him, parked, and joined him in the back of the Rolls. I nodded at Rogers, who sat in the front reading, gave my uncle a quick peck on the cheek, and got down to the business at hand.

"Uncle, who is Brenda Soldano? I've never heard of her."

"No one has. At least not by name. She is the mother of the bicephalic child that the *Post* was screaming about in its earlier editions. It's proclaiming some rock star's marital woes this afternoon," he added blandly as he reached for a glass of brandy from the tiny bar. He sipped delicately. "Huummm, excellent, excellent," he pronounced, pouring a glass for me. "I intend us to visit Mrs. Soldano, *mère*. I spoke to her over the phone and she's expecting us. She's quite distraught, as you may imagine. Brenda is her baby, so to speak—the youngest child and only daughter, the last one at home. To have first the attack itself and then the pregnancy has been quite a strain. They are devout Catholics and so abortion—even therapeutic abortion—was out of the question for them. Pity," he commented, shaking his head. "And now this deformed infant! It's driven the good woman to the wall, one might say.

"Of course, the child isn't expected to live, so the matter of its disposition is moot, but they had originally intended to give the child up for adoption. A couple had been found, in fact—good Catholics, I imagine. They've even, it seems, insisted loudly that they are still willing to take the child, which seems bizarre to me, but then people are strange." He shrugged.

"How on God's green earth did you ever find out her name?"

He chortled into his glass, clearly pleased with the effect he was having on me, and began to explain.

"Well, for starters, your friend Dr. Galveston was no help there, though he cleared up a few questions I had yesterday about Cousin Valdalene. He hadn't even heard about the infant till I told him—which may be a good sign in its way. He evidently does not read our more sensational tabloids. Nor do I," he hastened to add. "I saw the headline in the ferry terminal this morning (I never sit in the Rolls on the ferry, you know. Fumes! Very bad for one's lungs.) and bought a copy. The coincidence was too much to resist," he said, slapping his hand on his knee for emphasis and raising those snowy eyebrows of his, "and then, when I read of the bizarre circumstances of the conception—why—"

"I know, you put two and two together and got mooncalf. So did my editor."

"I was sufficiently curious to postpone a trip to the Bronx and head straight for Franklin General Hospital where, after passing out a generous supply of ten-dollar bills, I was given Brenda's name and address. My largess, by the way, did not get me so much as a glimpse of one pink toe of the infant.

"Well," he said at last, tapping on the glass panel in front of him and motioning Rogers to get started, "number twenty-seven is just down the way. Let's visit Madame Soldano, shall we?"

Uncle Jeremiah's Rolls stunned the neighborhood into amaze and opened the door to number twenty-seven as if by magic as

Rogers pulled her up to the curb before the small brick house with the maroon siding above and glass-jalousied sun porch to the side.

"It is fascinating what a rich old man in a Rolls Royce can get away with in life, my dear," he said with a twinkle. "Until she sees my somewhat sporty tweeds, I am sure the good Mrs. Soldano will assume I am the local bishop come to offer my sympathies."

"Oh, Uncle Jeremiah, you are a caution," I laughed.

"So I've been told—and the cat's meow as well, though that was a long time ago," he grinned, once more managing to look fleetingly like my father. We emerged from the car suitably solemn-faced and walked through the chain-link gate.

Mrs. Soldano was a short, plump, very bosomy lady in her late fifties. Her hair was still black, her dark eyes still vivid. If her face had not been so tired and anxious, she'd have been a fine-looking woman. She wore a simple black knit dress and an old-fashioned overall apron in a turquoise-blue flowered pattern.

She was curious as to who Uncle Jeremiah was, why he had called, what he wanted. I sensed that she made her home open to him, and to me as his companion, out of a sort of desperation. Whoever my uncle was, perhaps he could help, could answer her questions, explain *why* such a thing had happened to her family, to her Brenda.

She seated us on a green brocaded sofa and excused herself to go to the back of the house, toward the kitchen.

We sat uncomfortably, looking around the dim room, lit only by afternoon sun slanting in through closed venetian blinds onto green wall-to-wall carpeting. The walls were covered with faded green paper in a rose and trellis pattern that evoked the fifties. Scattered here and there on indifferent pieces of dark wood furniture were holy-water holders, vigil lights, madonnas, and saints tucked in here and there amidst vases of plastic flowers and framed snapshots of family members. On every wall were framed formal portraits of young couples in wedding garb or graduation gowns or holding newborn infants—the trophies of a large and loving family.

Mrs. Soldano came back into the living room bearing a silver tray, a decanter of amaretto, and three small glasses. We sipped our liqueur and talked—or rather Mrs. Soldano did, pouring out her puzzlement and fear.

"She's our youngest, our baby, and such a good girl, so pure. A saint. What's to become of her? She is ruined."

"Surely not, my dear lady," my uncle assured her. "She is very young and even such a terrible experience as this will fade in time."

"How could it happen? There has never been an abnormal birth in our family—nothing so much as a strawberry mark that big," she lamented, holding up her pinkie and marking the top joint with her thumb. "And never out of wedlock. Never."

Wiping her eyes, she apologized for her outburst and poured more amaretto in my uncle's glass.

"But please, Mr. Pearsall, why have you come? I do not really know—"

"Mrs. Soldano, I am a student of family histories. Such a bizarre occurrence as the birth of this child is so rare. It occurs to me the answer may lie in your family history. I realize how very distressed you are, and it seems to me that by helping you and your family to find the explantion, I may make things a bit easier for you. . . ." He spoke so gently, so calmly, that she was distracted from the fact that what he was saying had no real substance.

"Seventeen grandchildren, Mr. Pearsall. Never a deformity."

"So you say and I am sure you are correct. My dear lady, people, it seems, either know nothing of their family histories or else far more than anyone else cares to hear. It is farther back in the past that the answer may lie. I wonder if you have any family records . . ."

She shook her head.

"An old family Bible perhaps?"

At this, her eyes grew bright. She trotted into a bedroom and came out with a large box wrapped in brown paper and lined with dusty tissue paper. "This came from my mother. She was a Vescio. Her father's mother's mother's Bible, this was." In the box was a big, heavy early-nineteenth-century Bible with small, dense print, steel engravings of biblical scenes, and gaudy colored engravings of saints in agony. "Very ordinary," my uncle told me later, but I rather liked it and certainly understood Mrs. Soldano's pride in it.

Its value to Uncle Jeremiah, however, lay in a list as long as the generations of Abraham of the Vescio clan, which sprang from the DeAngelo clan, which had married into the family of the original owners of the Bible. They were Moores of Newtown, Long Island. He was hard-pressed to disguise his surprise. He sat back with an air of finality and grinned like a latter-day Teddy Roosevelt. "Mrs. Soldano, may I please have a few minutes to make some notes while you show my niece these lovely portraits of your family?"

Mrs. Soldano was grateful for such a happy distraction and gave me a tour of each portrait and photo in turn. While I made polite and not entirely insincere noises over various children and grand-children, Uncle Jeremiah scribbled furiously with a gold pen in his small, gold-mounted pocket notebook, transcribing information from the family records in the Vescio Bible.

In a quick ten minutes he had done what he needed to do, soothed Mrs. Soldano with a promise to see if his researches might not yield an answer to her daughter's terrible ordeal, and extricated us from the house on Peach Tree Lane without the necessity of another sip of amaretto.

We got back into the Rolls and Rogers drove up to where I had left my car parked. We pulled up behind the Mustang and I looked over my uncle's notes on the Soldano family history.

"Well?" I asked with a shrug.

He laughed. "It is easy to see that I cannot speak the shorthand of a genealogist with you yet, my dear. Didn't you ever even glance over those family charts that I sent you after your father's funeral?"

"Yes, of course I did, and tackled them again last night, as a matter of fact, sort of like a bedtime story. I can tell you right now that if those charts are accurate, then we have no Moore ancestry from Long Island. Our Moores were Philadelphia loyalists. See, I did read it!"

"Good girl. You are a quick study. True, our Moores are from Philadelphia and Chester County, Pennsylvania, but think of whence come the Pearsalls."

"Long Island—oh, no! Don't tell me that—"

He nodded slowly. "That is why I am going right to Forty-second Street to the public library from here. I don't want to go all the way back to Staten Island to my own library, so I shall stop in Room 315N—do you know it?"

I shook my head.

"Well, you should. It is a wonderful place. I study there often. These notes show there is a line leading from Brenda back to the Moores—a Samantha Moore, actually. I am off now to check a copy of *Some Descendants of the Rev. John Moore of Newtown, Long Island* for her ancestry. I have a feeling that I shall find some interesting connections. My dear," he said, "I want you to return to Nyack and wait for me. If you don't mind, I should like to join you for dinner."

"Mind? Why of course not. I'm delighted, in fact."

And I was delighted—at least until Uncle Jeremiah joined us for drinks in Meta's living room later that evening. I made the necessary introductions and then sat back in satisfaction as my uncle, my dear landlady, and my newest friend got to know each other. It was an easy process, since each of us was a conspirator of sorts in the mystery of the mooncalf—or was it now mooncalves?

"As I told Miranda this afternoon, the Soldano-Vescio Bible shows that Brenda and her mooncalf are descended from a Samantha Moore of Hempstead, Long Island. My own researches at the library just now show that Samantha Moore's mother was an Elizabeth Pearsall."

A cold chill went through me.

"I'll be damned. This is getting scary."

"Yes, I thought you'd think that. I'll have to check my Pearsall books when I get home. I didn't want to take the time to have them pulled from the stacks, but I want to see how far back I can take the line and where it connects with Valdalene."

Guy made a face. To him the connection seemed irrelevant.

"The rapist, by the way, is behind bars awaiting a trial date. He was arrested last September twenty-fifth on another rape charge and Brenda Soldano identified him in a lineup at the time. One of my friends in the coroner's office filled me in when I called earlier."

This was news that excited me. "Then he might be Valdalene's Mr. Smith too, or is that too much to expect? Damn, if only Ismeralda had seen him!"

Uncle Jeremiah reached into the inside pocket of his jacket and removed his gold-mounted memo pad, pulled the tiny gold pencil out of the hinged lid, and began to make notes. "I'll have to find out who the fellow's lawyer is and have a talk with him." He turned to Meta, who had been busy seeing to Duchess's dinner, and said, "Now I don't suppose, Mrs. Sullivan, that we might continue this conversation over our own dinner, do you?"

The four of us ate at Habebe's in Nyack that evening. The meal was delicious in spite of being accompanied by some of the most undelicious table conversation ever overhead by a Nyack waiter.

We discussed Valdalene Pearsall's autopsy report in detail, asking questions of poor Guy and probing things until a picture emerged of a young woman, drugged with heroin, five months pregnant, being brought to one of the vilest places imaginable to be rid of her suddenly painful and unwanted pregnancy.

Valda herself had died of shock and loss of blood, but the child had been taken alive and still strong enough somehow to fight for its own life, clawing and writhing until the strangling grasp of its murderer put an end to it. That was the real mystery of that dreadful room—not Valda's abortion, as strange as it was to have performed it under such horrendous circumstances, or even the fact of her dying as a result of it, but rather the prolonged survival of her fetus and its bizarre struggle against its destroyer.

"Miranda, you keep saying you think she was killed by a self-

styled midwife. Wasn't it more likely some old drunk of a doctor—
that old man who dumped the fetus maybe?"

"You didn't see him, Guy. I did, and I'll be my boots he's no
butcher."

"No, I didn't see him, but I did observe the girl's autopsy.
Whoever performed that cesarean and took that child was a professional. No surgeon perhaps, but he knew what he was doing and
must have done it before—under better circumstances, of course,
one hopes," he concluded dryly. He paused and then added quietly,
"The tox reports showed something else too, but I can't mention
it."

We all looked at him. "What's up your sleeve, Guy?" I asked.

"Never mind," he said, passing off my question with a shake of
his head. I glanced at Uncle Jeremiah and shrugged. We'd get it out
of him later.

"All right. Meanwhile, I am going to the Bronx tomorrow to
see what more I can learn from Ismeralda. It's her day off and she's
cleaning out Valda's apartment. She said I can come by. What are
you up to tomorrow?" I asked, turning to Uncle Jeremiah.

"Personally, I shall be content to leave Ismeralda and that area of
investigation to you, my dear, while I concentrate on this subtle
blood tie that seems to have popped up. I want to chart the Soldano
girl's ancestry. Miranda," he said abruptly, "I had better get from
you before I leave tonight as much information as you possess
about your mother's side of the family. I have never done charts on
the Chadwicks, you know."

"Is that really necessary? What good will it do?" I asked, feeling
a strange edginess at his request.

Uncle Jeremiah shrugged. "I am not quite sure. Just curious ever
since . . ."

"Ever since I said I found things like my mother's mother." I
completed his thought.

"Charts," Guy scoffed. "What next? Astrology?"

My uncle gave Guy a tolerant look. "Dotty, isn't it? You may,
in fact, be right, but I shall pursue it nevertheless. Not every

question is answered on the dissecting table, you know, or even in the law courts, and one has seen some strange things happen in the course of a long life; not all of them totally explicable. No, I shall pursue the heredity angle, and if nothing more comes from it than finding an interesting and remote new line of Pearsalls, why then, so be it. I'll just write a monograph for the American Genealogical Society and let it go at that." He paused for a moment, taking a sip of water. "However," he continued, "the fact remains that someone sought out Valdalene Pearsall and chose her to be the mother of his child. Suppose the reason is that she *is* a Pearsall?"

Guy shrugged.

"I, for one, would be most interested to learn why," my uncle added quietly.

"So would I," I agreed and Meta seconded me vigorously, digging into her chicken Fessanjan.

"Well, just to show you I'm not an ogre, I'll go down to Franklin General tomorrow and take a look at the latest mooncalf for you," Guy said with an expansive air. He patted my hand with a patronizing touch and began to tackle his shish kebab. "I'll get what information I can on the blood group and see if the paternity might be compatible with that of our fetus. If it's not, why that ends this mooncalf business and the 'Pearsall connection' right then and there."

"Excellent!" my uncle rejoined. He looked a bit complacent himself. Obviously he was betting on compatibility. "I intend to get in touch with the lawyer who represents the man the Soldano girl identified as her attacker. If he is guilty, of course, he's going to refuse to submit to blood tests that might indicate his paternity, but if he's innocent, those same tests might prove he could not possibly be the father. It's a risky business."

"Risky? Why? If he's innocent, what has he got to lose? The tests would prove he couldn't be the father." I looked from Guy to my uncle. Both were shaking their heads.

"What you uncle means, Miranda, is that while blood tests can prove nonpaternity, there is no legal way to prove conclusively the paternity of a child, so if this fellow has the blood tests and they don't prove his nonpaternity outright, then he's still not off the hook. It is a risky business for client and lawyer to gamble on. Eventually, of course, DNA testing will be used. That will be far more accurate, but speaking of blood tests," Guy went on, "I finally got medical records on Valdalene's children. None of them have any congenital malformations, save for the twin girls, who both show signs of the same slight carpal fusion that their mother had. It's a fairly common trait among people of African ancestry and nothing serious. Now Valda, as you may remember, was an Rh −, so I was curious as to whether she'd had trouble with any of her previous deliveries—"

"Oh, I don't think so," I broke in. "Her sister said that that was why she had agreed so readily to have a baby for this man. She hadn't had any trouble with the others."

"Well, I found that odd, given her Rh − blood factor, but the children's blood tests all bear out what the sister says. The first child, the boy Travis, was Rh − like his mother, so there was compatibility there. The twin girls, Taralene and Tonelle are Rh +, but since an Rh − mother usually doesn't have a problem with the first Rh + birth, again there was no trouble. The third child, the girl Valentine, is Rh − like her mother, so again Valda lucked out.

"Her luck ran out with this last pregnancy. The fetus was Rh +, remember, so the incompatibility contributed to the complications she was experiencing—apart from the gross deformities of the fetus itself."

"Interesting," my uncle remarked dispassionately.

"Well, luv, you and Mr. Fay and Guy are going to be busy investigating all sorts of things tomorrow. Now, what is there for me to do? I'm not going to be left out, you know!" Meta declared.

My uncle was delighted. "Of course you shan't, dear lady. I was intending to ask if you might have time tomorrow. Before I leave, I intend to write out a list of questions for which I need answers and the phone numbers of the people whom I think may be able to supply them. If you could act in the capacity of a sort of unofficial investigator on my behalf and ascertain the information I seek for me, I should be most grateful. Would you care to help?"

"Oh yes," Meta agreed. "I should enjoy that immensely."

"Well, since you will be by the phone, why don't we make yours the official command post," Guy suggested. "We'll call in any new information we come across and you can jot it down and pass it and any messages that we have for each other along to us as we report in." It was a splendid idea, but I wondered if we weren't all going a bit daft . . .

Later that evening, after Uncle Jeremiah had drawn from me every name I could conjure up out of my memory and my mother's old photo album, given Meta her orders, and ridden off into the night toward Staten Island, Guy and I finally had a few minutes to ourselves. We spent them walking Molly through the leaf-strewn streets of South Nyack, talking over the crazy turn that the investigation of the mooncalf seemed to be taking.

"I don't believe in all this spooky occult stuff about finding things and Pearsall blood going back into the mists of time. It's all just so much bullshit and you ought to be smart enough to know it!"

"Ah, but 'there are more things, in heaven and earth, Horatio, than are dreamt of in your philosophy,' " I said archly, wagging a finger in his face.

We walked back up the street toward the house. Meta's lights were blinking out one by one. Only mine remained lit on the floor above.

"It's late," I said. "I've got to get up early tomorrow and so, I imagine, do you."

"You aren't really going back down to the South Bronx tomorrow, are you?"

"See if I don't."

"You are a stubborn bitch, Miranda," he said gently, putting an arm around me. "You must have been told that before, I imagine."

"Yes, often, and in just those terms, too." I grinned, pulling

away as he tried to kiss me. I shooed Molly Brown up the front
steps and onto the porch.

"Good night, Guy. Dinner was lovely, the conversation as
bizarre as one could possibly wish, and the company superb.
Thank you."

"So, I get the brush-off and without even a good-night kiss."
He sounded like a spoiled child. He'd obviously forgotten our
conversation the other evening.

"Nobody gets a kiss from me these days 'cept cuddly old Uncas
and Molly Brown here," I said, picking her up, fourteen pounds of
squirming resistance, and kissing her fat mush noisily. She snarled
viciously and wriggled out of my grasp in fury at such an indignity.

"So what are you telling me?" he asked sulkily.

"Why, that it's a dog's life, love, that it's a dog's life," I laughed
and blew him a farewell kiss from the door.

Ten minutes after I got into bed, the phone rang.

"I never got brushed off like that after a date. How come you
didn't at least kiss the guy?"

"Max? Damn you, what were you doing, spying on me? We
have a noninterference clause, remember?" I was furious and even
a little frightened. The idea of Max lying in wait for me on dark
streets was scary.

"I wasn't spying. I just drove by to see if you were home and if
we could talk. I saw the son of a bitch try to kiss you. Why didn't
you let him?"

"None of your business."

"Come on, why? That's an easy question."

" 'Cause I don't love him."

"That was all I wanted to hear. Good night, honey."

Click.

Damn . . .

7

THE SPIDER FIXED
IN AMBER, CAUGHT
BY THE FLY

Ismeralda Jackson was in her sister's apartment, surrounded by boxes of children's toys and clothes and piles of bed linens and pillows.

"There's a man comin' to buy most of the living room stuff tomorrow," she said by way of explanation of the mess. "We gonna bring the kid's beds and stuff back to my place. They been sleepin' four to the bed and that ain't no good. Momma say we keep Valda's bedroom furniture too, but shit, I don't know where we put it all.

"Jovonelle have her baby last night. A girl, and she callin' it Valdalene, but she got real trouble—the baby come hard and Momma can't leave her just yet." She moved about, rummaging through drawers and boxes as she spoke. I felt as if I'd known her for years.

"Which means that all this is your problem," I said, looking around at the mess. The barren, dusty apartment looked all the worse for the disruption and shifting of furniture, the dirty windows denuded of their faded drapes. I kept away from the kitchen. I didn't want to encounter that mayonnaise jar.

"Shit, I don't mind. My momma'd only be in the way, goin' over everything and probily weepin' like a fawcet. I just look at it all practical-like. What we can use, I keeps. What's busted, I throws out, and what we can't use, I sells. Easy."

"I never asked you about Valda's doctor. Do you know who he was, or who she might have turned to for the abortion?"

"She go to Dr. Malik at Lincoln Hospital for her babies and her female troubles, but she don't use him last time. She go to some white man down the city what her 'Mr. Smith' take her to. But she wouldn't go back to him for no abortion, not with Mr. Smith lookin' for her." She shook her head slowly. "Not likely," she concluded.

"What about a local doctor? An older one perhaps, and not affiliated with a hospital?" I browsed idly through a small pile of envelopes on the coffee table, which had been shoved against the wall near the door. There were rent receipts, stubs of welfare checks, and an unpaid phone bill, but no messages or personal letters of any sort.

"Shit, honey, I don't know. She run off weeks before she die. She could of found damn near anybody in that time. The po-lice ax me all that and I can't tell them nothin' except about Dr. Malik. They already talk to him an' he ain' got nothing to do with it. He din't even know she be exspectin' again."

"Midwives, then?" I pursued. "Ismeralda, someone performed that abortion, and I've got to know who."

She looked at me curiously from across the room. "Honey, she sure got to you, din't she? I say on Saturday she be hauntin' you, an' I wasn't foolin', was I? Why? What you care so much for? What my black sister was to you?"

"Cousins," I said simply.

"What?" she said, her brow knitted, her eyes narrow. "You crazy, girl." She stood with one hand on her hip, shaking her head.

"Ismeralda, I mean it. She wasn't my sister, as she was yours, but we were descended from the same blood—what they call collateral relations, actually. According to my uncle, Jeremiah Pearsall Fay, Valda and I were both descended from a man named

James Pearsall and his wife, Forgiveness Basset, I through their first
son, Malachi and Valda through their third son, Jacob.''

She looked rather taken aback at that. "Cousins? Honest?"

"Honest," I assured her.

"Shit, if that don't beat all. How far back?" She hauled some
boxes out of the children's room as she spoke, huffing noisily but
waving me away nonetheless when I came forward to help.

"About six generations or so. The late seventeen hundreds."

"That's near two hundred years back, girl," she cried, standing
up straight, her brow furrowed.

"Yes, just about." I was beginning to feel foolish.

Ismeralda laughed richly. "You talkin' Roots, girl, real Roots.
You fixin' ta find Kunta Kinte or somethin'? Oh, Miz Miranda Fay,
you be one crazy white gal." She laughed again and looked around
at the mess that was her sister's apartment. "Shit, I can't work no
more for a while. Come on in the kitchen, crazy lady. I's gonna
fix us a cup of tea."

I followed her into the kitchen and stood looking out through a
window while Ismeralda filled the kettle and put it on the stove.
Across the back yard, with its inevitable ailanthus trees growing
amidst the garbage, through a narrow alley, I could see an expanse
of rubble dominated by the distant prospect of red-brick projects,
grim and towering on the landscape. Between lay a mile or more
of urban decay: bodegas and storefront churches, after-hours social
clubs and shooting galleries; buildings abandoned, buildings
burned out, and buildings being salvaged and refurbished, grimy
phoenixes rising out of their own ashes. Somewhere amidst it all
lurked the murderer of Valdalene and her mooncalf.

"I don't really think she'd go to a doctor. I think she was scared
and desperate and in pain, thinking herself beyond legal help. I
think she went to some woman that she heard about, some mid-
wife-abortionist who used to help women in trouble—"

I spoke as if in a dream, staring out through the dirty glass.
Ismeralda's voice, coming to me from the direction of the stove,
woke me from my daze.

"Honey," she said, "nobody need no abortionist no more. There are clinics all over now."

"Valda didn't go to one, did she?"

"She was scared Mr. Smith would find her."

"Precisely, so who'd be left but some neighborhood woman? All she'd have to do is listen to gossip in the supermarket, or call to mind the name of someone she'd heard about years ago or just ask around. That's all it would take."

The water began to boil. Ismeralda dropped a Red Rose tea bag in each of our cups, poured the steaming water on top of them, and brought them over to the old enamel-topped kitchen table. The mayonnaise jar was conspicuously absent.

Valda's sister regarded me seriously across the table, her brows knit in that familiar manner. "I got somethin' else. Valda use to wear this a lot. She leave it at my place when she run off. She always call it her lucky piece. I wants you to have it, honey."

A chill ran through me as she spoke, fishing around in her change purse. I didn't want Valda's lucky piece any more than I wanted Valda's luck, but I could hardly say no.

"She find it years ago and it tickle her so, she gits herself a little holder and chain to put it on." Ismeralda held a tarnished chain up in front of me. From it dangled a small silver coin holder. It rimmed an old silver coin that had been polished smooth by years of age and wear. "She say, 'Shit, girl, anybody can find themselves a peso or a Canadian penny. There ain't no trick to that, but who in hell eva fin' a English sixpenny piece in the Bronx?' "

"Who indeed?" I asked blankly as I reached out and took Valda's gift from her sister's hand. "Thank you, Ismeralda. It's very thoughtful of you." To cover my mixed emotions, I picked up the tea bag with a napkin and looked around for a wastebasket. "Where can I throw this?" I asked.

"Here's all the trash in this bag," Ismeralda said, waving one hand vaguely in the direction of a brown paper bag near the kitchen door. I noticed at once the Met Foods emblem on its side. I started to drop the napkin into it and saw the mayonnaise jar lying on its

side in the bag, together with a heap of its former contents and
some scraps of paper. I reached in and pulled out the crumpled
paper—the backs of old envelopes mostly, and a bit of lined
notebook paper as well—smoothing them carefully as I turned
back to the table and sat down.

"What's this stuff?" I asked.

"Jus' some old shoppin' lists she had stuck in the napkin holder.
I sees them when I was goin' through her junk for the coins and
old gold she fin'. No sense throwin' out money, is there?"

"No," I agreed absently. "What's Baby—Baby Derevenkon? Or
who, maybe?" I asked, trying to read one of the scraps.

"I don't know," she shrugged. "Valda neva did write a clear
hand."

"Valda didn't write this, did she?" I asked, sliding the paper
across the table to Ismeralda.

"No, that ain't her writin'."

"I didn't think so. It looks very old-fashioned and foreign. Baby
or Babi? No, Baba, I think. Baba Derevenkon. Strange. Sounds
Russian."

"Russian?" Ismeralda exclaimed. Clearly she was puzzled.
"Valda don't know nobody Russian."

"So it sounds to me. It's Derevenkov, most likely. K-O-V is an
ending for Russian names. I do know that." I picked up a phone
book from the floor next to the garbage bag and came back to the
table. Ismeralda was adding hot water to our cups. There were no
Derevenkovs listed in the Bronx directory, nor anything like Baba
that seemed remotely likely. "Damn, it looks like a dead end," I
started to say but checked myself. The words "Bab Derev" were
scribbled, this time in a different hand, on another scrap of paper
stuck in the phone book itself, together with the address 14 Willow
Terrace under it. Valda must have tried to find a phone number for
Derevenkov too.

"Ismeralda," I cried, "look at this."

She pulled the paper across the table and frowned at it. "Willow
Terrace. That be near where they found Valda."

"I know, I know. I remember seeing it on my street map. This could be the lead I've been looking for."

"Uh-uh," Ismeralda said, shaking her head solemnly.

"Uh-uh, what?"

"You ain't goin' over that place alone."

"So what are you? My mother? Of course I'm going."

"Shit, that's right by Saint Mary's Park, girl. That's all shootin' galleries and nigga trash hangin' out. You can't go there alone."

"All right. Come with me then. Between the two of us we ought to be able to defend ourselves against any wiseass dudes that try to hassle us, eh?" I broke out in a grin as I spoke—what is known in the vernacular as a shit-eatin' grin, I believe.

"OOeeeeeeh!" Ismerald shrieked. "Girl, you is goin' native for sure. 'Wiseass dudes.' Where you pick that up, girl?" She slapped her palm on mine. 'Gimme some skin, girl."

"I've had a liberal education," I retorted. "Now are you coming? Time's wasting. I've got my dog in the car, by the way, so we'll be a triple threat."

"I'm comin,' I'm comin'. I don't want no honky gal's murder on my conscience. You so crazy, you'd come back to haunt me— just like Valda hauntin' you."

"And not you?" I called over my shoulder as we bustled down the hall toward the front door.

"No, not me," she came back solemnly. "I's got enough to do for the next ten, fifteen years, keepin' those babies of hers alive. I ain't gonna have no time to be haunted." She stopped on the landing and fumbled for the keys to Valda's apartment. "That don't mean," she went on as she locked the door carefully behind us, "that I don't care about who did that to her. You wants ta get this abortionist, and I'm all for that, but then you gets this Mr. Smith, too, if you can. He be her real killer, honey. He be the real killer."

"Funny, that's what my landlady thinks, too. Maybe you're both right."

Willow Terrace, one block to the north, was not quite so devastated as Hawthorne Terrace, that nightmare street on which Valdalene Pearsall had met her brutal end. Perhaps because it faced directly on the park, most of its single row of graystone walkups had been kept up, each building still retaining its iron fences, its railings, and its windows intact. Garbage cans awaiting pickup at the curbs were filled to overflowing, but at least they suggested that order and occupation rather than chaos and decay lurked behind the crumbling facades.

We left Molly Brown guarding the car and walked up the steps of number fourteen. The tiny tiled vestibule listed the occupants, two apartments to each floor, five floors, ten apartments. A. A. Derevenkov occupied apartment nine, top floor left. Ismeralda pushed the button beside the ancient, grimy nameplate and to our mutual surprise, we received an almost immediate answering buzz. She pushed open the inner door and we climbed, puffing, to the top of the house.

The door to number nine was slightly ajar, the chain still on, when we got to the landing. A pair of large, frightened eyes peered warily out past the jamb.

"Are you from the doctor?" came a muffled query in a child's high, tentative shrill. I couldn't tell if it was a girl or a boy at first.

Ismeralda approached and peeked through the door. "Honey," she said kindly, "we came to see somebody call Der—Dere—Shit, you tell him, girl, I don't talk no Russian."

I stepped past her and smiled through the door. It was a small boy of perhaps ten or eleven who peered out at us. "A Mr. or Mrs. Derevenkov, young man?"

"You from the welfare?" he asked suspiciously.

"No, no, we're not," I assured him hastily . "We're just trying to find Baba or Babu Derevenkov."

"Babushka," he said brightly. "Baba. That what everyone calls her. Baba. She be real sick and I am—I'm—" His big dark eyes began to well with tears. "She a white lady," he explained, perhaps for my benefit. "She real old."

"Shhh, don't be scared, child. If the lady be sick, maybe we can help. I works at the hospital. You let us in, honey, right now." Ismeralda spoke with just that fortuitous combination of kindliness and authority to which a troubled child might respond and it worked. The door closed briefly, we heard the chain rattle, and then it was reopened to admit us.

The boy was skinny and small, with a dark, smooth, handsome face dominated by huge, clear black eyes fringed with remarkably long lashes. They glittered with unshed tears.

"Baba real sick. I be scairt she gon' die, Missus." He stepped back and we entered the living room only to be at once overwhelmed by the stuffy commingling of many odors: that indefinable old people's smell of sour, unwashed skin, of musty closets and unopened windows. Beyond that was the pungence of unchanged kitty litter, of spoiled milk and cat food cans left too long in the garbage bag.

Those were the first impressions, but as the boy led us down a narrow dark hall toward a back bedroom that would have been bright with sunlight had not the heavy brocade drapes been drawn, I could add other isolated scents to the mélange that assailed our nostrils: one was Djer-kiss powder just like my grandmother had used thirty or forty years ago. It was a dusty, overpoweringly sweet scent that did nothing to mask the acrid aroma of stale vomit. Someone had been ill—and recently. The boy saw the face I made and said apologetically, "She bin throwin' up all morning. I does my best to keep her clean, but there ain't but one clean towel left." He was on the verge of tears again.

"That's all right, boy. You be doing just fine," Ismeralda assured him gently as we entered the bedroom.

Baba Derevenkov or Mrs. Alexandra Alexeievna Derevenkov, the widowed Baroness Derevenkov, to give her the full panoply of titles to which she could make claim, lay in the center of an old-fashioned double bed, three mattresses high, propped up on a pile of pillows, some of which had white pillowcases and others of which were encased in greasy amber satin and brocade. They must once have been meant purely for decoration, but long since had been put to use. Mrs. Derevenkov was a large woman, fat and doughy. A white bath towel was tucked under her fat, wrinkled double chin. It spread down her heaving chest and great middle, giving her the bizarre look of an oversized baby.

The amber satin comforter and white sheet were shabby looking and in want of a change, but they were smooth and neatly folded over and tucked tightly around her thick body. Her motionless arms, bandaged from the backs of the hands to the midforearms, rested on the covers. She lay with her eyes closed, a compress across her forehead, moaning slightly in her sleep.

Ismeralda approached her and turned to the boy. "What your name, child?" she asked.

"Wesley. Wesley Nivens."

"Well, Wesley, you go open them drapes like a good boy. We needs some light."

"Baba say the light hurt her eyes," he protested feebly.

"Baba just gonna have ta lump it, boy. We got to see what be wrong with her. Now jump."

Wesley jumped. In the bright sunlight that streamed into the stuffy little room we could see the puffy, angry red skin that showed along the edge of the bandages. While Ismeralda examined the old woman with a clinical curiosity that impressed me, I turned to other matters.

On a cluttered nightstand next to the bed, underneath a small plaster lamp with an amber silk shade, bulb-burned and dry as paper, lay a scattering of small jars and paper pillboxes of a sort that I hadn't seen since childhood. One round box in particular caught my attention. It had an ancient label on which was hand printed the single word: laudanum. Beside it was a glass apothecary bottle of the sort that pharmacies used to use. Its glass label read Tr. Op. I lifted the stopper gingerly and took a whiff. It smelled horrible, like strong camphor—exactly what opium did smell like. No mystery there. The water tumbler near the edge of the stand smelled of alcohol and contained a chalky residue, again aromatic of camphor.

"Has she been taking any of this stuff, Wesley?" I asked as Imseralda removed the compress and felt the woman's forehead.

"She mixes some powder and drinks it off in the glass. I don't touch nothin' there," he said with a solemn nod.

"Miranda, this old lady be burning up with fever. She's sweating somethin' awful."

"She all the time cold. She always shiverin'," the boy said. He looked as if he wanted to cry.

"She's been dosing herself with laudanum and God knows what else beside," I commented, continuing to look over the things on the nightstand. One jar contained the remains of some greasy, noxious-smelling ointment with a dark, sulfurous yellow color. Smears of the same color were seeping through the gauze wrapped around her arms. "What's this stuff, do you suppose?"

"That be medicine. Baba make it herself. She real good at doctoring." The boy sounded proud of the old woman.

"So I see," I said dryly, exchanging glances with Ismeralda across the old woman's body. "Real good."

"She good," the boy insisted. "She real good, Missus. She deliver my little sister when my momma's time come so quick."

Ismeralda looked across at me. I nodded. It looked like we had found our midwife.

"Wesley," I asked, "who is her doctor?"

"She don't got one. She don't believe in doctors, but I so scairt she gonna die, I tell my little sister ta go for old man Weems, but she ain't come back yet."

"Who is old man Weems?"

"He a doctor. He the only one Baba like. He ain't her doctor though. They's just friends. He come if he be around, I know he would," the boy cried.

Ismeralda turned from the bed. "Then you run and get him, young man, and bring him here fast. Your Baba sure do need a doctor. We stay here with her."

He looked doubtfully from one of us to the other. On the bed, Baba Derevenkov groaned in her fitful sleep. "Git, boy," Ismeralda ordered sternly and young Wesley got.

"This is her, ain't it?" Ismeralda asked when the boy was out of earshot. Her voice was low and hesitant.

"I think so," I nodded. "I'm going to have a look around before this doctor gets here. If I were the police, it wouldn't be legal without a search warrant, but there's no law against being a nosey parker, is there?"

"If there was, honey, we'd all be in jail. You go on. I can watch her. If she gonna be sick again, I wants to see she don't choke in her vomit."

"I'd be inclined to let her choke."

"She may not be the one, you know, Miranda," Ismeralda called after me as I slipped back down the hall toward the living room. Almost unconsciously I moved like a footpad, lurking through a miasma of cat hair and unchanged litterbox that emanated from the bathroom. As I passed the open doorway of the kitchen, I stole a glance into the long, narrow room. What I saw made me stop dead and change direction. The living room would have to wait.

"Don't be too sure of that, girl," I called back over my shoulder toward the bedroom. "You should see this kitchen." It was a dreary little room with one window at the far end through which a bar of sunlight was trying to filter. The dirty glass and even dirtier curtains made it a thankless task. The kitchen contained, among other things, five or six fat, obviously well-cared-for cats who mewed politely and went back to sunning themselves on the kitchen table.

It was the other things that caught my interest. The room was lined on both sides with wooden cupboards: cabinets and drawers below, glass-fronted shelves above, all painted a cream-colored high gloss enamel in some distant year. The countertop and shelves were lined with worn and ancient oilcloth that had long since lost both its characteristic smell and most of its pattern of red roosters. Even the thumb tacks that held the lining in place had lost most of their original blue enamel. A brown paper Met Foods bag on the floor was filled to overflowing with garbage. She and Valda had shopped in the same market.

The wide countertop was loaded with more ancient apothecary jars like the one in the bedroom. Their gold and white glass labels read variously: Ol. Rosmarini, Tr. Gelsem, Tr. Valer. Amm., Tr. Antiperiod, and Ext. Trax. Fl. There were dozens of them, both on the counter and on the glass-enclosed shelves above. Scattered among them were other assorted bottles, most of them aged and of obsolete pattern, that had once held such mundane things as pickles or jelly or mustard, but which now held a variety of powders and dried herbs, suspiciously viscid liquids and poisonous-looking ointments. There were scores of dirty cardboard pillboxes, a white ceramic mortar and pestle, a tiny scale and set of weights.

In the drawers and cupboards below and on the shelves above were more jars, enamel pans, hot-water bottles, a rack of filthy test tubes, enema bags, and hypodermic syringes. Also behind the glass doors were a dozen or so books, antiquated, dusty, and printed in Russian. I took one down and thumbed through it briefly. I couldn't read the Cyrillic script, of course, but the line drawings told me all that I needed to know. It was a medical book and the subject was gynecology.

"Ismeralda, come take a look at this," I called down the hall.

"I can't, honey. I think she be comin' round."

"Oh, shoot, really? Here I come. Maybe we can talk to her." I laid the book down on the kitchen counter and walked back into the bedroom, where Valda's tough, capable little sister was soothing the old woman's brow, putting a fresh compress on her head, whispering to her comfortingly, telling her that she'd be all right.

She was fully awake now, moaning dreadfully, and calling for "Vasily," by which I was sure she meant the boy Wesley Nivens. Ismeralda calmed her gently and told her that he had gone for Dr. Weems, that she'd soon be well and that all she needed was proper help.

This last I doubted somehow. Whatever was wrong with her, it boded ill. Her fat old face was as pale as curd, the jowls and chin sagging dreadfully, suddenly a mass of fleshy wrinkles where before, I am sure, they must have been firm and full. Her small black eyes were glazed and sunken in pouches of translucent bluish flesh and her thin straggles of white hair lay lank and brittle on the pillow. She had broken into a profuse and pungent sweat, and her whole fat body shivered with chills. It was obvious, moreover, that she could barely stand the pain in her bandaged arms.

"Mrs. Derevenkov?" I said, coming up to her on the left side of the bed opposite Ismeralda.

"Mrs. Derevenkov," I repeated.

The glazed eyes rolled in the motoionless head and looked at me.

"Baroness Derevenkoff," she gasped out with a trace of testiness. Her accent was heavy. "I am da vidow off Baron Ivan Ivanevich Derevenkoff off de imperial Russian cavalry." She trailed off for a moment before going on. Clearly it was an effort to speak, though whether it was due to her pain or the opiate she had taken I could not tell. "I am all dot iss left." Again she paused, but this time it seemed she girded her strength and came back at me, forming the words grotesquely through white lips. "Who are you? Vat you doing here?"

"Baroness, are you a doctor, by any chance?" I asked, ignoring her question and asking my own.

"A doctor?" she repeated dazedly. "My fader vas doctor. Dr. Alexeiev, Prince Noblevski's personal physician. He vonce haff honor to treat da czar himself. Papa vas great doctor. . . ."

"Are you a midwife then?" I persisted, speaking very clearly and as near to her ear as the stench of her allowed. "Do you help women with babies? Women who are in trouble?" Ismeralda looked at me grimly across the bed. The old baroness was plucking at the towel with those bloated red fingers that peeped from her bandages, exhibiting every sign of increased anxiety. I must have struck a nerve.

"Babies?" she repeated. "Dot baby—" She broke off.

"Yes?" I prompted. "*That* baby. Tell us about that baby." My pulse quickened. I knew I had found my murderess. I had to hear her say it.

"Dot baby—it never come. It move and twist but it don't never come. Did you see it? So horrible, so ugly, and it don't die. *It don't die.*" She began to thrash around on the bed, raising her head from the pillow, trying to stretch her swollen arms toward me. "It don't die. Dear God, I tink it never die, an' she scream and scream an' I think she ain't never going to stop. . . ." She was delirious now, twisting her shoulders beneath our grasp as we tried to restrain her. Her eyes, bulging and horrible, stared beyond us at sights impossible for us to see, terrible visions that lay in her own mind's eye.

"Dot girl, dot girl," she said taking Ismeralda by the arm with her swollen, bandaged hands. Over the smell of stale vomit, Djerkiss powder, and perspiration I caught the sulfurous scent of the greasy ointment with which she had doctored herself. "She was black, like you, an' she scream and scream. God, the noise she make, an' I got nothin' that help . . ." Now Baba Derevenkov, like the old witch of the Russian fairy tales of my youth, Baba Yaga, was talking of evil and horror and death.

Ismeralda spoke suddenly, her words coming slowly from a mouth that threatened to crumple into a mask of tragedy. "She talkin' about Valdalene, ain't she?" Her eyes remained fixed on the grotesque old woman with a glassy stare.

"Yes," I whispered. My head nodded slowly on my neck and I felt as if my reflexes were winding down like an old Victrola that hasn't been cranked. I began to feel, in that strange, stuffy, amber-glowing room, as if I moved through warm, sunlit water, unable to breathe, my lungs full to bursting with foul, dead sir. "I think she's reliving the—the—" I couldn't say the word. "She's reliving Valda's death."

"Oh, shit, honey." Ismeralda, who until that moment had been a rock and a salvation to me though she knew it not, turned away from the bed and broke down, the tears coming first as a thin silver ripple down her plump cheeks, and then, at last, as a torrent. I came around the bed, took her in my arms, and held her, feeling the wracking sobs carry through her body and into my own.

"She shouldn't of died like that. . . . She weren't really bad. She just willful and foolish. She never hurt nobody and she tried to do right by them kids of hers. Why she got to die like that for?" She pulled away from me and turned back toward the bed again. The Baroness Derevenkov lay still against the pillows, moaning. She too was crying. The tears ran down from her glazed old eyes and mingled with the perspiration that sprang from every seam in her flaccid skin.

"Vere is da doctor? Vere iss he? I don't know vat to do. Dot baby don't come and her belly move so—I never see it like dis, never. She screamin' an' screamin' an' she spit up da laudanum. It don't work. I got nothin' to help her." Her anxiety was pitiable.

"Laudanum?" I asked and came around the bed again. "Baroness, she was a drug addict. Why didn't you give her heroin or something like that?" I wasn't sure I knew what I was talking about, but I did know that tincture of opium, or laudanum, was about as nineteenth century as one could get, and by the looks of the old woman's supplies in the kitchen, there might be no strength or virtue left in any of her pharmacopoeia. Aspirin might have been as effective as any drug this woman might prescribe.

She was lucid enough yet to respond with an abrupt shake of her head. "No drugs. I don't give no street drugs. She maybe already take before she meet me. I don't tink she need no more. She don't even know where she is. I don't tink there be no trouble," she said in her heavy, rasping voice. "But den dot baby don't come—" She broke off suddenly, sweating more profusely and writhing with spasms of pain. Ismeralda had gone into the bathroom. I could hear the sounds of retching and the flush of a toilet as counterpoints to the old woman's semidelirious account of the abortion. The sink taps ran full force for a moment and finally, after they were turned off, Ismeralda came back into the bedroom, looking pallid and drained, her face still wet from a fresh scrubbing. She carried a clean wet washcloth folded across her hands.

She placed it carefully on the Baroness Derevenkov's brow. "You didn't mean for her to die, did you?"

"No, no," the old woman moaned. "I feel sorry for her. She so afraid off him. Da fader, he was a devil—he born devil."

"You just helpin' her get rid of that baby, ain't you?" She stroked the old face almost lovingly. I could see that she was trying to come to grips with the horror of it all, trying to understand and perhaps even to forgive.

"Dot baby no good. Dot baby killin' her. She got to get rid—" The rest of her words were an incoherent garble interspersed with moans. She was rapidly becoming delirious as her temperature shot up. Her head was so hot to the touch that I began to think she might go into convulsions.

"Where *is* that child?" I asked, turning impatiently toward the door. I had just turned back, desperately worried, when the front door opened. Wesley Nivens ran down the hall, crying in his anxiety for the old woman.

"Baba, Baba, I got the doctor, Baba," he said, coming up to the bed and laying his cheek on the pillow beside her head. "Baba, don't die. Please don't die. I bring Dr. Weems. He take care of you."

Baba Derevenkov moaned and rolled her eyes toward him. She gave him a rictus grin, the closest thing she could manage, in her pain, to a smile, but it was a look of love and the boy knew it. He kissed her cheek gently and made way for the doctor.

Dr. Weems came slowly down the hall, his gait rather tentative and unsteady, his medical bag held before him in one thin black hand.

And then, looking up, I saw his face: his kindly dark eyes with their yellowed whites, his deeply seamed skin stubbled by two days' growth of gray beard. His wide mouth was fixed in a straight serious line. When he saw me, he stopped dead on the threshold, just short of the threadbare amber and blue Chinese rug.

We knew each other instantly. The startled look of recognition was mirrored in our two pairs of eyes, but I was the younger, and as it happened, the more sober of the two, so it was I who recovered the more quickly.

"We meet again, Dr. Weems," I managed to say in a reasonably calm voice, though my heart was pounding almost audibly in my chest.

"I remember," he answered me. He said something else too, for his lips continued to move, but his words were drowned in the sudden, incessant, wavering whine of an emergency services vehicle. It screeched to a halt on the street below and within a few minutes a team of paramedics from Lincoln Hospital had come bustling in and taken over the stuffy amber room, crowding Wesley and Ismeralda and me out into the dusty living room.

In less than a quarter of an hour, Baba Derevenkov had been strapped onto a stretcher and carried down five flights of stairs to the waiting ambulance. As if from nowhere a crowd had gathered to see her off, clusters of solemn dark-eyed faces. Those who knew her were obviously concerned, their mood punctuated here and there by the callous, smirk-faced humor of youths who think that dying is funny and the elderly a joke.

The boy, Wesley Nivens, his face stained with tears, had locked up the apartment behind us and gone back to his own flat on the floor below. Ismeralda had accompanied him.

Dr. Weems had stayed with Baba Derevenkov, holding her shoulder comfortingly as the stretcher negotiated each turn of the stairs. Just before they got her onto the street, as they maneuvered the stretcher through the double doors of the vestibule, the old woman came round again and, opening her eyes, saw me.

"I haff to do it. I haff to help her. I see da fader. I know vat he iss, I know vat he vant. Vay back, long time, even before da Nazis, I vork—I vork in—" Her voice began to fade. They bumped the stretcher and she moaned in pain.

"Watch it," I snapped at the paramedic, thinking not only of the old woman's pain but of Valda's and of Ismeralda's and perhaps even my own. I had to know as much as I could from her. "What is it?" I fairly shouted, keeping up with the stretcher as they got it out onto the stoop. "What are you trying to say? Baroness?" I stumbled down the steps, frantically trying to keep up as they lifted her down the stoop toward the gaping doors of the ambulance.

"I see da first baby. It was tera—terata—" She broke off with a scream of pain as the attendant brushed her arm. She closed her eyes resolutely as if to push back the agony and spoke again. "I know da fader. He vas—"

"Who? Who was he?" I was almost screaming myself as I tried to get into the ambulance with her. Someone pulled me back.

She rolled her eyes upward toward me as she was passed into the vehicle. "You can't get in there, lady," someone said. An arm grabbed at me but I shook it off. Baba Derevenkov was still trying to speak.

"He vas Dr. August—Dr. Augustin—Augustin . . ." She said no more. Dr. Weems got into the ambulance beside her and the paramedics climbed in and shut the doors. With a scream and a shrill of sirens they took off for Lincoln Hospital. The police dispersed the crowd and, finally, themselves. The show was over, save for Molly Brown, still in my little red Mustang, mournfully howling as accompaniment to the fading wail of the sirens.

"Dr. Augustin!" Those were the last words I heard from the lips of the old woman, for I never did see her alive again. She died at 4:05 that afternoon in the emergency room of Lincoln Hospital.

Alexandra Alexeievna, Baroness Derevenkov, born in 1903 in czarist Russia, the adored only child of a well-to-do doctor and his aristocratic wife, widow of an impoverished émigré baron. Dead in the wilds of the South Bronx in 1989, mourned by one bereft eleven-year-old black boy named Wesley and an alcoholic doctor called Weems.

∇

8

ELIJAH WEEMS

I took five minutes to give Molly a walk and came back into the building to find Ismeralda. I felt desolate and anything but triumphant. I had found the murderess, had seen her suffering, knew she would die. It had even dawned on me that her death might be the mooncalf's own revenge upon its destroyer. I had seen the angry, poisoned scratches on her wrists and arms and the import of those awful wounds was not lost on me. Yet I felt no sense of justice.

"You got some use for these, girl?" Ismeralda asked.

I looked up into the darkness of the stairwell. She leaned over the second-floor rail, dangling a set of keys in front of her temptingly. She had an impish grin on her plump face that made me think of little Valentine. The brass-plated Russian Orthodox cross that dangled from the key ring told me all that I needed to know.

"Ismeralda, you witch, where'd you get the keys?" I whispered as I climbed the steps toward her. A sense of mischief and conspiracy gripped me, sending that momentary feeling of dejection packing like a bad dream.

"From the boy. I told him we needs to get things ta take to the hospital—you know, nightgown, hairbrush an' like that."

We climbed back up to the top floor, tiptoeing like conspirators. "I doubt she's going to last long enough for hair-brushing," I mused, lowering my voice as we passed a door with the name NIVENS over the bell push. "He really seems attached to her. He's not going to take her death very well, I imagine, poor kid." I thought of the cats fed and the bed made, the clean towel spread under the old woman's chin so carefully and lovingly.

Ismeralda opened the door and we walked back into the Baroness Derevenkov's apartment.

"Oh, hell, what a stench," I exclaimed, going immediately into the living room to open a window. The cats, five of them—a Siamese, a Persian, and three gray angoras—came mewing in our direction from the kitchen as I looked around for a phone. I wondered vaguely what would happen to them now. They were fat and sleek and from the hairy look of the amber satin and midnight-blue velvet cushions that abounded, had led a sybaritic life until now.

I found the phone, hidden in an old telephone cabinet of the sort that was fashionable in the early days of that infernal machine. The buzz on the line told me the thing still worked. So the old lady had simply had an unlisted number, I realized, thinking of the blank I had drawn with the phone book. It seemed an unusual expense for one whose purse must have of necessity been rather slim. "Ismeralda," I called out, "I'm going to call my landlady. She's home taking messages at the phone all day. I want her to tell my uncle where I am if he calls."

I told Meta as briefly as possible what had happened, where I was and so on, left the baroness's phone number and rang off. Ten minutes later my uncle called from Mineola. He put Rogers on for instructions to Willow Terrace and told me to sit tight. Within another forty-five minutes he was making history of sorts as the owner of the only 1937 Phantom III ever to park on that mean and desolate street. I had a feeling that the baroness would have loved it.

"The natives seem to think it's a new form of pimpmobile," my uncle remarked jovially as we looked down onto the street from

the living room window. There was a small band of sightseers,
mostly children and teens, gathered around for a closer inspection.

"Why, Uncle Jeremiah," I exclaimed, "you shock me! Such
language." We laughed, and suddenly, after that awful afternoon, I
felt that the coming evening would be safe. With admiration I
watched Rogers, a handsome man in early middle age, on the street
below us. He leaned against the front fender with an air of both
dignity and nonchalance, his arms folded against his broad chest,
his face passive. To the little gaggle of potential troublemakers he
gave a stern "Look but don't touch" glare, though he seemed to be
answering questions affably enough. It was only later that I learned
of a licensed Luger he wore beneath his maroon and gray tunic; he
could afford to look relaxed in his strange surroundings.

After being introduced to my uncle, Ismeralda had gone into
the kitchen in hopes of finding something other than Puss 'n Boots,
kitty litter, and Pop Tarts. She came back into the living room
shaking her head. "Honey, there ain't enough fixin's to make tea
for a mouse and I wouldn't know that old lady's tea from poison
anyways, she got so much funny stuff in there."

"Does she now?" my uncle asked with undisguised curiosity.
Turning on the charm like a true Fay he steered Ismeralda back into
the kitchen with the suggestion that while tea wouldn't do even if
it could be found, ice would be very much in order. The same
charm sent me downstairs to Rogers, who supplied a decanter of
bourbon and real cut-crystal tumblers from the nicely stocked little
bar in the Rolls. It was fascinating and not a little heady to run the
gauntlet of onlookers carrying such elegantly packaged booze.

"To our absent hostess," my uncle said solemnly, without any
trace of the facetiousness that the situation might suggest. He raised
his glass toward an empty chair—overstuffed, greasy, and obviously much used—which sat beside the front window. It was easy
to imagine the long years in which the baroness sat at that window,
her fat arms resting on a pillow on the sill, watching the ebb and
flow of life on the changing streets below her. Stale ice from her

old Kelvinator clinked in our glasses as we touched them one to the other and sat down. None of us took the chair by the window.

"Miss Jackson has shown me the kitchen and the bedroom nightstand in your absence, Miranda. The lady is possessed of a bizarre pharmacopoeia to say the least. The medical books are terribly old and out of date, which would be bad enough if they were British or American to begin with—but Russian! I shudder to think of being treated by someone using Russian medical books from the eighties and nineties. Yah!" he concluded with an ostentatious shiver followed by a good swig of his velvety smooth bourbon.

"They must have belonged to her father. She said his name was Alexeiev and that he had treated the czar once."

Uncle Jeremiah nodded. "That is the name on the flyleaf of the books I glanced at—Dr. Alexander Alexeiev. I imagine most of that stuff she has belonged to him. Half of it belongs in a museum, the rest in the garbage."

"While we were waiting for you to get up here from the city, Ismeralda and I went through her desk. No, don't look at me like that. We didn't disturb anything and we didn't take anything. All we wanted to do was see what her full name was—she's A. A. Derevenkov on the mailbox and the door. Her full name is Alexandra Alexeievna Derevenkov. She is a baroness—really—and she and her husband evidently lived in France for years before and during the war. They were admitted to this country, according to their passports, in nineteen forty-eight."

Ismeralda spoke up. "I found her husband's death certificate in the desk. He die in nineteen fifty-nine of cancer. He was about twenty years older than her. She got a will in the desk too."

"A will?" my uncle asked, his eyes taking on a lawyerly glow. "Sealed?"

We both nodded. "The envelope is inscribed 'To be opened by my lawyer in the event of my death.' The lawyers are in Manhattan," I explained.

I reached over the arm of my chair, pulled a long business

envelope off the top of a cluttered little desk in the front corner of the room, and handed it to my uncle. He read the inscription frowningly.

"Duvall, Duvall, Rickaby and Romford. Yes. Interesting. I know of this firm. They are old and reputable. She must have *some* money, it would seem. They'd not be likely to deal with her otherwise."

"Look at these," I suggested, passing him a pair of bank books. "There is about seventy, eighty thousand, all told. She didn't do Valdalene's abortion for need of money from the look of things." I told him about the small luxury of an unlisted phone number and the paid-up rent and utility bill receipts that were also in the desk. She had had Social Security and a small annuity too.

"Hummm, no, it would seem that whatever her reasons for what she did, money was not the motive. Well, it's a bad business all around. Miss Jackson," he said, repeating the name once or twice until he roused her from her reverie, "you were starting to describe the Baroness's symptoms when Miranda came back upstairs with the bourbon. Would you please continue?" And Ismeralda described the old woman's condition in detail, my uncle listening attentively all the while.

"There's something else," I put in. "Just before the paramedics got here and took over, Dr. Weems—who is my old gentleman on the path, by the way—"

At this, my uncle's white eyebrows went skyward. He nodded vigorously for me to go on. "Dr. Weems cut the bandages off her arms. They were hideously red—the skin really angry-looking—and scored with fine gashes that ran from the backs of her hands right up the forearms. Do you remember what Guy said about—"

"I remember," my uncle broke in. "You realize don't you, both of you, that this is a police matter now? We have enough circumstantial evidence to accuse this woman of illegal abortion, manslaughter—in the case of your sister, Miss Jackson," he said, turning toward Ismeralda with a softened voice, "and murder, in the case of the child, which was, as you know, born alive and then strangled. From what you two describe, the woman is suffering from septicemia."

"Blood poisoning," Ismeralda declared.

"In the kitchen, there are several boxes of disposable syringes and the refrigerator contains a supply of insulin," my uncle explained, "which implies that the baroness is a diabetic. That being the case, she is a prime target for pyaemia as the shivering and the sweating seem to indicate. That," he pointed out before I could ask, "is an acute form of blood poisoning in which abscesses form not only at the original site of infection—in this case, the scratches on her arms—but also in the deep tissue of the body—lungs, kidneys, liver, and so on. It is a very unpleasant way to die."

"Then you think she will die?" Ismeralda asked flatly. She sounded neither triumphant nor vengeful.

"Oh, yes, Miss Jackson," my uncle replied matter-of-factly. "An elderly, overweight, malnourished diabetic with pyaemia! I should say she'll not live more than a few days at most, if the infection was introduced during the abortion, which Dr. Galveston tells me must have taken place on the third of the month. This is the eighteenth. The bacteria have had over two weeks to migrate. The entrance wounds were, moreover, on both arms. She is, I would say, a prime host."

"She was indeed a prime host, sir."

The voice we heard in the gathering darkness of late afternoon was cultured, with a softly accented southern drawl most pleasant to the ear.

"Are you a doctor, I wonder?" the voice asked.

We all turned toward the hall door, which I had evidently not locked behind me when I returned with the bourbon and glasses. Dr. Weems stood there, tall despite the dejected stoop of his shoulders. He swayed and took hold of the jamb unsteadily.

"You had better help the doctor in, Miranda," my uncle suggested. "He does not seem well."

Indeed he was not. His breath was rank with bad liquor and his yellowed eyes were glassy. He had been weeping. Tears still lingered in the deep creases of his leathery old face. He reminded me for an instant of little Wesley Nivens in the apartment downstairs. The boy's cheeks were smooth, but the tears and the sorrow were the same.

"She was a remarkable woman, the Baroness Derevenkov. She had led a remarkable and tragic life. I—I shall miss her, dreadfully. Dreadfully . . ., " he repeated softly to himself. He closed his eyes and more tears came, squeezing through the lids and running down his cheeks until they fell onto his lapels.

I took his overcoat from him, noticing as I did a pint whiskey bottle, wrapped in a twisted brown paper bag in the big side pocket.

"You were friends then?" I asked.

"Friends," the old man mused. "I suppose—or perhaps just companions in life's adversities. The last twenty-five or so years of our lives we have grown steadily closer together, deeper in our understanding and—tolerance, perhaps. My wife died, her husband, her health began to fail, my son was killed in Vietnam, my practice began to fall off. That was nothing really. She had seen worse, lost more, far more than I, but we understood one another. I—it is not to say that I approved of her—of some of the things she had done over the years, but I did understand. . . ."

I hung the coat on a hook inside the closet door, making sure that my uncle saw the pint bottle in the pocket as I passed his chair. He caught my eye and nodded.

"Miranda, see if you can find a clean glass in that kitchen and some more ice. Being a southern gentleman, I suspect Dr. Weems appreciates good bourbon."

The old doctor managed a faint smile. "Thank you, sir. It's a long time since I've had the luxury of good bourbon, and frankly, I am not ashamed to admit I rather need it at the moment. I hadn't seen her since—since the day after the—the—" He trailed off and could not speak for a moment. I came back in with a glass for him and fresh ice for us all.

He took his drink and held it, staring at it as if he dared not indulge. "Wesley told me that she had forbidden him to come to me, that she treated the scratches herself with peroxide—God knows how old the stuff was—and some of her poultices." He shook his grizzled head sadly. "She was a foolish, foolish woman. She didn't trust doctors and she was afraid, I suppose, that if she went to a hospital they'd find out how—find out what had happened and that it would implicate me. Wesley told me that she had read all the papers and knew that they were looking for an elderly black man who might have scratches on his hands. She died trying to protect me," he said to his glass, shaking his head again with a sort of finality. "Remarkable." He drank suddenly, raising his glass and taking a gulp that must have seared his throat going down. He winced and fresh tears came to his eyes.

"My, that was foolish of me. This is too fine a liquor, sir, to treat in such a cavalier manner."

My uncle nodded sagely. It seemed to me at that moment that the room held only those two old men speaking softly to each other in the gathering darkness. Ismeralda and I were simply dumb witnesses to their colloquy.

"I can see why she wished to avoid the hospital, but why did she not send for you when she grew worse? She must have known that you would come," my uncle said.

Dr. Weems shook his head wearily. "Shame, I suppose. She knew that I was horrified and disgusted. She was herself, for that matter, and I think she must have been very frightened.

"I should have looked in on her. I know all that I should have done, what as a doctor and as a gentleman I was bound to do, but . . . one does not always act as one would wish to act. I drink, sir, as I am sure you must have noticed." He said this with calm and dignity, pulling himself erect in the chair that I had vacated upon his arrival. "I did not in my youth, nor even very much after my wife died. Moses was my only son, my only child."

The old man paused again, mastering himself, sipping at the bourbon delicately, appreciating its texture, beginning slowly to regain something of the real man—the man whose essential qualities I saw on that early morning along the rim of the Hudson below Hook Mountain.

"I began to drink after he was killed. All that I had worked for and struggled for seemed to be . . . dust. I—there isn't much more to say. My practice began to fall off long ago. I still have a few old patients of long standing, but that is all. I have ceased to keep up with current medical practice. It is all but over for me.

"The baroness might have come to me, but she would not have found me in, or, if in, she would not have found me conscious. I have not been seeing patients recently. I have been seeing . . . ghosts, I suppose."

The old man turned toward me, looking as if he were seeing me for the first time. "You are the one who found it. I recognized you at once. You saw it. You did see it . . .?"

"Yes, I saw the child, but I saw the mother, too" I replied. "I saw Valdalene Pearsall, Dr. Weems."

"Then perhaps you can understand why I have—" He looked at me with pleading in his eyes. "I have had neither the courage to go to the police, nor the callousness to forget. Can you understand that, sir?" he asked, turning from me to my uncle.

"Yes," Uncle Jeremiah said, nodding thoughtfully, bridging the tips of his fingers together before his face. He looked then as I imagine he must have looked for forty years and more to the countless anxious clients who had come to him for advice and counsel. "Yes, I think I can understand. People are often foolish out of fear, Dr. Weems. It is not always easy to be wise or sensible."

"I didn't kill that young woman—or the child either, for that matter, but I am an accessory. That much I do know."

"Humph," my uncle mumbled. "Yes, well." He considered for a moment or two, "Before we get into that, I think that introductions are in order. A man ought to know, it seems to me, with whom he is drinking, and I do have the advantage of you." He sounded very calming and pleasant as he spoke, modulating his voice and motioning to me to replenish the doctor's glass.

Dr. Weems smiled faintly. "Yes, you do have that, sir." His soft voice was rich with gentle irony. The contrasts between the two old men were many.

"I am Jeremiah Pearsall Fay—" and here Dr. Weems started visibly at the familiar name. "Yes," my uncle went on, "the name is the same, and I am, as it happens, a collateral relation of the victim as is my niece here, Miss Miranda Fay. You might say that it is an odd twist of fate that has pulled first her and then myself into this peculiar situation. It is a remarkable coincidence, to be sure . . . if it is only coincidence.

"I am also a lawyer, as I think it only fair you should know. I am no longer in practice, however, and am not acting on behalf of any client. The other young lady," he continued, "is Miss Jackson. She happens to be the most immediately involved of all of us for she is Miss Pearsall's sister. I doubt any of us here can properly imagine or share in her sorrow."

Dr. Weems looked at Ismeralda. "I—it was too late. I couldn't save . . ."

Ismeralda shook her head violently as if to blot out his words. He seemed to understand and fell immediately silent. She started to take another sip of bourbon, stopped, looked at the tumbler in Dr. Weems's frail, trembling hands and put her glass down on the cluttered table beside her resolutely. Instead she got up and began walking from lamp to lamp, putting each on in turn. Since none of them had anything higher than a forty-watt light bulb, the stuffy apartment still remained dim and murky, swimming in icons and cat hair.

"Thank you, Miss Jackson, that is a help," my uncle said kindly. Observing the dim light for a moment, he then asked the doctor a question. "She was a diabetic, I know, Dr. Weems, but did she also have glaucoma?"

The doctor nodded. "It had been getting worse. She could still see, but bright light was painful and her field of vision was narrowing rapidly. In another few months, a year, she'd have been blind, I imagine. The only things she'd let me prescribe for her were the insulin and the drops for her eyes. They relieved the pressure, but her condition was too advanced—"

"Indeed, indeed," my uncle broke in, and then, non sequitur, "Anne Arundel County, I should guess. Maryland. Am I correct?"

Dr. Weems looked rather taken aback.

"You are very good, Mr. Fay, very good indeed. Is it my accent? They say that experts on language can tell a man's place of origin right down to the street in the town by the way he speaks."

My uncle chuckled and shook his head. "No, no, my expertise lies in the field of genealogy. The Weemses, originally spelled 'Wemyss' in Scotland, are an old family in Anne Arundel County. Our own ancestress, Williamina Weems," my uncle explained, nodding toward me, "married John Moore, king's collector of customs in Philadelphia in the eighteenth century. Her brother— David, if I am not mistaken—settled in Anne Arundel County and was a man of large estate there."

Dr. Weems nodded slowly. With great dignity he acknowledged Uncle Jeremiah's remarks. "My great-grandfather," he said, "took his name from that family. My grandfather, Elijah, for whom I was named, was born in slavery on the Weems plantation in eighteen fifty-nine. I have no reason to believe, however, that the blood of the Weemses flows in my veins. I would prefer to think that it does not, if you can understand and take my meaning."

Uncle Jeremiah sipped from his glass and smiled. "I most certainly take your meaning and understand fully," he said amiably. "I meant only to imply that your name, combined with the still strong suggestion of a distinctive Maryland accent, gave me, as a student of family histories, a likely point of origin. I am something of a monomaniac on my hobbyhorse. I cannot resist delving into people's histories."

"Well, you are a good detective, sir," Elijah Weems acknowledged, raising his glass to my uncle's honor, "and a splendid judge of good bourbon into the bargain." As he grew more mellow, his accent became even smoother and more southern.

"You say you didn't kill Miss Pearsall?" Uncle Jeremiah remarked suddenly, delivering a one-two punch that took not only Dr. Weems, but also Ismeralda and me by surprise.

"No, I did not," the old man gasped. He took a pull of his drink, gulped, and began to explain, casting first a wary eye on Ismeralda, who nodded grimly at him. Her expression indicated that she had dug in with every intention of hearing his story. "She was barely breathing when I arrived. I—I could hardly believe the scene that I came in upon."

"Excuse me," my uncle interrupted. "You were not there from the very beginning? You were not the—the abortionist?" He had the modulated sound, as he spoke, of a lawyer gathering his facts.

"No, no, sir, I was not, and never would I have been, under such conditions as those that prevailed in that room. I have never liked abortion—most doctors don't, I think, though I admit I performed many abortions in the past before the laws were liberalized, and with good conscience in most cases. This time, no." He shook his grizzled old head emphatically. "I had no idea that such a thing was even contemplated. If I had, I should never have allowed it to be performed as and where it was—or by the baroness. It was sheer madness."

He paused as if gathering his strength and continued. "She sent young Wesley to fetch me. It was late on a Monday evening. I had no idea what the problem was, where he was taking me or even why. He was overwrought, undoubtedly affected by her own state, which was near hysteria, and I couldn't get a sensible word out of him other than the bare fact that Baba Derevenkov needed me."

"Had you been drinking?" my uncle asked quietly.

"Yes," Dr. Weems conceded. "Yes, I had had a drink, maybe was on the second when he rang my bell, but I was not drunk. I was quite sober, in fact. I suppose if I hadn't been, I'd never have been able to deliver the child alive. That, at least, I was able to do." He paused thoughtfully, looking at the bottom of his empty glass.

"I couldn't believe the condition of the building that the boy took me to. It was hardly habitable. I decided that the baroness must have been injured chasing after a cat or trying to rescue a litter of kittens. She did things like that. What I am trying to say, I guess, is that I was totally unprepared for the scene that I came in on. It could hardly have been worse."

"Wesley, that little boy, saw—?" I asked in horror.

"No, no. I pushed him back out the door and told him to go home. I can't imagine a child seeing such—such goings-on. The baroness had had him posted in the hall outside the room to act as a lookout, I suppose.

"When I arrived, things were in a deplorable state. There was a young woman screaming—I had never seen her before—and she was twisting on the bed. The baroness had tied her to the mattress as best she could to try to keep her still. She said she was afraid she'd injure herself more. She had been tearing at her belly from the pain, it seems." He stopped and turned to Ismeralda. "Really, Miss—Miss—? I am sorry. I cannot remember—"

"Jackson," Ismeralda answered quietly. "Ismeralda Jackson."

"Miss Jackson, surely you ought not to hear this.'

"Dr. Weems, we have no right to tell a grown woman what to hear or not to hear. If it were my sister, no one could stop me either."

"That's right. Thank you, Miranda," Ismeralda said, and, rising from her chair, came across the small crowded room to sit beside me on the couch. I took her hand and squeezed it reassuringly. "Please go on, Dr. Weems. I wants ta hear."

He sighed and shook his head and continued.

"There had been some bleeding to begin with, the baroness told me. By the time I saw her, however, she was hemorrhaging. Her screams subsided just after I entered the room. She was extremely pale and sweating profusely, beginning to go into shock, whether from blood loss, pain, or the effect of drugs, I could not readily tell. Most likely blood loss was the immediate cause, but all three must have been factors in the end. She had almost no pulse.

"The baroness said that she had attempted to abort the child, but that it had not come and that instead it had begun to thrash about violently in the uterus. It sounded impossible, such a thing, but I saw the belly for myself. The girl was in shock by then, clammy to the touch, breathing shallowly, almost no pulse—very near death—and yet the child was moving vigorously in her belly. You could actually see it; not an occasional listless thump as if it were in extremis, but a constant, insistent writhing the like of which, sir, I can assure you, I have never seen. It was—unsettling to say the least." The old doctor leaned back in the chair and sighed. It seemed as if he were gradually unburdening himself of a great weight as he told his story.

My uncle nodded but said nothing. Outside it was dark. In the stuffy room with its half dozen forty-watt bulbs, it was almost equally night. The cats had padded in unnoticed and now mewed around our ankles, wanting their dinner, their milk, their Baba, but now, in the dark, no one paid any attention to their subtle cajolery. Dr. Weems sighed again and went on with his tale.

" 'How far along is the child?' I asked her. She shrugged and said five or six months. She wasn't sure. Of course, no such attempt should have been made under those circumstances, to begin with, but at the end of the second trimester—unthinkable. It seemed like a nightmare. Indeed, it was a nightmare. It was no place for a woman that far along. I couldn't give her anything. She was in a state of shock as it was and near death. I did give her Adrenalin—"

"You did?" My uncle broke in sharply. The old man nodded. I knew what Uncle Jeremiah was driving at. The tox reports on Valda had shown Adrenalin had been administered. That information had, however, been kept out of the papers and could only have been known by the person who administered it to her. We had only just wheedled that news out of Guy over dinner the evening before.

"It hardly increased her pulse at all, and then only briefly. I was beside myself. I couldn't convince the baroness to call the police and I was too busy trying to stabilize the girl's condition to fetch them myself. And then—" He bowed his grizzled head and shook it forlornly. His eyes were shut tight as if against the images his words had conjured, and his dry old hands convulsed around the empty glass from the Baroness Derevenkov's awful little kitchen.

"She died. I knew that she would. Without a transfusion, without proper attention—no doctor coming into that room with just his bag could have saved her." He stated that matter-of-factly, with no pleading in his voice. It was simply the truth, bald and unvarnished, and none of us could doubt it for an instant.

"The child was not dead, however. It still moved. I—I don't know quite what possessed me. I performed a cesarean. I have performed many in the past, though not in some years. I have no young patients these days. I opened her and took the child—a monstrous child with a great, deformed head and a body like a— like a—" He shuddered. "It was born screaming—screeching, rather—like a trapped rat or a wild possum. The voice was animal-like and it was furious. Its eyes—lidless eyes—rolled about wildly. I gave it to the baroness and told her to cut the cord while I cleaned up. I don't think that I was quite myself by this time. I think that I was actually frightened of the thing. I know I could have used a drink," he said with a wry smile that crossed his weary face for an instant and was gone.

"She took it from me on a towel and laid it on the floor by the bed. She cried out for me to look at it. She said her eyes were bad and that the candles were glaring. Was it really so horrible as it looked? Was it teramorphous? I told her that it was."

"She said that? She used the word 'teramorphous'?" my uncle asked.

"She did. It didn't surprise me that she should. The Baroness Derevenkov knew something about medicine. Her father had been a physician in Russia. They had had bad times during the Great War and the revolution. They made their way out through Siberia when she was a child. She assisted her father at times and under horrible conditions. She never studied medicine herself, however. She was a prime example, was the baroness, of the adage, 'A little knowledge is a dangerous thing.' What she knew drove her to help your sister, Miss Jackson," he explained, turning to Ismeralda, whose face he had been studiously avoiding during his story. "What she didn't know killed them both."

"What happened then?" I asked.

"It wouldn't stop squealing. It writhed and squirmed in her hands. She said something strange then, something about having seen the father." I glanced at my uncle and caught his eye. We both held our breath. "She said that she knew who he was. Those were her very words, in fact. 'I saw the father—long ago. I know who he is. I know *what* he is.' She cried out then that the baby wouldn't die. She sounded frantic. I could hardly understand her. The accent, you see. I said that we must bundle it up and get it to the hospital, that she should find something to wrap it in.

"She laughed at me and told me that I was a fool, that if I knew what she knew, I'd kill it myself. It was then that I realized what she was doing. I came around the bed and looked down. She was kneeling on the floor in a pool of light cast by several candles—and she was strangling the thing with its own umbilical cord. It was struggling wildly, its hands and feet clinging to her wrists and arms as a kitten might do. It seemed to have claws like a kitten, in fact. I tried to pull her up, but she was a heavy woman, and strong, and she shook me off. She kept tightening the cord until the thing finally stopped struggling and died. It was horrible—horrible. The most terrible thing that I have ever witnessed."

He sighed again and continued. "There was nothing more I could do. The woman was dead, the child murdered before my eyes, and my old—my only—friend bleeding and hysterical from the ordeal. I put alcohol on her wounds, bound them with gauze, gave her a shot, wrote out a prescription for an antibiotic, and sent her home. Wesley was out in the street waiting for her. He took her home, I believe."

"I found the prescription on her desk. She never filled it," I said quietly.

The doctor shrugged and went on. "I went back into the apartment, picked up the child, and put it into a bag that I found. The baroness had brought her paraphernalia in it, it seems. I put the child in the bag and rolled it up into a small bundle. I wiped the basin and whatever else I thought she might have touched so that there would be no fingerprints.

"I sat in my consulting room all night drinking. It did no good. I stayed awake and sober and frightened. I was terribly frightened, sir." The urgency to be understood sounded in his voice. My uncle pursed his lips and nodded at his fingertips, bridged comfortably across his vest as he slouched in one of the baroness's chairs. The doctor went on.

"I remembered so many things that night. So many good thoughts of my wife and my little boy and the way things used to be. I had a car in the old days and we'd take long rides in the country. We used to picnic along the Hudson at Nyack. My wife had cousins who lived in Haverstraw. We'd walk along the river and feel we were in another world, so peaceful and isolated and away from—" He stopped and looked from my uncle to myself and then to Ismeralda. "Well, away, at any rate."

"At dawn I got up and put the bundle in my overcoat pocket, took the crosstown bus, and went over to the George Washington Bridge. I took the Nine-A bus and went up to Nyack. It was along walk from town but I knew where to go. It hadn't changed so much in thirty years. I don't even know why I did it. I could have dropped the bag in any garbage can anywhere and probably nothing would have been discovered. Instead, I took it to a wooded path along the river, where it was found in a matter of days by a dog. Ironic," he said with a small shrug.

"You should have gone to the police," my uncle said mildly.

"So I should, and if it were not for the baroness, I probably would have."

"But then, if it were not for the baroness—," I said.

"There would not have been a bungled abortion, a manslaughter case, and a murder," Uncle Jeremiah said, wrapping things up succinctly.

$\triangledown$

9

ENTR'ACTE

My landlady, in true Mrs. Hudson fashion, was waiting for me with a drink, a baked ham sandwich, and a couple of nice juicy pickled walnuts: pure ambrosia. Even Sherlock himself could have expected no more. Her reward for her efforts was a detailed account of our afternoon with the baroness and our evening with Dr. Weems, after which she filled me in on the news from her end. Uncle Jeremiah had left it to Meta to tell me of his early-afternoon activities, since she had been acting as his liaison and knew exactly what had happened in Mineola, Long Island.

"He saw Brenda Soldano's accused attacker at the county courthouse where he's being held. His name is Vincente Rocco and he is an unemployed auto mechanic with a wife and three children and another on the way." She took a small pad and pencil out of her apron pocket and consulted it. "His lawyer," she went on, reading from her notes, "is one Anthony Di Certo, hired by the family and not a legal aid lawyer. Your uncle says he thinks the young man is sharp. He had the blood tests done as soon as he could on Monday. They indicate with ninety-nine percent certainty that Vinnie Rocco could *not* have fathered the infant that Brenda Soldano gave birth to on Sunday. Also, all of the Rocco children are normal and the pregnancy in progress is, so far as is known, perfectly uneventful. The other rape charges against him, which involve two other women, both older by several years than Brenda, will not be challenged, but the lawyer expects that when he gets a hearing, the Soldano rape charge will be dropped. Therefore, your uncle concludes, the father of Brenda Soldano's child is still unknown. The baby, by the way, was still alive as of three this afternoon."

"Well," I mused, "Uncle Jeremiah said I'd find what you had to tell me interesting. I guess he was right. Who fathered that baby, then?"

"Oh, and, love, speaking of the baby, Guy called at six-fifty and I gave all this information to him. He said he talked to a doctor at Franklin General. The child's blood type is not—here I have to quote him exactly," she said, putting her glasses on the end of her nose and peering through them owlishly. "The child's blood type is *'not inconsistent* with the blood type of the Nyack mooncalf and therefore does not rule out the possibility that they were fathered by the same man,' " she read precisely from her pad.

"But doesn't prove that they were, either," I concluded glumly. "Damn all the double-talk. If they weren't, then none of this matters at all. If they were . . . What else did Guy say?"

"Oh, that he missed you when he called this morning. He is a bit sweet on you, I think, luv." Meta looked pleased with this intelligence.

"Spare me, please. I have enough problems with Max. Did you tell him what I told you about finding the midwife and the things in her apartment?"

Meta nodded. "And I told him she'd been taken to Lincoln Hospital and gave him the number where you could be reached. I also filled Guy in on your uncle's activities and told him that Jeremiah had planned to go to the Bronx. That relieved his mind. He didn't like to think of you being there alone."

I made a face, not in the mood for being overprotected, and ignored the remark.

"There'll be an autopsy on the baroness, I imagine. They'll try to link things up with what Guy found during the mooncalf's autopsy—blood, skin samples, so on—and check it with Dr.

Weems's official statement, and, if it all fits, which one supposes it will, this whole sordid little mystery will have sorted itself out." I sounded flat and let down even to my own ear.

She leaned across the table and handed me a copy of the new *Nyack Stop-Press*. "Here, luv. It's your article."

"Tell me, Meta, why in hell do I feel so bloody let down?" I asked, glancing over the paper and admiring my name on the byline. Even that didn't cheer me much.

"Because you think it's over," she said simply.

"Well, isn't it?"

It was after midnight when I took Molly for her final walk of the night. We ambled along for twenty minutes or so, finally completing our tour by rounding the corner of Piermont Avenue and crossing through the bushes behind Meta's garage. At the edge of the rhododendrons, Molly raised her hackles and began to growl.

"No, no, M. Brown. No raccoon hunting for you, please." She refused to budge, and instead began to bark and lunge on the leash furiously. At that, something a damned sight bigger than one of our local raccons took off at a trot, thrashed through a small copse that divided Meta's property from a big, talf-timbered Queen Anne house on the next street, and ran along the slate sidewalk in hard-soled shoes.

"Damn you, Max," I yelled after the retreating sound. "Beat it! Leave me alone. I've had it! Do you hear?"

In another minute a door slammed, a motor started, and a car took off toward South Broadway. I heard it turn left and head south. Right toward the entrance ramp for the Tappan Zee Bridge, if I were to hazard a guess.

I stooped to pet Molly. "What a good girl you are," I said, still shaking a bit from both anger and fright. Max was beginning to make me nervous. This was the second time now he'd been spying on me.

I had just finished brushing my teeth when the phone rang.

"Max, you son of a bitch—"

"Tch, tch. Language, my child," my uncle's thin, cheery voice came over the wire.

"Oh, Uncle Jeremiah, I am sorry."

"Quite all right. Think nothing of it. I take it that you've had some words with the fellow?"

"No, no words, actually. He's watching me, hell-bent on catching me out with Guy or some other poor hapless date. The jerk was actually lurking in my landlady's bushes, but never mind that. I'm all right."

"Good. I've called to ask you to have lunch with me at my club tomorrow. Guy is going to try to make it as well, if he can get away from his cold steel slab for a bit."

"Which club?" I asked with a laugh, remembering the list of memberships he had rattled off the other day.

"Why not the Genealogists' for a start? West Fifty-fifth. Twelve-thirty. That will give us plenty of time for a drink and a look round before luncheon."

"Perfect." I was just about to say good night and hang up when I realized with a pang that I was lonely—and even a little scared. I didn't like the idea of Max being nutty enough to lurk in my landlady's rhododendrons. "By the way, Uncle Jeremiah, what do you make of Elijah Weems?"

"Ah, Dr. Weems," came my uncle's reply, "well, I think that he's an honest man and a troubled one, of course. It is quite sad, actually, but I see in him a man stalked by the White Camel. It has been behind him and closing for a long, long time."

The White Camel, I knew was a symbol for Death in Arab legend. "The White Camel stalks us all," I said soberly.

"No, no, not really," my uncle of over eighty replied vehemently. "I haven't heard the Camel's bell yet myself, and I am eight or ten years Dr. Weems's senior, but when I do hear it, when I am overtaken, it still shall be in one sudden, swift movement. There shall be the padding of the great feet, the insistent tinkling of the bell, the sweep of the great beast's rhythm—and then *finis*. All swift, you see, and only frightening for an instant.

"Elijah Weems, on the other hand, has heard a damned, slow incessant tinkling for years. He never forgets that it is just behind him and closing . . ."

"That, I suppose, is why he drinks . . ."

The Genealogists', one of the more obscure and elite of New York's many elegant little clubs, has quarters in a graystone sliver of townhouse designed by McKim, Mead and White in 1900, the very same year that an unknown teenybopper called Evelyn Nesbit first became a Floradora Girl. It is even possible, though by no means certain, that Stanford White himself may have had a hand in its design. However, be that as it may, it remains to this day the quiet, sumptuous apotheosis of everything tasteful and extravagant in turn-of-the-century New York architecture and interior design. Moreover, while its library swells with inherited volumes of exalted lineages and its walls glower with the painted visages of stern-demeanored deceased members, its wine cellars and kitchens are justly famous for quality befitting the American descendants of stalwart refugees from the royal and aristocratic houses of England, France, and the Holy Roman Empire—or so the lawyers, doctors, tool- and die-makers, and other assorted businessmen whose preserve it is like to think.

"Wednesday is ladies' day," my uncle said by way of greeting. "Otherwise you'd never have got past the mail slot in the front door." He ushered me from the grand foyer up a flight of carpeted stairs replete with brass stair rods and into a long narrow library with tall stained-glass windows at each end and several thousand leather-bound volumes behind glass panels and bronze grills. Glass-topped display cases containing hand-illuminated coats of arms, spidery-handed manuscripts, and assorted memorabilia stretched down the room in long ranks. Shaded reading lamps and uncomfortable chairs abounded.

He waved a hand. "This is the world's largest repository of

uncut pages. No one comes here to read or study, but merely to bask in the printed proof of one's worth. 'Man's Folly Fossilized' is what I'd title a still life of this room if I could paint as well as your father did." My father, among other things, had been a gifted amateur in oils.

"The luncheon, however, will be excellent," he added jovially. "That I promise you. Now, let us descend to the smoking room for a brandy and soda before they serve. I have something to show you."

The "something" turned out to be a chart of the first ten generations of my ancestry—not only my father's line, with which I was familiar, and which in turn represented only a tiny portion of my uncle's years of research into the more remote generations of the family—but also that of my mother, Ann Claire Chadwick.

I glanced over the pages of the chart in amazement. "You've done all this since Sunday evening? From those few names and dates that I gave you, you've come up with all this? I can't believe it."

"I didn't do much," he shrugged modestly. "Your landlady did a great deal for me by phone, calling cemeteries and state records offices and churches. I haven't gone back nearly as far, nor in as many lines as I would have liked. Some of it will take real digging, for which I haven't the time right now. As soon as I saw the Mesereaus and Bedells—Long Island families again—I concentrated on them. Played a hunch, so to speak, and as you see, it paid off." He pointed out one section of my mother's chart that he had underscored in red.

"Your mother was a Pearsall through her great-grandmother, Elizabeth. Elizabeth Pearsall Bedell was a direct descendant of a James Pearsall and his wife, Forgiveness Basset. As you know, on my side of the family, your great-grandmother, Lydia Pearsall Van Voorst was also descended from the same couple. Consequently, you, my dear, have a double descent—at least a double descent— from them." He turned away and riffled through the papers in his briefcase.

"Now, of necessity, I've only done a very sketchy chart for most of Cousin Valdalene's line," he said, handing me another, single sheet of paper, "but I have found that her father, Edward Pearsall, is also a direct descendant of the same James Pearsall and Forgiveness Basset who appear in our charts." Uncle Jeremiah slipped yet another chart out of his case and laid it on my lap on top of the others.

"Brenda Soldano," he said softly. "I told you she was a Pearsall, but I didn't know exactly what the connection was until about two o'clock this morning. Look."

Underlined in red were the names James and Forgiveness Pearsall.

"It's awfully coincidental, isn't it?" I asked somberly.

My Uncle Jeremiah frowned, caught up totally in the intellectual puzzle of it all. "Perplexing is the word. There are hundreds of Pearsall lines, of course. There's no mystery in that. Why, Clarence Pearsall's book alone runs to three volumes, but that each of the lines in these particular charts would lead back to one couple who had such a relatively small family to begin with! I think that there were only three live births of ten recorded pregnancies. Now I've pored over all my Pearsall material, not only Clarence Pearsall's book, but also all my own material, which is extensive, and so far as I can tell, none of the three sons of James Pearsall had more than one or two children at most. It was not a prolific line and yet you yourself have two descents from it and these other young women at least one each. Peculiar. The odds against such a coincidence must be fantastic."

"What can it be about the Pearsalls?" I asked. "Who was this James Pearsall? Was he important or famous in his day?"

My uncle shrugged. "Neither, I'm afraid. According to what information I can find, and information is admittedly scant, he was merely the eighth and last son of a Long Island farmer named Charles Pearsall. His mother went by the more exalted name of Olivia Chandos. Her line is quite interesting, by the way, though irrelevant, I think, to our current project. Now James, given his birth order, should have been apprenticed out to some artisan or craftsman or other and led a humble, impecunious life. Somehow, however, he managed to be a landowner and successful farmer by the time he was in his early twenties. That would be in the seventeen twenties or thereabouts, I imagine, which was at just about the time he seems to have taken his wife, as a matter of fact. I am tempted to postulate a connection there, but be that as it may, he and his wife and seven infants are buried together in Sandhole Methodist churchyard near what is now Lynbrook. At the time he died, his land holdings were large enough to be divided amongst his three surviving sons and provide each of them with a living.

"Where that land came from—or the money for it, rather—seems to be the mystery. I want to trace the record of the original purchase or grant. That may help." He frowned and fell silent, motioning to our waiter for another round of drinks.

I thumbed through the charts again idly, first my own and then, out of curiosity, Valdalene Pearsall's. Her father's line was straight-forward enough and at least in the paternal descent went back ten complete generations. It was in her mother's line, that of an Audrey Williams, that a lesson in the social history of the black American cropped up.

"Look at this," I said, shaking my head, "no information any farther back than a maternal great-grandfather born in eighteen sixty-two. Named Lincoln, no less! Lincoln Debbins," I read aloud from the chart in my hand, "born on November tenth, eighteen sixty-two, died nineteen eleven. Married Freeborn—, surname unknown. With a name like that, she must have been born in eighteen sixty-three, just after the Emancipation Proclamation, I'll bet. Married young, all her married life she'd be called first Momma and then Grandma Debbins and her own name forgotten forever."

"Debbins," Uncle Jeremiah repeated. "There's a story in that name too, as it happens. Debbins is thought by many genealogists to be a Southern Negro corruption of the name De Bains. A Francoise De Bains owned a plantation in Louisiana in the eighteenth century. He was the second son of an old Norman French family of that name. He died intestate and without legitimate issue in seventeen eighty-seven and his property reverted to the senior brother in France. The interesting thing is that he had a son living, the bastard son of a black slave woman, and he actually did intend to give the boy his freedom and make him his heir. The papers were, in fact, already drawn up and awaiting his signature when he died suddenly, or was poisoned by agents of the brother. One never knows in such cases. At any rate, the son lost his attempt to establish his birthright and inheritance, and disappeared from history, most likely sold as part of the very estate that should have been his.

"In any case," he concluded, sipping his drink carefully, "the name Debbins, obscure and rare as it is, is thought to be a corruption of Francoise De Bains's surname and, it is assumed, indicates descent from his only child, Phillipe De Bains. Now that strikes me as being as sad a story as one can hear: to be deprived of one's true birthright and very freedom, in fact, for want of a signature on a piece of paper."

"Unc, you are a repository of the damnedest information," I said, raising my glass to toast him.

He chuckled, obviously pleased with my comment. "I have idled away a lifetime in reading. My brain is a sponge. Squeeze it and I drip useless information drop by drop."

He was about to say something more, but looked up from contemplating the color of his drink and spied Guy Galveston following solemnly in the wake of the blank-faced club servant who ushered him toward us at a stately pace. "But now in good time, here comes our jolly 'medical crowner,' " he cried out heartily. " 'Here's a corpse in the case with a sad swell'd face, and a medical crowner's a queer sort of thing.' " The butler, without the flicker of an eye, withdrew, leaving Guy to join us.

"I know. I know," he said, throwing up his hands, "the Ingoldsby Legends. I had a prof in med school who loved to rag us with that." He shook hands with my uncle, bent to peck my cheek chastely, and plopped into a deep club chair with a luxurious moan of ecstasy and an accompanying whoosh of air and aroma of old leather. He looked around the room appraisingly. "Nice place you've got here, sir. Restful, and I need rest, God knows. I've been in for more cutting, sawing, slicing, and sectioning in the last five days than I can begin to comprehend. Just witnessed the old woman's autopsy—your baroness, Ms. Fay, and by damn, I'll lay odds that when the final report is in, forensic evidence proves beyond a doubt that she killed that mooncalf of yours. Sure as hell. Your old doctor'll be off the hook, because whatever charges they come up with against him, murder and manslaughter will be out. The fact is, he can say he was called in on the case and that he administered Adrenalin in an attempt to save the mother. The child's live birth and vigorous, if brief, survival back up his story that he tried to salvage one life at least. I can come up with plenty for you, Mr. Fay."

Uncle Jeremiah grinned and raised his glass. "Splendid, but not for me, my boy. I think, however, that I've a good lawyer for him. A young fellow and hungry for a bit of notoriety."

Guy had a drink of his own by now. He sipped at it avidly, gulped, and began to speak again. I could tell he was still wound up. "Miranda, I told you after I did that first autopsy that the skin samples from under that thing's claws would catch us a murderer. Well, the irony is that little monster caught his own murderer and actually avenged himself posthumously."

My uncle looked at us with that broad grin of his that so much reminded me of my father. "I find it all rather pleasing," he said cheerily. "It smacks of a sort of cosmic neatness not unlike Cassius in *Julius Caesar* dying on his own birthday. Shakespeare's full of that sort of touch," he rattled on expansively. "The mooncalf destroying its own destroyer is fine melodrama."

"Poetic justice," I agreed.

"But getting back to mooncalves, the next autopsy I witness— at three," Guy said, glancing at his watch, "is in Franklin General. The Soldano teras. It finally died—early this morning."

"Then you *will* get a look at it?" My uncle was suddenly very serious. "Any chance—?"

"Yes, if you want it. I know the man who's doing the autopsy and he was happy to agree. I told him that you were a retired colleague. . . ."

"How very splendid," my uncle chortled.

"My friend Matthews wants to get this examination done fast before the county medical examiner snaffles the corpse for his little black museum. The Soldano family wants the baby buried at once and was very reluctant to release it to Matthews in the first place. He convinced them that in the 'interests of science,' etcetera, but the M.E. must be having dreams of sticking the thing in formaldehyde for his collection, so Matthews wants to get the thing opened up, take a quick look, and then get it to the funeral home fast. Besides, the M.E. has a two-headed baby already," Guy grinned, "so fuck him."

"You're too much," I laughed, shaking my head.

"And where do you go from here, Miranda?" he asked. "Not back up to the Bronx, I hope?"

"No, no. In quite the opposite direction, actually. To the august precincts of Duvall, Duvall, Rickaby and Romford on Park Avenue to interview Mr. Judd Romford. He is handling the Baroness Derevenkov's estate. I want to get as much biographical material as I can for what is most likely my last article on the mooncalf murder. I may not use it all though," I added thoughtfully. "I may keep some back for the book—that is, if I decide that there's enough material for a book in the first place."

We rose then, at the sound of the dinner gong in the hall and made our way into a chaste oak-paneled dining room hung with scores of hand-illuminated coats of arms framed in flat antique gold frames against hunt-green damask walls. It was the sort of place where toast came in silver racks and the wine was decanted. White napery, gleaming silver flatware, cruet sets, shaded candles in silver sticks, and hunt-green-and-white china emblazoned with the arms of the club were set out on each table with the same perfection and luxury one might expect from the oldest and finest of London's private clubs.

"This is just too lovely," I whispered as we sat down.

"I rather thought you'd like it, my dear," my uncle said primly. He got no further with his remark before we were interrupted.

"As I live and breathe, here is Jeremiah Pearsall—and the lovely Miss Fay. This is too, too fortunate. It must be the reward of a good life. I helped my aged mother across Fifth Avenue not forty minutes ago, like the good Boy Scout that I am. They do say that good deeds pay and here's the proof."

All this was said at rapid fire in a loud tenor by Gilbert St. Mauger, who crossed the dining room from a table in the far corner as quickly as his great height and broad girth would allow. He clapped one huge paw on my uncle's shoulder familiarly and took my hand with the other, bending ponderously to kiss it with embarrassing fervor. His grip was unexpectedly gentle, the hand warm and dry and not at all unmanly. Somehow that hand surprised me—quite pleasantly, as it happened.

I heard Guy mutter a quizzical "What in hell?" under his breath and hoped that St. Mauger had not heard him. One never knows with people who are rather odd just what they hear and how they may feel, however oblivious they may seem to the effect that they are having on others—and certainly Gilbert St. Hilaire St. Mauger seemed oblivious to the many pairs of eyes that slewed around in his direction as he made his effusive greeting.

"Gilbert," my uncle exclaimed heartily and with every appearance of delight, "how nice. Do join us for lunch." Uncle Jeremiah introduced Guy, who looked at St. Mauger as if he were a subject for his slab. Guy gave Gilbert only the barest greeting and one could sense the contempt that he felt. The look and the reaction was returned almost in kind by St. Mauger himself, save that underlying his cool expression I sensed something almost like malice. It would have been a dreadful luncheon.

"Alas, Jeremiah Pearsall," he said, "I wish that I could, but this being ladies' day, I am forced into a dutiful lunch with my sister, more's the pity. She insists, and since her grief is only to be assuaged by a granting of her every tiny wish, perforce, I must dine with her in that quiet corner yonder. I expect it is one of those duties for which one is rewarded in the next life. I look upon it philosophically, as a chance to accrue karma, which I can only hope will be meted out as the luxury of one day returning as an only child. What a penance one's sibling can be," he sighed shooting an enigmatic glance in his sister's direction. Her black-clad back remained rigidly and, I thought, rather pointedly, toward us.

I laughed politely at his remarks, sensing an undercurrent in them.

"You agree with me then, Miss Fay?"

"Well, I am an only child myself, and since that state of being has always been a pleasure to me, I must suppose that my karma has already accrued."

"You are an angel. You do understand." He took up my hand once more, bending over me almost intimately. His smooth, choirboy countenance came between me and Guy, who sat beside me like a bulwark. I felt that it was quite deliberate. "Tell me, Miss Fay, are you free this afternoon, or has your uncle filled your whole card?"

"My card, Mr. St. Mauger, is quite blank after about three-thirty," I replied, taking up his quaint turn of phrase with delight. His charm was genuine, and his question gave me a chance to bring home to Guy the fact that I was an independent woman.

"Then shall I meet you for an hour or so at the Metropolitan? Whenever I am in New York, I pay my respects to my ancient Egyptian soulmates at the Met, and I confess I have not yet done so this trip. Shall we say four o'clock at the Temple of Denderah?" He still bent over me, gripping my hand warmly. His voice was gentle, deep, and quite other in tone from his usual fussy manner of speaking.

"I should be enchanted. Four o'clock at Denderah, then," I

echoed, liking the idea more and more. It sounded like an invitation from one of Charlotte Hungerford's romantic novels.

After Gilbert St. Mauger left us, my uncle chuckled under his breath and said something about my having made a conquest.

Guy, on the other hand, looked like thunder. "Who in hell is that fat faggot, and why did you say you were free?"

"Well, I am free," I shrugged, "and if you think he's a faggot, then why are you so upset? It's the nonfaggots of this world, I should think, that one might be jealous of—"

"Oh, stop it, you two. Don't let's get into a squabble. St. Mauger's all right and it is very nice of you, Miranda, not to turn him down. I suspect that he's a rather lonely fellow underneath it all and can use the company. Anyway, it is his sister who is the predator in that family."

"Do tell?" Guy looked hard across the room and catching sight of the lady in profile as she turned and raised her head toward a waiter, gave a low wolf whistle. "That's the sister? She's a knockout. How old is she?" he asked, giving me a sly look out of the corner of his eye.

"The lady is nearly sixty by now, I imagine," my uncle said placidly.

"Sixty," we both said in near unison, exchanging glances of wonderment. I knew from the first that her age was ambiguous, but this was ridiculous.

"Well, fifty-eight, fifty-nine at least. Thirty years ago, when she was still a young woman, and before she had begun to go to Switzerland—Vevey is the town, I believe—for treatments and injections and face-lifts and the like to preserve her youthful looks by unnatural means, she actually tried to seduce me. . . ."

"Seduce you," Guy gulped. "And you turned her down?" Clearly Guy would not have been so foolish.

"I did."

"Why?" I asked. "I—I mean, well, you were a widower, weren't you? And she must have been lovely then, if she is so beautiful even now. . . ." I glanced across the room and reflected on Hillary St.

Mauger. No wonder that despite her seeming youth, she moved in the slow and rather stately manner of a dignified middle-aged woman. Shots and lifts and tucks might keep her looking youthful, but nothing has yet been invented to erase the marks and scars of life from one's heart and mind and soul. Inside, at least, the aging process still went on.

"She was," Uncle Jeremiah conceded. "But, as I say, predatory. Moreover, she had an ulterior motive. She wanted a child. Not marriage, mind. Just a child. It was not a proposition I could entertain—not because I wouldn't have liked a child of my own, or even because a night of love with her was so abhorrent . . ." He paused thoughtfully.

"No, it was the idea of Hillary St. Mauger raising a child of mine alone, somewhere in France or Switzerland amongst all her debauched and degenerate friends. To say nothing of how such a thing would have sullied the memory of my dead wife and the love I bore her." He shook his white-fringed head solemnly. "No, I turned her down quite flat."

"And that is why she hates you," I concluded.

"That is why," he agreed simply.

"But she had a son, after all. That, by the way, is why she is wearing black, Guy. She's in mourning for her son who died—when?" I asked, turning to my uncle.

"Last fall or winter sometime, in Vevey. I didn't see her for the longest time and then about—oh, it must be eighteen or nineteen years ago, I heard that she had had a son. A friend of mine who knew the story sent me a clipping from a Paris paper announcing the birth of a son to Madame Hillary St. Mauger, a son to be called René St. Hilaire St. Mauger. Of course, she was never a 'Madame' in her life. She is Mademoiselle St. Mauger and always was. She never cared anything about marriage any more than St. Mauger has."

"What did he die of?" Guy asked bluntly. "The boy, I mean."

"Funny, I don't know," my uncle answered. "Gilbert never said, but leave it to a medical examiner to ask that!"

∇

10

AN AFTERNOON IN EGYPT

THAT Wednesday in mid-October was quite gray, the sky shedding leaden light through the great glass wall of the Sackler Wing onto the small perfect Temple of Dendur, a thank you from the Egyptian people to the people of America for their help in rescuing the Temple of Abu Simbel from the rising waters of Lake Nasser, formed by the completion of the Aswân High Dam.

Beyond the glass, across the Eighty-sixth Street Drive through Central Park, the trees were bright with gold and orange against the gray sky, a strange vista for those ancient stones. I sat on one of the granite benches that face the temple gate and watched thoughtfully as the twentieth century tried to absorb the mysteries of ancient Egypt through the medium of those 651 displaced blocks of stone.

"Penny for your thoughts."

St. Mauger stood looming above me, blocking the temple with his big presence. He held a shiny new penny between his thumb and forefinger.

It was such a silly, literal gesture that I couldn't help but laugh. "You'd never believe me if I told you."

"Of course I would. Try me."

"All right then, I was thinking of this poor little temple so far from home, encased in glass and concrete against a sky more somber than it has probably ever seen before. . . ."

He stared at me so penetratingly that I actually had begun to stammer and blush. He broke the spell suddenly by stepping aside and casting the penny into the large shallow black granite reflecting pool that surrounds the temple.

"There, I've made a wish," he said, staring with his dark eyes into the water. There were hundreds, perhaps thousands of coins on the black bottom. "It's odd, Miss Fay. You have a strange sensitivity to atmosphere, rather like a cat. Or a lioness," he murmured, regarding me with hooded, thoughtful gray eyes. "Perhaps you were a priestess once. Oh, not of some little temple like this one here," he said, waving his hand dismissively at the Dendur monument. We began to walk toward it, and then slowly down the steps and along its side. "No, you would have been a priestess of Bast, I should think, during the twelfth dynasty most likely, when she still wore the guise of a lioness—at Beni Hassan, of course. That was the site of a high priesteshood of Bast, you know. Now I have always fancied that I must have been a priest of—"

"Osiris," I suggested quickly.

"Oh, no, no. Not Osiris. One of the more obscure mysteries, I should think, rather—of the Apis bull, perhaps, or of Min." He blushed. "Well, you know what I mean, my dear. Something perfumed and Oriental and debauched." He took my hand in his and began to lead me back toward the temple again. He turned and looked down at me laughingly. I laughed too, but only for a moment, for suddenly there came to that great cold, echoing hall, full of shuffle-footed, murmuring museum-goers, a whiff of incense and the elusive sound of a sistrum tinkling brassily on the dry air. I thought, as we passed it, that I could see ropes of flowers floating across the surface of the pool, and hear, beyond the noises of our surroundings, the faint whisper of suggestive voices, as of lovers laughing in the shadows of the stones behind us.

The feeling lasted for only a moment, but it was powerful while it did, lovely and quite palpable to my senses. I looked up at Gilbert St. Mauger in surprise. He looked back at me questioningly.

"You were a magician back then, I think—or still are now. You've turned this dead great hall into an instant of ancient Egypt for me with your conjurings. Really you have," I insisted.

"Yes, I know," he said simply. "Now shall we spend the next hour visiting the mummies?"

We did indeed visit the mummies, followed through each room by curling fingers of incense, by the fragrance of lotus flowers, and the elusive sound of lovers whispering over the faint tinkling of the ancient sistra in the temple. If I had not loved it so, I might have thought myself going mad and become frightened by it, but actually I believed, as I experienced that strange phenomenon, that I had never been so contented or so enchanted in all my life.

At five o'clock, out on noisy, bustling Fifth Avenue, surrounded by scattering hundreds of other museum-goers, Gilbert St. Mauger was once more a mere mortal twentieth-century man, blinking in the brightening afternoon light, his scrubbed choirboy cheeks looking rosy and benign. The ithyphallic god Min indeed! I reached up and pulled the lavender MMA button off his lapel rather unceremoniously.

St. Mauger pursed his lips and looked pleased. "Thank you, Mama, and now we must have tea," he said emphatically and hailed a cab—which came to an instant stop at his feet, since by his height and size he overshadowed all the lesser beings on the curb who were attempting the same. He opened the door and, pushing me in before him, cried in that odd manner of his, "I am simply ravenous. Aren't you?"

We ate at the Palm Court: tea, little sandwiches, biscuits, jam, and finally a selection of terribly rich, terribly delicious cakes. St. Mauger ate delicately and with impeccable manners, but the amount he managed to stow away was astounding, to say nothing of either unhealthy or expensive. He might have had an excuse for such a ravenous appetite if he'd missed luncheon, but the fare served at the Genealogists' at one o'clock was of the sort to keep one stoked til a traditional dinner at eight—or so it would have been for anyone but my burly companion, and burly was the correct word. There was nothing fat about him in the traditional sense of the word. He was simply tall, broad, and big around, with large hands and feet rather disproportionately small, though they carried him well enough. He gave the impression of being both strong and gentle. I felt constrained to be kind to him, as if, despite his great size, he was actually quite fragile.

"So, my dear," he said in the same precise, automatic tone so common in a good, efficient, old-fashioned nurse, "tell me all the latest about your mooncalf. I read your second article about that black whore—quite dreadfully delicious." He bit into a cucumber sandwich and chewed thoughtfully, ruminating like a cow over its cud. "You have a knack for grotesque detail that had me virtually smacking my lips with relish." He wiped his mouth then, as if to confirm the impression that he had meant his words literally. "And now you've actually found the midwife! How clever of you. There was a small article in the afternoon edition of the *Post* about her. Some old Russian woman—"

"The Baroness Derevenkov. She's as strange a person as one could imagine being mixed up in illegal abortion."

St. Mauger buttered a biscuit carefully, his eyes focused on the task so nicely that they appeared to cross for a moment. "Really? A baroness? That is odd. Was she insane or just senile, I wonder?" He had a far-off, speculative look in his eye, being, of course, as avid a true crime buff as my Uncle Jeremiah and I.

"Insane or senile," I repeated thoughtfully. "Perhaps neither, and yet a bit of both. Her father was a doctor . . ." I began to talk of Alexandra Alexeievna Derevenkov and of her apartment full of medical books and apothecary bottles, of cats and icons and the shabby memorabilia of her strange, eventful lifetime. It helped me to talk about her, sifting in the information I had just learned this afternoon from her lawyer with what Dr. Weems had been able to tell us. "She and her father were refugees from the nineteen seventeen revolution. Her mother had died by then, so it was only the two of them, father and daughter. She had a harrowing adolescence in Siberia and the Far East until the early twenties when they were able to get into France as refugees. Her father practiced medicine among the Russian colony in Paris until some time in the mid-thirties when he died. In nineteen thirty-eight, she married Baron Derevenkov. He was a widower twenty-three years older than she. He was not in good health and she must have been more of a nurse than a wife, I imagine. They never had any children, so far as is known.

"Between her father's death and her marriage, she worked briefly in a small private hospital outside Paris. Her father had been affiliated with it, it seems. During the war, when things were so difficult under the Occupation, she went back to work there. That, it seems, is when her troubles began."

"Oh?" St. Mauger asked quietly. He had begun on the petit fours.

"It was during that time that her husband had his first stroke—although he eventually died of cancer—and she needed help. The doctor whose hospital it was treated her husband in exchange for her services as a nurse—although she was never a certified nurse at all. The war, I suppose. Those things matter less at such times. What she did not know, or at least claimed not to know, was that the man she worked for was a Nazi collaborator. He and many of his associates on the staff worked with the German Occupation medical staff—with the blessings, so it appears, of the Vichy government. God knows what it means or what went on at that hospital during those years. The lawyer wasn't sure, but he didn't care for the implications any more than I do.

"At any rate, they almost were not allowed into this country because of the work she had done. They had tried to come here as early as nineteen forty-six, but they didn't make it until nineteen forty-eight. Old Mr. Duvall handled their legal matters and he finally got them into the country.

"There isn't much more to say. She has left her estate in trust for a little black boy who lives in her building, for his education, one would hope. There's an outright gift of ten thousand dollars to a friend of hers, the elderly doctor who got rid of the mooncalf for her. I must have mentioned him the other night at dinner."

"Humph, yes, I suppose you must have done. Interesting, interesting. What very strange lives people lead. Anything else?"

"Anything else?" I repeated, watching idly as passersby glided past us over the broad red and gold carpets of the hall.

"Well, gory details. How did she die, her last words, all the bloody details that make my silly sister cringe."

"Well," I said, hunching over a trifle and whispering confidentially to placate the child in him, "the scoop is that the mooncalf I found, and whom she murdered with her bare hands, actually managed to avenge himself on her posthumously. My next article will be gory indeed. It was his tiny, malformed claws that wounded her and introduced the infection that eventually killed her." I leaned back and reached for my cup. "Talk about poetic justice! My Uncle Jeremiah just loves the perfect irony of it, and Guy—he's my friend, the assistant county medical examiner, whom you met at the club today—" Did I detect a flicker of that same malice I had seen in his eyes before lunch? "Guy is in love with the forensic evidence. He thinks it's perfect."

"*It* killed her?" He asked.

"It did."

"By God," he exclaimed, "the mooncalf killed her. How splendid! This is a cause for celebration." He called back our waiter, who had already been made weary by his many trips to the pastry table, and ordered champagne cocktails.

"To poetic justice," he proclaimed loudly, snatching the glasses off the tray as they arrived. He handed one to me and raised his own so high that the palm fronds above us were christened. "And to your scoop, my dear. It's quite, quite bully."

Uncle Jeremiah called me at about seven o'clock. I had just walked in the door and now sat on the sofa in my living room kicking off my shoes, fending off Molly Brown, who wanted her walk and her dinner in any order that came.

"You wouldn't believe what a time I've had. He got me snockered on champagne cocktails at the Plaza—we must have had half a dozen apiece—and then he took me down to Grand Central, stopping the cab, by the way, while he ducked into a shop and came out with a three-pound box of Godiva chocolates that he insisted I have to 'see me on my way.' " I looked at the box, lying unopened on my coffee table, and marveled. "It must have cost the earth, really, by the look of it. When we got down to the train, he bought me *Town and Country, Architectural Digest,* and *Vogue* for the trip to Tarrytown. He'd have got my ticket too, if I hadn't already bought a round-trip ticket in the morning.

"My God, Uncle, he's right out of the middle ages, he's so courtly. He must have kissed my hand ten times if he did it once and he stood on the platform outside my window like a sentinel until the train left. He actually stood there and waved as it pulled out, with every weary commuter on the five-fifty to Tarrytown looking at him as if he was nuts. He's compelling in his fashion, I must say, and I can't help liking him in spite of myself."

"Nor can I," my uncle agreed. "I have known him since he was a youth and I have always found him to be a delightful companion. There is a strong streak of the romantic in him, I think."

"There certainly is. He thinks he's been reincarnated, which is an appealing thought, I admit, but it is really too romantic a notion. Shades of *Portrait of Jennie!* Well, enough of that. I didn't mean to go on about him so, but as I say, I just walked in and I'm sort of wound up over him yet. My coffee table's laden with expensive magazines and a jillion calories' worth of luxury chocolates. It tends to make an impression."

"I daresay it does," Uncle Jeremiah's thin chuckle came over the wire pleasantly, "but I really should like to hear what Judd Romford had to say about the baroness."

"Judd Romford!" I cried, obviously still wound up and not a little tipsy. "It was their firm that helped get her and her husband into this country after the war . . ." I gave him the complete rundown on what I had learned in the law offices of Duvall, Duvall, Rickaby and Romford.

My uncle was silent for a moment or two after I had finished speaking. "Yes, humm, well, I suppose there's nothing there, but still, I'm getting a strange sense of déjà vu, you know, as if I'd heard all this somewhere before. It helps to explain the lady's peculiar desire to perform the abortion, I suppose—the medical background, I mean." He paused again and sighed. "Strange, how that strikes a bell with me, though. Ah, well, must be getting old. Memory isn't what it used to be."

"How was your afternoon?" I got up as I spoke and trailed the cord into the kitchen to feed Molly Brown.

"It has been a long while since I witnessed an autopsy, but this was fascinating, utterly fascinating. Oh, and I spoke to the Soldano girl's parents at the hospital. They took her home today."

I opened Molly's can of Alpo and dumped it into her dish. "Well, say something. You haven't told me the results."

"Humm? Oh, ah, yes, well, I'll let the 'medical crowner' himself give you the gory details. He was quite excited when he left me and mentioned that he was going to call you as soon as he got home. I think he was a bit put out that you agreed to meet St. Mauger. He rather likes you, I think."

"Good. I like him too, but I need friends and uncles and puppy dogs right now. Not romance."

"Perhaps you are right, my dear. And now," he said brightly, "I must phone your charming landlady, Meta, and find out what she has to report. I've had her calling all sorts of places for me. I'll ring off now, dear. Keep the line open for Guy—and be nice to him. He's not a bad chap, you know."

"Yes, I know. I will, Uncle. Good night and pleasant dreams. Oh, and thanks again for lunch. I loved your club—and I love you."

"I love you too, my child."

Guy didn't call till twenty after ten that evening.

"Sorry, Miranda. I got home at six, couldn't get you, and then fell into bed as if I'd been poleaxed. I woke up two hours later with an idea that just wouldn't wait. I'm up in Pomona now in my office. I've just had your mooncalf on the slab again."

"Again? Why?" I turned off the TV and scrambled through the clutter on the coffee table for a pad and pen. "What's up?"

"Me. Every time I look at you."

"Seriously."

"Oh, shit. I am serious. Tell me, why is it that I can't get to first base with you?"

"Maybe because we're not playing baseball. Now what about the mooncalf? Why did you take it out again?"

"A hunch. I took a look at that child today—the Soldano baby. For one thing, the extra head and external third arm were not the only duplicated parts. When they opened it up they found that a growth that they had spotted in the X rays was actually a good portion of a second, very small twin growing against the rib cage where the third arm emerges. Very bizarre, though not, of course, unheard of. In fact, it reminded me of a book I read about six months or so ago on the subject of twins. It's by a woman named Cassill and it's quite interesting. There was a chapter on phantom twins that was right on target with the baby I saw today."

"Phantom twins. That's a new one on me." I pushed the Moll's insistent nose away from the coffee table. She was not going to root around in a fifty-dollar box of chocolates if I could help it.

"Well, it's not really all that new. It's just that with sonograph and other new techniques, we're learning more about human reproduction all the time and so doctors are becoming aware of the phenomenon. I'll try to explain." He cleared his throat and began.

"Now the Soldano child actually should have been twins, but somewhere early in the pregnancy something went wrong. One fetus absorbed most, but not all, of its twin. This evidently happens more often than we know. In other words, twins are conceived, but by a mechanism that we can't yet explain—perhaps a genetic tendency or even a spontaneous mutation, we don't know—one is actually absorbed by the other early in the gestation period and the result is a normal singleton. The Soldano baby must have begun the process of absorbing its twin, but for whatever reason, the process didn't begin soon enough or was not properly completed. The result was a teras or monster."

"Academically fascinating," I agreed, "but what does all this have to do with the mooncalf? It didn't have two heads, just one big hideous one."

"But nonetheless, I decided to take a second look. Just an eerie hunch. Now listen. Down in the pelvic area, attached to the interior surface of the left hipbone—to use layman's terms, my dear—I found a tiny blastema. It's a tumor containing embryonic material. The vestigial traces, in other words, of a phantom twin." Guy was excited now, tripping punchily over his words and syntax. He sounded like a boy with a new video game.

"Honey, it proves to me at least—beyond a shadow of any doubt whatsoever—that the Soldano baby and your mooncalf were fathered by the same man, a man with a genetic tendency toward the conception of terata."

"So there are actually two mooncalves," I said thoughtfully, reflecting on the import of his words. The story wasn't over then, and wouldn't be until the rapist who impregnated Brenda Soldano was arrested. "And there is a Pearsall connection."

"Oh that! Shit, how the hell do I know? All I'm saying is that scientifically, medically, forensically, what have you, I'm willing to stake my reputation on the fact that both those creatures were fathered by the same man. The blood work that I've done and now this second incidence of phantom twinning—the odds are too great for it to be a coincidence. Look, can I come by and show you what I'm talking about? I've got some sketches that I've made and the blastema's here in a bottle."

I glanced at the clock. It was almost eleven. "No, no, please don't. It's late, you're all the way up in Pomona . . ."

"Giving me the gate, huh? Now that you've got the articles all written and the mystery solved . . ."

"Oh, you idiot," I laughed. "I'm not giving anyone the gate, least of all you, and remember, if both these mooncalves were fathered by the same man, then the mystery isn't solved at all. It means that there is a nut still loose, which is both perplexing and a little scary too. I was about to suggest, before you got so defensive and sorry for yourself, that you come by tomorrow evening and I'll make you dinner while you show me the blastema and your notes. I haven't even begun to tell you what I've learned about the baroness."

"Oh, damn, I forgot all about the old girl. Her autopsy was classic stuff—out of a textbook, by the way."

"Good. Tell me all about it over dinner. Seven, all right?" I must have sounded abrupt although that was not my intention.

"Sure, strictly business. I bring my bottle of blastema and we talk forensics all evening. Or can I bring a bottle of wine and expect to get a little cozy with you?"

"Really, Guy, you are a devil, aren't you? Now do be a good boy and say good night. I'll see you tomorrow around seven," I answered merrily and hung up. Keep it light, Miranda.

That night I dreamed that I floated down the Nile with Gilbert St. Mauger. We glided on the gentle current in an ancient reed boat, the tightly caulked bundles of papyrus creaking rhythmically under the slow motion of the red-skinned oarsmen as we lay serene and idle amongst a heap of silken cushions. I trailed my fingers in the cool waters while St. Mauger plucked at the petals of a lily, dropping them on the surface of the river where they drifted in our wake.

Then, without warning, Guy, naked and draped with water weeds, rose up out of the riverbed like old Nilus himself and upset the boat. As I tumbled from my nest among the cushions and bolsters, falling endlessly in the fashion of dreams, I could hear

Max, safe on shore, laughing viciously and insistently with all the mindless menace of a hyena.

So much for a peaceful night's sleep . . . or a serene breakfast either, if it were up to Peter.

"Boss man," I laughed resignedly, "why can't I just once have a quiet breakfast at the Skylark without you tracking me down? Do you have a bloodhound somewhere in your family tree, or do you just pester me for the fun of it?" He strode along the broad aisle and slid into the booth opposite me, rumpled his wide mouth into a silly smile, and crossed his eyes at me.

"What'd you order, Grumpy?" he asked.

"My usual," I replied, crossing my eyes back at him. "And I ain't grumpy. I'm just sick of men this morning. I'd like to put you all in a monastery and throw away the key."

"I don't know what I've done to deserve such treatment, but for God's sake, consign me to a convent instead. I may be old but I'm still randy." He grinned broadly at me.

"Are you?" I asked thoughtfully. "But then, why shouldn't you be?"

"You know, I haven't seen you since Sunday, and every time I phone either there's been no answer or the line's been busy. Even your good landlady's been incommunicado. Who is this Russian woman the Post's been going on about? In short, my dear cub reporter, what the hell is going on?"

I grinned at him and groped among the purse, notebook, and assorted newspapers on the seat beside me. "Be patient a minute. Ah, here it is." I slid a copy of my finished article on the Baroness Derevenkov across the table at him. "She was, dear Peter, the midwife, the abortionist, the murderess, the whole shebang. It's all there," I said, tapping the envelope.

Peter slit it open and began to read. His dark eyes glittered. "This looks marvelous," he mumbled, riffling through the pages.

"I think it is, actually. And it's a scoop, Peter, a real scoop. No paper in the city will have so much revelation and so much detail." I paused. "You know, Peter, I thought last night when I was writing this that it would be the final one in the mooncalf murder series, but now . . ."

"But?" The waitress put our plates down before us.

"But I think that it's not over. I'm sitting on something hot, very hot. Remember your 'Monster Born on Long Island' the other morning? You thought that there just might be a connection with our own little Nyack monster?"

"A quaint notion that you pooh-poohed out of hand," he reminded me.

"Well, I was wrong. There is a connection."

"Hot damn, no fooling?" Peter looked like a happy bloodhound who's just been given a nice ripe sock. I told him all about my uncle and how he had found out what the press had yet to learn—the name of the girl whose baby the monster was—and how he and Guy Galveston had been witnesses just the day before to the child's autopsy, and about the "phantom twin" blastema that Guy had found in the mooncalf. "He is sure that the coincidence is too great to be ignored. He's willing to swear on his forensic life, if you will, that these two things were fathered by the same man."

"So add to the crime of buying babies the crimes of rape and sodomy. The guy's a peach."

"Now, look at these charts." I slid several Xerox copies of genealogical charts across the table to him, explaining what they represented and how my uncle had compiled them with Meta's research assistance.

Peter read them over his coffee and shrugged. "So?"

"Both of these young woman have descent from the same man, James Pearsall."

"That's the Pearsall connection that you keep rattling on about, I take it." He looked over the charts more carefully and made a sound in his throat. "Do you know how many ancestors we each have going back ten generations?"

"No, not exactly, but a hell of a lot, I know."

"A *hell* of a lot, kid. One thousand and twenty-four to be exact," he declared, after doing a quick calculation in his head.

"Now, for us native New Yorkers of British, Dutch, and French ancestry, the odds increase greatly that ten generations ago we were related—many of us, I imagine. Fourteen generations ago, we're most likely to be cousins at least once, and even double cousins, so I doubt that these charts of your uncle's mean a goddamned thing. Stick with the forensic angle. If there is a connection, that's where it lies."

"You're right," I said decisively, finishing the last of my coffee and setting the cup down in the saucer firmly. "I know you're right."

$\triangledown$

11

THE POOR MILLER'S
PRETTY DAUGHTER

THE voice on the phone was youthful and unsteady, the words coming singly or in short bursts, tentative and stammering. Yet in spite of that, the young woman sounded as if she must be articulate and well-spoken as a rule.

"M—Miss Fay. Miranda Fay?"

"Yes."

"You write for the papers? I read—the mooncalf, you call it?"

"Yes."

"I read in the paper—the *Bergen Evening Record*—about this woman, this prostitute who had the baby—?"

"Yes," I prompted as patiently as I could. I wanted to shout "Yes, yes, get on with it," but she was so nervous that I forbore, fearing that she might hang up.

"Miss Fay," the voice came back clearer and a bit stronger.

"I'm still here." I wondered if Max might have put someone up to this.

"I read an article of yours in the *Record* last week. It was real interesting, you know, but I didn't really think much about it. Then yesterday, there was another article, about this black woman—the mother—"

"Yes." This was getting to be tedious.

"Well, I'm not black and I'm not a prostitute, but I am pregnant and a man is paying me . . ."

I sat up in the chair, jerking my legs off the desk with a crash. All suspicion that Max was behind the call was forgotten in seconds. "A man is paying you—?"

"Yes, but he's really nice," she said hastily. "It's not like with her. It's all legal, part of a surrogate mother program. So you see, he'd never beat me up or anything like that, I'm sure. It's just that it seems so strange—the coincidence, I mean."

"What coincidence?" I fairly shouted into the phone.

"Miss Fay, my name is Jennifer Pearsall."

Baumgart's has been on Palisades Avenue in Englewood, New Jersey, seemingly forever and is still there now. As I walked in, the memory of all the hot fudge sundaes with pistachio ice cream and all the BLT's on white toast with mayo that I had consumed through junior high and high school came flooding back on the cool air inside. Even the squeak of the tall counter stools sounded the same to my ear.

I found Jennifer Pearsall as I climbed the three steps up into the large back dining room. She was huddled against the semicircular banquette of a booth in the left-hand corner of the room. Her swelling stomach was swathed in the sort of awful, cheap maternity smock that makes a woman look like a great white blimp. The hem of the smock was rucked up, showing the bottom edge of the patch of elastic stretch fabric in the belly of her brown maternity slacks. She looked dejected and wretched to begin with. The outfit didn't help.

She didn't see me at first, so I had a moment to observe her. She appeared to be a tall girl, a natural strawberry blond of about twenty-two. Her pale, freckled-skinned and snubbed nose worked against beauty, but she was certainly not ugly, or even, strictly speaking, plain. When her face was not bloated with pregnancy and her expression compressed with anxiety, she might actually be pretty.

Beside her on the bench seat were her purse, a thick spiral notebook, and a couple of psychology textbooks. In front of her on the surface of the round table was a paperback novel, open but unread. She stared through it rather than at it.

I made a noise in my throat and crossed the floor to her table. She jumped at the sound and looked up at me with large, startled brown eyes.

"Miss Pearsall?" I asked gently.

"Miss Fay?"

"Yes, but call me Miranda." I slid into the booth and edged my way around the curve until I sat opposite her. I smiled reassuringly. "You're scared as hell, aren't you? And maybe over nothing. Pearsall is a fairly common name, you know. Why, as it happens, I'm a Pearsall three times over, myself."

"Has anyone hired you to have a baby?" she asked, looking down at her trembling hands placed before her on the table. She wore a plain gold band on the appropriate finger.

"No, not yet," I answered softly. "You read that article of mine on Valdalene Pearsall and it's got you spooked, which is understandable. On the face of it, there are strong similarities and the coincidence of the name. Now it seems to me that the best way to get to the bottom of this and find out if you really have anything to worry about is for you to tell me how all this came to happen."

Before she could begin, a waitress came and took our order—a vanilla milkshake for Jennifer and a hot fudge and pistachio ice cream sundae for me, for old time's sake.

"Where were you born?" I asked to prompt her.

"Philadelphia. I'm nearly twenty-one." I winced. She was a baby herself. "I go to Fairleigh, the Teaneck campus. I've been going there on and off since I was a sophomore. I ran away from home, sort of—"

"Sort of?" I repeated.

"Well, I mean I tried going to Temple and living at home, but I don't get along with my parents and I couldn't afford an apartment in center city. That's downtown Philadelphia. I started at Temple

University, but when I was a sophomore I switched to Fairleigh to get away from home. My father got mad and stopped helping me, so I've been working to support myself ever since. I quit school last year to try and save, but it didn't work out too well. It's hard to make enough to make ends meet, let alone go to school too.

"Then late last spring—it was early May, I think, I got this letter in the mail. My mother had forwarded it from home. It was from a doctor."

"It came to you at your parents' home," I broke in, musing aloud. "Was it unopened?"

"Oh, yes. She just crossed out our address and wrote in my address in Hackensack. I live in Hackensack. That's why it was so easy for me to meet you here in Englewood. I just take the bus. I live in a furnished room. It's cheap."

"Okay. Now, what about this letter you received?"

"It was a sort of form letter, saying that this doctor was starting a surrogate mother program in the Northeast and that young women of college age—healthy, intelligent, and in need of funds for their educations—were considered ideal candidates for the program. It said all medical, clothing, and household expenses would be paid during the length of the pregnancy, and that at the birth, ten thousand dollars would be paid for the mother's services. There would be no record of my having given birth since the child would be born with the father's name. I would be completely protected legally and all dealings with the doctor would be absolutely confidential." She repeated all this last by rote as if she had read the letter over so many times that it had been nearly memorized.

"There was a phone number to call too. I read the letter over and over again. It seemed awful. I even threw it in the garbage, but that night at the diner where I work some creeps hassled me and I got upset. The boss was in a foul mood—he was always coming on to me anyway, you know—and he said it was my fault, that I don't treat the customers right. He fired me. No notice, no severance, nothing. I went home and lay awake all night thinking of what a mess I was in and what I was going to do, how I'd never get back to school this fall . . ." She paused and glanced at me sideways, shamefaced and red with embarrassment.

"The next morning I fished the letter out of the garbage and called the number it gave—collect like it said—and talked to the doctor. He sounded so nice—really fatherly and yet businesslike, you know. Very reassuring. He said I should come into New York for an interview and an examination, all expenses paid and fifty dollars for my trouble."

"Very generous," I commented dryly. "Where is the office?"

"On Fifth Avenue near Fourteenth Street in an old office building. I had no trouble finding it at all. It was a regular doctor's office—neat, clean, sort of old-fashioned, you know. I remember being disappointed in a way. I sort of expected everything to be real modern and sleek and efficient like on TV. Surrogate mother programs, you know. They're so recent."

"Yes, they are," I agreed. Her logic had been right on target and her first wary instincts sensible. "Yet you went on with it," I said, "despite your misgivings?"

"Oh, it wasn't misgivings exactly. It was just that it wasn't quite what I had expected, that's all."

"What is the doctor's name?"

"Kennedy. Terrence Kennedy, M.D. His nurse is Mrs. Sidney. The name on the door is The Kennedy Center for the Perpetuation of the Family. I remember thinking how nice that sounded. It must be awful to want a baby and not be able to have one." She slid her hand over her swollen belly and cast her eyes down madonnalike. "It's not so bad, really, having a baby. I'm not having any trouble at all, and Dr. Kennedy says it's going to be an easy birth."

I drew in my breath, trying not to show any reaction. "You are still under his care then?"

"Oh yes, I go once a month. The father sends a car for me and I go into the city to see the doctor and then to have dinner with him."

"With the doctor?"

"No, no, with the father," she said and blushed. "I told you over the phone. That's why I know that Pearsall woman couldn't have been a surrogate mother for the Kennedy Center. They wouldn't let the kind of man who'd beat up a pregnant woman use their service, would they? I mean, they screen people, you know? It's just so funny that the name is the same," she said, looking perplexedly into her milkshake. She had hardly touched it, so it had become a thin, milky fluid in a sweating glass.

"What is the father's name, by the way?"

"Leigh. James Leigh. He's a widower. His wife died giving birth to their child—it died too, and he was so inconsolable that the only thing he could think of was having another baby right away. It's so sad, really," she added mawkishly.

Christ, what a story. "Why didn't he just get married again?" I asked thoughtfully, eyeing her reactions. A sudden, lurking suspicion had crossed my mind.

She looked crestfallen and avoided my eyes as she answered with a shrug of seeming nonchalance. "Oh, he loved her too much for that, and he's sort of old too. In his fifties, I guess, and he's kind of past getting married again, he says. Anyway, I guess."

"In his fifties. What does he look like?" I asked. My heart was racing. Brenda Soldano's attacker was in his thirties or early forties and Valdalene had merely described her Mr. Smith as old. Would the descriptions tally at all, or was it merely a coincidence after all?

"Well, he's got gray hair and he's fat—really fat—with a mustache and big glasses—thick, you know, like he's got bad eyesight. He's very kindly . . ." She trailed off thoughtfully. I thought it best to change tack.

"All right then, Jennifer. Let's get back to the doctor. He convinced you to become a surrogate mother obviously."

"Yes."

"What was the procedure?"

Jennifer Pearsall didn't speak for a long moment and then at last her face crumpled and the tears began to fall. I handed her a napkin from the holder on the table and waved away an approaching waitress. The girl trembled, the freckled whiteness of her skin almost as pale as the white cotton smock she wore.

"He, the doctor, asked me if I was a virgin. I said 'no' and he seemed pleased. He said that that was good because he found that the quickest conceptions and the healthiest babies were those made, you know, the 'normal way.' He said that if I wanted, he would perform artificial insemination, but that the best way was if I spent a night with the father and conceived naturally." I passed my hand across my brow at that one.

"Since I wasn't a virgin," she went on, "and the father was single, you know, there would be no problems, he said, and it would mean an extra thousand dollars right away."

"In addition to the ten thousand for the baby?"

She nodded weakly, as if telling the story made her begin to see the flaws in it. "Miss Fay," she pleaded, "a thousand for one night or maybe two in a motel with a stranger—it may sound cheap and wrong to you, but I was getting a dollar and thirty-five cents an hour plus tips for a sixty-hour week in that tacky old diner with a sixty-year-old boss trying to make me on the side, and I get fired yet! I—it meant I could go back to school and get my diploma and get a decent job and maybe be somebody someday. I mean, like who'd ever know, really?" She wiped her red-rimmed eyes and looked at me like a wary child.

"You do not have to defend yourself to me, Miss Pearsall," I assured her quietly, trying to calm her. "I'm not here to make moral judgments on you. This age in which we live is far too confusing and difficult for all of us. But I *am* concerned for you on general principles, so please, forget the apologies and tell me the rest."

"Well," she sighed, "I needed the money and the doctor assured me it'd be all right and he'd give me something for my nerves in case I got scared. He kept saying it would be a faster conception and that I'd have a healthier baby. That seemed to make it okay. I mean, I'd rather be conceived like a person and not out of a tube, wouldn't you? And the thousand dollars extra right away was a godsend." She paused and blushed, looking down at her hands, playing with the cheap gold-filled band on the third finger of her left hand. "He introduced me to James Leigh last June in his office. I had sort of dreamed that he'd be young and good-looking, which was silly, I guess. He was sort of old and fat instead, but he was as nice as he could be. He had a way of making everything seem fine. We had drinks and dinner at a real nice Italian restaurant in Greenwich Village, a place where the waiters sing arias."

"You must mean Asti's."

"Yeah, that's the place, and he talked about his wife and how much he missed her and how he had wanted a baby—'even a girl,' he said and he laughed. He was joking. He said if she looked like me he'd be real happy, but she'd probably be dark like him. He's such a gentleman and real refined. I—I really got to like him," she said wistfully. "He'll make a nice father," she added, again caressing her stomach with that tender, unconscious gesture of motherhood.

I looked at her sharply, but she didn't notice my expression. By damn, but she was in love with the man! I realized that she must have been building fantasies around him and around their baby for months now. As I watched her hand lying across her belly so affectionately, that faraway look in her eye, it gave me the willies. If what I suspected was true, that this surrogate mother program was mighty fishy, and that James Leigh was Valdalene's Mr. Smith, then God knew what was going to happen to this girl. She snapped out of her reverie, saw the look on my face, and drew her hand away abruptly.

"He drove me to a motel out near the Jersey Turnpike and we spent the night together—or I stayed there all night. He left at about three in the morning, I think. Anyway, he left me fifteen hundred dollars in cash and had a car service come round to take me home the next day at checkout time."

"Fifteen hundred? I thought you'd agreed on a thousand?"

She blushed. "We did but—" She avoided my eyes.

"Go on," I urged. "You had better tell me everything."

"I—I was really high, you know, when we got to the motel, but he told me I should take the pill that Dr. Kennedy prescribed anyway. You know, so I wouldn't be nervous."

I nodded helpfully.

"Well, I guess it was too strong or something. Maybe it was the wine at dinner, but I passed out for a while and when I woke up it was late, real late. Mr. Leigh was already dressed. I—I didn't remember what had happened, but I hurt all over, you know, and—and down there, you know. I mean front and—and behind too. I was kind of bloody and sore. I got very upset at first, but he was so nice. He explained how before I passed out, how high I got and how I turned him on. He said he hadn't had any—you know, since his wife got pregnant and that was almost two years ago and so he said he sort of lost control, you know. He felt so bad about it and he said that if I'd promise to forgive him and not think bad of him, he'd give me an extra five hundred dollars."

"You forgave him," I suggested dryly.

"Sure." She shrugged. "I didn't even remember what happened, and he really didn't mean to—"

"Did you ever have to—? Did you conceive that night or—" I tried to think of a polite wording for my question.

Jennifer Pearsall nodded emphatically. "Oh, I got pregnant that night for sure. Dr. Kennedy figured the timing just perfect. And ever since, once a month I see the doctor at his office and then I have dinner with Mr. Leigh. That's when he gives me my expense money and rent."

"In cash."

"Yeah. Then it's all off the books, you see. No tax."

And no evidence, either, I thought to myself. "When was the last time you saw him?"

"On October the fifth."

"You see him next when?"

"November the fourth. At Dr. Kennedy's office."

"Can you get in touch before that time?"

"I could call the doctor, I suppose," she said reluctantly.

"But not Mr. Leigh?"

She shook her head and looked mournful. "No, not him. It's all done through the doctor's office. Mrs. Sidney, his R.N., arranges things."

I had a sudden inspiration. "Tell me, have you met any of the other mothers in the program?"

"No," she answered, her eyes flickering. Clearly I had given her something to think about. "But then I wouldn't, would I? The program's only just started, so there wouldn't be many yet, and each mother must have her own visiting day just like I do. That way we each have privacy and anonymity, just like the doctor promised. Then the parents too have privacy. All the other people who want babies are couples. Dr. Kennedy only took Mr. Leigh's case because he felt so sorry for him and because he's rich and can hire proper nurses and a governess for the baby. It won't really miss not having a mother. . . ."

She looked down at that swelling belly again with that same awful, wistful look of hers and whispered, "And anyway, maybe Mr. Leigh will change his mind and get married again after all. . . ."

I shuddered at the strange gullibility of this girl. She was like a creature from the moon. Even Valdalene with her hopeless dreams of being an actress seemed more understandable to me.

"Yes," I said as cheerfully as I could, "maybe he will. Wouldn't that be wonderful, for everyone. . . ."

Peter Polhemus was the last to arrive. He crossed my living room, took the drink I handed him, made a funny face at me, and sat on the sofa next to Uncle Jeremiah and Meta. Guy sat apart in the oak throne chair, spinning the ice in his glass with an insistent motion that betokened impatience.

It was nearly seven on Thursday evening and I had had a busy afternoon on the phone since leaving Englewood at half past three. I had scrapped my plans for a fancy dinner for two and had stocked up on buffet food for our whole little band. Now I forced a smile and addressed the gathering.

"There is a young woman, a college student, and to my mind probably one of the most gullible creatures on God's earth. She's from Philadelphia originally, but she lives in Hackensack right now, and she is pregnant. She is serving as a 'surrogate mother' for a rich, kindly, fat old man who enjoys raping and sodomizing women who've first been drugged into insensibility. Sound familiar?"

"How'd you get onto her?" Guy asked thoughtfully, over the general uproar that followed.

"I didn't actually. She called me. She's worried, downright spooked, in fact, by my two articles that she read in the *Bergen Evening Record*. It was the second one, all about Valda, that got to her. There is a certain similarity." I paused dramatically, looked directly at my uncle, who sat watching me so intently, and quietly dropped my bomb. "Her name is Jennifer Pearsall."

After the dust had settled I told them the rest of the story.

"I didn't like leaving her in Englewood in that condition when I could so easily have driven her home, but she insisted that she didn't want me driving her. She's had the feeling on and off for a week or so that she may be being watched. I chalk that up, I hope, to pregger lady's nerves, but anyway she insisted.

"Uncle Jeremiah, this," I said, handing him a page torn from my notebook, "is all the information she could give me offhand on her family—mother, father, aunts, uncles—especially her father's Pearsall line, of course. She also gave me, very reluctantly, her parents' phone number in Philadelphia. They don't know anything about her pregnancy or the surrogate mother program."

He perused the paper thoughtfully, sucking on his white mustache as he read.

"Well, I can tell you this right now, Miranda. She's a cousin of ours for a certainty. Her father's name is John Seaman Pearsall and I happen to know for a fact that my grandmother, Lydia Pearsall Van Voorst, had an only brother called John Seaman Pearsall. Their

mother was a Seaman and their father was your great-great grandfather, John Titus Pearsall. It won't take much checking to tie this
one up to Valda and Brenda Soldano." He fell silent and I could see
he was trying to jog his memory further.

"So there is a Pearsall connection, just as you've been saying all
along, Mr. Fay," Meta said firmly, casting a wicked eye at Guy
and Peter, the two scoffers.

"Well," Uncle Jeremiah said with a sigh and a shake of his head,
"there is no doubt that this girl is another direct descendant in the
paternal line from James Pearsall and Forgiveness Basset."

"I knew it," I said, quietly pouring myself another whiskey and
water—only I forgot to add water. "Uncle Jeremiah, I made a
whole bunch of calls after I left her this afternoon. There is no Dr.
Terrence Kennedy listed by the A.M.A. as licensed to practice
medicine in this state; no one on the Nurses Register of New York,
for the last five years at least, by the name of Mrs. India Sidney,
R.N.; and there is no surrogate mother program in the entire
country calling itself The Kennedy Center for the Perpetuation of
the Family."

Peter chuckled richly. "This whole thing is layered with tinges
of irony," he said. His eyes sparkled as the wheels turned in his
head. He was on the scent of the newspaperman's dream: a unique
and interesting mystery. "Have any of you realized yet the incredible psychological insight being used in sizing up these women? I
mean, Valda was a natural for the limousine, the dinners out, the
white john who wants a baby—*her* baby. She was set up perfectly
and simply and five grand was enough to bait the trap.

"But you couldn't use an approach like that with this other
young lady. She's very middle-class and proper. Everything had to
be legal, medically sound, and aboveboard, hence the surrogate
mother program. It was the only thing that would sound reasonable
to a girl like that, and of course, the ante'd have to be higher to
override that middle-class upbringing. The fact that she's desperate
for money and doesn't get along with her father only helped. It

didn't take long for this 'doctor' and 'James Leigh' to tumble to her weaknesses. They've played the 'kindly father' image to the hilt.''

"That they have," I agreed. "She's more than half in love with this bastard, whoever he is, already."

"Valda was simpler, more venal, and more pragmatic. She'd have blinked and said 'Huh?' if they'd sprung a surrogate mother program on her—totally unnecessary claptrap—but poor Jennifer Pearsall needs all the official sanction of doctors and nurses, and even then, it seems, it hasn't kept her from having her doubts." Peter looked up at me frowningly. "You know, those articles of yours may actually save her from something terrible. She should see another doctor and have herself examined."

"I suggested that. I think she may. Anyway, I promised to keep in touch, naturally. I didn't want to panic her till I knew there really was a problem."

Meta spoke softly then, "And the only way to get an innocent Italian Catholic virgin pregnant, short of marrying her, would be rape." She crossed herself piously. "He'd be sure that if a child was conceived, it would be, poor soul, carried to term. Abortion—even therapeutic abortion—would be out of the question for such a girl." She shook her head sadly.

"Which means that whoever offered to adopt the baby was in on it—!" I fairly shouted out the words. We all looked at each other and began to talk at once.

"May I use your phone, Miranda?" my uncle asked loudly, cutting through our excited chatter and bringing us to silence by the import of his question.

"Hell, yes," we all chorused and he made for the desk in my writing alcove.

"Well?" I asked as he put down the receiver and rejoined us.

"Mrs. Soldano says the couple was named Sidney. The wife's name was India. They were middle-aged, both in excellent health, moderately well-to-do, devoutly Catholic, and came highly recommended by a private adoption agency in Manhattan—"

"Don't tell me," I breathed.

My uncle pursed his lips and, looking down at his tiny note-book, read, "The Kennedy Center for the Perpetuation of the Family."

"Uncle Jeremiah," I said suddenly as my thoughts came to-gether, "how is it possible—? No, wait. Let me phrase it properly. Valdalene Pearsall and Jennifer Pearsall and Brenda Soldano . . . Now, granted that two of them have the same surname, but still, so must hundreds of others in this area, and Soldano sounds about as far from Pearsall as you can get—

"So how," I continued, "would anyone know who . . . ? Know which names were the right ones? I mean, were they just pulled at random from a phone book or what? How would anyone know which people were related, what particular women were descended from James Pearsall?"

"That's actually fairly simple to answer, my dear," Uncle Jere-miah said thoughtfully, staring into space as he spoke. "If one has a starting point, as we all have in, say, our mother's surname or our father's, we simply begin there and gather as much information as possible from living sources and then start to trace our line back-ward." He paused and then continued, "But suppose—just sup-pose—we did just the reverse and started, for whatever reason, with a particular name from out of the past . . ."

"James Pearsall," I put in.

"James Pearsall," he repeated with a nod. "Well, if we were to start with that name and do all our standard genealogical research, go through those same records, but mind you, working forward into the future rather than backward into the past, eventually we'd have a file of family group tables that would bring us to the present. We'd have found the current descendants of the person we started with. Most likely nowhere near all of them, for records can be very spotty and hard to find, but we'd have a good many, I should imagine. That is, assuming that the person we started with had descendants into this present generation. Lines do die out as well, you know. We'd be able to verify recent descendants easily enough for accuracy by sending for birth certificates, checking cemeteries for dates and so on, just as one does in the course of ordinary research."

"So, assuming we did start with this James Pearsall, we'd have come across Valdalene Pearsall, Jennifer Pearsall, and Brenda Soldano," Peter said, ticking off the three names on his fingers as he spoke.

"And we'd have found Miranda Fay too," Meta said slowly, looking at me with sudden realization. "Oooh, luv." She looked worried.

I smiled reassuringly. "No, we wouldn't actually. Daddy was working on a bridge-building project in Venezuela when I was born, and so my birth was recorded in Caracas, not in New York, or New Jersey, where I was raised."

Meta looked relieved.

Uncle Jeremiah frowned. "I wonder, my dear, just what is in the head of the man who is fathering these mooncalves? For whatever reason, he seems to prefer to link himself to a particular bloodline, however obscure the origins of it and whatever the difficulties entailed thereby. Now, I'm most likely being an alarmist, but under the circumstances, I believe that we should keep mum about your own Pearsall descent from now on—and for God's sake don't mention it in any of your articles for the *Stop-Press*."

"Well, I haven't so far, and naturally now I won't."

"Good," he said, "and now, Mrs. Sullivan, I shall have some more research for you to do tomorrow. Will you be free?"

Meta preened self-consciously. "Why, of course, Mr. Fay. I love helping out."

"Well, what happened to that dinner we were supposed to have— alone?" Guy asked as we stood at my living room window and watched Peter Polhemus stroll up Piermont Avenue toward town. Uncle Jeremiah had left earlier for Staten Island and Meta was giving Duchess and the Moll their last walk of the evening.

"I guess tomorrow night will have to do," I smiled, "since you don't count soup and sandwiches for five as a proper dinner."

"I'd count popcorn and hot dogs as a great dinner if I was alone with you. It's the crowd I object to. I notice that you didn't serve the wine I brought. Does that mean something?"

"It means that it will be nice and chilled for tomorrow night at seven when I shall make up for tonight with a real dinner strictly tête-à-tête." I walked back to the center of the room and began to clear away glasses and coffee cups. Guy's jar of blastema in formaldehyde sat among the inevitable clutter. "How about broiled filet of blastema amandine?"

"Oh, Christ, don't let me forget that, will you? And my notes. I've got to be at the office early tomorrow. We've got a drug O.D. from Pearl River and another burn victim from Haverstraw."

Meta knocked just then and came in with Molly and Duchess in tow. "She's spent a penny, luv, and had a treat, so she's set for the night."

"Oh, thank you, Meta. What a dear you are. We'll come down with you. Guy has to be up with the birds tomorrow." It was sneaky of me, but at least it got him out and onto the porch without a wrestling match on my sofa. It wasn't that I was too old for such shenanigans. I was simply too bloody tired.

Downstairs, Meta said a discreet good night and left us alone to walk across the lawn to Guy's car.

"I'll see you tomorrow night, then?"

"Same time, same place," he said, and before I knew what had happened, I was in his arms with his warm lips against my cheek. "This is more like it," he whispered. His kisses were exactly what I had expected—fervid and insistent and very arousing. I gave myself up to them for longer than I should have, but finally I struggled and broke free. My cheeks felt hot and I panted to catch my breath.

"Oh, Guy, please. This isn't what I want."

He smiled down at me benevolently. "Well, it's all I want—at least for now. Stop resisting me and, for Pete's sake, stop fighting your own self. There's nothing wrong with two adults desiring each other."

I didn't argue. "I'll see you tomorrow," I whispered.

"See you then." He smiled complacently and got into his nice sleek Datsun 280ZX, winked at me, and took off down Piermont Avenue, turned left onto Clinton and was gone. Somewhere in the next block, another motor started and sped away, leaving the night silent once more.

I walked back into the house thinking not of Guy at all. It was Gilbert St. Mauger—big, shy, romantic St. Mauger—who seemed to move my own romantic soul.

Friday night wasn't going to be easy.

The building in which the Kennedy Center was located had been built back in the twenties and was full of the forlorn offices of dying businesses whose owners had not the means or the spirit to vacate for other, more modern premises. In the small vestibule, on the wall over an ancient cast-iron steam radiator, an equally ancient directory board listed the occupants in dirty white lettering that snapped piece by piece into black slots.

Squeezed in out of any alphabetical order were the two words "Kennedy Center" followed by a six to indicate the suite number and a fourteen to indicate the floor. It was a nervous ride I took in the wheezing self-service elevator, which rose reluctantly, the chains of its ancient mechanism clanking ominously, and ground to a halt on the fourteenth floor.

The faint staccato of typing came from the office of an underwear wholesaler at the far end of the hall, but other than that, there was no sound. Even the elevator remained open and waiting behind me. There was evidently no one below either.

I found Suite 1406 easily enough. It had a dirt-darkened oak door, quite locked, with a frosted glass panel above and a brown ceramic doorknob and an unpolished brass mail slot below. There was no lettering on the door such as Jennifer Pearsall had described, and no answer to the steady tattoo I beat on the panel. My knuckles came away sticky from the surface of the glass, which gave me pause. I stopped knocking and ran my fingers over the surface slowly as if I were reading braille. There was a pattern to the gummy feel, consisting of a curving arc on top and several lines of varying length ranged horizontally below. It didn't take much imagination to envision the stick-on black and gold letters that Jennifer must have seen during her visits, or the ease with which they could be removed once her monthly visit was over. Talk about covering trails!

Although maybe not so covered up after all! Mail had evidently been delivered quite recently, for the tiny point of an envelope stuck out of the mail slot. It was so small an end that I had to use the nails of my thumb and forefinger like a tweezer in order to get a purchase on the paper, but by carefully grasping it with the nails of my right hand and pushing up the flap of the slot cautiously with my left, I was able to pull the letter back out into the hall. I pocketed the small envelope unopened and dashed for the elevator.

Out on Fifth Avenue once more, in the thick of a lunch-hour crowd, I made off like the thief that I was, sure in my heart that ere long Uncle Jeremiah would be citing by number the statutes I had broken and the penalties attendant thereon. The only place that I could think of making for was the Book Review Restaurant, a coffee shop on the corner of Fifteenth Street just south of Barnes and Noble.

My heart thumped with guilty delight like Nancy Drew, Girl Detective, as I slid into a booth and contemplated the stolen envelope in my hand. I gave an order for a cheese omelet and a cup of coffee and perused my prize like the map of an ancient treasure.

It was addressed to The Kennedy Center for the Perpetuation of the Family and had in the corner a return address in Madison, Wisconsin. The name of the sender was a Mrs. Allan Howard and the only thing I could tell about her was that she was an even more indifferent typist than I was myself.

Having weighed the consequences of my mail theft against the Kennedy Center's mail fraud, I made my decision: The Kennedy

Center lost. There was only one proper expedient. I slit open the envelope carefully with a knife and pulled out a sheet of notepaper—a Hallmark pattern with embossed apple blossoms that I recognized immediately. It was rather incongruous under the circumstances, but then Mrs. Howard probably didn't expect to have to write a letter like the one I now read. It was admirably short and to the point:

> Sirs:
>
> I do not know how you come to have my maiden name in your files, or what information about me has possessed you to think that I might be a candidate for your "program," but I can assure you that you are in error.
>
> I neither agree with nor approve of any form of surrogate mother program such as you suggest and the idea of my being part of one is ludicrous.
>
> Kindly cease and desist from any further contact with me or I shall be forced to seek legal recourse.
>
> Pamela Bedell Howard
(Mrs. Allan Howard)

Short, sweet, and to the point. I did like the dudgeon of Pamela Howard—and I knew without any recourse of my own to my Uncle Jeremiah that Mrs. Howard would turn out to be a distant cousin on my mother's side and therefore a Pearsall descendant as well. There were too many Bedells buried in the original Bedell-Mesereau-Chadwick plot in Greenwood Cemetery for it to be coincidence. Guy couldn't scoff any longer. Someone was after the descendants of James Pearsall.

I stashed Pamela Howard's note in my purse, gulped down the last of my lunch, and headed back uptown to Washington Heights. I had come over the George Washington Bridge that morning, left the car on a side street, and taken the A train downtown.

It was at the newsstand on the platform at Fifty-ninth Street and

Columbus Circle, where I made the switch from the D to the uptown A, that I saw the headline on the afternoon *Post:*

ROCKLAND MED EXAMINER IN MURDER TRY
CAR OVERTURNED BY MYSTERY VAN—SEE PAGE 4

I bought a copy and read what little there was to read in seconds. It didn't say anything about the extent of his injuries or when the incident had occurred or even to what hospital he had been taken.

By the time I got to 175th Street and the bridge, I was beside myself. I didn't know if Guy was alive or dead, but I had a horrible suspicion that I knew who it was who had run his car off the New York State Thruway.

$\triangledown$

12

DOWN CORRIDORS OF TIME

META sat beside me on a slick leatherette couch in a waiting room at Nyack Hospital, alternately holding my hand and blowing her nose into a tiny square of Irish linen. She was taking the accident hard, for she liked Guy and had begun to entertain the sort of high hopes prevalent in ladies of late middle age whose own marriages had—at least in retrospect—been happy and worthwhile. She wanted us to fall in love and live happily ever after.

Peter came down the hall toward us with a big blond young highway patrolman at his elbow.

"Miranda, this is Officer Herrmann of the state police. He was on the scene last night when Guy was found. He'll tell you what happened."

And he did, succinctly describing how Guy's car had been forced off the Thruway at high speed, and how it had rolled down the steep embankment of an overpass onto a grassy cloverleaf. Witnesses had seen a metallic-brown van bear down on the Datsun and sideswipe it repeatedly until Guy finally lost control and went off the road. There was no doubt on the part of witnesses that it had been a deliberate murder attempt.

Guy had been removed from the wreck unconscious, with head trauma and possible internal injuries. His collarbone was broken. That was all the officer could tell me, except that when the van sped away none of the witnesses had been able to get the license number.

I waited till the officer was out of earshot before I spoke. "You know, don't you, what I'm afraid of? Suppose it was Max? He drives a gray Buick, not a van, but he could have rented one, or maybe his company has one, and I know for a fact that he's been spying on me. He even admitted as much on the phone the other night, and last night after Guy drove away, I heard a car take off right afterward. Suppose it was Max following him? I'm awfully worried. Is Guy going to be all right?"

The answer to that was yes, thank God. Pete had talked to Guy's father and the doctors earlier. Guy had a concussion, and cuts and lacerations, and the doctors had said he looked worse than he was, but they'd be monitoring his vital signs and watching him for internal bleeding. So far, he was stable and occasionally conscious. He'd been sleeping a lot, which was normal, and he was not comatose. "That being that," Peter concluded, "let's get out of here," and he steered us through the halls, out into the bright sunshine, and drove us home.

That evening, the phone rang just as I was putting dinner on the table. I dropped the plate and made a leap for my desk, hoping I'd hear Guy's breezy voice saying he was okay and able to have visitors.

It was Gilbert St. Mauger.

"Oh, how nice of you to call," I said. "I enjoyed our visit to ancient Egypt so very much the other afternoon."

"Yes, so did I. In fact, my dear, that is why I am calling. I thought we might while away a pleasant couple of hours at the Cloisters on Sunday next."

"Oh."

"Not a good idea?"

"Oh, yes, yes, it's a lovely idea as a matter of fact. It's—it's just that I'm in rather a state right now and can't begin to think." I told him about Guy and his accident, omitting the fact that it was actually a murder attempt and that I was afraid it was my crazy husband who was responsible.

"But you say that he's out of danger, my dear?" he remarked persuasively. "Then by Sunday there should hardly be an impediment to your escaping for a bit of pleasant diversion. The calm medieval surroundings of the museum and the cloister gardens are an ideal distraction for a troubled spirit."

With that argument he struck exactly the right cord in me. "You know, Gilbert, you are absolutely right. Serenity is precisely the right prescription. I feel as if I'd been shot out of a cannon at the moment. Shall I meet you there?" It was an impulsive decision and one that I began to regret almost as soon as I had spoken.

"Excellent," he said heartily. "At one, shall we say?"

"At one," I agreed.

"Pray do not forget," he admonished lightly.

I had just put my cold quiche back in the oven to reheat and begun to pick at my salad when the phone rang again. This time it was Ismeralda Jackson informing me that her sister's viewing would begin on Monday afternoon at two. The following morning there would be a funeral service and interment at St. Raymond's Cemetery in the Bronx. I wrote down the address of the funeral parlor and told her I would be there on Monday.

The Cloisters, which is a museum of unusual beauty and serenity, sits on a bluff in Fort Tryon Park at the northern end of Manhattan. With a little imagination one can sustain briefly the illusion that one has returned to the early Middle Ages, to a French cloister in Normandy. The museum, however, is set not in that remote place and age, but sits like a jewel in the dust and glorious grime of late twentieth-century New York, looking west across the Hudson to the New Jersey Palisades.

I pulled into a parking spot on the short curve of courtyard just below the entrance, counting myself lucky to get so close. As I locked the car, I looked around and spotted St. Mauger on the parapet before the upper entrance and waved.

He returned my greeting and motioned me to the left, up a long path that swept around and up to where he stood in front of the covered entrance to the museum. I picked my way along the cobbled road, dodging immense acorns that fell from the great old oaks that embowered the walk. They pelted onto the stones like tiny bombs, dropped by a bevy of sleek, velvety black squirrels who worked their way industriously from branch to branch, sending their harvest to earth for later gathering. Further along the road, blue jays and mockingbirds worked their way through their own meal of gleaming red dogwood berries, shrieking and cavorting with sheer joy in the early afternoon sunlight.

I grinned and made an all-encompassing gesture toward the scene for St. Mauger's benefit. "Isn't it too gorgeous for words?" I said as we met at the top of the cobbled road. "God's in his heaven and all's right with the world."

"It can indeed seem so on a day like this," he said austerely, bending to kiss my hand. "But for some, nothing can ever be quite right with the world. How is your friend, Dr. Galveston?"

"Guy is fine," I assured him. "Quite on the mend, but Mr. St. Mauger, Gilbert"—I corrected myself before he could say anything—"you sound so sad today. Would you rather not have come?"

"Oh, no, no. Quite the contrary. If I am sad at all, your good company shall cheer me. You are observant to have noticed. You take great joy in life and in nature, do you not?" He glanced at the oaks overhead and at the bright blue sky beyond them.

For some reason I blushed, as if it were an embarrassing admission. "Yes," I confessed. "Sometimes the beauties of nature are all in which one can find joy."

Once having opened up to him it grew easy. St. Mauger was a very good, almost too intent listener. I told him how worried I had been that Guy's accident had been the work of my husband. "It wasn't, though. Guy got a look at the driver and he was nothing like Max. You can't imagine how relieved I was to hear that!"

"Your husband?" He seemed startled. "I didn't realize that you were married."

"Well I am, more's the pity. But not for long, I hope. We're separated for the time being and I'm trying to get him to agree to a nice, easy, civilized no-fault divorce."

"So you can marry Dr. Galveston?" he asked nonchalantly.

"Guy? Good God, no. In the first place I've decided that I'm not ever going to marry again, and in the second, he's already married though he's separated and a divorce is in the works. No, there is nothing between us but a friendship that has sprung up quite naturally during this mooncalf investigation. He's been enormously helpful. My articles have been very detailed and convincing thanks to his help and I've actually made a little money from them. There may even be a book out of it eventually, when the whole story comes out."

"The whole story? I thought when they found the old Russian woman that rather finished it?"

"I can't say much, you understand, but actually there is quite a good deal more, as it happens. I'm following up leads so extraordinary that I may get a fat book contract out of it. The Nyack mooncalf is not the only mooncalf, and if I'm right, one day you shall have another true crime volume to add to your collection— one dedicated to your dear friend Jeremiah Pearsall Fay and written by your obedient servant, Miranda Fay."

"You amaze me, my dear. You are a fit niece for such a man as Jeremiah Pearsall. I cannot tell you how much I admire him." He bowed to me, offering his arm with an angelic choirboy smile. "Shall we, my dear Miranda?"

"We shall indeed, Gilbert," I smiled back, and, taking his arm, stepped into the cool, shadowy entrance hall, as if into another world.

St. Mauger, whimsical and serious by turns, led me through one cool stone room and chapel after the other and finally out into the garden of the Cuxa Cloister like a guide who has come back through time. He seemed to know so much that he might have been a contemporary of the stones and columns and ancient door panels themselves. Not for us now the insinuating, sistrum-sounding, scent-laden mysteries of ancient Egypt which he had so magically evoked at the Met. Rather we entered into the strange inconsistent life of a medieval monastery with its alternating moods of chaste austerity and earthy sensuality. He seemed to revive with his words and his manner as he escorted me through the maze of rooms, the forbidden sins and lurid whisperings of a monastery full of passionate, alive men bound by vows and tormented by the breaking of them; hell-fires licking at their sandled feet. No professor, no book had ever conjured for me such images and sensations as Gilbert St. Mauger conjured on that bright afternoon in October.

We came to rest in the Pontaut Chapter House, an ancient stone room complete with stone benches lining the walls and long slitted window openings that looked out to the Palisades. We sat in a companionable silence on the cold stones and listened to the sound of recorded Gregorian chants echoing all around us against the smoothly worn, pockmarked surfaces.

As a counterpoint to the steady monotony of the chant, came the sound of many chickadees beeping through small, twisted fruit trees; the splash of water in the marble fountain. It was a miniature vista of utmost peace and loveliness, and brought to me as I gazed over it, a sense of tranquility deeply welcome after the last few weeks of strange happenings.

St. Mauger's eyes were closed, his big head back against the stone frame of one of the glassless slits of window behind us. He might almost have been asleep, but his long forefingers betrayed the illusion. They kept time to the slow insistence of the chant. As I gazed at him, I felt myself overcome by a deep feeling of compassion. He was like a homely, sleeping child, for whom one feels an unaccountable tug of one's heartstrings, an urge to bend and kiss the sleeping cheek.

He opened his eyes and caught me watching him. I smiled. They were large dark gray eyes, made vivid in the pale, plump face by the fringe of long black lashes that circled them. He looked at me quizzically at first and then, his eyes still on mine, he found my hand and took it into both of his very tenderly.

"I felt your eyes on me, you know. It was like being covered in a warm blanket. Very comfortable." His words startled me. I did not want him to misunderstand, to think that I felt any deep affection for him.

The chant ended just then, breaking off just as abruptly as it had started and breaking with it St. Mauger's thought. It saved me from comment. We rose and walked around the cloister and through a pair of huge iron-studded wooden doors.

"How lovely," I murmured as we walked across the Romanesque Hall and approached the steps of the entrance to the twelfth-century Langon Chapel.

"Yes, yes, all very well, altars and tabernacles, if one likes that sort of thing, but you are missing the best of all," St. Mauger said, reverting momentarily to that fussy manner of his that made me think of eunuchs and viziers and the Arabian Nights. He stopped at the foot of the steps and made a grave obeisance to the two nearly life-size stone figures that flanked the opening. "Clovis, King of the Franks, and his son, Clothair, our Frankish forebears. Have you no respect for your ancestors?"

"My ancestors?" I asked dubiously.

"Of course. We each, you and I, can claim descent through many lines from Charlemagne and through him from his forebear St. Arnulf, Bishop of Metz, and through Arnulf back to Clovis the Riparian, Frankish king of Cologne and kinsman of our Clovis here."

He spoke as matter-of-factly as if he were speaking of a grandfather or two, reaching out to pat the effigy of King Clovis on the knee. A voice addressed us across the hall: "Hands off the art." The guards were earning their keep with eagle eyes. St. Mauger colored and withdrew his hand slowly.

"My family," he said, "no longer has the holdings that once it had, but there was a time when we could have cut out a man's tongue for addressing us in such a manner." I smiled at his conceit.

"Really, my dear, I am being quite serious, you know. You share your uncle's pedigree, being sprung, so he has assured me, from his elder brother Luke Van Voorst Fay. Your esteemed uncle and, therefore, you yourself are descended several times over from the loins of the dukes of Normandy, among them William the Bastard, Conqueror King of England, through both his legitimate descendant Joan of Acre, Princess of England, and also one of Henry I's bastards, Robert of Caen, Duke of Gloucester. These and other lines stretch back in time to Charlemagne and to his supposed forebears. It is all quite simple really. It just takes research."

"Fascinating."

"Yes. Most lines dilute and die out, of course, but there are those of us who have many duplicated branches of descent. I myself am a descendant many many times over of an uncle of your ancestor William the Conqueror. He was Mauger, Archbishop of Rouen, and in his day one of the most powerful and famous men of Normandy. We are, here in this building, my dear, quite within our element."

He pursed his lips complacently, shot a glance over his shoulder at the guard, and led me across the room to a small doorway that led out onto the West Terrace, which overlooked the Hudson and the sunlit day. It was almost blinding to go from the dim chapel into such brilliant light. I blinked until my eyes adjusted. St. Mauger was already leaning against the stone balustrade, looking south toward the silver-gray span of the George Washington Bridge.

"Tell me, sir," I said, coming up beside him and taking his arm playfully, "what hanky-panky went on back in what must have been—ten sixty-six or so that you can claim descent, and many times over at that, from an archbishop? I thought that sort of thing was frowned upon by Mother Church?"

He took my hand and drew me toward him, his long arm feeling strong and hard around my back and waist.

"He was the bastard son of Richard the Good, Duke of Normandy, by a woman called Papia of Evereau. She was Norman, of course, but little is known of her. She may not even have been legitimate herself. Certainly she was no better than she should be," he added prissily. "She had another son by the duke who was called William, Count of Arques. The two brothers were close. Mauger de Rouen was born in ten seventeen. In ten thirty-seven his father's brother, Robert, Archbishop of Rouen, died. It became expedient to find a successor who would be able to keep the immense power and wealth of the See of Rouen in the hands of the ducal family. They were a rapacious lot, and fit descendants of our original Norman forebear, Rollo the Viking, first duke of Normandy. The miter of the archbishop was placed on the twenty-year-old head of Mauger.

"It was, of course, rather unfair. At twenty, a young man is usually more inclined toward making women than church law, so it was only to be expected that he should stray from the path of celibate righteousness into the iniquitous ways of fornication and ribaldry. He had several bastards by his concubines, and to add even more to this deliciously scandalous brew—there is no proof of this, mind"—St. Mauger cautioned with gossipy delight, enjoying his tale of ancient devilment immensely—"but it is generally supposed from some of the things written at the time that the mother of his third son and my direct male line ancestor, Mauger St. Mauger de Rouen, was none other than a daughter of Count William of Arques and therefore his very own niece. A delicious bit of incest there, what?" He said this with a funny little movement of his mouth that made me think of Robert Morley playing Oscar Wilde.

"So let's see, we have illegitimacy, violation of the sanctity of holy office, nepotism, concubinage, fornication, and a bit of incest thrown in for good measure. They were wild times, weren't they?" I said merrily.

St. Mauger was disposed to be serious and he answered me with something of the air of a lecturer. "Sensuality and passion have existed in all ages. In ancient Egypt, for example, lust, passion, and even incest were all part of the accepted mores, at least for the higher levels of society. Despite the advent of Christianity in the West, the same passions still existed. They had simply become sins. In fact, it took the Puritans to make life the hell of repression and sin that it has become in modern times. Sin has so little glamor any more. It was infinitely more fun, I imagine, to stray in Archbishop Mauger's day. No one asked him how he felt about his mother or whether he was a bed wetter or not. They simply allowed as how he was a sinner, possessed of a devil, or given to the lusts of the flesh. No Freudian mumbo jumbo then."

"Did Mauger never get his comeuppance?" I asked.

"I'm afraid he did rather. He made an enemy of his nephew, William the Duke, who had the church fathers bring him up on a variety of charges—simony, unchastity, filiation. One might think that a bit high-handed of William. After all, there must have been some who thought that a bastard duke was not much better than a bastard archbishop. The ducal office was, after all, a holy one, its accession celebrated with church rites and a Mass. However, William won out and Mauger was dispossessed of his offices and revenues and exiled to Guernsey in the Channel Isles. William, of course, was your ancestor, you know."

"Well, please don't hold that against me," I said, throwing up my hands defensively. "I'm all for sensual, fun-loving archbishops."

"So he was, I imagine," St. Mauger said, looking down at me with a smile. "Pray do not worry. I shan't hold a grudge, not after nine hundred years."

"What happened to him then? Did he stay in Guernsey?"

"Yes, till he died."

"What a terrible fate for the sort of man he must have been: to go from an archbishopric and rich preferments—wine, women, and song, so to speak—to life in a dull backwater like Guernsey."

"Actually he was quite popular with the islanders, had many

visitors, loved sailing and wenching. His spirit was not crushed, it would seem. After his death, the islanders venerated his bones—"

"Of course, and then he was sainted. I should have realized," I put in. "How ironic to have been justified at last. Too bad it had to be a posthumous honor."

St. Mauger coughed delicately. "Well, not quite. It is true that his remains were enshrined and that pilgrimages were made to his tomb and that his youngest and evidently most beloved son, my direct male forebear as I have said, took the surname St. Mauger— as a gesture of loyalty and defiance, one presumes—but the church never canonized him. In fact, he was ignored in death even as he had been castigated in life, though it seems that the little cult that grew up around his tomb on the island was a source of irritation to the church fathers for the next two centuries or so. Gradually the cult died out except for a few members of the family who kept the traditions alive. Then in fifteen sixty-two a raiding party of Huguenot rabble came to the island, destroyed the tomb, and ground Mauger's bones and regalia into dust beneath their feet. Ironically, those same marauders had just a few weeks earlier raided St. Peter's in Caen where William the Conqueror was buried and scattered his bones as well. What irony."

Speaking with great animation, though he kept his voice low, Mauger guided me from the West Terrace, and we returned through the Chapter House to the Early Gothic Hall. He paced along the open cloister into the hall with immense, erect body and noble carriage, bearing his corpulent midsection before him like a badge of office. I thought that he would not have looked out of place in the gaudy regalia of a medieval archbishop himself, for one thing was certain—St. Mauger had nothing of the cloistered monk or hair-shirted hermit about him. He was a sensualist, not an aesthetic, and a fit descendant, I suspected, for a line of illustrious, renegade voluptuaries.

Clearly, in that quiet medieval atmosphere, the injustice, as he saw it, done to his ancestor and namesake rose up and agitated him mightily. Over tea at the Plaza he might have told the same tale with the light-hearted affability of a raconteur. But, like the cat he had said I was like myself, he too was prey to the atmosphere and mood of his surroundings. It was something else, apart from descent from Rollo, the Viking Duke of Normandy, and Charlemagne, Holy Roman Emperor, or reincarnated Egyptian souls, that we shared in common. We were both intensely romantic and given to indulging our romantic natures. A far and refreshing cry from Max, the egocentric realist.

I left St. Mauger in the Gothic Chapel, looking intently at the stone effigies of medieval nobles and their ladies, and made my way through the Halls of the Hero Tapestries and the Unicorn Tapestries and down the stairs to the ladies' lounge. I wanted to make a phone call and see how Guy was and tell him that I'd see him during evening visiting hours.

"Hi, how are you?"

"Lousy," he grumbled amiably. "I'm sore all over, my arm and collarbone are in a cast that make me look like the Mummy, my head aches like the devil, and you ask how I am. And where the hell are you? Why aren't you here to hold my good hand and offer solace in my hour of pain?"

"I thought I ought to leave you alone to rest, so I've come to the Cloisters with Gilbert St. Mauger. I'll see you tonight at about eight. Meanwhile, calm down or you'll wind up on your own slab having your brain dissected to find the blood clot that killed you, love. Bye."

I hung up chuckling to myself. I had just caught a choice pair of cuss words as I dropped the receiver.

I found St. Mauger hovering outside the ladies' lounge, trying to look nonchalant.

"I was afraid you got lost," he said petulantly.

I took a note from his mother's book and adopted a severe tone. "Don't be naughty, Gilbert. A lady has to have time to herself

occasionally. Now come along. I want to see the Bury St. Edmund's Cross in the Treasury."

"I am not interested in crosses. After what Christendom has
done to our family, we St. Maugers have all been rabid nonreligion-
ists—all save Mama, who insists on being a Catholic despite
everything."

"Well, she is a St. Hilaire, after all. Maybe they didn't have their
saint treated quite so roughly as yours," I suggested.

"That is sheer nonsense, Miranda. The St. Hilaires are our
cousins. Mama has as much of St. Mauger in her as I do myself—
well nearly, anyway," he corrected me with a pout. He continued
to sulk as I pulled him into the small Treasury Room to look at the
ivory cross that stood in solitary simplicity in a display case in the
center of the floor.

"This has nothing to do with religion anyway, my dear. This is
art. Now do behave." I could hardly believe the way I spoke to this
great hulk of a middle-aged man, yet he seemed to love it. He
obeyed me at once, tagging along, a teasing gleam in his great dark
gray eyes. He stood on the opposite side of the case from me,
crouching so that he could catch my eye through the Plexiglas.
Several people in the room turned to look at us, and a strange pair
we must have seemed—a short, slim lady in slacks and blazer and a
huge, bulky man, six-foot-four if he was an inch, in a charcoal-
gray pinstriped business suit replete with gold watch and chain
strung across his ample, vested middle. He looked like a banker
and behaved like a five-year-old.

"You are a very bad boy, Gilbert," I whispered, and, taking his
great paw in mine, led him out through the gallery into the serenity
of the Trie Cloister.

He quited down at once. "There," he said triumphantly, "isn't
this better than looking at nasty old crosses in a stuffy little room
like that? Look at the flowers in this garden. Listen to the music."
He walked over to a small placard that told what chants were being
played. "Conductus, Benedecomus Domino, Compostela XII

Century! How cheerful. How bell-like the tones." He cocked an ear and listened intently.

I sat on the stone wall between two worn old pink marble columns and listened, lost in the mood and peace of the moment. St. Mauger, who had stepped out into the tiny overgrown garden, came round one of the columns and hung over me, watching me with an intensity that was unsettling to say the least. I looked up at him, smiled weakly, and looked away, pretending to be absorbed in the music. Still he stared. I could feel his eyes on me, gentle and intense, willing me to look up at him. I didn't.

He gave up at last and slid down onto the stone wall. He faced outward toward the garden, the opposite way from me, the slender pink column standing as a barrier between us. We neither of us said a word till the music stopped briefly. It was followed a few seconds later by another slow, solemn Gregorian chant. Again our mood changed with the music.

Gilbert St. Mauger slid his hand around the column and stroked my cheek lightly with one long wide forefinger. I loved the feel of it in spite of myself and turned to look at him. He leaned his whole bulky upper body around the column almost sinuously and taking my jaw in his hand, pulled my face toward his. Our lips met lightly, gently at first, and then his great hand slid round the back of my neck and I found my lips pressed hard against his mouth with such force and passion that hot sparks seemed to ignite between us and run down into me like a river of molten fire. I shivered and trembled and cursed the damned column that stood between us like a wall, keeping me from his arms and the fierceness of his embrace. It was a moment of sheer physical hunger.

He thrust my face away almost as abruptly as he had drawn it to him, and rising to his feet, tugged on his vest nervously. He looked down at me with a wild, hot look in his eye, the look of a man surprised by his own passions. He said, almost angrily, "What are you trying to do? Seduce me?"

I looked up at him aghast, helpless to express the indignation I felt at his words. My cheeks grew hot, but hotter still was the irrational surge of passion and desire that he had aroused in me with that one kiss. Damn him, *he* was annoyed with *me!*"

"I did not ask you to kiss me," I said coldly. "I did not lead you on in any way. I have not the slightest desire to—to 'seduce' you, or any other man for that matter." I walked partway round the cloister and stopped, looking out through one of the slitted window openings.

Growing tall and straight from the earth far below was a huge old pine tree. The afternoon sun shimmered through the boughs, gleaming on the clusters of long needles and turning them to shivering shards of silver in the autumn light. Streaks of sap, bleached a skeletal white, stretched like bony fingers against the black roughness of the bark. A pair of nuthatches tripped down the trunk, pecking jerkily at insects as they wandered.

It was an odd moment. I could see all the minute details of nature through the stone-bound opening before me, and yet I could still sense Gilbert St. Mauger standing two or three feet behind me, looming over me with both his hands open and outstretched inches from my shoulders. He did not touch me, yet still, somehow, I could feel his fingers as surely as if he actually gripped me. He wore a long gown of finely woven wool, burgundy in color, and over it a robe, stiff, fur-trimmed, and caught at the throat by a pair of ancient clasps of curiously wrought gold and enamel. From a chain around his neck hung a large gold and ivory cross. It rested on the swell of his corpulent stomach. His fingers were long, wide, well cared for, and each bore a ring, massive and set with crude stones—emeralds, rubies, pearls, and rock crystals as delicious looking as pieces of Christmas candy. His garments exuded the scent of myrrh; his breath, the rich, stale odor of red wine. His face I could not see and of that I was secretly glad.

I was smaller, thinner, paler than myself, clothed in a sort of crude, stiff saffron velvet, heavy and uncomfortable to wear. My hair was coiled on my head beneath a covering of some sort, and my hands, which trembled on the stone sill before me, were small and pale and naked save for my right forefinger, upon which I wore a delicate gold band set with polished peridots and tiny gray pearls. The nails, unlike my own, were bitten to the quick.

Whoever I was at that moment, whatever other me stood there within me or beside me, I knew only two things:

I was afraid.

And I loved Mauger.

I don't know how long it was that we stood like that, but as quickly and as insidiously as the spell had come over me, it left, vanishing like smoke, without a trace, making me wonder if I had felt what I had felt, seen what I had seen. I turned slowly and looked at Gilbert St. Mauger and knew.

He was stricken. Ashen, in fact, his eyes faraway, his lips compressed and nearly blue. Without seeing me, he took my elbow and ushered me from the shadows of the Trie Cloister where we stood and through a door into the open, sunlit garden of the Bonnefont Cloister with its intricate pattern of walkways, its espaliered apple and pear trees, its masses of herbs, and four low, twisted quince trees, heavy with fat green fruit.

We picked our way along the paths together hand in hand without speaking, wandered along the covered walk, through the Glass Gallery and up a flight of steps into the Gothic Chapel. We walked through room after room and finally came to the Great Tapestry Hall, long, high, and dark with old wood. We had not spoken or looked at each other since that strange, passionate kiss and its weird aftermath in the Trie Cloister half an hour earlier.

At the far end of the Tapestry Hall, I entered a small door that led into the spacious high-ceilinged Campin Room, built of stone-work and paneling. It had tall leaded-glass windows set in deep embrasures fitted with pairs of stone window seats. It was peaceful, empty of browsers, and lit only by a gray north light that was a relief after the strong sunlight of the cloister gardens.

"Oh," I sighed, "this is perfect." I crossed the room and sat on one of the stone seats, looking out the window onto the very drive up which I had walked two hours earlier.

St. Mauger followed silently and sat on the narrow seat opposite me in the embrasure. He was poised delicately on the edge of the stone with his big hands folded over his stomach.

"This must be the sort of room in which your ancestor Mauger lived," I said with forced cheer, trying to break the silence between us. "It's so spare and serene and civilized."

"I've been a scholar all my life. A dilettante and a dabbler. Ask your uncle. He knows. I've delved into history, into the distant past—until dead ancestors like Mauger and the St. Hilaires and de Baynes are more alive to me than any living man—or woman . . ."

"That sounds very lonely," I murmured, knowing something of what would follow. This was, as my uncle had suggested, a very lonely man.

"I know, have always known, the sort of figure I cut. My sister is very beautiful and vain and keeps herself magnificently. Such outward vanities are important to her. She has known many men, had the adoration of many lovers—" He broke off and wiped his eyes, delicately blinking as he did. I suspected that he fought back tears.

"The figure I cut, my size, my—my grossness have put me beyond . . . I am more a figure of fun than of romance, I know," he said with a gesture as I started to protest. "No woman has ever been in love with me. I knew no one ever would be, you see, quite early on, and so I have always kept to my own world—my studies, my collections, my books—until . . ." He paused again, reflecting on his polished, well-manicured nails.

"I have never kissed a woman the way I kissed you a little while ago. Oh, I have a way about me, kissing hands or a cheek with a sort of comic exaggeration. A defense mechanism, a psychologist would say, I suppose, But before, in the cloister, that kiss—it was from the heart, *my heart,* and it happened without a thought or reservation or fear."

"Fear?" I echoed, and then I understood. Fear of rejection.

"And you responded. I am not such a fool to think that you wanted to, mind, but you did," he said hastily, raising his hands protestingly, his eyes fixed on the oak trees beyond the glass. "But you did respond. You were as moved as I and I—I don't quite understand it. All I know is that I have never felt such a moment before in my life—never."

"Never?" I must have looked amazed.

He shot me a glance and smiled crookedly, almost laughing. "Oh, my dear, I am not a virgin. That is not what I meant at all. Any man, even I, can have women if he is willing to pay the price. No, it is heart's love, heart's desire of which I speak. That I have never had. That I have never felt—"

I interrupted him deliberately, breaking into a cynical smile. "Well then, Gilbert, perhaps you are fortunate. Heart's love and heart's desire I *have* had, and a fat lot of good it's done me."

He ignored me. "Heart's love, heart's desire. Something that goes as deep as the spirit, that rises above"—he shook his head and made a funny little gesture of depreciation—"above a great, fat hulking body like St. Mauger's." The expression of pain that crossed his face as he blurted out that declaration was hardly to be borne.

"Oh, Gilbert," I whispered, reaching across the embrasure to take one of his big hands in mine. It was so warm and firm, so dry and strong, that I felt as if I could have curled up in it and slept like a creature in a cocoon. "Dear St. Mauger, you make too much of your size. You are a big, strong gentle man and even though I may resist you or Guy Galveston or any other man right now, it's only because I've been hurt and am sick to death of the male sex. You are such a dear, and a man very very worthy to love and be loved. Surely you must know that?"

"You responded to me in spite of yourself, as a woman," he persisted doggedly. "I know you did not want to, but you did! Can you deny it?" He leaned toward me and lifted my hand to his lips.

I pulled away. "No, I can't deny it, but my dear, dear man, I don't want to respond to you—or to any man right now. I don't want a lover."

I got no further with my protestations before he acted, taking me by the shoulders and pulling me toward him so that I found myself suddenly yielding and dropping to my knees in the embrasure. He lifted my face to his and bent to kiss me, this time without the preliminary tenderness of his first attempt.

I reached up blindly, throwing my arms around his massive shoulders, finding the thick muscles at the back of his neck with my fingers, stroking his dark hair lovingly, returning with all the strength I had the force of his lips on mine.

Never had I felt such desire and such hunger and such passionate satisfaction in one moment of—of what, I wondered? It wasn't simply lust; it wasn't even love. It was something far stronger and deeper than either, though it had elements of both. There was something of sheer perversity in it, perhaps. All I knew was that I was bewildered by it, drawn and repelled in the same instant.

Suddenly he pulled away and I felt my cheeks unaccountably wet. I opened my eyes and saw his face above me. We were both drenched with his tears. He cupped my face in one hand, wiping his tears off my cheeks with the other. It was a touching gesture.

"I'm sorry," he said. "I'm so sorry, I never meant—" He broke off in a strangled sob. "Oh, my dear, I am as surprised as you by this, by what I find myself feeling. Forgive me, I have to leave—"

With that, he rose, and wiping his tear-stained face on his sleeve like a child, stumbled blindly from the Campin Room and through the Late Gothic Hall to the exit. I started after him and then thought better of it. Instead, I sank back down onto the window seat and looked out onto the curving cobbled drive in time to see St. Mauger stride hastily down the walk, wiping his eyes with a handkerchief fastidiously, oblivious of the acorns under his feet or the squirrels that scampered away at his approach; oblivious too of the massive, gliding form of Mauger, deposed Archbishop of Rouen, who kept pace behind him on the cobbled road. If he had looked, I remember asking myself, would Gilbert St. Mauger have seen him too? If I looked now, I wondered, would that little band

of peridots and pearls be on my right index finger? I rather thought
it would, though I dared not glance down and be sure.

At the foot of the path he stopped and waved toward a limousine
in the small semicircle of parked cars. The driver sprang to attention and started the motor. St. Mauger turned and looked up to
the window in which I sat, saw me watching him, and opened his
arms in a gesture of despair. He shook his head sadly as if to ask
forgiveness. Behind him, Archbishop Mauger smiled sardonically
and faded from my sight, smoke in the autumn light. The car
pulled up at his feet and St. Mauger got in. One gentle kiss blown
from his fingers and he was driven away.

Whatever I might think of the figure cut by Gilbert St. Hilaire
St. Mauger, at the moment, "comic" was the last word that would
have occurred to me.

▽

13

OBSEQUIES

It was late October and the long Indian summer had finally ended.
Overhead, waves of birds migrated south on the crest of a cold
front that swept down out of Canada, killing off the lingering
summer gardens and bringing dry, frigid air down the steel blue
funnel of the Hudson. I left Nyack early and headed down the
Sprain Brook Parkway in a dazzle of sparkling, windswept
beauty—and then I hit the Bronx! The funeral home where Valdalene "reposed" was at 162nd, across a bare triangle of what passed
for park from the old Forty-second Precinct Station House.

I parked the car at the corner of Elton Avenue and 161st Street,
left Molly on guard with a rawhide chewy and a bowl of water to
keep her happy, and walked the block or so to the Williams
Brothers Funeral Chapel, which was housed in a buff brick building that occupied the whole of a wedge-shaped lot on the corner.

It had been designed long ago in pseudo-Gothic style with
pointed stained-glass windows and a wide oaken door bound with
massive iron bands and huge hinges. Over the years, and with the
evolution of the surrounding neighborhood from solidly middle-
class German to black and Hispanic poverty, the funeral home had
changed hands and been altered drastically. The windows were no
longer of glass, but had been fitted with sheets of plywood painted
gloss white. Stark black lettering, hand done and nonprofessional,

announced the name and ownership on each boarded window. There was a maze of iron guard gates. The place looked like a fortress.

The door was opened for me even before I could ring by a middle-sized, middle-aged black man in immaculate black pinstripes with a white carnation in his lapel.

The air inside the Williams Brothers Funeral Chapel was humid and overheated, suffused with the scents of roses and gladioli, chrysanthemums and ferns, mingled with a faint whiff of the damp papier-mâché pots and sodden Oasis sponge that held them. No flowers, however, in any funeral home I've ever been in, have overcome successfully the elusive but ever-present and evocative aromas of embalming fluid, wax, and thick, creamy cosmetics that lie at the heart of their operation. The Williams Brothers had been no more successful than the rest.

"Miss Pearsall resides in the King Room. Will you sign the book, please?"

I signed, one of the few who had arrived early, and stepped into the King Room, so named in honor of the man whose photographed portrait hung on a wall at the narrow end of the room.

Valdalene's casket—of necessity closed—was covered in some gray embossed, velvetlike cloth with silver-plated fittings. On it rested a blanket of pink and white roses, a gift from my Uncle Jeremiah, I knew, and on that was the large framed photograph of her that I had seen in her sister's apartment. Her beautiful face smiled out at me with all the force of a living person. It was a jolting sight, somehow more jolting than it would have been to see a waxen dead face lying exposed on a pillow of white crepe smocking. One expects death to look like death in such circumstances. It is the living countenance that jars one.

I walked down the aisle between two rows of empty wooden chairs, each with its "Williams Brothers Funeral Chapel" stenciled on the back, nodded at Ismeralda, who smiled back wanly, and knelt briefly at Valdalene's coffin. Rising, I turned my attention to Ismeralda, alone in the first seat of the row. She wore a black skirt

and white blouse with a little black ribbon at the throat. She looked
like a schoolgirl—sweet, worried, and vulnerable.

"Thanks for coming, honey," she said, taking my hands in hers
as I bent to kiss her. She had been crying.

"Nothing could have kept me away. I figured you needed all the
moral support you could get. How are you holding up?"

She shrugged her plump shoulders. "I's okay, but it's worse
now my momma come home. She's been carrying on something
awful."

I looked over my shoulder at the empty room behind us.
"Where is she?" I asked.

Ismeralda cocked her head and rolled her eyes upward. "Up in
the ladies' room with her sister, my Aunt Rayetta, and a neighbor
lady. She started wailing to break your heart when she come in and
saw that casket and Valda's picture sitting on it. It looked so bare.
Then they started coming in with the flowers. Valda'd be so
proud—all them flowers." She shook her head again and smiled at
her sister's picture amidst the roses on the coffin.

At two-thirty, Uncle Jeremiah arrived, confounding the brothers
Williams with his dapper sartorial splendor, his utterly impeccable
graciousness of manner, and the aplomb with which he suffered
the effusive embrace of Valdalene's mother, Mrs. Audrey Jackson.
She hugged him to her ample pouter pigeon's bosom, thrust him
away dramatically, flung her arms wide, and wailed shrilly, in that
excess of emotion that is the legacy of all wailing, bereft women
from time immemorial.

It was not until some time later that the two of us were able to
steal a few moments for a chat in a quiet corner of the hall outside
the King Room.

"Since we shall be attending the services and burial tomorrow, I
suggest that you come home with me and spend the night on
Staten Island," Uncle Jeremiah said. "I tried to call you earlier
when it occurred to me, but you had already left. Now, we have a
great deal to catch up on—this Kennedy Center business in partic-

ular, so let us see if we can't make a swift exit. People have begun
to arrive in numbers, so it should be easy." We rose and walked
back down the hall just as the front door opened.

It was Elijah Weems, tall, spare, and tentative. He hovered in the
tiny vestibule, unable to make up his mind whether to enter or
not. When he saw us, he smiled wearily and signaled a desire to
speak privately. We led him back to the nook from which we had
just emerged.

He coughed into his hand nervously. "I am not sure that I
should be here, but I felt I had to pay my respects. I don't want to
upset anyone—" He broke off huskily, his soft southern drawl
raspy from lack of sleep. Leaving the two men together in the
nook, I tiptoed into the King Room and caught Ismeralda's eye.

She came into the hall, mastering her emotions enough to shake
the hand that Elijah Weems offered and listen to him with somewhat impatient politeness.

"Miss Jackson, I—I realize that my presence might distress your
mother, but I could not let this time pass without expressing to
you my—my deep sorrow. I—"

"Dr. Weems, I understands. I accepts what happen to Valda, but
you can't exspect me to—"

"To forgive me, no. I don't expect that, Miss Jackson. It had
been my intent to attend the service tomorrow at St. Anselm's,
where I would be able to pay my respects without intruding on
you and your family, but I have just been informed by her executors
that there will be a memorial service for the baroness tomorrow
morning at the same time. She was cremated Saturday, you know.
I must attend that service, of course. There will not be many
mourners, I think, and so I thought I would come here today. I
want to make my peace with you, Miss Jackson, if you will be so
kind—"

"It—it weren't your fault. I knows you did what you could,"
she declared reluctantly. She shook her head restlessly and then,
nodding, she concluded, "Okay, peace." She didn't look at him as
she spoke, but she did offer her hand to be shaken once more.

He thanked her in a choked, dry voice and then turned to me, taking my hand and looking at me with a searching look in his tired yellowed eyes. I tried to smile reassuringly at him.

Finally, looking hard at Uncle Jeremiah, he grasped his hand in turn. I could barely watch their farewell. The depths of sorrow in those weary eyes of his, so small and bloodshot from lack of sleep, were such a contrast to my uncle's bright eyes and ruddy good health.

"You have been very kind, sir, and helpful beyond measure," Dr. Weems said in that languid drawl. "The young lawyer you recommended has kept me out of jail. He is negotiating a waiver of immunity and release from all criminal charges in exchange for my statement before the grand jury to close the case on the baroness. It seems I am more valuable to them as a material witness than as an accessory." He smiled a sad ironic smile. "Under the circumstances, I have much to thank you for. You are a true gentleman, Mr. Fay."

"I believe I can turn that remark around, Doctor, without flattery. It is a pity that our paths have crossed under such unpleasant circumstances. Perhaps time will change things for the better and we shall sit over another glass of bourbon together one day."

"Perhaps. I should like to think so, sir."

With that, Elijah Weems nodded and left us, walking down the hall with a slow step, his heavy black overcoat hanging from his shoulders shapelessly. Only his innate dignity kept him from appearing a picture of complete dejection.

As the door closed on him, Ismeralda shrugged and looked at us defensively. "If it wasn't for Momma, he could of stayed. I wouldn't have cared if he stay. Shit, I forgives him. It ain't his fault that old lady done to Valda what she did. Shit . . ."

I followed Uncle Jeremiah down into the city, parked my Mustang in his private garage space in a building on Fifty-sixth Street, and joined him in the Rolls for the rest of the trip to the island. Molly, clearly loving every minute of it, rode in front with Rogers.

My uncle poured us each a Scotch and water, and we settled back to enjoy in comfort the long afternoon traffic jam down the West Side Highway to the Battery and South Ferry. The drink, the fragrance of the soft butternut leather upholstery and my uncle's soothing voice all served to lull me into a sense of tranquility.

"I spoke to Guy this morning. He should be out of the hospital by Wednesday. He told me that you had been afraid that it was this husband of yours who ran him off the road." He cocked one white eyebrow at me questioningly.

"Well, it seemed like an obvious possibility at the time," I said sheepishly. "There is a streak of repressed violence in Max."

"Guy told me that the man who ran him off the road was very slender and pale, small, wrinkled, and appeared to be toothless, or nearly so. Sunken jaws and thin, mousy hair. Sound like your Max?"

I laughed out loud at that. "No, 'my Max,' as you put it, is middle-sized, middle-aged, well toothed, and very handsome." I paused for a moment, lost in thought. "I have not heard a word from Max, as it happens. He usually calls several times a week just to nag me about coming back to him, but there hasn't been a peep in a few days. Anyway, it wasn't him."

My uncle stared thoughtfully out the window, slowly rotating his hand to stir his drink. "I had another idea entirely, one that has evidently not occurred to either of you. Suppose it is the man we're looking for—the father of these two mooncalves? He has shown himself quite capable of violence toward women. Why should he stick at trying to kill a man intent on investigating the case? Guy's name has been in all the papers—and on that very day, I believe, in connection with the autopsy on Baroness Derevenkov. I suggested it to Guy and he reminded me that the man has been described variously, but never as slight of build or toothless, and never with light, lank hair. I reminded him that false teeth and toupees have been in common usage for some time now, but we wound up in a draw. Slight builds do not become heavy at will, or the reverse either. It was just a thought." He waved his hand to dismiss the conversation and took a pull of his drink.

"By the way, I never told you about my trip to the Kennedy Center on Fourteenth Street last Friday." I related my adventure. "I spent part of Saturday calling the management company that handles the building and found out that Suite 1406 is actually for rent. It is one of about six or eight empty suites in the building. Whoever is behind the Kennedy Center just goes there on the day the client is supposed to show up, and I assume now Jennifer may be the only one, sticks the letters on the door, and opens for business. They probably pick up their mail every few days or so, but I'll bet not oftener."

"That's taking a bit of a risk, isn't it?"

"Why?" I asked. "There isn't a regular super on the premises and if you'd seen the janitor, you'd realize how lax the place is. They chose their locale very well. They probably looked at the place with the agent originally, managed to diddle a copy of the key, and have been going back at will ever since. They might have been noticed, I suppose, moving their furnishings in, but believe me, five bucks and bottle of muscatel would take care of the janitor if he were conscious enough to notice anything, which, as I say, I doubt." I paused and took a sip of the whiskey. "Jennifer Pearsall told me the furnishings were old, by the way. They undoubtedly leave them in place and could simply abandon them if they had to. It renders them damned near untraceable."

My uncle looked out across the wind-whipped river toward the gray, dismal Hudson County shoreline with its factories and wharves and ugly new high rises that dwarfed the ancient Palisades against which they clustered. "Our earliest Van Voorst ancestors settled Hudson County when it was called Communipaw. They survived Indian attacks and God knows what privations to carve out farms and build churches over there, and look at it now." He shook his head. "I'm sorry, my dear. What were you saying?"

"Here." I pulled Pamela Howard's letter to the Kennedy Center out of my purse and thrust it at him defensively. "I had intended to call you on Friday night or Saturday and tell you about it, but Guy's accident knocked it right out of my head. I'd like your advice on what I should do about it."

He glanced first at the envelope and then across the seat at me. "You 'swiped' this, I take it?" he asked dryly, using a word more suited to my father's earthy vocabulary than his own refined one.

"I prefer the word 'purloined,' if you don't mind," I said with a haughty sniff. "It was lodged in the mail slot—"

"I should be angry with you, young lady, but the information it gives us more than justifies your transgression. This young woman, it would seem, is a Bedell, which indicates to me that she may tie in to the Pearsall line from the same Bedell branch that you have on your mother's side."

"That's what occurred to me the minute I saw the name."

"Yes, well, with the help of your esteemed landlady, I'm still in the throes of tracing the present-day descendants of James Pearsall. He had at least six great-grandchildren, and one, I know, did marry a Bedell. Her name escapes me at the moment, but I shall find the tie-in presently. This is a big help."

Rogers drove the car onto the ferry while we got out, went into the terminal, and walked on board as foot passengers, enjoying the chance to stretch our legs and breathe the fresh air at the tip of Manhattan. We hadn't long to wait before the warning bell rang, the wide doors to the ferry opened, and we were swept along in the beginnings of the afternoon commuter rush back to Staten Island.

"I forgot to mention it, but I saw your friend St. Mauger again yesterday . . ."

"Gilbert? Did you?" he asked, looking at me in surprise. We stepped out onto the deck and watched as the ferry moved away from the slip, its engines grinding softly somewhere below our feet.

"He's a very strange man, isn't he? And sad too," I added. "You are very right about him, I think. He is lonely, but he's a remarkably compelling person as well. I—" I broke off, quite at a loss.

Then, inarticulately, groping for each word, I told my uncle about our meeting at the Cloisters, the strange moods that had been evoked in each of us by the atmosphere, the intensity of our feelings, the final kiss, and his emotional departure from me in the Campin Room. Finally, and with trepidation, I even spoke of the weird feeling that had come over me of having been someone else, of the ring on my hand, and of having seen Mauger de Rouen dogging Gilbert's heels on the cobbled road to the parking area.

We were well across the bay now and the wind coming up the Narrows was brutal. We retreated behind the doors at our back and leaned against the bulkheads of the narrow inside walkway facing each other.

"And then suddenly to find *myself* attracted to him! It is too perverse for words. I simply cannot explain it." I shook my head vigorously.

My uncle turned from me, pinching his lower lip between thumb and forefinger in what I took to be another of his lawyerly mannerisms.

"You have explained the phenomenon very well, actually—better than I could have myself at the time. I was every bit as caught up, you know, with Hillary, every bit as fascinated at the time. 'Perverse' is the right word. It took me a while to understand, but I think I do. It's a form of hypnotism, I expect. I'm not at all sure they are even aware of it themselves, of the power they exert. It's in the blood, of course. There's no other logical explanation that I can think of, and since they are so inbred, it is far, far more marked than it would ever be in the average person. Then too since we are collateral—very distantly collateral, actually—perhaps we are particularly subject to their appeal. . . ."

"Hah, then by that token, Gilbert and his sister should be drawn to each other. No two people have closer blood ties than siblings, and the St. Mauger bloodlines are, as you say, multiplied many times over. Besides, Gilbert seems to believe in reincarnation, not bloodlines." I was being funny.

Uncle Jeremiah looked at me askance. "I hadn't wanted to mention this, as it is only just the most malicious of gossip, but at the time of her son's birth, no one could discover who among Hillary's lovers was the father. The only one often in her company at the time the child must have been conceived was Gilbert."

"Oh, Uncle Jeremiah."

He shook his head. "As I say, it was only malicious rumor. Hillary St. Mauger has her share of cast-off lovers. She is not a well-liked woman and gossip in Europe amongst the bored elite can be vicious. At any rate, I understand what you went through yesterday."

I smiled. "I was afraid you'd think I was mad."

Uncle Jeremiah smiled back and put an arm around me sympathetically. "I do understand, and you are far from mad, my dear. Very similar things happened to me thirty years ago when Hillary began to pursue me. I must admit that I was half in love with her at the time, but I was a bit afraid of her as well. She alternately repelled and attracted me. I began to think of her as a Medusa, with the face of a lovely woman and the soul of a snake. She is a descendant several times of Mabel Talvas of Belleme, one of the most notorious women of the early Middle Ages—an accomplished poisoner who was beheaded by some of the enemies she had made and buried sans skull. We are descended from her as well, though only in two lines that I've been able to trace. In any case, I've always wondered . . ." He broke off briefly and began again on a new thought. "Yet Gilbert himself I like immensely—and have since he was a boy."

"How did you happen to meet the St. Maugers? I've been meaning to ask."

"It was after the war. I was living in London and working with a firm of solicitors in the city. We were sorting out legal claims of Americans in Europe and Europeans in the States. The war caused all sorts of havoc, you know. Madame St. Mauger and Gilbert had spent the war years in England. Hillary had been caught at school in Switzerland in thirty-nine and sat out the war there. She came over in early forty-seven and that was when I met them. We had interests in common and eventually things began to happen. It wasn't long before I was something of a surrogate father to the boy."

"So he said. Where was his own father?"

"Oh, his father," Uncle Jeremiah clucked with a dismissing shake of his head. "He was something in the Vichy government, I believe. The St. Maugers never speak of him quite naturally. He was tried for war crimes in nineteen forty-seven and died in prison the following year. I never had anything to do with that aspect of their legal problems, but as I say, they were alone, they needed friends, and I was one of them." He shrugged. "Funny, but I haven't thought of all this in years."

"What was Gilbert like back then?" I asked.

"Much the same as he is now. Not quite as heavy, of course, but he has always had that prematurely corpulent middle. Shy, naturally. Much more so than he is now. Petulant, brilliant, spoiled. He could have taken honors at any university in England but his mother would never part with him. He was tutored at home and never permitted to go to a public school where he'd be prepared for university. It was quite a shame really, because without the discipline of a solid school behind him he became as he is now: a dabbler and a jack-of-all-trades rather than the disciplined, well-schooled intellectual he might have been.

"He has never shown me this compelling, mystical side that you describe, nor have I ever found him repellent in that particular way that his sister has with me. I still find her so, you know, though it often occurs to me that I should like to have taken her to bed—at least once—just to see what she'd have been like, fire or ice." He mused momentarily and then looked at me with a red face. "Do I shock you?"

I shrugged. "Not in the least. His tales of his ancestor Mauger were very interesting, by the way. Was the archbishop really so wronged by our ancestor William the Conqueror, or was that just Gilbert's ancestral pride showing?"

At that Uncle Jeremiah shook his head, tossed it back, and roared with laughter. "Oh, my dear, of all the hobbyhorses man ever rode, Gilbert St. Mauger on Archbishop Mauger is the maddest. Here, we are coming into St. George. Let's go outside so we can get up the gangplank ahead of the rush. Remind me to tell you all about Mauger de Rouen over dinner. It makes quite a story, though not nearly so refined a one as Gilbert is wont to tell."

We did not speak of Archbiship Mauger over dinner after all. Our conversation turned instead on the tack I should take in trying to get information about the Kennedy Center from Pamela Bedell Howard when I called her, which we had decided was the thing to do.

We rose from the table at seven forty-five after an early dinner and took our coffee into the library, where I could use the phone in comfort. Getting the number was easy. There isn't, one supposes, much reason for having an unlisted number in a place like Madison, Wisconsin.

"Hello."

"Mrs. Howard," I said lightly, "I am Miranda Fay. You don't know me, but I hope you will be kind enough to hear me out." I paused, throwing myself at the mercy of her good manners.

"Yes," she said tentatively.

"Thank you. I have reason to believe that we are both being harassed—that is the best word, I think—by a surrogate mother program calling itself the Kennedy Cen—"

I heard her draw in her breath on the other end of the line. "How did you know? How did you get my name?" She was clearly alarmed now, but curious as well.

"Please don't be upset," I pleaded. "I live in New York, not far from the city. I've been receiving letters from these people and finally got so infuriated that I went in to their offices to complain to them in person. There was a letter of yours open on the receptionist's desk in the outer office. It was easy to see that you were as incensed as I about receiving such mail, so I made a note of your name and address. I hope you don't mind."

"Yes, I sent them a letter recently," she said guardedly. "What is it you want?"

"Well. I am highly indignant that they would have contacted me in the first place," I said. "I have very strong convictions against such procedures and have no idea how they could have thought—"

"So do I," Mrs. Howard broke in eagerly.

"Well, I think I may want to carry this thing a bit farther than just refusing them and getting them to take me off their mailing list. I am contemplating filing complaints with both the A.M.A. and the postmaster here. I can't believe they have the right to solicit such services through the mail with impunity."

She cleared her throat. "No, I don't want that kind of involvement. I don't want my name used." There was a pause. "I suppose I could send you a copy of their last letter, though, if that would help. That is the only one I saved." She hesitated. "You won't drag my name into it?" I reassured her that I would not. "As far as why they selected me, or where they got my name from, I have no idea and up until now I really haven't given it much thought. I was married this year, but I suppose they had no idea about that. After four letters, I finally answered the last one. I figured that if they saw I was married, they'd stop. I'll send you a copy of it. After all, they shouldn't be sending things like that through the mail. Some little girl could get one."

"Yes, I agree. Thank you. May I ask how old you are?"

"Twenty-six."

"And do you know of anyone else who has been approached by these people?"

"No."

"None of your friends at school—or relatives? A sister? Perhaps a cousin?"

There wasn't a sound on the other end of the line and for a moment I thought I'd lost her.

"Miss Fay? That is it? Fay?"

"Yes, Miranda Fay."

"I—I had a sister. She was studying in London at RADA, the Royal Academy of Dramatic Arts. In January she was attacked and raped and beaten. She—she died, and so I haven't got a sister any more." Her voice cracked and became that of a little girl.

"Oh, Mrs. Howard. I am sorry. I didn't mean to rake up any past troubles. I had no idea naturally."

"My parents are both gone. If it weren't for Allan, I don't know what I would have done. She—her name was Samantha—she'd have been twenty this month. She was so beautiful, and very talented too. She was going to be a really fine actress. Everyone said so. He raped and sodomized her, the bastard. Oh, forgive me," she added, "Allan says I'm not supposed to say things like that. It—it's not Christian—but I just can't forgive him."

"Did the police find the man?"

"No, no. They have no idea who he is. She never regained consciousness. She could never say who it was, but they think it was an acquaintance. She knew so many people. She was very popular—and a little, you know, reckless. I don't mean bad or anything. She was just very trusting and confident of herself. She made friends easily. The case isn't closed yet. I keep hoping they'll find him. Don't they say that Scotland Yard always gets its man?"

"Something like that," I answered distractedly. "Mrs. Howard. I am truly sorry to have revived all this for you. I'm just sick about your loss. It must be dreadful for you."

"Thank you," she murmured. "You can see why I don't want to have my name used or to be involved in any way in what you are doing. I had enough of reporters and police in London. I've got to put it all behind me, and this surrogate mother thing—"

"Yes, of course, I understand completely. Just let me give you my name and address and you can send the letter, or copy, rather, on to me along with anything you can think of that seems like it might be pertinent." We said brief good-byes and I set down the receiver gently with a low whistle of relief.

"Well, I'll be damned. Uncle Jeremiah, I may be jumping to conclusions, but—"

For the next ten minutes I jumped to every conclusion I could think of.

∇

14

THE WHITE CAMEL CLOSES

U NCLE Jeremiah stood before the fire toasting his hands distractedly. He looked over his shoulder at the immense grandfather clock
against the wall by the hall door. "Damn that six-hour time
difference. It's too late to call London now, but what I wouldn't
give to have a rundown on the file they've got on that murder right
this minute."

"Samantha Bedell," I mused. "It's a pretty name. Sounds like
just the kind of old-fashioned name that would pop up in one's
genealogy, you know, like Forgiveness Basset. They certainly
sound like names from another century, don't they?"

"Rape and sodomy again," my uncle murmured under his
breath. "Last January, she said?" he asked aloud.

"Yes, why?"

"Oh, oh nothing, just a passing thought." He shook his white-
fringed head and went back to contemplating the fire.

"Care to join me in the garden while I walk the Moll?" I rose
from the leather comforts of the couch and stretched. "The fresh
air will do us good. Now, where is the little monster?" I asked
rhetorically as I looked around the room for her. "Oh, there you
are, baby." She was sitting as alert as a cat in a corner formed by
the joining of the side of the deep fireplace and the massive
bookcases that stretched along the walls to either side of it. "Well,

look at this! Uncle Jeremiah, you must have mice. That's Moll's hunting position."

Molly Brown sat upright, her fat little bottom firmly planted, her front legs quivering slightly in anticipation, and her head cocked to one side and bowed toward the baseboard of the bookcase. She stared intently. Behind the wood there was a faint scrabbling sound. At that, Molly flopped down and thrust her nose into the corner, sniffing furiously. She whimpered and began to claw insistently.

I pulled her away by the collar. "Oh, Uncle Jeremiah, I am sorry. Has she done any damage?"

He roused himself from his reverie, and bent to inspect the woodwork. He shook his head. "No, but she is a very clever dog, your Molly Brown, every bit as good at finding things as her mama."

"Not another mooncalf, I hope."

He chuckled and patted Molly affectionately. "No, no mooncalf, but she has located the entrance to the tunnel."

"As in secret tunnel?" I asked. He nodded, grinning at my girlish delight. "I love reading about secret tunnels, but I've never actually seen one or been in one. Oh, show me."

"I can't." He shook his head regretfully. "It is behind this bookcase, more or less boarded up for the past eighty years or so. Your father and I had a way of sliding back the panels at the back of the lower two shelves and worming our way into it, but that was seventy years ago at least. It hasn't been touched since then. The mice must use it as a freeway into the house, I suppose."

I picked up the Moll and carried her, slung unceremoniously under my arm, to the door. "Who built it?" I asked. "Where does it lead?"

Uncle Jeremiah opened the door to the hall and looked out. Then, in a low tone, he answered me as we made our way down the hall to the front door. "Well, this house, you know, was built by your great-grandfather, Luke Fay, Jr., and his wife, Mary Gibbs Fay, back in eighteen sixty-eight. In eighteen seventy, her brother

Fenton Gibbs bought the property across the road and built what is a nearly identical house—"

"St. Mauger's house," I interjected as he opened the front door. We stepped onto the front porch and into crisp, cold night air under a sky full of brilliant stars. I put Molly down and she took off down the steps and began rustling through the fallen leaves in the garden. Uncle Jeremiah went back into the house for our coats.

"Yes, St. Mauger's house," he repeated as he helped me on with my jacket. "Fenton Gibbs lived there with his parents. He never married. Now, here's the interesting part. During the construction, the two brothers-in-law, quite unbeknownst to the few neighbors that they might have had back then, dug a tunnel between the libraries of the two houses—for the convenience, one supposes, of not having to go out of doors, or even, I have always suspected, simply for some nineteenth-century love of fun. Now since the tunnel traverses Dissoway Drive, which is public property, it was and is quite illegal—so, of course, no word was ever breathed outside the family."

"A real family secret if ever there was one!"

"Quite. As I have said, Fenton Gibbs never married. When he died in eighteen ninety-three, his parents were long dead and his sister, your great-grandmother, was his sole heir. She gave the house as a gift to your great-aunt, Laura Gibbs Fay, who was assumed to be a spinster since she was over thirty and still unmarried. Well, she fooled them all and in nineteen hundred and two ran off to San Francisco with a sea captain. Your great-grandfather was furious, but there was nothing he could do. She put the house up for sale. He couldn't buy it himself at the time to keep it in the family—he'd been badly hit by the depression in the late nineties. And my father was just starting out. He had a wife already, but your father was on the way and I was not even a twinkle in his eye. He lived in this house with Grandpa Fay as it was, and would eventually inherit it, so there was no help for it. The house across the street passed out of the family.

"Before the sale went through, my father and your great-grandfather went through the tunnel, bolted the panels of the entrance in the other house, and then came back through and had that extra section of bookcase built into the corner of the fireplace to cover the entrance. They had another section built in on the other side of the mantel to balance the room, and that was that. The tunnel passed into legend—or so it was until one day when your father and I managed to get into it. No one ever knew we could do it, you see, so we had quite a bit of fun when we were boys." He laughed softly and fell silent as if remembering the happenings of long ago. "We even managed to work back the bolt and open the other panel." He chuckled again. "How bad we were!"

"Then the tunnel was never filled in?" I asked thoughtfully. "It still exists?" I began to form a little fantasy around the idea of rediscovering it.

"No, it never was. It would have been too expensive, I imagine, and far too much trouble. By the way, for God's sake, do not tell Gilbert about it. He, of course, has no idea of its existence, and I shudder to think of what would happen to my privacy if he did. You and I are the only two people living who know of it now. Even the Lynches and Rogers, who have been with me for decades, have no idea it exists and I wish to keep it that way."

I laughed lightly. "Have no fear. I won't breathe a word, but I am glad you told me. It is a wonderful secret to have. How did Mauger ever come to buy that house, by the way?"

"He was in New York—oh, ten or twelve years ago now—twelve, actually, and came to visit me. The Whitleys, who had had the house for twenty years and more, had just put a great, god-awful sign—FOR SALE BY OWNER, it read—up on the palings across the street. Well, when Gilbert saw this house and then saw the once across the road and heard that it had been built by a relative of mine, he went wild. He was like a child who wanted a new toy.

"Much to my horror, he bought the place the very next day and moved in within the month. I had, as you may imagine, grave misgivings at first. I had no wish to play Amos Wilde to his Andrew Bentley, but fortunately things have worked out quite well. He is, for the most part, an absentee neighbor. So, since I travel so much myself, I have not yet had occasion to find his presence intrusive. In fact, it is only this last year that he has been in more or less constant residence, but that is only because he has found his sister's and his mother's mourning over the boy so depressing. He came here to get away from them. They, however, have followed, so he's stuck anyway, poor sod.

"So, as I say," Uncle Jeremiah concluded, "it has all worked out quite well, after all. The house is so big that some dreadful Moonie cult or outpatient drug clinic might have taken it over. This neighborhood is not what it once was, I'm afraid. Now, shall we go in? It is getting quite cold."

"By the way, uncle mine, who are Amos Wilde and Andrew Bentley?" I asked as we hauled Molly out of the rhododendrons and climbed up the porch steps and back into the house.

"Who are they?" he clucked. "And you profess to read the literature of the supernatural? Reread your Derleth, my girl. . . ." Then, of course, he lent me the appropriate bedtime reading.

Uncle Jeremiah had placed his first call to London at six in the morning, well before I was awakened by Mrs. Lynch. An hour later over the breakfast table in a sunny little room at the back of the house, I heard his tale of frustration.

"Now I realize I'm old," he said with a shake of his bald head as I kissed him good morning. "That young inspector at the Yard whom I expected to ask about the Bedell murder?"

"Yes?"

"Well, he's now a retired chief inspector who's on holiday with his grandson, fishing in Scotland. And I still see him as an affable young fellow of thirty or so. If that's not a sign of age, I don't know what is."

"Do stop," I chided. "You know that you are a boy in your heart, which is where it counts—and besides, he's given up the tracking down of mysteries and you're just getting warmed up again, so who's showing signs of age?" I poured our coffee from a lovely Georgian silver pot that Lynch had set beside me. "I take it you had no success then?"

Uncle Jeremiah grinned at me through his white brush of mustache. "On the contrary, my dear. They were the soul of courtesy. I dropped as many names as I could summon to mind and finally got through to a detective inspector I had dealings with back in the early sixties. He's *not* retired, I hasten to add, and was quite cooperative. I told him I had given up my law practice, and that I was now in partnership with my niece in a private inquiry agency."

"Uncle Jeremiah!" I put down my butter spreader with a clatter.

"I told him we'd been hired to look into the rape-sodomy of a Connecticut girl who happens to be the cousin of the girl whose murder they are investigating, that the family has begun to suspect some sort of personal vendetta is involved. I told him that this was a family with money and a social position and they haven't wanted to get the police involved at all till they have something concrete to go on. That is a situation any Englishman would understand. Besides, I had a very good rapport with this fellow years ago and he remembered me quite well. He agreed that we ought to exchange information. He's going to look at the Bedell file and get back to me."

"Humph! They must be getting old reruns of Perry Mason over there. I suppose they think it's just typical American private-eye stuff."

My uncle twinkled. "Well, if I am Perry Mason, my dear, you make a lovely Della Street."

That, I decided, deserved the kiss I planted on his blushing cheek!

Valdalene's funeral service was at St. Anselm's on Tinton Avenue in the South Bronx at ten, so we were out of the house and in the terminal at St. George shortly after eight. It was as we waited to board the ferry back to Manhattan that we saw the headline on the morning edition of the *Post:*

REVEAL DOC'S PART
IN
PROSTI "MONSTER"
ABORT-MURDER

"Oh, bloody hell," he muttered as I nudged him and indicated the headline. He bought a copy and carried it onto the upper deck with us. The article was brief and not terribly informative when one analyzed it, but it did its damage nonetheless, for it dragged the name of Elijah Weems before the public eye for the first time.

It described him as the "longtime friend and companion" of the late Baroness Alexandra Derevenkov, thus using the age-old jargon of yellow journalism to hint at things suggestive and forbidden. It described him further as an "accessory and material witness in the abortion-murder" of Valdalene Pearsall and her "baby-for-pay mooncalf," thus lifting my term and using it as their own.

"This is terrible," my uncle muttered, looking furious.

The article went on to state that Dr. Weems was free on his own recognizance pending a grand jury hearing, yet the whole tone and implication of the thing, though the facts were essentially correct, was damning. It managed to flirt deftly with libel without being legally libelous—a nice gratuitous hatchet job done on an old man for the sake of a big dirty headline to sell the morning edition and beat out the *Daily News,* which was rapidly gaining by default the stature of a *New York Times* of the tabloids.

"It's such a rotten shame. Here my article comes out today in the *Stop-Press* and tomorrow on the wires and I was so careful to keep his identity a secret. Now some bastard leaks this. He's going to take this hard, I think."

"I'm afraid you are right, Miranda dear," Uncle Jeremiah said solemnly, squinting through the morning sun at the Statue of Liberty, clad in her mantle of vivid green. He shook his head. His broad, high forehead was a mass of wrinkles. "He is no fighter, at least not at this stage of life. If he could only get angry. . . . I shall try to reach him after this funeral and talk to him, but"—he mused for a moment—"I'm afraid Elijah Weems is a sensitive man."

That evening the three networks outdid themselves with coverage of first Valdalene's funeral and then the memorial service for the baroness. It was television news coverage at its most bathetic.

Mini-cams had not been allowed inside St. Anselm's, which for all its grim brick exterior turned out to be a dramatic Romanesque-Byzantine fantasy of glazed tile built during the South Bronx's palmier days. Blue-green light had shimmered all around us as the sun streamed through the stained glass of the clerestory and bathed Valda's mourners in the serene tones of a forest floor. Outside, beyond the incense and the ringing chime of the altar bell and the flowers and the sobs of Valda's mother and children, was the insistent wail of police sirens, the thump and yelling of a basketball game going on in a nearby playground, and the shouts of all the milling throng that waited to see the spectacle that the TV cameras would record at the end of the service.

Meta clucked disapprovingly at the television as the camera pressed in on Valda's weeping mother. "Why can't they leave people alone at a time like that?" my esteemed landlady fumed, sloshing more sherry into her glass.

"What, and deprive the public of a chance to leer voyeuristically? 'Prosti Abort-Murders' are big news."

We sat in front of my set, in the shade of two vases of roses that had arrived in my absence, the first on Monday and the second Tuesday afternoon. They were from Gilbert.

I got up and moved one of the vases off the coffee table and onto the top of the T.V. "I'll have to drop St. Mauger a thank-you note for these." Somehow they made me uneasy. One bunch was acceptable. Two was excessive.

The next news segment dealt with the memorial service for the Baroness Derevenkov, which had been arranged according to her instructions by her lawyers. It had been held that morning at the

Russian Holy Father's Church on West 153rd Street in Harlem.
There was no sound on the tape at first, but while the camera dwelt
on a silent, morose Elijah Weems, a reporter's voice-over repeated
his story essentially as it had been outlined in the papers that
morning, minus, happily, a few of the more libelous implications.
At last the sound on the tape came up and we heard reporters
asking, "Just what was your relationship with the baroness? How
did you two meet? Had she performed other abortions to your
knowledge? What kind of deal did you make with the D.A.'s
office?" Endless questions, stolidly ignored.

Dr. Weems, escorted by his young, earnest, fresh-faced lawyer,
ran this gauntlet with dignity from the moment he stepped out of
the church with its blue onion dome until he was able to cross the
wide, crowded stretch of sidewalk and enter the hired limousine
that took him away.

The camera, frustrated at the loss of its prey, turned from the
departing automobile and panned across the tiny group of mourners that drifted away from the front of the church. Among these
was a small, slender woman in deep mourning, accompanied by a
stocky man of middle height dressed in the plain black cassock and
three-armed cross of a Russian Orthodox priest. The image was
cut off abruptly and replaced by one of Chuck Scarborough
bantering with Pat Harper about Al Roker's upcoming weather
report.

"Well, I'll be damned," I blurted out. "It can't be! What on earth
would she be doing there?" I stared at Meta. "Of course, I only
met her once, and this was barely a glimpse. It could have been
anyone."

Meta opened her mouth to ask, no doubt, what I was going on
about, but she was too late. The phone rang that very moment. It
was Uncle Jeremiah.

"Miranda, are you watching the news?"

"Yes, yes I am."

"Channel Four?"

"Yes."

"Then did you see what I saw?"

"Well, yes, I think so, Uncle Jer—"

"Miranda, what would Isabelle St. Mauger be doing at a memorial service for the Baroness Derevenkov?"

When I awoke the next morning, it was with a sense of foreboding. I lay in bed, wide awake, stiff from sleeping in one position all night long and exhausted from the turmoil of my dreams.

By eight-thirty, the second cup of the Skylark's strongest brew had begun to percolate through to my sleepy brain. A plate of French toast and crisp bacon was doing its best to rev up my idling motor.

"Miranda dear, I'm so sorry. You must feel bloody awful." Peter slid into the booth opposite me and reached across the table to pat my hand.

I blinked at him uncomprehendingly. "I know I *look* like the wrath of God, but I don't *feel* quite that bad, Peter. Besides, you don't look so great yourself," I retorted. "I just need another cup, that's all. I've got to pick Guy up at the hospital at ten. They're releasing him this morning."

He frowned, his wonderful face rumpling like old leather. "Then you haven't heard? Your uncle didn't think you would have yet. He said he's been trying to get you to break the news since before eight."

"What are you talking about? When did you see my uncle?"

"I didn't. He couldn't get you on the phone so he tried first Meta and then me. He wanted someone you know to break the news. It's about Dr. Weems. They found him about seven. His lawyer had been trying to get him since the night before. Finally, he called the police and met them at the office—he had an office and a room to sleep in in a tenement somewhere down in the South Bronx."

"He lived a block or so away from the Baroness Derevenkov," I said quietly.

"Well, they found him in his office—dead."

"He killed himself, didn't he?"

Peter nodded solemnly.

"He hanged himself from a ceiling fixture. He evidently planned it very carefully. He left a note for the medical examiner and a copy of his will. He must have decided on it after he saw the papers, because yesterday afternoon after the memorial service he went to a lawyer up in Harlem—just walked in off the street, it seems—and made out a will." He hesitated. "It sounds like he wanted to do it and didn't want to be stopped. You know what I mean, kid?"

I heaved a sigh and signaled the waitress for more coffee. "Yes, I know. It can't be helped. I am so sorry," I said softly. So, the White Camel finally caught up with Elijah Weems.

"Oh, Peter, I should get to a phone and call Ismeralda. She's going to feel terrible about this, too." And guilty, I might have added remembering how torn she had been at her sister's viewing on Monday.

"Not necessary. Your uncle said he was going to call her after we hung up."

I began to cry in earnest now. Peter handed me a wad of napkins from the dispenser on the table. "Here, kid," he mumbled awkwardly, and sliding out of the seat opposite, he moved in beside me and took me in his arms. He held me against the warm flannel of his shirt, letting me sob against him quietly until the first flush of my sadness was spent.

I looked at Peter and blinked back the rest of my tears. "You are the nicest man in the world. How many bosses let their cub reporters bawl all over them?" I leaned over and gave him a quick peck on the cheek.

"Damn few," he said heartily, and I noticed he blushed ever so slightly. "And fewer still pay their breakfast checks too," he added as he took my bill from the table and stood up. "Come on, we'll go pick up your boyfriend at the hospital before he thinks you've forgotten all about him."

I scurried down the aisle after him, pulling on my jacket as I went. "He's not my boyfriend, and besides, I have an hour yet. I want to call Uncle Jeremiah."

"You can't," Peter declared as he opened the door for me. "Your uncle must have taken off by now."

"Taken off?" I asked. "Where to?"

"London. He booked a seat on the nine-thirty Concorde, he said. It seems he has a date with somebody at New Scotland Yard this afternoon."

Leave it to Uncle Jeremiah.

$\triangledown$

15

TWO SHERLOCKS, A
WATSON, AND MRS. H.

GUY lazed around all Wednesday afternoon, shifting idly between my apartment above and Meta's below, nursing his Valpo cast tight to his chest and looking like a cross between Boris Karloff as Karis the Mummy and Jackie Coogan as the Kid. When he had nothing else to do, he glared at St. Mauger's two dozen roses as if he'd like to chuck them in the garbage.

I threw a copy of the afternoon *Post* down on the coffee table in disgust and snorted. "ABORT DOC HANGS SELF," the headline screamed. Didn't anyone ever feel remorse or guilt? Is that what it was like to become one of the "ink-stained wretches" of big-time journalism? If so, I wasn't at all sure I wanted to be a part of it. Better stick with biography, where the search is still for truth, or resort to novels, where fiction is still called fiction.

"What's with you?" Guy asked, looking up from the *Times* crossword puzzle.

"Not a damned thing," I snapped. "People I know kill themselves every day."

"He was an old man, for Chrissakes. He'd reached the end of his line."

"And that makes it okay, hah?"

It was then that my doorbell rang. Molly Brown barked and ran to it.

"Ah, saved from further bickering by the bell," I declared with a toothy grin as I went to answer it. It was Gilbert St. Mauger.

"Gilbert, I—why, how nice. What a surprise." I hoped I did not look as stunned as I felt, for he was the last visitor I either expected or wanted. Before I could say another word, he thrust an armful of red roses at me and murmured something about their beauty not doing justice to my own.

"Oh Gilbert, how sweet and how utterly lavish. You are overwhelming me with roses, you know. You really shouldn't." God knows I certainly meant it.

He followed me into the living room, where his previous two days' offerings still dominated the coffee table and the top of the television console. The place was beginning to take on the look and smell of a Mafia funeral, and Guy's baleful expression did nothing to dispel the impression.

"I believe you two have met," I said cheerily, though even to me my voice was unconvincing. "Dr. Guy Galveston, this, you may remember, is Gilbert St. Mauger. Guy was just released from the hospital this very morning," I said brightly, hoping to smooth over what was a terribly awkward silence.

"I had hoped that we might talk," Gilbert said pointedly, ignoring my remark and turning his back on Guy.

"Guy," I said politely, "would you mind being a dear and asking Meta if she has a large vase I can borrow—for the roses."

I shot him a glance pregnant with meaning. He made a face but took the hint and left us. I placed the roses on the kitchen counter and came back into the living room. St. Mauger was still standing, looking glum. He shifted from foot to foot, his normally placid countenance frowning. He looked as ever like an earnest, scrubbed choirboy.

"Gilbert, please sit down. You look so uncomfortable standing there."

"Would you mind locking that door? I shouldn't like your friend to come barging back in here."

"Of course."

"I can't stop thinking of last Sunday," he began, after I'd locked the door to the hallway. His back was to the light that streamed in the dining-room windows, so that I couldn't see his face in the glare. "It would be so wonderful, so utterly, unimaginably wonderful, if you could return always the feeling—dare I say it?—the passion that I felt for you and that I think you felt for me.

"I have never harbored any hope that I would ever be loved by a woman such as yourself, but what we felt on Sunday transcends any dream I have ever had. Such feelings, I believe, are capable of surmounting any obstacle, any impediment. Such feelings might endure through the ages, perhaps as Mauger's love for Adeliza D'Arques and hers for him rose up against all odds and endured even beyond death." He spoke so earnestly and with such anxiety that I was at a loss.

"Gilbert, please," I said at last, trying to be gentle, "you—you romanticize too much. We were caught up in the mood of the moment, that's all. It was the atmosphere of the Cloisters itself, the medieval music, your fascination with your ancestor—"

"Or was it our two souls, reincarnated at last, coming together out of ages past?" He spoke with sudden power. "You are as much a descendant of Adeliza as I am of Mauger, and they were great lovers . . ."

"Oh, Gilbert, please. You are not making sense."

"It was she who found him, you know. She searched and searched, swearing she would never give up until—"

"Stop it," I cried. "It is nonsense."

"Is it?" he asked, tears welling in his eyes, his voice cracking like a child's. "Didn't you feel it? Didn't you feel something Sunday that—?"

"I—I did, it's true, feel something strange," I admitted reluctantly, "but it wasn't love, my dear, dear man. It was a mood, only a strange mood that caught us up for a few minutes and swept us along." I felt terrible saying what I said, but he had caught me off guard, first with his unannounced visit and then with the directness of his approach. I could only answer with honesty, however painful it might be. "Gilbert, it wasn't love, really it wasn't, not on either of our parts."

He crumpled, the intensity draining from him like water. He sank down onto one of the chairs at the dining table and bowed his head in what seemed to be defeat. I came toward him slowly. I was torn, wondering what to do when, for the second time in half an hour, I was saved by the ringing of a bell.

"That's the phone. I'd better get it," I said softly. As I lifted the receiver I half-expected it to be Guy calling from downstairs, but it was not.

"Hello? Oh, Jennifer. Yes, yes, how are you?"

Her voice was sweet and little girlish. "You went to the funeral for that black girl, didn't you?" she asked. "I just saw your name in the paper."

"My name?"

"Yeah, here it is, in the story in the *News*. 'Among the mourners was Miranda Fay, the woman who found the fetus that had been aborted at the time of Pearsall's death.' I went to the other doctor again this morning—just, you know, to be on the safe side."

"That's good! What did he say?"

"Oh, only that I'm fine and the baby is fine, only he thinks maybe I'm going to have twins. There are two heartbeats."

"Twins?" I wondered instantly why the doctor at the Kennedy Center hadn't detected two heartbeats—unless, of course, he was no more a doctor than I was.

"Yeah, isn't that something? Miss Fay, I just know that the names are only a coincidence. I mean Jennifer and Valdalene Pearsall, you know. My Mr. Leigh just isn't that kind of man. He just isn't like that. He'd never beat up a woman. I just know he wouldn't."

What could I say to her? I had no proof. I had no way of convincing her of the fact that her pregnancy was part of some mad, sick plot, the aim of which was still unknown. And if I did manage to convince her, what would she do? For the time being, all I could do was placate her, calm her fears, and keep in touch.

Her next visit to the Kennedy Center was scheduled for early November. It was a date that I would keep with her.

"Jennifer, listen to me. I'm sure you are right. There can't be any connection. After all, Valdalene Pearsall was not part of any surrogate mother program. It was simply a very unorthodox private deal. It is just the coincidence of the name that links you." I ached to end the conversation. Gilbert was making restless, shifting sounds across the room. "Please don't worry," I urged, trying to bring the call to a conclusion.

"I know," she said in a small voice. "I only wish . . ."

"What do you wish, honey?"

"That I could call Mr. Leigh and tell him about the babies, that it's twins. I think he'd be glad and, maybe . . ." She paused. "I mean, he's a widower and all, and I'm their real mother. He's old, sort of, I know, but I like him. He talks so soft and nice to me. I— I'd make him a good wife and I'd take care of the babies. . . ."

"Jennifer, Jennifer, listen to me. What about college? What about making something of yourself?"

"Miss Fay, I love him. I keep on thinking about him. If only he'd marry me, everything would be perfect. I just know it would."

Guy was knocking on the door, Gilbert had risen from his chair and was pacing the living room like a caged animal, and Jennifer Pearsall had burst into tears on the other end of the line.

"Jennifer, honey, can I call you back? I have company and someone's at the door."

"You can't call me. I'm at a pay phone at school. I'll be okay. It felt good just to talk. I'm so glad it's twins, aren't you?" She stopped crying and blew her nose.

"Yes, honey, I am. I'm very glad for your sake. Now calm down and have a nice quiet evening, okay?"

"Okay," she sniffed, and said goodbye.

"Who was that?" Gilbert asked abruptly. He was wiping his eyes with a large silk handkerchief.

"Was that Guy at the door?" I asked.

"Yes. I sent him away. I said we were busy. Who was that on the phone?"

"Oh, a girl I know. She's carrying a baby—twins, she thinks—for a man she hardly knows, as a surrogate mother."

"Oh?"

"Oh, indeed." I smiled ruefully. "It's a sad case because he has no interest in her personally and she's made the mistake of falling in love with him. Let's not get into it. It's more than I can cope with now."

"Of course," he said austerely. "Miranda, perhaps you misunderstood me. I have spoken of passion, of feeling, but I haven't made myself clear. I wish to marry you." He was cool again now, masterful and compelling. He crossed the room and put his arm around my shoulder, turning me toward him.

"Marry?" I was shocked. My mind raced to find a gentle answer. "Gilbert, I am married. My separation from Max isn't even formal enough to lead to a divorce yet. I can't possibly think of marriage—"

"To me?"

"To you or to anyone. It may be a year or two before I'm free and then I doubt that I shall ever marry again." He turned my face to his and tried to kiss me but I pulled away. I was afraid of my reactions should he kiss me again the way he had at the Cloisters.

He stepped away, still watching me. "Don't you want a family?"

"A family? You mean children? No, of course not, not at my age, and besides, if I had ever wanted children, I'd have had them already. After all, I've been married twice. Why, I look at that poor girl, big as a house and expecting twins, no less, and I think to myself, there but for the grace of Margaret Sanger go I!"

"What about love?"

"Now that's a different story. I've always wanted love, but as I told you on Sunday, it tends to play us false. Why, look at that poor child, Jennifer Pearsall. She's in love, and it's all to no avail. I loved Max and that's turned to ashes. I don't think I believe in love any more."

Strangely, in the moment I spoke, the image of a face passed unexpectedly and unbidden before my mind's eye, and was gone. Gilbert looked down at me oddly. I turned from him, fearful lest he try to kiss me again, but he didn't. He walked instead, slowly, ponderously, to the couch, and picked up the hat and gloves that he had shed upon his arrival.

"I'm sorry, Miranda, to have troubled you. It was foolish of me. You are quite right. I let the passion of the moment sweep me away, always an unwise thing in a man such as myself, but I risked appearing the grotesque and the fool because—because I am like your friend Jennifer: alone, vulnerable, and in love with someone who does not return my feeling."

"Oh, Gilbert, oh, I—"

Gilbert, erect and with all the majesty that his ancestor Mauger the archbishop might have mustered before the high altar of the Cathedral of Rouen, opened the door and strode from the apartment.

Guy, hearing St. Mauger close the lower door, came out of Meta's living room and bounded up the stairs.

"What'd that fat fag want?" he asked.

"Shut up, Guy."

"What'd he want?" he persisted.

"None of your goddamn business," I snapped. "Now leave me alone. Go finish your crossword puzzle or something."

Just before dinner the phone rang again. It was the overseas operator with a call from London.

"Hello, Uncle Jeremiah. So you really are in London. Peter said you'd taken the Concorde, but I wasn't sure if I should believe him." Guy perked up and cocked an ear to listen. I winked at him across the room to let him know my mood had passed. He winked back. "Yes, yes, Peter found me having breakfast in town. He told me. I feel just awful about it. By the way, Gilbert stopped by this afternoon."

"In Nyack?" he asked querulously.

"Yes, here. Guy is here now, and Meta just came upstairs with dessert. We're going to have dinner together."

"Can't talk, I gather. Will it keep?"

"Yes, it's not really important, just personal. But about our mystery, Jennifer Pearsall called to tell me that she's expecting twins." At that, Guy, who was listening unabashedly to my conversation, looked ready to turn cartwheels.

For the next few minutes Uncle Jeremiah gave me a rundown on what he expected to accomplish in London and read off a list of things he wished me to do in his absence.

"Rogers will stop by tomorrow before noon with some material for you and Mrs. Sullivan to collate for me. I'm having him bring an *Orderic Vitalis* for you. I have two sets, so you might as well have one. I expect you'll enjoy browsing through him. He's very readable and has quite a bit to say on our friend Mauger de Rouen."

"Thank you. I can hardly wait. I'll do everything you say and have everything ready when you get back. Promise. Bye now, love you."

"To Guy," I said, raising my wineglass in toast, "may you mend quickly and be back to cutting and slicing in no time at all."

"Oh, it was a near thing, luv," Meta murmured, patting Guy consolingly as I cut his steak for him.

"Meta, or perhaps I should revert to calling you Mrs. Hudson since you are a full-fledged investigator, Uncle Jeremiah wants us to go over your notes on the descendants of James Pearsall and collate them with the material Rogers is bringing up from Staten Island in the morning. He wants us to put it all in chart form, and by the way, he solved one mystery for us, Meta. It *was* Madame St. Mauger we saw on the news last night. He asked her, and it seems that back in the thirties when the St. Maugers lived in Paris, she knew the baroness as Miss Alexeievna, the doctor's daughter. When she read about the baroness in the papers and realized who she was, she decided to pay her respects for old time's sake."

Over dessert Guy expounded on the news of Jennifer Pearsall's twins.

"Boy, would I like to get a look at those babies when they're born. If the same man fathered them as fathered the other two, they should prove the link conclusively. I've already told you I think the man has a definite genetic tendency toward the conception of terata. If Jennifer Pearsall's babies are in any way deformed, hell, it will be terrific. I'm willing to bet that the blood types will be consistent with the blood types of the two we've already got."

He rubbed his hands together with an enthusiasm that I found hard to generate myself. A cavalier attitude toward the cadaver on a slab was one thing, but Jennifer and her unborn babies were alive and breathing and human.

"At the risk of spoiling your fun, I prefer to hope that she gives birth, full term, to two bright, happy, pink babies who are pretty and perfect in every way."

"God bless them, yes," Meta said, putting down the bowl of trifle to cross herself piously.

I said not another word, but poured the coffee in a thoughtful silence. God might bless them and I might have high hopes for them, but in my heart of hearts, I knew how likely Guy was to be right when the final score was in.

It was a prospect that did not bear thinking on.

That night, to amuse myself as I drifted off into my unquiet slumbers, I harked back to the conversation that Uncle Jeremiah and I had had in the Rolls going up the East Side Drive to Valda's funeral the day before. It had been a sunny, gusty day and as we watched the wind whipping up whitecaps in the East River, I had asked him to tell me about Gilbert's ancestor, the archbishop.

Uncle Jeremiah had chuckled softly and run a hand over his shiny pink dome, smoothing his fringe of silver hair neatly. "Mauger, eh? Well, did Gilbert tell you he was the bastard uncle of William the Conqueror?"

"Oh, yes, and that he was tried by the church—at William's urging—for simony and fornication and all sorts of debauchery."

My uncle had gone on, unfolding the tale like a fable. "Oh, he was tried all right, and convicted. He had, it seems, made an enemy of his nephew by condemning William's marriage to Matilda of Flanders—after he had, in fact, performed the ceremony. The condemnation was as much a matter of church politics as anything else and was actually ordered by the pope rather than Mauger. In any case, William was hardly pleased by the action, and so when Mauger compounded his first offense by aiding his brother William d'Arques, the Conqueror's other bastard half uncle, in a scheme of rebellion, why that tore it.

"William convoked a gathering of the church fathers and engineered Mauger's explusion from the See of Rouen. Mauger was stripped of his authority and his income and exiled to the island of Guernsey, where he held a randy and lavish court not much less dissolute than the one he had held in Rouen, it seems. He was a gregarious man, always surrounded by his concubines and bastards, his hangers-on and his companions in debauchery. Amongst this rabble he included poets and scholars, so there is evidence that he was no ignoramus.

"He must have been, by any standards, let alone those of his own day, a most peculiar man. He claimed to consort with demons—no mean feat for an archbishop, I should imagine—and was known to entertain his guests at table with the appearance of his very own pet demon, a familiar spirit whom he claimed was under his thrall and at his constant command. He carried on conversations with this demon, whom he called Thoret or Little Thor. It was shocking behavior for an archbishop, as you may imagine, and undoubtedly contributed to his downfall. As I said, he was ultimately condemned by a church tribunal and expelled from Normandy.

"His court in exile was, as I said, lavish. He was accompanied to Guernsey by several of his women, and his surviving sons, Michael of Baynes and young Mauger, known as the Bastard of Rouen. It was he who later took the ironic surname St. Mauger and became the direct ancestor of Hillary and Gilbert. There was a coterie of hangers-on and retainers as well. Thoret was in the company, evidently, for several chroniclers mention specifically how difficult he was to manage at the time of his master's death. Nobody has ever quite understood those passages in *Orderic* about the demon, by the way. They are ambiguous reading to say the least."

I pulled my eyes from contemplation of a chunky little tugboat on the river and looked askance at my uncle. "Quite a story. No wonder Gilbert left out a few details."

"Well," Uncle Jeremiah mused, scratching the back of his head idly, "since Thoret was hardly a demon, he may have been a jester of some sort—a dwarf, perhaps. Some scholars have gone so far as to suggest that Mauger was a ventriloquist, though I find it rather hard to imagine a debauched and libertine archbishop entertaining his dinner guests with some sort of demonic eleventh-century Charlie McCarthy perched on his knee. It just doesn't fit."

I giggled. "Edgar Bergen with miter and crosier and Mortimer Snerd with pitchfork and cloven hooves."

"Still," my uncle continued, "they did take it rather seriously back then, and since it was an age of avaricious, practical men, there must have been something to it. The trouble is, no one knows quite what."

"How did Mauger die? Gilbert was very sketchy on the subject."

Uncle Jeremiah came back from his reverie and chortled. "And well he might be, my dear. Mauger was out sailing somewhere in the waters of the Channel Islands, drinking heavily, eating lustily and, one supposes, satisfying his other appetites as well, when he felt the quite understandable urge to heed a call of nature. I put it delicately."

"So I see," I agreed dryly. "Do go on."

"Well, he loosened his belt, dropped his hose, and began to relieve himself. The stockings slipped down his legs—as stockings will do—caught, it would seem, around his knees, and in that unfortunate condition, he lost his balance, fell overboard, and was swept away in the strong current between the islands.

"You can see why Gilbert might be reticent about the demise of his favorite ancestor. It does rather take away from the story to end by saying that he died taking a leak off a pitching boat in a rising sea."

"His body was never recovered, I take it?"

"Oh, on the contrary, it most certainly was. In fact, the story of the recovery is told in one of the more outré passages of *Orderic Vitalis*. They found the body lodged in the rocks on one of the islands, but couldn't retrieve it at first because of Little Thor. He seems to have set himself over the body like a watchdog. It wasn't until some days later, when Thoret himself died—evidently from exposure—that they were able to carry off the corpse."

"That's rather ghastly."

"Yes. You know, I must, just for the fun of it, get out my *Orderic* and look it up again. I wish I had a copy of the original Latin text. I might try my hand at a new translation of those passages and see if I can make some sense of them. Might even publish a paper," he speculated. "Gilbert would love that!"

Meta spent Thursday morning making phone calls, collating the information she had already collected from various churches and cemeteries she had contacted for my uncle, and awaiting the imminent arrival of the chauffeur, Rogers, with a stack of Uncle Jeremiah's material on the descendants of James Pearsall. On top of those chores, she was also seeing to the needs of Guy, whom she had invited—"Poor lamb, all alone"—to sleep in her back bedroom, a situation that I was not happy about at all. It smacked too much of her matchmaking.

When I came downstairs to tell her where I'd be all day, I found Guy sitting at her breakfast table munching his way through a bowl of Skinner's Raisin Bran and bananas while Meta bustled about her kitchen, poaching him an egg.

"Isn't this a cozy little scene," I chaffed. "You two planning to make it legal?"

"I would if she'd have me," Guy retorted. "She sure knows how to take care of a man," he added pointedly.

"I don't doubt that," I agreed. "She's just like the girl that married dear old dad. Aren't you, Meta?" I called into the kitchen. "I'll be off now to the library at Queens College to track down the grant for James Pearsall's original farm. I'm meeting one of the history professors there at noon. Uncle Jeremiah still thinks it's strange that such a young man should have been so well possessed. If I'm lucky, they may have the original land grant and any subsequent sales, hopefully one to James Pearsall himself."

I could have spent several months of my life quite happily picking through the vast collection of books and documents stored behind the doors of Room 101 of the Queens College Library

Professor Sandor Markowitz, one of the leading lights of the history department, had made time for me strictly on the "open sesame" of Uncle Jeremiah's name, and now, five minutes late, he met me at the locked door to Room 101.

He was a big, bearded man of about fifty-five or sixty in a blue oxford-cloth shirt, rust sweater, brown cords, and a brown tweed jacket; affable, rumpled, and, quite typically, with that dazed air of a man with his mind on too many things at once. He shook hands absently and after fumbling with his keys opened the door, switched on the overhead lights, and indicated I should take a chair at one of the tables in the center of the room. A man of few words, obviously.

I opened my leatherette folder and pad and tore off the sheet with the names of James and Forgiveness Pearsall, the date of their marriage, the location of the original farm, and a list of several subsequent land acquisitions that James had evidently made in later years. It added up to a fair-sized chunk of what is now southeast Queens and western Nassau County.

The professor humphed and tapped a pencil against his big front teeth. He wore L. L. Bean duck shoes, of which I had a splendid view, since he sat back in his chair with his feet up on the formica top of the table across from me. He glanced over the material for a few minutes as if digesting it, handed the paper back to me, and rose slowly from the table.

"Come on," he said and led me through the room between gray steel stacks of books and along an aisle of map drawers and microfilm viewers. "We'll blow away the dust and begin on these," he said, taking a set of maps from a long, shallow drawer and setting them on top of a cabinet.

"The area in question was once called Pearsalls. Now its Lynbrook and environs. Back in the sixteen sixties, after the taking of New Amsterdam by the English, a lot of the land was reclaimed from the original Dutch and English settlers who had located there before patents and titles were thought to be necessary. The Pearsalls were among those who lost a good deal in the transition to English rule, so in effect, they had to start all over again.

"Now let's see," he murmured, "that'd be about seventeen twenty-five or so, wasn't it?" He sifted through the survey maps on the cabinet, handling them very carefully, for they were brittle with age. "Hummm, yes. That'd be—well, here's a map dated seventeen twenty-five that shows J. Pearsall as the owner of a tract. Now what we need is some of the earlier ones."

While I looked at the faded, ancient vellum with its slashes of pale brown ink made in a large, round hand by some clerk of nearly three hundred years ago, Professor Markowitz went to another drawer in search of earlier survey maps.

Idly, I turned the map over and saw a list of names, the names, as it happened, of those landholders whose properties were set out on the reverse. There among them were the words "James Pearsall, his mark," followed by the shaky "X" of a young man of means but no education. This very sheet of vellum had been handled and marked by an ancestor of mine, one of the remote fonts from which flows the blood in my living veins. It was a moving moment of realization.

"Yes, here's what we want," the professor boomed with mood-shattering gusto. He brought over another of those great, stiff vellum documents. "This one's dated seventeen twenty. It shows that particular piece of land belonged—damn, the ink's faded," he muttered, squinting through his thick horn-rims at the pale lettering.

He put the map down in front of me and went back down the aisle to fetch a magnifying glass from a desk near the door, but I with my sharp eyes didn't need a glass to read the words "F. Basset" in bold round strokes, which were quite readable by the scratches of the quill pen that had made them, though not by the long-faded ink. After the name "Basset," in small square lettering, less faded, as if the pen had been redipped in the inkpot before going on, was a phrase in Latin: *nothus putatino filia Mordake generosus N. X. N.*

My Latin, suffering from twenty years and more of neglect, failed me shamefully. *Filia* meant daughter, and I could guess at *putatino*, which has the same root as our word putative, but that was as far as I could get. Professor Markowitz, brandishing his trusty magnifying glass, came to my rescue. "Literally, 'F. Basset, illegitimate, reputed daughter of Mordake of noble birth.' The *N.X.N.* stands for 'Christian name not known.' He obtained it by right of his wife, evidently, as a marriage settlement. If she was, as this suggests, the bastard daughter of a nobleman, a dowry like that would serve as a powerful inducement for any prospective husband."

"I wonder if there's a record of her birth anywhere."

"Most likely she was not born on Long Island," the professor said with a shake of his head. "If the father was of noble birth, as *generosus* suggests, she may have been born in England and sent over here to get rid of her and avoid embarrassment. America was a convenient dumping ground for by-blows in those days." The professor had lost his initial disinterest and was as curious as I now to find out more. It was the instinct of the scholar at work, his natural curiosity aroused. "Where were they married? Do you know?"

"I'm not sure. New York certainly, but I don't know what church. Uncle Jeremiah probably knows . . ."

Professor Markowitz strolled down the stacks, pulled a book in a standard black library rebinding off the shelf, and thrust it at me. "Here. See if they're listed in this. Try both Basset and Pearsall. If they were married by the reading of banns rather than by posting of a bond then we're out of luck, but try anyway."

The book so unceremoniously thrust at me was entitled *Names of Persons for whom Marriage Licenses were issued, New York, Previous to 1784*. It had been published in 1860 and listed all those persons who had obtained a marriage license by the posting of a five-hundred-dollar penal bond recorded in the office of the secretary of state of New York. Neither a James Pearsall nor a Forgiveness Basset were listed, nor any Mordake, which I tried as a long shot.

"Damn," I exclaimed, snapping the book shut. "Nothing."

"Drew a blank, huh? Well, don't be discouraged. Sometimes you've got to scattershot your way through the indices of half a hundred books before you hit it right." He continued to sift persistently through stacks of old survey maps. "Take a look at the ships' passenger lists while I keep looking for the original patent granted to F. Basset."

I found the books to which he referred. There were dozens of volumes for various eastern ports and national groups. Some, like books specifically of German immigrants to Pennsylvania and others for Irish immigration or Huguenot, were completely irrelevant to my search, but finally, in a recently published book of ships' passenger lists for New York in the years prior to 1750, I found what I was looking for.

September 25, 1701. Ship *Rose of York*, Joseph Crowell, Master, from Portsmouth, last from Dublin, Ireland. 255 passengers.

Among the passengers were listed:

Basset, Ivy, fem. ae. 17 and infant daughter ae. 1 yr. 2 mos.

It was a heart-stopping thrill to read those words and know the excitement of discovery. "This is it," I called, bustling down the

narrow aisle between the stacks to where Professor Markowitz had
spread out his pile of documents.

"These are land patents issued by the British governor of New
York between seventeen fifteen and seventeen twenty-five. Fortunately, there aren't too many to go through," he said absently,
poring over one of the nearly illegible patents with his magnifying
glass, à la Sherlock Holmes.

"Look at this," I urged excitedly, pushing the book toward him.
"She arrived here as an infant. She must have been born in England,
or perhaps Ireland, since the ship stopped in Dublin, in—let's see—
seventeen hundred, it must have been. Why, her mother was just a
child herself—only seventeen. Ivy Basset. I'm sure this will be new
to my uncle. He's never mentioned the name of her mother and it's
not on his genealogical charts."

Sandor Markowitz looked at the book and then at its publication
date. "It will be new to him, I imagine. The book only came out
last year and it's a new acquisition. Unless he's seen it somewhere
else, he probably doesn't even know of it. See if you can find a
marriage record for Ivy Basset. She may have married once she got
over here and settled."

After a fruitless ten minutes, I finally came across a copy of the
three-volume Pearsall book of which I knew Uncle Jeremiah had a
set in his library at home. I took down the thick third volume,
looked up Forgiveness Basset in the index, and turned to the one
page on which she was listed.

> James Pearsall, son of Charles Pearsall of Hempstead, Long
> Island, New York, Chapter 30, section 1a, resident at Pear-
> salls, now Lynbrook, L.I., N.Y. Died December 12, 1758;
> buried in Sandhole Methodist Protestant churchyard near
> Pearsalls, now Lynbrook, L.I., N.Y. He married Forgiveness
> Basset at St. George's Church, Hempstead. She died October
> 14, 1739, ae. 39 years; buried Sandhole M.P. churchyard.
> Children—

It wasn't much to go on, but on a hunch I asked the professor about church records and he directed me to a shelf at the far end of the stacks. I drew another blank looking for Sandhole M.P. church, but there was a book entitled *Records of St. George's Church, Hempstead, L.I.* in which I found the date of their marriage, which was January 7 of 1722, and the baptismal record of their first living child, my ancestor Ezekial Pearsall, in February of 1724. Their firstborn, Ivy, had been buried in the churchyard in December of 1722.

Most interesting of all to me was the entry for April 4, 1731, of the burial of one Ivy Mordake, widow, age forty-seven. Over the years, it would seem, Ivy Basset had taken unto herself the aura of widowhood and its consequent respectability. I came back to the table where Professor Markowitz was still poring over his patents, holding the book before me as an offering, but my findings, interesting as they were to me and would certainly be to Uncle Jeremiah, held no brief with him.

"Here's what we're after," he said gruffly and shoved a chair in my path. "Sit down and have a look at this."

He presented me with a large, flattened, but once much-folded sheet of thick vellum bearing a red wax seal and a date in April of 1701. It turned out to be, when the professor had deciphered the crabbed, old-fashioned script for me, a patent conveying to E. Mordake, *generosus*, two adjacent parcels of land on Long Island described as consisting of pasturage, farmland, and woodland. Attached were changes of title dated September 30th of the same year, transferring ownership of one parcel to an Ivy Basset and the other to her custody during the minority of her infant daughter, F. Basset, *nothus*, or, to put it succinctly, bastard.

"That ties it all together for you, I think. She was the illegitimate daughter of an E. Mordake who had the wealth and influence necessary to obtain a patent of land and have it transferred to his mistress and her child. Things of that sort did happen, as I told you earlier." He slapped his hands on his knees and stretched.

"Well, now to the microfilm to tie it all together for you." Within another twenty minutes we had confirmed that James Pearsall was the heir-in-chief of his mother-in-law Ivy Mordake. It was the name "Mordake" that was the key to all we had found.

▽

16

OF BIRTH AND DEATH AND
THAT WHICH LIES
BETWEEN

My discoveries in Queens had been so exhilarating that I even beamed on Guy when I arrived home at three-thirty and found him stretched out on my sofa with his feet up, his socks off, and a stack of my books beside him on the floor. He could not have looked more settled in if he'd tried.

"You look comfortable. How's the old collarbone? Mending, I hope."

"Mending," he said, wiggling the finger that peeped from his cast, "mending. I've been browsing through some of your dusty tomes here, Sherlock. You've got quite a taste in weird reading."

"Browsing barefoot, I see. All you need are cheeks of tan. Now do put that book down and listen to me," which he did patiently, not once but twice at least and then heard it all again when Meta came up to join us for soup and sandwiches at seven.

"You keep mentioning that name Mordake," he said. "I've got the strangest sense of déjà vu every time you say it."

"Maybe you knew someone by that name once," Meta suggested.

Guy shook his head. "No, no, it's more recent than that. I came across that name in something I've read recently." He rubbed his eyes and temples distractedly. "Shit, this concussion of mine isn't helping. I could swear—"

Twenty minutes later, he stopped speaking in the middle of a sentence, got up from the table, and with the triumphant cry of "Monsters!" began searching through the pile of books that he had left on the floor by the couch, haphazardly scattering them across the floor with his good arm. "Eureka," he shouted. "You and your uncle may be a pair of Sherlocks and Meta may have Mrs. Hudson's role sewn up, but I make a pretty mean Dr. Watson myself. I knew I'd seen that name—E. Mordake, isn't it?"

"That's it," I confirmed.

"Well, here, read this—or better yet, I will myself. Now listen," he urged and began. The book from which he read was *The Mystery and Lore of Monsters*, a reprint that I had picked up in a remainder bookstore years ago.

" 'One of the most extraordinary, as well as pathetic instances of human deformity is related by Gould, in reference to a young man, Edward Mordake, who is said to have been heir to one of the oldest peerages in England. His figure is said to have been remarkable for its grace and his face was that of an Antoninus, but upon the back of his head was another face, that of a beautiful girl, lovely as a dream, yet hideous as a devil.' "

"Oh, how dreadful," Meta said with a shiver, crossing herself like a nervous Transylvanian villager.

Guy ignored her and went on with relish. "Listen, it gets better. 'The female face was a mere mask, occupying only a small portion of the posterior part of the skull, yet exhibiting every sign of intelligence of a particularly malignant kind.

" 'It would be seen to smile and sneer while the face of the young man was weeping. The eyes would follow the movements of the spectator and the lips would gibber without ceasing.

" 'No voice was audible, but the young man averred that he was kept from his rest at night by the hateful whisperings of his "devil twin," as he called it, "which never sleeps but talks to me forever of such things as they only speak of in hell. No imagination can conceive the dreadful temptations it sets before me. For some

unforgiven wickedness of my forefathers, I am knit to this fiend—
for fiend it surely is. I beg and beseech you," he said to his
physicians, Doctors Manvers and Treadwell, "to crush it out of all
human semblance, even if I die for it." ' "

"Oh God love the poor soul," Meta exclaimed. "Don't read any
more, please."

"Well, there isn't much more anyway. It seems he never claimed
his title and he wound up poisoning himself at the age of twenty-
three."

I put down my spoon and extended my hand across the table
toward Guy. "That's a helluva story. Let me see." I read the short
passage over again to myself. "Can it really be true?" I asked as I
browsed through the rest of the book, which was profusely illus-
trated with line drawings and woodcuts of grotesque human
"monsters" quite obviously taken from a variety of even earlier
sources. "I read this book so long ago that I had forgotten all about
it. The name certainly is coincidental. Edward Mordake is not
exactly Smith or Jones. There are no dates mentioned and no
internal evidence to tie this Edward to the E. Mordake who seems
to have been Forgiveness Basset's father. I suppose though, if I were
the sort of monster that Edward Mordake was and I fathered a
normal child, as one supposes Forgiveness must have been, I might
consider that the 'wickedness' of my forefathers had indeed been
forgiven. The name of the child would be appropriate to the
situation."

I flipped to the back of the book and checked the bibliography.
"Gould and Pyle, *Anomalies and Curiosities of Medicine*, eighteen
ninety-seven. It would be a good idea to look this up. There may
be more information."

Guy volunteered to see if there was a copy in the medical library
up in Pomona.

"I wonder what Uncle Jeremiah will make of all this," I mused.
"I wish he'd come back home soon. There's so much to tell him."

As it happened, I had only to wait till midnight before speaking to my uncle. He called then to say that he'd be on the Concorde from Heathrow the next morning at ten-thirty.

"The blasted thing arrives in New York at nine twenty-five in the morning, which means I shall be arriving before I left, so to speak. Oh, this modern age," he laughed, and I could hear his self-satisfaction carrying three thousand miles via laser beam and telcom satellite all the way from London.

"You've had some success, I suspect, Uncle Jeremiah, haven't you?" I asked.

"Just wait until tomorrow morning. Meet me at International Arrivals and we'll go in to the city for lunch. I've got much to tell you, but nothing so vital that it won't hold. Now, what have you found out on that end?"

"Hold on to your hat. Only the name of Forgiveness Basset's mother, and, by inference at least, her father. She was the bastard daughter of a wealthy man, so the farm James Pearsall owned did come to him through her. The father's name seems to have been E. Mordake."

There was silence on the other end of the line.

"Uncle Jeremiah?"

"Oh, sorry. I am just rather stunned at your success. Mordake, did you say?"

"Yes, E. Mordake. And there's something very funny about it too. By one of those peculiar coincidences that happen now and then, Guy was browsing through a book of mine on anomalies and human mon—"

"Yes, I know. Edward Mordake. He was an example of a janiceps, or two-faced monster. It's an awful story, fairly well known, actually. Now tell me exactly what you found out."

"This must be costing you a fortune. I'll tell you tomorrow."

"No, tell me now," he said, with an abruptness that surprised me, and so I did, going through all the discoveries that I had made at Queens College with the help of Sandor Markowitz. I ended up with Guy's recognition of the name Mordake in my book on monsters. "I drove him home to Pomona just a while ago. He's going back to work tomorrow—not slab work 'cause of his arm being in a cast, but he's got a ton of paperwork to catch up on."

Once again I had the feeling that I was talking to the empty air. "Any news about Elijah Weems's suicide?" he asked at last with an absent tone.

"Nothing new really. The papers and television have been having a field day raking up his 'past'—they've even uncovered a few abortions that must have been done ages ago, from what he said to us—but they're blowing it up into a one-man abortion ring. It's very ugly and I've been trying hard to ignore it all. I'm reading your *Orderic Vitalis*, in fact, as an antidote to the realities of present-day America."

"Good, you do that," Uncle Jeremiah said with what I could sense was an uncharacteristic false heartiness. "But do meet me at Kennedy tomorrow, and bring all the notes you've made. Did you and Mrs. Sullivan make those charts I asked for?"

"Yes, this evening after dinner as a matter of fact. There didn't seem to be any surprises. Oh, and I got that Xerox of the Kennedy Center letter from Pamela Howard. It came in today's mail. It's no help at all by the look of it, but I'll bring it along tomorrow anyway."

"Good. See you tomorrow at nine-thirty. Good night, my dear."

It was strange, driving my uncle, who was used to the spiffiest of antique Rollses, in my nose-bluppy little Mustang that still retained an aura of Molly Brown, despite the fact that I had left her at home, but then Uncle Jeremiah never did, for all his natural elegance, stand on ceremony.

We dined at a quiet table on the east side of Windows on the World at the top of the World Trade Center, overlooking, from the eighty-fifth floor, the incredible panorama of metropolitan New York. Over a nourishing Bloody Mary, I told him about St. Mauger's roses, his visit, and his rather offhand proposal of marriage. Uncle Jeremiah's mind seemed to be on other matters, so I cut my tale short and told him again of the discoveries that I had made with the help of Sandor Markowitz, this time omitting no detail.

By the time our salads had arrived he was telling me all about his visit with Inspector Brent of Scotland Yard and what he had learned about the death of Pamela Howard's sister.

"Samantha Bedell was no random victim of a stranger who followed her and pushed in the door after her in typical New York style." He frowned and shook his white-fringed head in exasperation at the waste of it all. "She was beaten senseless in her own bed by someone whom she knew and perhaps had dated, someone she trusted enough to have brought into her flat. She was a popular girl, well-liked, and had a great many friends. She did have one fairly steady boyfriend, but he was cleared almost at once. He had been on tour with one of the RADA acting companies." He hesitated for a moment and then reached down beside his legs for his briefcase. "She was a very beautiful girl," he said, handing me a picture, and indeed she had been: strong yet refined bone structure, chiseled features, and flawless, creamy skin. Her hair had been chestnut, her eyes green. It was a striking combination. "You would not want to see that face after he got through with it," Uncle Jeremiah said softly. "The man was a sadist.

"It would seem," he continued once our appetizer was put before us, "that she had a date that night. No one—none of her friends— seems to know who he was."

"Not her roommates?" I interrupted.

He shook his head. "Unfortunately for her, as it turns out, the Bedells are quite well-to-do. She had complete control of her inheritance from her parents and did not need the inconvenience of sharing digs. Too bad, that. It might have saved her life. Well, she evidently brought the date home and they had intercourse. Later on, she seems to have admitted still another man—the killer—to the flat. There was no sign of a break-in and no sounds were heard. The only other occupants of the building, in the flat below, were on holiday in the south of France at the time. There must have been a hell of a struggle, though. The bedroom was wrecked, but in the end she was beaten senseless, sodomized, and left for dead. The char found her when she came in at seven the next morning. She was in a coma for two weeks before she died."

I scowled at my escargots, suddenly not relishing them as I had when Uncle Jeremiah placed the order. "How do they know it wasn't the unknown date who killed her? He never came forward, I gather?"

"Uh-uh." He shook his head. "The man with whom she had intercourse that night was not the same man who sodomized her. Both were secreters, so their blood types could be determined from semen samples taken at the crime scene. They indicate two different blood types and therefore two men. I've got copies of all the lab work, by the way. I'll have Rogers bring copies to Guy. I want him to take a look at them and see how they may tie in with what he's got on the Soldano rapist."

"And don't forget paternity. He can determine whether the blood types, either of them, are possible matches with these mooncalves of ours. If neither of them is compatible with their paternity, then it indicates that there is no connection between her attack and what's going on here."

"I can't be certain, of course, but I think you'll find that one of them will match. Look at this."

He handed me a photocopy of a page from Samantha Bedell's appointment book for Friday, January 16th. Among the neatly written entries for various class times was the notation "Dinner with J. Leigh—seven-thirty."

"James Leigh!" I exclaimed sotto voce. "It's got to be Jennifer Pearsall's James Leigh. It's too coincidental!"

"It looks that way, doesn't it?" he asked. "There's something else. The girl smoked pot occasionally—there's no getting around that—and she had smoked some that evening evidently, but the major finding of the toxicological report was the large amount of alcohol and barbiturates in her blood. She may, it seems, have been drugged."

"Just like Valdalene and Jennifer. In fact, Brenda Soldano was rendered unconscious too, wasn't she?"

My uncle nodded. "Chloroform in her case, I believe." He shook his head again slowly. "If it were not for the fact that the semen samples showed two distinct blood types, I'd be inclined to go along with a scenario in which he came home with her, had sex, and then either came back later and was readmitted or else had snapped the latch and returned after she had retired for the night to attack her. Either way, it doesn't work. There were definitely two men—one who had sex with her in the conventional manner and one who sodomized her during or after a violent attack. I don't like it," he concluded with a solemn shake of his head.

He picked up one of the charts I had given him. It covered all the known generations that descended from James and Forgiveness Pearsall and represented the collation of the information that both he and Meta had been able to compile. "I especially don't like it when I look over these charts you've put together for me.

"Jennifer Pearsall, age twenty. She has a nine-year-old sister, Janet, and a fifteen-year-old brother, Michael. She is a fourth cousin of yours, and she is carrying the child—or children, actually—of a man who calls himself James Leigh and who used a fictitious organization called The Kennedy Center for the Perpetuation of the Family to contact her.

"Pamela Bedell Howard, age twenty-six. She has also been contacted by this same Kennedy Center, though they have not been successful in their attempts to use her. Samantha Bedell, her only sister, age twenty, was murdered in the course of what may have been an attempt to impregnate her. She knew someone named J. Leigh. Both she and her sister are—or in Samantha's case were— fifth cousins of yours." He looked at me across the table briefly, and went on reading.

"Valdalene Pearsall, age twenty-seven. She died during the course of an abortion to rid herself of a child conceived for pay by an unknown man called Smith. She also was a cousin of yours, though many times removed. Now she does have a sister, but Ismeralda Jackson, being a half sister on the mother's side, is not a Pearsall and therefore appears to be out of all this.

"Brenda Soldano, on the other hand, age nineteen, is one of many children but is an only daughter. She was raped and sodomized and as a result of the attack bore a child by this unknown father. Adoption had been arranged through the auspices of this same fictitious Kennedy Center. Only the monstrous birth and subsequent death of the infant prevented the adoption. Brenda Soldano stands in a distant but nevertheless quite firm cousinly relationship to every one of you."

"Of us," I murmured, taking my uncle's point readily enough. The chart also showed that I too was a female descendant of James Pearsall and Forgiveness Basset, and, oddly enough, on both sides of my family. The fact had begun to frighten me in spite of the cavalier attitude I had adopted about my own position in the scheme of things.

"You know, I was unable to find any other female descendants of James Pearsall beyond those we already know, which means that whoever it is behind this is as accomplished in this sort of research as I am myself. He seems to have found all there was to find— except for you." He paused, throwing down his fork and gnawing nervously on his mustache. "And you know too that you are descended from both Malachi and Ezekial, two of the three sons of James. Therefore, you constitute a double descent. . . ."

"Yes, but what can that mean?" I asked.

"I do not know, but if someone wants to unite in blood with one line, why then how much more desirable would be a double descent from that very line?"

"But I'm over forty, for heaven's sake. These were all young women and girls."

"You are not yet too old to bear a child, are you?"

"No," I replied soberly.

"Well then, until we get to the bottom of this I do not want you to be alone anymore. It's too bad that you had to send Guy packing back to Pomona last night. I'd rather have him staying there in the house to protect you."

"What, with a cast on his arm?" I laughed. "He can't even cut up his own dinner." Uncle Jeremiah ignored my levity. "Besides, it doesn't even make sense—uniting bloodlines that separated ten generations back." I watched as Uncle Jeremiah pulled out the individual charts that had been done, some of them weeks ago now, on the women involved in the case. He perused Valdalene's chart closely and then mine. "Why a Pearsall connection?"

"I don't know," he repeated thoughtfully. "Wouldn't it be odd," he muttered more to himself than to me, "if there were no Pearsall connection after all. . . ." He put down the charts and stared blindly through the tall window at which we sat, looking out over the vast expanse of Brooklyn, Queens, and Long Island toward the gray infinity of the Atlantic. "No Pearsall connection at all. . . ."

Saturday morning dawned uninvitingly gray and cold. It was the first morning in over a week that I had nothing pressing to do, so I rolled over and slept late.

At eleven, just as I was finishing breakfast, the phone rang. It was Peter, sounding slightly odd. I couldn't quite put my finger on it, but there seemed to be a strange note in his voice. It wasn't until a week later that I learned that Uncle Jeremiah had asked him to keep an eye on me. He asked me to join him on a trip to Cold Spring to pick up some copy from a contributor to the paper. He needed the company, he said.

With each mile north along Route 9W, I felt the tension of the past weeks leaving me at an ever faster rate. I heaved a sigh and leaned back luxuriously into the deep bucket seat of Peter's Mercedes. The trees were almost bare now this far up the Hudson, but the woodland floor was still a blaze of vivid oranges and golds against the gray of the day.

"What's the sigh for?" Peter asked, not taking his eyes off the winding, narrow road.

"Contentment," I answered. "I haven't had more than a day or two since the beginning of this month to just relax and think of nothing at all. It's all been mooncalves, autopsies, pregnant ladies, rape, sodomy, hospitals, and funerals." I shook my head in a sort of wonder at it. "It's been too much, really. I think it's finally caught up with me."

Peter gave me a thoughtful look, wrinkling his mouth into a wistful smile. "What you're saying is that you need a break. I'm glad I called."

"Me, too," I murmured almost drowsily. We drove in a companionable silence for a while, exchanging occasional glances at times when our unspoken thoughts must have turned on each other. Then we passed by Hootersville, which lay directly across the river from the Indian Point Nuclear Power Plant. The huge domes and ugly stacks hove up out of the Westchester County landscape with the relentlessness of a nightmare.

Peter rumpled his seamy leather face and nodded at it. "God, look at that monster—sitting on top of the Ramapo Fault like a disaster waiting to happen."

With the juxtaposition of those two thoughts, monsters and disasters, my idling mind returned to gear. "A disaster waiting to happen," I mused. "That's sort of the way it was for that old man, Elijah Weems, wasn't it? His life was in shambles already. The final disaster was just waiting to happen and it did."

"What got you off on that subject, Miranda?" Peter asked.

"Just after you phoned this morning I got a call from Ismeralda Jackson. She was in tears, very upset. It seems that Dr. Weems made out a will the day he decided to kill himself. He left everything he had—insurance, the residual from a small annuity, and the ten thousand due him from Baroness Derevenkov's estate—to Ismeralda, to help her raise Valdalene's children. She is to use it in whatever manner she sees fit.

"You know, Peter, on Wednesday night when I watched the news coverage of his suicide on the networks, I was struck by the callousness of people. They brought their Minicams onto the street outside his office and asked people about him, got them to tell about abortions he had performed and the times when he'd fallen down drunk in the street. No one said a word about the bills he must have forgotten over the years—he wasn't rich, God knows— or the lives he must have saved, the ear he must have given to people in distress, or the loss of his family." I became lost in a reverie, my mind's eye picturing a wide-eyed, street-smart Hispanic boy of about fourteen who had smiled into the camera lens like an infant Erik Estrada and told how, unlike some neighborhood doctors, he refused to sell pills and tried to "talk to them dudes who think they smart, man, an' do drugs, ya know. Nobody pay no 'tention to him, like you know, man, but they respec' him, man, fo' trying to keep the little kids clean."

But that was not enough epitaph. That was not the final word on Elijah Weems any more than suicide by hanging, strung up by the length of those two worn leather belts, was his last act. His last act on earth had been a bequest, an attempt to right in some small measure what had been a terrible, terrible wrong.

It was as if Peter had read my mind. He whistled softly for a moment and then said, "He must have been a helluva decent man. You know, it occurs to me, would you like a column or two for a short windup piece on him? I've got the space."

"Thanks, Peter, I'll take you up on that offer. I do want to say a few things before the world forgets him." I smiled across the seats at him, feeling grateful and relieved. "You're a dear man, Peter."

The rest of the afternoon was perfect. We whizzed over the Bear Mountain Bridge, drove along 9D through Garrison and, after picking up the copy from a local Cold Spring writer, we parked the car and walked down the long main street of the town toward the river, browsing in and out of antique shops.

We walked along the river eating ice cream cones in the cold gray light, with the granite skeleton of an ancient mountain loom- ing over the narrow river across from us, and finally, much later, stopped at a country inn in Garrison for dinner.

I sipped a whiskey sour and watched Peter as he read the menu through a pair of black horn-rimmed glasses perched halfway down his long nose. His thick salt-and-pepper hair was still tousled by the wind along the river and his grizzled eyebrows were knit in concentration. As I watched him, I realized that of all the men I knew, he was the most attractive, the most comfortable to be with, and the most appealing as a human being—Uncle Jeremiah excepted, naturally.

Age had worn him, refined and polished him, but age had not made him old. He wore his sixty-three years quite well. He was easy, kind, good-natured, and usually cheerful, with none of the self-centered middle-aged neuroses and depressions of a Max or the impatient, insistent, youthful callousness of a Guy.

Peter looked up over the top of his glasses just then, and did a small double take at my expression. "What's up?"

I shook my head. "Nothing. I was just looking at you. You're a very nice man."

"Just finding that out?" he said easily and went back to perusing the menu. The tiniest of smiles appeared in the corner of his wide mouth. "The sweetbreads are very good here, you know," he said quietly.

It was as simple as that: a small jolt in the region of my heart, and I had fallen in love . . . and for once in my life, it didn't seem to hurt.

On Sunday morning I awoke in Peter Polhemus's great-grandfather's bed—a monstrous carved walnut thing that must have been the ultimate in luxury circa 1860. It looked like it belonged in the Lincoln bedroom at the White House. I yawned and stretched, and, leaning up on one elbow, began to trace the carved roses with my fingertip.

From the bathroom across the hall I could hear the homey sound of tapwater running. "Like that bed, do you? I was born in it, you know." Peter came into the bedroom naked, still lean, still well-muscled despite his age, drying his face in a towel. "I thought I'd better shave before—" He left the rest of the sentence unspoken, but since he was obviously ready to continue where we had left off the night before, no further words were needed.

Our lovemaking was long and intense—passionate love, noisy and sweating, culminating in one last incredible, convulsive shudder that left us both spent and joyous. We lay together for a long while after that, each lost in our own thoughts.

"What are these?" he asked, playing with the two silver sixpence pieces that hung together from the chain that Ismeralda had given me. I had been wearing them since the previous Monday at Valdalene's funeral.

"You were with me at the Hudson Street Tearoom the day I found that coin. It was in the dirt in the garden, remember? Well, Valda found the other one. She considered it to be a lucky piece. We both find—or found—things. I don't know what it means."

"What things?" Peter asked gently.

I shrugged, avoiding his eyes. "Coins, bills, pins, broken lockets, rings, all sorts of stuff. You name it. We both found things. I found her baby—"

"Your dog found the baby," he corrected. "Maybe you find things because you're searching for something," he suggested.

I was puzzled. "Searching? What do you mean?"

"Tell me, do you think Valda was happy with her life?"

"No, of course not."

"Are you?"

"What? I—I don't know. No, I suppose I'm not. I need—"

"What do you need?" he asked, nestling me closer to him.

"Love, security, contentment. A sense of belonging. A place that's my own where I feel I belong. I don't have that yet."

"So, you find things. Maybe when you find what it is you're searching for, the finding things will stop," he suggested.

I thought about that for a moment. It was simple psychology and sounded plausible, yet I hesitated to accept it as an explanation of what has been a lifelong quirk. I had the feeling that St. Mauger would be more likely to understand the underlying mysticism of it and to tolerate the eerie feelings I had when I thought of Valda and her Grandmama Williams who had been a Debbins and me and my two grandmothers. Of the five, four were descendants of James Pearsall—and all "finders of things."

"You think so? Is it really that simple?" I reached up to my throat and felt the warmth of the two coins, each in its circular holder, lying side by side against my skin.

"It's not simple at all. It's as complex as the human mind, but it's not magic. My point is that there's no psychic bond between you and a dead hooker." He stroked me gently as he spoke. "Sorry. That was a harsh word, but you know what I mean." He began to kiss me softly, following the curve of my neck down to my breasts.

"Maybe you're right," I said, but not because he had convinced me that he was correct. Rather, I had come to realize quite suddenly that there really was no "psychic bond," as Peter called it, between Valda and me or between me and my grandmothers. The bond, if it existed at all, linked all of us with someone else.

By my three o'clock deadline, I had completed my little article on Elijah Weems and handed it in to Peter with a sense of relief. Without giving the details, I gave the thrust of his last will and testament and tried to mitigate the harm done to his reputation by those paragons of yellow journalism in the city. It was the last small thing that I or anyone else could do for him.

I came into the apartment just in time to pick up the phone before Guy gave up.

"Hello."

"Hi, happy Halloween," he crowed cheerfully into the receiver. Behind him I could hear a babble of shrill voices engaged in some sort of nerve-racking altercation. "Or happy tomorrow anyway. It's actually tomorrow."

"Halloween? Is it really? God, so it is. I totally forgot. Thanks for reminding me. I'll have to get some candy for trick or treats."

"That's not why I called, and I've got the kids with me for the day. You know, the weekend-father bit. In fact, we're on our way to McDonald's for dinner. I just want to read you something— from Gould and Pyle, remember?"

"Oh great, you found the book," I cried.

"Well, the references to the Mordake janiceps are almost word for word the same as in the edited-down version reprinted in Thompson. There is, however, one very interesting portion that I want to read to you. Now listen to this. 'In spite of careful watching by his faithful personal servant, Thomas Basset—' "

"Basset!"

Guy chuckled. "I thought that'd get you. Listen, there isn't much more. '—careful watching by his faithful personal servant, Thomas Basset, he managed to procure poison, whereof he died, leaving a letter requesting that the "demon face" might be destroyed before his burial, "lest it continues its dreadful whisperings in my grave." At his own request he was interred in a waste place, without stone or legend to mark his grave, and "my issue, if it live, to be sent away from this place forever." ' How do you like them apples?"

"Holy smoke," I murmured, scrounging through the notebook on my desk for the notes I had made in Queens. "Guy, Forgiveness Basset was born in July of seventeen hundred. Does it say when he took the poison?"

"It just mentions the date as 'in seventeen hundred and one' but no specific month."

"Close enough. Christ, wait till Uncle Jeremiah hears this. Thanks so much. This is great."

"Thought you'd be happy. Well, on to McDonald's for me."

It wasn't until a full three minutes after I had hung up that the implications of this new information hit me.

First, all of us who were descended from Forgiveness Basset— Uncle Jeremiah, me, Valdalene, Jennifer Pearsall, and the Bedell sisters—were descendants of Edward Mordake as well.

Second, there was no Pearsall connection. There wasn't even a Basset connection per se. The thread running between the pieces of this mad patchwork of mystery was Edward Mordake—and Edward Mordake had been a mooncalf.

$\triangledown$

17

EXEUNT AN EIGHTEENTH-
CENTURY GENTLEMAN

I spoke to Uncle Jeremiah at once, telling him excitedly about Guy's call and the fact that Edward Mordake had had a personal servant named Basset. His phlegmatic reaction was hardly what I had expected. It took me rather by surprise.

"Yes, my dear. I've already made that discovery. I have a copy of *Anomalies* here in my own library. I found Basset's name Friday afternoon when I returned home."

"And you didn't call? Isn't it important?"

"Oh, my dear child, forgive me, but I have been so busy. And yes, it is important. For one thing, it means that we have all sorts of new lines of inquiry to pursue vis-à-vis our genealogy. Moreover, its implications in regard to this mystery of ours are leading me to some very disturbing possibilities, ones of which I hardly dare think. I have been following down leads into the wee hours of every night, and frankly I am becoming brain-weary."

"You do sound tired."

"I am, very, and I am concerned as well. I am on the verge of putting it all together. I know that, and yet, for some reason I cannot seem to concentrate. The solution is there to be found, yet it continues to elude me. . . . I almost get the feeling that I do not want to know. Psychologists call it denial, I believe," he concluded dryly.

"Uncle Jeremiah, we are all of us descended from Edward Mordake through our ancestress, Forgiveness Basset, are we not?"

"So it would seem, though of course, conclusive proof is lacking."

"Then we are all descended from a—a mooncalf—a teras, if you will, and someone knows it, has known it for some time, and for God only knows what insane reason, wants to beget a child with that particular heredity. That is it in a nutshell, isn't it?" I didn't wait for an answer. "Now, Guy has been saying all along that he thinks the father of these mooncalves of ours is—oh, damn, what is the word I'm groping for?"

"Teratogenerative," my uncle suggested.

"Yes, that's it. Now, if this man is teratogenerative and seeks by fair means or foul to link his bloodlines with those of the descendants of another possibly teratogenerative line, then—"

"Then the man must be insane," he suggested very softly.

"Insane, yes," I agreed enthusiastically, "but mustn't he also have a great deal of very specialized genealogical knowledge if he knows about Forgiveness Basset's ancestry? I mean, you didn't know, did you?"

There was a pause at the other end of the line. "Yes, that is true, Miranda," he said at last. "In all my years of research, and especially since my retirement, when I began my studies in earnest, I have never traced the Basset line. Of course, there seemed to be no compelling reason to do so, you understand. So many lines in a genealogy end in a blank wall that one gets used to it. One simply drops that area of research and goes on to other, more promising ones, but if I had taken the time to go to the original documents as you did for me on Thursday, why, I might have stumbled onto this Mordake connection years ago. How I wish that I had."

"That's water over the dam, Uncle Jeremiah. The point is we are hot on the trail now. Suppose I come down there tomorrow and we'll go over all our notes and the lab reports and everything and try to put it together. I'll bring every scrap of information I've collected ever since the first mooncalf was found and between us maybe we can lick this thing. You know what they say about two heads being better than one—the Soldano baby excepted, naturally."

"That might be a good plan," he murmured thoughtfully.

"Uncle Jeremiah, it's got to be. We haven't much time. Remember, that kid, Jennifer Pearsall, is carrying twins for this madman and we've got to have a way to prove that what we believe to be happening really *is* happening. How do we hope to convince her or the police or anyone that someone is out to create a monster? How, for heaven's sake, do we save her from whatever is going to happen once these infants are born?" I stopped to catch my breath for a second and then continued headlong. "And another thing. She's got her monthly checkup with the Kennedy Center in a few days. I'd rather like to join her on that visit to the center, and have the law right behind us all the way."

Somehow, the more I talked the better I felt. It was as if I sensed the end was in sight and that with the discovery of the Mordake connection, the secret of the mooncalves was within our grasp.

"You sound very enthusiastic," my uncle commented.

"Aren't you, Uncle Jeremiah?"

"Well, yes, I suppose I am. I think it is just plain brain-weariness that's got me down. I'm here at my desk surrounded by legal pads, charts, genealogical references, a copy of Burke's *Extinct Peerage and Baronage*, and heaven knows what else. I've even been dipping into *Orderic Vitalis* for light reading.

"In fact," he said, his voice brightening as he relaxed a bit, "I've borrowed Gilbert's copy of the original Latin text. Thought I'd try a new translation of the passages concerning Mauger and his devil, Little Thor, if only just to take my mind off our mystery for a few hours. Sometimes distraction is good for the little gray cells, and I find myself rather drawn to that peculiar old puzzle."

"Yes, I've been dipping into the *Orderic* you gave me, too. Now, shall I come down for a visit tomorrow?" I persisted.

He sighed in resignation. "Yes, do, my dear. Plan to stay

overnight, and bring Molly Brown along as well. She can catch a mouse for Mrs. Lynch."

At that I laughed. He sounded better and I felt relieved. "I have shopping and laundry to do in the morning. I'll aim for midafternoon." I started to say good-bye when something else occurred to me. "Oh, Uncle Jeremiah, please, if you see St. Mauger, don't tell him that I'm coming down or invite him over. I'd feel rather funny, you know, having been proposed to and so on."

"I wouldn't dream of it. Besides, he's packed his mother and sister off to Europe—for good, I presume, by the vanload of luggage his caretaker loaded and drove off with last week. I haven't seen hide or hair of him since Friday evening when I borrowed his Latin *Orderic*."

"Good. Now I shall wish you a good evening. I'll see you tomorrow about three or so," I said. "Oh, and happy Halloween, Uncle Jeremiah. Tomorrow's the thirty-first. Love you."

"Happy Halloween," he chuckled, "and I love you too, dear."

Whatever Meta may have thought of my sudden liaison with Peter, she had been discreet enough to say nothing about it when I arrived home late Sunday morning. It was a slightly different story, however, when she came up to visit on Monday morning after breakfast. It was five after nine and Peter had only just pulled away from the curb outside the house when she knocked, so I was sure she was aware he had been with me all night.

"Hi, landlady mine, have a cup of tea with me?" I chirped as I opened the door and returned to the kitchen.

"If you like, luv," she said solemnly as she followed me across the living room floor.

"Peter just left," I said, taking the bull by its horns.

She made a prim face. "What about Guy? He's very fond of you, and Peter's a bit old, isn't he?"

"And I'm fond of him, but what about him? If anything, he's a bit young for my taste. Besides, I suspect he carries, hidden behind his back, the same sort of collar and leash that Max slipped around my throat not so long ago. Peter at least has both hands out in the open where I can see them: no strings, no collars, no leashes. Besides, to quote the immortal Burt Reynolds, 'the older ones are so grateful.' What Burt evidently hasn't learned yet is that the same applies to men."

"That sounds very cynical," she said, looking mortified.

"I am cynical," I agreed cheerfully as I set the teapot on the dining table and brought her a fresh cup. "You know the old saying 'Sufficient unto the day is the evil thereof'? Well, my new motto is going to be 'Sufficient unto the love affair is the sex therein.' I may just embroider that sentiment on a pillow, in fact."

Meta looked across the table at me balefully.

"Oh, hell, Meta, I'm sorry, really I am. I don't mean to be flip. I just happen to need a nice, solid, sensible, strong father figure right now, and Peter fills that bill to a T. The fact that he happens to be a superior lay is just icing on the cake."

She winced slightly and reached across the table to pat my hand and say she was sorry. "I shouldn't interfere, I suppose. It's just that I don't understand you modern young women."

"I'm not so sure we modern women understand us ourselves, and thanks for the 'young.' "

"Just be happy," she said, and I knew she meant it.

By noon, I had done some much-needed laundry, shopped, and made up a hundred or so little bags of well-wrapped trick-or-treat candies for the local children. I was just about to bring my basket of goodies downstairs to Meta, who had agreed to give them out with her own after I left for Uncle Jeremiah's, when the phone began to ring.

"Collect call for Miss Fay from Jennifer. Will you accept?"

"Yes, yes, operator. Is that you, Jennifer?"

"Yes, it is, but not Jennifer Pearsall," she giggled, and for one brief instant I thought she must be high.

"Not—?"

"Not any more I'm not. Can you imagine? I'm Mrs. James

Leigh now. Really. I'm a married lady. Isn't it wonderful? Can you imagine? I was just telling you how much I love him and now it's happened. He loves me, too."

"How—how wonderful for you, darling." Through the buzzing in my head I began to think more clearly. "Now, slow down and tell me all about. How did it happen? Where?"

"I can't talk long. I'm—oh, you can't guess where I am! I just know you can't." She was burbling on like a child, and my dismay and shock were rapidly turning to exasperation. Behind her there was a low babble of voices that aroused misgivings.

"Tell me, dear," I urged.

"I'm at Kennedy Airport. I'm going on a honeymoon, a real honeymoon, to Paris—"

Oh, God, no. She was married to a madman and on her way out of the country.

"Is he there with you at the phone? Can I speak to the bride-groom to wish him well?" I tried to sound bright.

"No, he's down by the gate with his family. I said I had to use the ladies' room. He's got to stay here and wind up some business, but he's coming over after us in a few days. That's when our honeymoon will really start. I'm going to buy clothes in Paris so I look good for him. Oh, Miss Fay, I'm so happy. I'm so lucky."

"Yes, yes, you are, I'm sure. Tell me how he proposed, dear. Where were you married?"

"What? Oh, yesterday in Baltimore. You only have to wait forty-eight hours after you get the license in Maryland. We didn't even need a blood test. It was so easy."

"What made him propose? When you spoke to me last Wednes-day—"

"He came by that very night and said—oh, it was so romantic. He said he got Dr. Kennedy to give him my address, even though it's against the rules, you know, 'cause, you know, he couldn't stop thinking of me. He asked if he could take me out to dinner. Oh, I could hardly believe it."

"Go on, Jennifer, please."

"I told him it was twins and he was so happy. He said twins run in his family. He kissed me—my hand—which was so romantic, and he nearly cried, honest. He said that it gave him courage to hope maybe I could overlook how old he was and homely—he's not homely, really, just kinda fat—and he asked if I would become his wife and raise the babies with him. He said he was lonely.

"Oh, Miss Fay, we both cried and I said yes and we all drove down to Maryland—his family and Mrs. Sidney and Dr. Kennedy and—oh, I'm so happy."

"His family? Who—?"

"Uh oh, they're calling our plane. I've got to run. I'll send you a postcard—"

Before I could say another word, she had hung up and our tenuous connection was irretrievably broken.

It began to sprinkle just as I opened the car door. I had an overnight bag, notebooks, file folder, and bag of dog food cans and biscuits in hand, and Molly Brown, tangling me in her leash, at my heels. Meta saw me from the window and came out with an umbrella for me.

"They say it's going to pour this afternoon, luv, and maybe even snow before midnight. You'd better have this."

"Thanks, you're a dear," I said as she slipped it through the driver's side window onto the back seat. She noticed that I was upset and I wound up telling her about Jennifer Pearsall's call.

By the time I rolled the car off the ferry at St. George, it was windy and raining in fine, horizontal silver needles. Large yellow maple leaves slapped themselves against everything—cars, pedestrians, shop windows, and fences, their wetness gluing them to whatever they touched.

As I drove up the winding, hilly street that was Dissoway Drive, the first hardy trick-or-treaters, in damp costumes and still loaded with school books, were beginning their trek from door to door carrying optimistically large shopping bags or one of the gaudy neon-orange plastic pumpkin heads that have replaced the mellow burnt-orange papier-mâché jack-o-lanterns of my youth. They made a colorful contrast in their bedraggled finery and ragamuffin patches to the polished, leaden gray sky overhead and the stark wet blackness of the bare tree trunks rising to either side of the winding road. The fleeting image of little Valentine, who was going to be a Smurf on this day of days, passed before my eyes and I smiled faintly at the vision.

To my surprise, the big iron gates of the driveway were pulled almost shut, though, by the way the padlock and chain hung, I could see that they were not actually locked. I turned into the drive, honked once to announce my arrival, and got out to pull the gates open. Molly shot past me, scurried through the narrow opening, and scooted into the garden, barking joyously.

After I had pulled the car up as far as the porte cochere, I walked back down the path to close the gates again. A gaggle of trick-or-treaters approached, grumbling at having been turned away from St. Mauger's house across the way. I waved, told them to take the main path to the house, and, cutting across the wet lawn to beat them to the front door, I rang my uncle's doorbell. There was no answer.

It was then I noticed that, like the driveway gates, the front door had been left slightly ajar.

I pushed the door open and immediately noticed a huge bowl of lavishly bulging trick-or-treat bags, each one neatly tied at the top with an orange ribbon. It sat on a table by the door in readiness for the afternoon and evening.

Calling out and receiving no answer, I turned and handed out a bag to each of the children as they came up the steps. I wished them a happy Halloween and called Molly into the house. I'd get my things from the car later.

There was something in the atmosphere—an emptiness that went beyond mere lack of occupancy. There was a strange, chill sense of something nameless that repelled me before I could properly define it. Molly sensed it even more quickly than I. She trotted around the perimeter of the front hall, clicking her claws on the parquet between the Oriental throw rugs, sniffing the air busily. Her raised hackles bristled along the length of her back like those of a boar. Having circled once, she ran between the open doors of the library and disappeared out of sight in the direction of my Uncle Jeremiah's beautiful eighteenth-century pedestal desk. In no more than a second I heard her give out the most bloodcurdling, heart-stopping howl that I have ever heard from the throat of an animal.

I felt my own hackles rise. It was as if I had ceased to breathe or to feel. There was no further sound after that one long achingly poignant cry of Molly's; neither the sound of blood rushing in my ears nor of my heart pounding in my breast. It was as if all the senses of the world had stopped and in their place was only dread.

The eighteenth-century gentleman was dead. I knew it even before the double doors swung fully open to reveal his body, upright and lifeless, at his desk.

I did not know then how he had died, only that he was dead and that he had been so for some time. If I had touched him, which I did not, I knew his skin would have been cold already to the touch; his hands, which rested on the burgundy leather arms of his chair, rigid and stonelike. Already his eyes, wide open as if surprised by that White Camel of his fancy, were glazed and opalescent.

For one brief moment my eyes welled with tears. For one brief moment, before the numbness descended upon my heart, I felt an agony impossible to describe. But the numbness did fall over me like a merciful veil, the doorbell did ring, and Molly Brown did run to the door barking. I followed in her wake like an automaton, hearing as if I were in an echo chamber the voices of children shrieking out their threat of tricks or treats on the porch.

I opened the door and handed out my Uncle Jeremiah's treats. The trick had already been played.

I am not sure how long it was before Mr. and Mrs. Lynch pulled up to the house in a battered old Hillman-Minx with the trunk and the back seat full of the week's grocery shopping, but I do know they must have thought me mad—standing in the open door giving out candy to wet, lively children in garish, ghoulish costumes while Uncle Jeremiah sat cold at his desk.

Mrs. Lynch, once they had discovered what was wrong, led me away from the door, wrapped me gently in an afghan, and sat me down in a chair in the big, warm kitchen at the back of the house. She poured a glass of blackberry brandy that seared my throat as I drank it, bringing tears to my eyes and making me shiver.

Lynch himself, looking ashen, came into the room from the library and shook his head slowly, confirming what I already knew and had not wanted to face.

"I've called his doctor and the police. They're on their way. Rogers just pulled into the driveway. I've instructed him to move all our vehicles into the garage to make way for the—the ambulance." He spoke with the calm authority of a good and faithful servant, trained to manage and to keep his reserve no matter the occasion. A great depth of feeling lay beneath the serene surface he presented to us that afternoon, and I admired him for it.

Mrs. Lynch, a soft-faced, plump woman in her fifties with red hands and lank hair, lacking her husband's professional discipline, gave way and wept copiously into a linen dish towel, her every tear a counterpoint and a reproach to the numbness that had descended upon me like a pall. I heard, I saw, I spoke, but I neither felt nor thought nor reasoned. It was not until long after that I realized what the Lynches had known all along: I was in shock.

Little else is as calculated to bring one back to a semblance of reality as the solid presence and flat voice of a policeman doggedly asking questions in pure New Yorkese, and so it was that by questioning all of us—the Lynches, Rogers, and myself—the police were able to reconstruct the events of the day as they must have happened, and by doing so, bring me back to myself.

Rogers had been the first to leave, setting off from Staten Island at about eleven. He stopped along the way for lunch, finally delivering the material from London to Guy Galveston at his office in Pomona at about one-thirty or so. He returned home at a leisurely pace, knowing he was not needed for the rest of the day. He had pulled up to the gates on Dissoway Drive just behind the Lynches in their Hillman at about three twenty-five.

Mrs. Lynch had spent part of the morning making up the trick-or-treat bags that I had found on the hall table and preparing menus for the week to come. Her husband had served my uncle his lunch on a tray in the library at twelve-thirty. This was not his usual habit, but he had not wanted to take time from his research for a more formal meal at the dining-room table. As a consequence, the couple had left for the nearest Food Emporium over the ferry in Manhattan to do the week's shopping rather earlier than was usual for them.

By the time this information had been elicited from the others, I was sufficiently aware of reality to describe my arrival, the dog's reaction, and then my discovery of my uncle's body.

Brandy, hot tea, and the necessity of answering the officer's questions had brought me around so that I was quite aware of the hushed bustle in the hall that signaled the removal of Uncle Jeremiah's body to the mortuary van that stood under the porte cochere at the side of the house.

From somewhere in the front garden I heard a shout and a cry and then the fall of light, swift footsteps on the porch. "I must be allowed to enter. I am practically family. Please." The voice, shrill and nearly cracking, was that of Gilbert St. Mauger.

I shut my eyes and passed a hand across my forehead.

"Oh, damn, tell them to let him in, please. He's an old friend and neighbor of my uncle's. This will be a great shock to him."

Lynch had directed Gilbert discreetly away from the library, where the police, an assistant medical examiner, and my uncle's doctor were still in consultation, and led him into a small parlor behind it. I entered just after him and Lynch left us alone, closing the door in his wake.

"Oh, Gilbert, I'm so sorry you had to find out like this. I should have remembered you were home."

"I wasn't. I just arrived this moment," he said abruptly. "I didn't expect to find you here."

I nodded. "It's Uncle Jeremiah. He's . . . gone." I could not bring myself to use any more final word than that. "I found him . . ."

"Yes. I came home just in time to see him . . ." He turned to me, dry-eyed but anguished. "I can hardly bear to think that I shall never see him again or speak with him."

Not knowing quite what to say, I filled the silence between us with parroted facts. "The doctor says he had a mild heart attack a few years ago," I said, drawing closer to Gilbert and putting my hand on his arm.

"He never seemed any age at all. He was like a father to me, you know. I cannot think of life without him. I shall miss him dreadfully." He began to weep copious tears, the drops falling down those smooth, plump, choirboy cheeks of his like rain. For a moment I found his display of emotion actually repellent, but that was unfair of me. He had loved Uncle Jeremiah after all, and known him far better than I. Upon that thought followed an overwhelming rush of quite unreasonable jealousy. I couldn't speak.

"If only," he said at last, "if only you had accepted me last week, how very different things might have been." He paused and sighed deeply. "We could have held and comforted each other in ways that now cannot ever be. It is too late, and too much has changed." His words were spoken softly with a tone of regret and yet there was a note of dispassion and reproach. "Now it can never be," he repeated firmly as he drew away from me. "I must be alone now, Miranda. I shall be across the way if you need me. You'll let me know about the funeral, of course."

"Yes, yes, of course," I stammered.

I felt somehow incredibly guilty, as if all this were my fault— his pain, my pain, our isolation from each other even as we embraced and wept together in our mutual sorrow. His manner had grown so reserved that it constituted a rebuke. He passed one plump hand across his moist eyes to wipe them dry. Gray afternoon light from the tall windows glinted on his wet cheeks, on the bright gold of the ring on his hand, and on the last silvery teardrop that hung from his smooth, round chin.

"I'll let you know, naturally," I said. "The plans will be handled by his executors, I expect."

He turned and left without another word. I heard the front door close behind him.

By five, Uncle Jeremiah's house was empty, not only of his presence, but also of his doctor, the police, the medical examiner's assistant, ambulance attendants, and of all save Rogers and the Lynches, who sat around the kitchen table like lost souls, drinking strong tea or whiskey in morose silence.

I had made no calls, no plans, done nothing at all since Gilbert's abrupt departure, except to walk Molly through the wet garden while rain ran through my hair and dripped down my neck in icy trickles. A northwest wind was blowing, bringing colder air with it, so that finally, feeling quite chilled, I was forced to go back into the house. I tiptoed into Uncle Jeremiah's library as if it were a shrine of my own particular devotion. If only I had not pulled him into this situation. Perhaps the guilt that lay on me like a sodden blanket was well earned.

His chair was empty now, and the great flat expanse of his pedestal desk bare and eloquent of his passing. The pens lay neatly in the trough of the pen tray that matched his big bronze inkstand; his yellow legal pad, carefully squared with the edge of the desk, was blank and inviting, waiting in vain now for thoughts that would never come. A stack of books rested on the corner of the desk nearest me, as carefully squared as the notepad, awaiting hands that would never open them. I cocked my head idly and read the titles: *Great Tales of Terror and the Supernatural*, a battered copy of *The King in Yellow*, *Famous Ghost Stories*, and a new biography of William Rufus, king of England.

In the corner of the library was the narrow spiral staircase that led up to his lounge and bedroom suite on the second floor. I climbed the steps and wandered around the lounge, past all the neatly ranked shelves of books and the comfortable rump-sprung leather sofas set before the fireplace, finally coming to the double doors in the far wall, beyond which his bedroom lay.

What was evidently his latest bedtime reading—two aged John Dickson Carr "locked-room" mysteries—rested on the nightstand with a pair of reading glasses. His elegant carved mahogany bed with its pineapple finials and exquisite silk brocade spread awaited him in vain.

Perhaps it was that old Dell paperback edition of *The Three Coffins* and a newer copy of *The Judas Window* lying on the bedside table, perhaps it was the neat blankness of the pad of yellow ruled paper on his desk down in the library, or perhaps it was the titles of the books that were *not* on his desk . . . or in the lounge beside the comfortable sofas . . . or even on the shelves where they belonged . . .

I had always been good at solving the mysteries I read. This, however, was a real mystery, and the clues—or lack of them—were staring me in the face. I walked back through each room—the bedroom, the lounge, the library—checking shelves, reading the titles of books that lay in neat stacks on various surfaces, riffling through the blank notebooks and pads that lay on his desk and nearby chairs, until I had satisfied myself thoroughly.

With each passing minute, with each new realization of what I saw and did not see, the sorrow and the desolation of my loss—and even some of the guilt—drained from me, leaving in their place a cold, implacable fury and a bitter craving for revenge.

I picked up the telephone on my uncle's neat, well-ordered desk and made my first call of the afternoon. It was to Guy Galveston, to ask his help and to tell him that Uncle Jeremiah had been murdered.

"Are you sure they'll do an autopsy?" Guy asked.

"No, I'm not sure. He had a wonky heart, but his doctor did not want to sign a death certificate. He hadn't expected anything like this and so he's reluctant, naturally. But now I'm certain it was not his heart, and I want an autopsy done. I'll give you the doctor's number if that will help." I reached for the leatherbound address book beside the phone and read it off to him.

"Listen, Miranda, before you hang up, your uncle's chauffeur dropped off those lab reports from London this afternoon. I've looked them over. Do you want to hear what I found or would you rather put it on the back burner for a while? Under the circumstances—"

"No, no, tell me right now." I started to reach for that blank pad, instantly thought better of it, and found some letter paper. "I've got a pen and paper ready. Go on."

"First, neither of the blood types of the two men whose semen samples were found on the girl matches the blood type of the suspect they were originally holding for the Soldano rape-sodomy, and since Brenda bathed before she reported the attack, there's no way of checking either sample against that of her attacker.

"However, I've made note of some interesting facts. Both of the blood types are very much compatible with the blood types of the Soldano monster and the original mooncalf that you found in Nyack. One of the two in particular is an extremely good match. It's my bet that the same man who had sex with Samantha Bedell in London last January—not the one who sodomized her—is the father of these two mooncalves of ours."

"Are you sure?"

"Well, I'm not going to stake my career on it, but between you and me, the evidence is all but overwhelming. There's something else too. The blood types of these two men are different, of course, but there are certain genetic indicators that imply to me that they are possibly siblings. You know blood-typing is a lot more complicated and refined these days than it used to be. It's not simply a matter of A or B or RH- any more. I'd have to do a lot of testing to be more certain."

Guy, caught up by his academic interest in the English lab reports, continued enthusiastically. "Boy, I wish I could get hold of some amniotic fluid from around those babies Jennifer Pearsall is carrying. I could blood-type those kids before they're even born and confirm everything I'm thinking this very minute. She wouldn't submit to amniocentesis, do you think?"

That brought up another topic. I told him briefly about the call I had received that morning, neglecting to add that my uncle and I were the "business" that Jennifer Pearsall's new husband had to wind up before he left on his honeymoon. It was strange. I knew so much now, and yet I had proof of nothing and still did not have the answer to the most puzzling question of all—why? Madness was not answer enough . . . though possibly it would be the only answer.

"Now please, Guy, enough about Jennifer. I can't for the moment even think of her problems. There's so much to do and so little time to do it in. Just see that they do an autopsy on my uncle."

I sat in the dark library for a long, thoughtful few minutes after I hung up. Finally I reached across the too-neat, too well-ordered desk and switched on the antique brass desk lamp. The room, lit only by that one dim pool of green light, came to uncertain life. Tiny glints of color reflected off gold-tooled leather, brass, porcelain, and waxed wood surfaces all around me.

I roused myself from my reverie and pulled the blank pad toward me, fished a lead pencil out of the center drawer, and began to brush the side of the pencil point lightly across the top sheet of paper, in the manner of a child making a graphite rubbing of a coin on a piece of paper. Gradually, a few faint white lines began to appear in the gray graphite. With much care, I was able to recover the last few words Uncle Jeremiah had written before his murderer tore the sheet off the pad, reshelved or stole outright the books on and around his cluttered desk, and calmly walked out of the house carrying his victim's books and briefcase full of genealogical charts, lab reports, and copies of so much information that had been amassed during the investigation of the mooncalf murders. Logic would tell the killer, after he looked over that material, that however far ahead of me Uncle Jeremiah may have been in his researches, I would not be far behind. Yet, like so many killers before him, he had gone too far in his precautions.

That bare desk had been his biggest mistake. It was like the curious incident of the dog in the nighttime; it should have barked and it didn't. Uncle Jeremiah's desk should have been cluttered— and it damned well wasn't.

Eventually, I dialed Peter's number at the *Stop-Press*.

We talked only briefly, long enough for me to tell him about Uncle Jeremiah, what I thought had happened, and what I had to do about it. He wasn't happy when I refused to allow him to come down to be with me or to fetch me home. My next call was to Meta.

"Oh, luv, no," she gasped. "It can't be. Why, I only talked to him—"

"Talked to him?" I echoed. "When?"

"Oh, it can't have been—it was just before one, I think. I had the news on. They're saying there's a snowstorm on the way, and I was worried about you driving home tonight or tomorrow. He called and asked if by chance you hadn't left yet and were still with me. I told him you'd been gone about a quarter of an hour. He didn't chat me up the way he usually does if he calls. He seemed upset." She hesitated, starting to cry.

"He said something about putting it together and not liking it. He mentioned a name, something about Bentley. You know, like the car."

"Bentley? What was it, please? What did he say?"

She cleared her throat and began to speak calmly, her voice still heavy from crying. "Well, he called and asked if by chance you might still be here. You hadn't answered your phone upstairs. I told him you'd started on your way to him already and he said, 'Oh, damn,' and then apologized for his bad language and said he'd feel better if you stayed away after all."

"Stayed away! He said that?"

"Yes. Oh, luv, that's it. He said, 'Oh, damn, Mrs. Sullivan, I wish she wasn't coming after all. I've been going into this mooncalf business very minutely and I think I've got another Andrew Bentley on my hands.' Yes, that's it exactly: 'another Andrew Bentley on my hands.' Then he apologized and said he'd have to ring off. There was someone at his door. He seemed suddenly very preoccupied."

"He had a visitor, then? That's why he hung up?"

"Yes, luv, that's what he said. He said he'd have to answer the bell himself. He was alone, you see."

"And this was just at one, you think?"

"Yes, dear. Maybe it was that man. Maybe it was Andrew Bentley," she suggested hopefully.

"Yes, Meta," I said thoughtfully. "Andrew Bentley. That is exactly who it was."

I thanked her and hung up, every bit as preoccupied as my uncle had been five hours earlier. Pushing the phone out of the way, I reached across the desk toward that neat little pile of books and picked up my uncle's copy of *Famous Ghost Stories* . . .

The Central Research Library, or the Forty-second Street Library as it is commonly known, was still open when I arrived at seven-thirty, but it already echoed with the air of a place gearing down for the night. I raced up the marble steps two at a time to keep from waiting for the big, slow, stainless steel elevators.

I paced the immense North Hall of the main reading room like a flea on a hot griddle, waiting for the books that I had ordered to make their way up from the stacks and listening to the sounds that echoed in that cavernous block-long room divided in two by the massive oak return desk. All around were ranks of long oaken tables, green-shaded reading lamps, and heavy yellow oak chairs. Every sound, from the whir of microfilm machines behind me in the northwest corner to the slap of books on tabletops, the raucous scrape of chair legs on terrazzo floors, the faint scratching of pens on paper, the sporadic cough or sneeze of a reader, strummed my already twanging nerves.

After a good ten-minute wait, my call number light flicked on on the big indicator board in the corner of the room, and I went to collect my books. I carried them into Room 315N, the local history and genealogy division, and began the process all over again, consulting the card files, filling out request slips for each book, and entering a seat number so that the page could bring the books to my seat. I submitted my requests to the clerk at the desk and sat down.

I began to look through the books I had selected from the main reading room: *Orderic Vitalis* in both Latin and the 1856 translation and an unabridged Latin dictionary. I began by rereading the passage in *Orderic* on Archbishop Mauger's death.

> And so, in that unfortunate manner, Mauger was swept away from his craft and died in the sea between Guernsey and Herm. His body, being lost for upwards of a day and a night, was found at last among the rocks on the northwestern shore of the Isle of Herm by Adeliza, Lady D'Arques, whose eager and frantic search along the shore at last bore its unfortunate fruit.
>
> It was yet another day, however, before his body could be recovered due to the violence of his minion Thoret, who, refusing all food and drink offered by the hands of the Lady D'Arques, at last wasted and died by his master. At that time Mauger was taken up by the servants of the Lady D'Arques, who had loved him in defiance of God's holy law, and his body borne back to Guernsey, where her master was buried with all honor and wearing upon his finger that ring with which he had pledged to her his unsuitable troth. The other, called Thoret, was torn from his master and burnt to ashes and his remains scattered in the sea.
>
> This was the ignoble end of Mauger de Rouen whose blood carries his name to this day by means of his bastards born to him by the Lady D'Arques.

Opening the Latin text to the same passage, I tried to tackle a new translation. So engrossed was I in my task, so caught up in the effort to dredge my four years of high school Latin out of the mire of twenty-odd years of accumulated neglect, that when the page brought the rest of the books I had requested, I scarcely took notice.

I covered six pages of my notebook with barely legible scribbling in two languages before I at last gave up and opened *Burke's Extinct Peerage and Baronage.* It was then that answers began to come thick and fast. Before I was through I had a pretty good idea of why Uncle Jeremiah had been killed, and, incidentally, why those two coins I wore made Valda and me so very special—even more special than Jennifer and Brenda and the Bedell sisters—and what it was that linked us down a spiraling double helix of time with another lady who found something once, long, long ago.

I spent several minutes making a hash of notes from *Burke's,* since it took so long to get anything copied at the Forty-second Street Library, and finally returned to the Latin *Orderic,* comparing it to the English version and trying to see if I could recapture my Uncle Jeremiah's train of thought from those last few words he had written on that yellow pad on his desk.

"Why *dissepare?*" he had written. "Why not *depallare* instead? *Appendix* odd choice of words. *Membrum diabolicus*—trans. wrong. That devilish member correct as in orig. Can orig. text have been bowdlerized?!! Suspect so! Translation certainly is *Thoret membrum diabolicus*—? Like Mordake calls 'devil twin'?"

At the bottom of the page he had added in a larger hand:

"Mauger / Thoret
Mordake / devil sister
Little Thor / little brother
IS IT POSSIBLE THAT—? But it is *insanity* . . .
I have never seen any sign—"

What, given my creaky Latin, could I ever make of that? What had been the thread of his thought?

What was it that was POSSIBLE? What was the *insanity?*

18

THE END OF THE PASSAGE

I was lost in research, trying to remember my Latin conjunctions and divine the subtle nuances between words of similar but slightly different meaning, following the trail left by my uncle. It wasn't easy, and it didn't help to have my concentration broken by periodic warnings that the library was about to close in fifteen minutes, in ten, in five . . .

When I finally roused myself from my studies sufficiently to be aware of my surroundings, a gray-uniformed guard was calling to me from the doorway. I was the last person left in Room 315N. The library clerks were putting on their coats at the door and a page was switching off the lights at the master control beside it in a series of resounding clicks. They all gave me dark looks as I collected my impedimenta, and huffed off leaving me to the long-suffering young guard, who hurried me through the catalogue room into the rotunda to the accompaniment of ringing bells, the distant scurrying of feet, and the occasional hollow slamming of doors.

It was then that my mind, filled with mooncalves and Mordakes, Bayneses and janiceps monsters, played me false. The vast rotunda of the library was now a dimly lit cavern, illuminated primarily by the eerie red glow of an exit sign down the hall to the right of me. I turned toward it instead of making my way left toward the elevator bank at the north end of the building that led to the Forty-second Street exit.

I hastened toward the beckoning red sign, through a corridor that seemed narrower in the dark than I had remembered it to be, and found, at the end, not the exit I had expected, but another turning to the right. At the far end of this even narrower passage was another red light over a door in the left-hand wall. Beside it, on the wall facing me, were an ax, an alarm box, and the large glass pane of a fire box containing a length of accordion-pleated canvas hose. Above this was a large round alarm bell.

It was silent now in the vast building behind me. The warning bells were no longer clanging, no doors slammed, and it seemed that no footsteps scraped along the terrazzo floors but my own.

In that I was wrong.

Behind me, far back in the passageway, I could hear the quick light click of a steady footfall and, ever more faintly, the slight whistle of exerted breathing. Some sixth sense told me that this was not one of the easygoing, lethargic guards who earn their keep like complacent watchdogs, with one eye open, nor even some hapless lamb like myself who had taken a wrong turn and strayed from the flock.

This was the wolf and he was ravening at my heels.

I kept on going, past the ladies' room on my right and the Rare Book Room on my left, hurling myself with force against the exit door, slamming it against the wall with a deliberate crash as I went through. Noise, I reasoned, could only be my ally. The landing was lit by one bulb; the stairs themselves were a dark void at my feet. Breathless now, more from nerves than exertion, I clutched the banister with one hand, my notebook and purse with the other, and plunged down the staircase blindly, slowing my pace at the next landing simply because in the blackness I dared not miss my step.

I reached the second-floor landing, lit by its one low-watt bulb, and saw through the glass panel in the door that there was nothing but blackness beyond. No help there. Even during normal library hours the south wing was never open to the public. Now it must be completely deserted. I hurtled around the banister on the landing and plunged recklessly down toward the first floor, which, I could see, also lay in darkness.

Behind me the footsteps were closer, the wheezing breath louder and more terrifying, the gasps coming so thick that it was disconcertingly like the effort of two labored breaths, rather than that of one murderer, one cold villain.

The door to the first-floor hall was heavy, and, as with the door above, I smashed it against the wall recklessly in hopes of attracting someone with the noise. In the blackness of the corridor, I was momentarily blind, but at last I could make out the faint line of light that streamed in under a door at the far end of the hall to my right.

I raced down the slippery terrazzo floor, literally sliding into the door and groping in the darkness for the knob. It was locked. "Hey," I screamed at the top of my lungs, "don't leave me here. I'm locked in." Behind me I could hear the tread of my pursuer as he came into the corridor behind me, that weird wheezing gasp a hideous sound in the blackness. "Help, help," I shrieked, pounding on the door with my fist.

From the sound of his gasping breath, I knew that he had come within a few feet of me. For one brief, terrifying second, I felt my neck grazed by bony fingers and sharp nails. Pulling away, I dropped suddenly to my knees and scrambled past him on all fours, getting to my feet as quickly as I could and hurtling in the opposite direction, toward the faint red glow over the fire door through which I had just come. By its light I could make out fire apparatus like that which I had seen on the floor above. I pulled the long red ax out of its holder and turned toward the figure in the corridor behind me, brandishing it clumsily as my notebook and bag slipped to the floor at my feet.

"Stay away from me, you bastard," I shrieked. "I've got a

weapon and so help me, I'll kill you. There's a fire alarm here. If I pull it, all hell will break loose. Stay away from me!"

Miraculously, he did. With an oath, muttered in French in a high thin voice that I had never heard before, a large, dark figure plunged past me and through the fire door at my right. I had a strong whiff of a particularly vile and powerful body odor as he passed by and I instantly thought of Valda telling her sister that Mr. Smith stank and of Brenda Soldano's mention of her attacker's body odor. The door closed after him but I could still hear his swift tread recede into the lower depths. Moments later I heard faintly the short sharp screech of an alarm bell and the muffled echoing slam of a door.

Suddenly, in the darkness, over the sound of my own searing breath I heard the jingle of keys being rattled merrily. At the far end of the hall, the locked door swung open and a stream of yellow light spread down the corridor toward me. In its rays was silhouetted the welcome form of a security guard.

"Hey, sweetheart, what's all the noise? We ain't gonna lock you in. You're okay. Now I bet you got caught in the ladies' room up on the third floor when all the lights started going out, didn't you? Happens all the time," he said with a cheery chuckle and a shake of his head. "Someone's supposed to check those rooms up there, but half the time they're in too much of a rush to bother, and tonight, with this crazy snow comin', they're all anxious to get home. No need for you to panic, though. We always got staff on duty." He chortled at the thought of my fright and let me out the revolving door onto Forty-second Street. "Don't worry, we'd have found you eventually," he called as he waved me into the snowy night.

Yes, they'd have found me eventually, at the end of a locked corridor in the darkened library, and I'd have looked like Samantha Bedell did when they found her in that flat in London.

I stood for a moment at the top of the steps leading down to the sidewalk to catch my breath and get my bearings. The freak early-season snowstorm that Meta had said was supposed to arrive around midnight had begun early. Plump, wet flakes fell softly, melting instantly on the rain-wet streets. Only in the bushes and fallen leaves of Bryant Park was there any trace yet of accumulation.

There wasn't much traffic, so I noticed a van moving slowly along the curb toward me as I headed west toward Sixth Avenue. It was a dark metallic brown. The face and figure of the driver were obscured by the snow and the rapid sweep of the windshield-wipers, but I could see a pair of bony white hands clutching the wheel. It was enough. Every instinct told me that I was still in danger, that those bony hands were the ones that had grasped at me in the darkened corridor of the library. I picked up speed and raced past and along Forty-second Street, ducking into the IND subway station, which was well lighted and busy. I asked a transit cop where the nearest phone was and made a call to have Rogers pick me up in St. George.

On Staten Island the snow was already sticking, the roads mushy with accumulated slush. As we rode up to Dissoway Drive from the ferry, I asked Rogers a few questions about limousines, vans—particularly metallic-brown ones—and the living arrangements of servants, those apartments over garages so favored for their privacy and comfort, as well as all manner of neighborhood gossip. If he thought me slightly mad, he did not give any indication.

I sat up for what seemed like hours in Uncle Jeremiah's library with a plate of sandwiches and a pot of incredibly strong tea to sustain me. Molly snoozed on the rug before the cold fireplace. Only the sound of the grandfather clock ticking loudly in the snow-muffled silence of the night kept me company.

By two-thirty or so, I knew as much as was possible for me to know without Uncle Jeremiah's thoughts and stolen notes to aid me. As it was, I knew a great deal.

I knew that Valdalene's Mr. Smith, Brenda Soldano's rapist, Samantha Bedell's murderer, Pamela Howard's harasser, and Jennifer Pearsall's new husband, James Leigh, were one and the same man.

I knew the reason the Baroness Derevenkov had helped Valda. Somehow, by some accidental sighting perhaps, she had seen Mr. Smith on the streets of the Bronx, or perhaps picking Valda up at the grocery store, and had recognized him. Because she knew who the father was, she had tried to help Valda to rid herself of his child.

I surmised too that had the baroness not died in her own way, she would eventually have been discovered and killed as Guy had nearly been killed and as Uncle Jeremiah had been this afternoon. It was no longer, of course, a case of who. Given the circumstances of Uncle Jeremiah's death, that was relatively easy to figure out. Until now he had been a faceless, nameless victimizer and brutalizer of young women, a begetter of monsters—but now I knew him for what he was: the cold-blooded murderer of my uncle. It was not even a matter now of the "how" of it, though that must be answered in good time. Most of all, it was for me, as it had been all along, the "why" of it.

Why?

What madness lay behind this bizarre and complex scheme to beget a mooncalf?

I had spent some time puzzling over the passage in *Orderic* that had so interested my uncle. There was something very strange about it. If his notes had been left, and the copies of the volumes themselves, I'd probably never have paid them any mind or connected them in any way with our mooncalf mystery. That research, after all, was merely a diversion for his amusement, not part of the mystery itself. Yet those notes and the books had been removed with the other material.

Translating Medieval Latin, even with the help of an English text, was a bit much for me. I threw down my pen in disgust and despair. The answer lay among the things that had been taken from the desk after he was murdered. At the worst, they were already destroyed; at best, they were inaccessible.

The clock creaked, groaned, and struck three sonorous notes in the silence of the library. Molly roused herself, blinking and sniffing as she rose stiffly from the hearth rug and stretched.

From behind the bookcases came a noisy squeak so loud that I could hear it halfway down the room. It galvanized Molly, who leapt into action and took up her hunting stance in the corner of the bookcase by the side of the fireplace. She whimpered pleadingly and began to scratch at the baseboard as she had done that night a week before. For a moment I sat stupidly and watched her, reflecting on how horribly things had changed from that one pleasant Monday evening to this nightmare Monday night, and then it hit me.

I locked M. Brown in the kitchen with a bowl of water and a large can of tuna fish, the best reward I could find in the larder short of a tin of beluga caviar, which I thought would be a bit rich even for Molly. I raided the drawers in the butler's pantry and the kitchen cabinets and came up with a small pair of pliers, a screwdriver, a stubby end or two of candle, some matches, and a flashlight, all of which I carried back to the library with me, carefully locking the door behind me as I entered. What I was about to do would not bear the light of discovery.

The cupboard at the bottom of the bookcase nearest the fireplace was filled with a collection of miscellaneous boxes, magazines, books, and files, all of which I removed and stacked in proper order on the hearth rug. The two shelves were adjustable. I lifted them off the small metal pegs that held them in place and took them out.

The cabinet was built of walnut and seemed quite solid, but remembering what my uncle had told me the week before, I began to sound the back of it, pushing and tapping at it carefully until at last the whole backboard, which was actually made up of two panels, began to shift, creating an aperture two feet high by two feet wide. Behind it there was no trace of a wall, only an uninviting blackness and a draught of cool, damp, earth-smelling air.

I took the flashlight and peered into the opening. It was actually the top of a narrow flight of shallow brick steps that led to the right, parallel to the outside wall of the house and flush with it. I could not see very far down into the stairwell, but the top step, which was wide and made of wood, and the brick ones just below it were thick with dried mouse droppings and smelled strongly of rodent.

Wriggling through the opening and onto the landing, I managed to stand upright. I was on a platform approximately two feet by two feet square. There was open space above me to the height of the ceiling of the room from which I had come. At my back was the brick wall of the fireplace, to my right the inner plaster-and-lathe wall of the library, and to my left the outer stone wall of the lower story of the house. Some feet ahead of me was a joining of these two walls at what I gauged to be the front corner of the house. Below yawned the flight of narrow brick steps that led to the old Fenton Gibbs house across Dissoway Drive.

I crouched down and, reaching through the opening at the back of the bookcase, took the candles, matches, and tools, stowing them in the various pockets of my blazer and slacks. Finally, flashlight held before me, I descended into the blackness of the secret passage that no one had entered since my father and uncle had explored it three-quarters of a century earlier. How strange a legacy to have left.

Once I was below the level of the first floor, both walls were of stone to a depth of about twelve feet, the level of the basement, I imagined. The steps were all of old brick, shallow, steep, crumbling, and not easy to negotiate. About twelve feet ahead, the tunnel began. It was approximately five feet in height, two and a half feet wide, and had a packed earth floor. It ran nearly level for fifty feet or more before it dipped to what appeared to be bedrock and narrowed to just two feet. Regularly spaced brick columns held up the roof, which was made up of thick flagstone slabs. At each joining, thin, limy stalactites of mineral deposit hung like icicles. Corresponding spines of stalagmite crossed the floor below them;

small, shiny, wet-looking mounds like the infant beginnings of the Howe Caverns.

The brick steps at the far end of the tunnel corresponded exactly with those I had descended, but they ended at a long, narrow panel that I could see opened like a sliding door, rather than in a pair of bookcase backboards like those through which I had come. Before Great-grandfather Fay closed it off at his end, the entrance into his own library had probably been similar.

The panel into the Fenton Gibbs house was bolted closed with a slide bolt and socket of wrought iron in a fancy molded pattern of long ago. The original black paint had long been frosted over with a layer of rust, but, working patiently, I was able to loosen the screws of the bolt-plate just enough to shift the bolt itself and slide it out of the socket.

After that, sliding the panel to one side in its wooden channel was fairly easy, though rather slow going since the wood had warped over the years. What made me cautious was the thought of what might await me on the other side of the wall, in the library beyond.

The room was in darkness, of course. I shone the beam of the flashlight across the floor and over the furniture to take my bearings. The panel opened just behind a dusty, overstuffed lounge chair that had been new in the early thirties. Beside it was a brass-plated floor lamp with a cream-colored alabaster slab set two feet up from its base to serve as a table. On it was a dirty ashtray. On the far wall, flanking the door to the hall, were arrangements of medieval weapons: pikes, crossbows, morning stars. Gilbert's contribution to the decor, I imagined. The room smelled dusty and unaired.

Uncle Jeremiah's briefcase lay on the floor beside the rolltop desk that sat against the far wall near the front windows. Above the desk hung a portrait of a man, painted fifty years ago or more, but jarringly familiar. Stacked on the floor next to it were two sets of *Orderic Vitalis*, one in English and one in Latin. On the desk blotter lay my uncle's copies of *Anomalies* and *Burkes Extinct*

Peerage. From the pages of the latter protruded several sheets of yellow lined paper.

I knew already what it was Uncle Jeremiah had found in *Anomalies,* and I had read the illuminating entry on the Mordake family in *Burke's* just this evening at the library on Forty-second Street. It was the contents of those yellow sheets that fascinated me with a lure almost too tempting to resist. I was strong, however, at least for the moment, and left the papers where they were. I picked up the briefcase, the four volumes of his English *Orderic,* and Gould's *Anomalies* and carried them back across the room to the secret panel, setting them on the steps just inside the opening.

Carefully skirting the lounge chair and the lamp, passing a dingy oak book table, several other chairs, and floor lamps with frayed, antique wiring that spread across the shabby blue Oriental carpet like so many snakes, I returned to the desk by the single beam of my flashlight and sat down. The house was silent. I felt safe, and I had found what I sought. Now I had to know what it was Uncle Jeremiah had found that solved the mystery for him and made him wish to keep me away, that made someone wish to kill him.

One of the sheets contained the annotations that I had already deciphered from the pad left on his desk at the other house. Another contained a list of words he had obviously used in making his final translation. The third sheet was his own new translation from the original Latin of the passage in *Orderic* that deals with the death of Archbishop Mauger and his burial. It differed in only a few key phrases from the 1856 translation that I had read earlier in the evening.

In such fateful manner, Mauger was swept away from the boat, drowning in the sea between Guernsey and Herm. His corpse, being lost for nearly a night and a day, was at length found lodged in the rocks on the northwestern shore of the Isle of Herm by Adeliza D'Arques, whose vigilant and frantic search along the shore at last bore its unhappy fruit. Her frenzy and grief at the loss of her lord and lover was passionate but her duty to him made her continue her service to his vile appendage, which yet lived and which none dare approach save her.

In consequence, the body of Mauger lay on the beach, where it was found yet another day for fear of Thoret, that devilish member whose violent behavior and watchfulness struck terror into the hearts of all who saw. At last, refusing all food and drink even from the hands of the Lady D'Arques, that vile appendage wasted and died. It was only then that the body of Mauger was taken up by the servants of the Lady D'Arques, she who had loved him in defiance of the holy laws of God and Man, and his body taken back to Guernsey, where she caused her lover to be buried with all manner of honours, however ill-befitting his scandalous life and shameful manner of death. By her order those two, master and devil, were torn from each other, the one to be buried with sanctity and honour and wearing the ring once given to her in pledge of his incestuous troth, the other to be burnt on a pyre on the wild shore and its ashes scattered over the sea.

Such was the end of Mauger, once Archbishop of Rouen, though his blood and the seed of his devil carry on his name to this day through his bastards born to him by his brother's daughter, Adeliza D'Arques, whom, some said, was bewitched of him and his devil member. Of that, none can say, for in her subsequent life she was exemplary in character and devotion, living as a recluse, walking the shores of Herm and the other isles in search, some said, of her lost love. She died mad in her eightieth year.

I sat quite still in the deep silence of that dusty room in the old Fenton Gibbs house, thinking about the translation I had just read. Uncle Jeremiah had been right. The 1856 text had been bowdlerized, but probably only because a straight translation made no sense. "Master and devil torn from each other." "Vile appendage."

It had meant something to Uncle Jeremiah, but it was still Greek to me.

The only thing that was clear—and that had been clear enough in the passage I had read earlier in the library—was that Adeliza D'Arques, common ancestress of all of us females involved in the mooncalf murders, had searched for and found Mauger, and that somehow her search was bound up with the fact that Valdalene and I were "finders of things"—or, as Peter would have it, "searchers for things," which might be nearer the mark, actually. The how and why of it I could not fathom, but it seemed to be our common link down the ages of time that separated us from Adeliza. I knew too, though it was not described in *Orderic*, that the ring that Mauger de Rouen had worn to his grave was a small circlet of peridots and gray pearls. But still, what in Uncle Jeremiah's translation had driven someone to murder him? Or was it the juxtaposition of that translation with all the other things he had surmised? Was *Orderic* just the last link?

I folded the three pages and stuck them in my pocket. The copy of *Burke's* lay open before me to the Mordake entry, where the papers had been thrust when my uncle's murderer had gathered up the things on the desk and fled to safety. It was foolish of me, but I stopped to read.

Mordake of Baynes Parva
Lineage

The name of Mordake is ancient, though its appearance in Cornwall begins with the use of that patronymic by William of Baynes, third Baron Baynes in the time of Edward I, in right of his wife, Lady Cicily Mordake, daughter and heiress of her father Rolf or Ralph Mordake.

Michael de Baynes, 1st Baron Baynes, son of Mauger, deposed Archbishop of Rouen, in England from the time of Henry I, *Beauclerk*, ca. 1200, had grants of land in Cornwall, Essex, and Kent. Made a baron by Henry ca. 1209, m., despite the forbidden degrees of consanguinity, his niece,

Lady Eleanor St. Mauger, dau. of his brother, Mauger St. Mauger de Rouen, Sire de Guernsey, posthumous son of the aforesaid Mauger and his niece, the Lady Adeliza D'Arques, thus establishing a pattern of intermarriage between the two branches of the family St. Mauger that continued into the early eighteenth century. His descendant,

Walter Mordake, 11th Baron de Baynes of Baynes Parva, Cornwall, born in 1654, married Ann St. Mauger de Bains of St. Hilaire, France, and had issue Edward. He died in 1700. His son,

Edward Mordake, a recluse of uncertain health, who made no attempt to take up his title, was born in 1680 and died without legitimate issue in 1701 when the title is considered to have become extinct.

The families de Baines, St. Mauger, and St. Hilaire, all in France are branches of this ancient family.

To that discreet entry my uncle had added in his small, neat hand the additional comment: "The family de Bains became extinct in France upon the death in eighteen thirteen of Sebastian St. Hilaire de Bains. Madame Isabelle St. Hilaire St. Mauger is the last of the St. Hilaire line. Gilbert and Hillary are the last surviving St. Maugers. With their deaths, the family becomes extinct in all direct lines from Mauger de Rouen. Interesting. Valdalene and Miranda."

He had written no more, but I understood what it was he had meant. Our double descent—at least double descent, for other lines may have entailed cousinly intermarriage that we had not yet discovered—constituted something special in the eyes of the man who was behind all this. Valdalene had been an especially desired target, as I would have been myself, had my birth records been accessible.

Perhaps it wasn't that we "found things," she and I. Perhaps it was that somewhere in our genes, in our blood, if you will, or perhaps, as Gilbert would have it, in our previous incarnations, we had been a part of her, a part of Adeliza, the Lady D'Arques, who had searched and searched among the rocks of Herm for her beloved, for her Mauger and his devil, Thor. Our common ancester, their posthumous son Mauger St. Mauger, had from the womb shared in that terrible search. Perhaps somehow, in the anxiety of our own lives, which we ached, each in our own way, to change, we searched and in that unconscious search called into play the echo of that ancient search of our common ancestress for her dead lover. And how many times over was she our ancestress must be beyond counting, so intertwined were those incestuous early bloodlines. Yet all of the victims of the mooncalf murderer were of the blood to a greater or lesser degree. A child born to any one of us would be more a St. Mauger than anyone living, save Gilbert and Hillary themselves.

That much had become clear, but still there was that one last sane question in the face of all the insanity that had gone before. I closed the book and sat bent over it, my head in my hands, spent with a weariness that went beyond the body and into the very soul of me. The flashlight cast its single yellow beam across the desk.

"Why?" I muttered. "Why?"

"If you come down the hall and into the dining room, my dear, I shall explain why."

Gilbert St. Mauger stood silhouetted against the open door to the hall, immense and scrubbed as ever. He must have bathed, for the offensive body odor that he had exuded during our scuffle in the library at Forty-second Street earlier in the evening was no longer evident. He wore an elegant burgundy silk dressing gown with a deep shawl collar of quilted paisley wool piped in twisted silk cord. The gown was secured with silk frogs and belted by a tassled silk cord that girded his ample middle. From beneath the hem peeped shiny burgundy leather slippers. He was the picture of a sartorial splendor that had been left behind on the pages of a Victorian gentleman's magazine.

In one hand he held a plate of sandwiches and in the other a tall tumbler of milk. Nothing could have been more prosaic than this, the great chubby master of the house with his midnight snack in hand. I realized with faint heart that if I had not stopped to read the entry in *Burke's*, I would have been well away by the time Gilbert's hunger pangs had struck.

"Come," he commanded with a motion of the hand that held the plate. Turning, he ambled flat-footedly across the wide hall and into the dining room, which was poorly lit by a single circle of small naked bulbs, flame shaped, in an old-fashioned bronze chandelier that had been converted from a gas fixture. He sat at the head of the table in a huge, heavy nineteenth-century copy of an early Gothic throne chair. I took a similar one at the foot of the long table, some twelve feet away, feeling as I did some instinct to keep my distance.

If I was nervous or afraid, I did not feel so, or perhaps even appear so to Gilbert. I felt instead a rather keyed-up tingling of the nerves, a heightened awareness of the sights and sounds and colors in the dimly lit room, paneled in yellow oak with its battered dark oak chairs and table. There was a massive sideboard on my left, its dusty carved surfaces festooned with animals and leaves and sinuous branches of flowers and fruits all done in high relief. The drapes at the end of the room, at Gilbert's back, heavy panels of moss-green velvet faced with worn, age-stained yellow silk, looked as if they had not been removed or even dusted in decades. The rug was Chinese, in blues and greens and amber, threadbare and showing constellations of white knots through the thinning pile. I had the feeling that he had moved in and left everything just as it had always been, down to the very spiders in their webs on the wall.

For a long time there was no sound at all in the room. Gilbert sat in his seat in silence, staring fixedly at the plate of sandwiches before him, fat things full of slabs of baloney and butter on large, thick slices of spongy, tasteless white bread, a glass of thick whole milk completing the strange picture. Its whiteness made me think of the snow outside, falling with a soft, pillowy swiftness that muffled every sound.

If the silence around me gave me a weird sense of being deaf, those dim, naked bulbs in the chandelier above me made me blink and rub my eyes as if my sight were failing as well, as if the last thing that I would ever behold was Gilbert St. Mauger and his midnight snack in a grimy room in a dark house.

At last, he stirred and spoke.

"Forgive us," he said, "but we are hungry, quite hungry."

It was then that they began to eat.

19

LITTLE THOR / LITTLE BROTHER

It was a strange, almost surreal moment. I might have been Adeliza, Lady D'Arques, sitting at the table of her lord and uncle the Archbishop Mauger, watching him amuse his guests with his personal devil Thoret.

But I was not Adeliza, I was Miranda Fay, and it was not Mauger de Rouen, but rather his last direct descendant, Gilbert St. Hilaire St. Mauger, who sat at table with me—and Gilbert had his own personal demon. Gilbert had his own Little Thor.

The creature peeped out from the deep V of the dressing gown like an animal from its den, eyeing the food on the table before it with an avid gleam. It glanced down the long board toward me, chittered slightly like a nervous squirrel, looked up at Mauger as if for reassurance, and then, with what appeared to be a shrug and an evil, monkeylike grin, it stretched its neck and slithered a pair of narrow, slug-white shoulders from the dressing gown where it had been nestling and reached with scrawny, long-muscled arms toward the plate to snatch animal-like at one of the sandwiches. Its fingers were long and bony with ragged talons like those on the unborn mooncalf I had found in Nyack.

It had, this caricature of a human being, a wide mouth and nearly toothless gums, obscenely pink and bright. The soft bread pleased it no end and it crooned sensually to itself as it ate, its bright, dark eyes closed as if in ecstasy. Its hair was lank and pale and it looked old, like a skinny, toothless old man; like the man who had driven Guy's car off the road from behind the wheel of a metallic-brown van; like the hands I had seen on the wheel of the van on Forty-second Street. The thought of this creature out in the world, doing its evil deeds, gave me a shiver of dread.

It appeared to sit on St. Mauger's lap precisely like a ventriloquist's dummy, exactly the Mortimer Snerd with miter and crosier that I had joked about with Uncle Jeremiah no more than a week ago. Occasionally, it would eye me askance down the long table and mutter something in French under its breath. There was evil in that wizened face; a small dwarfish being, malignant, shrunken in its skin like an almond left too long in the shell.

I saw what I saw, but still did not understand, really *understand*— or perhaps I did even then, but could not bear to accept the full realization. . . .

Gilbert reached for one of the sandwiches himself, took a wolfish bite of bread and baloney, chewed, and swallowed with a large gulp.

"What are you doing here?" he asked at last, his voice still soft but with a dangerous edge to it that was not lost on me. "How did you get in?"

I didn't answer.

"Jeremiah Pearsall must have had a key, I suppose," he said with an expansive, self-satisfied smirk, pleased at his own deduction. "I never bothered to change the locks and by the look of them, nobody else has in a hundred years either."

"I came," I said after a tense silence, "to retrieve the things you stole from my uncle's desk when you murdered him." The thing on his lap chittered happily at my remark, seeming to find it humorous. He stuffed his mouth with bits of fallen bread like a greedy child.

"I suppose I ought to ask what gave us away," he said languidly.

I shook my head. "Such a small thing at first. Uncle Jeremiah said he thought he had another Andrew Bentley on his hands. Bentley, if you remember August Derleth's story, 'The Return of Andrew Bentley,' was the wicked neighbor of an elderly scholar named Amos Wilde. Who else could he have meant but you?"

Again a long pause while Gilbert took another bite of his sandwich and sipped daintily from the tumbler of milk, which he shared with the creature.

"You are quite wrong, you know. I did not kill Jeremiah Pearsall," he said decisively as he wiped the milk from his upper lip with a fastidious gesture of his handkerchief. "I didn't kill Jeremiah Pearsall," St. Mauger repeated firmly. "I loved him like a father—better than I could ever have loved my own. It was my brother. It was little brother, little Thor." He glanced down at the dwarfish creature on his lap, watching him gabble and gum the baloney sandwiches with a strange mixture of pitying affection and fastidious distaste. "Thor was jealous, of course, always jealous of him, for he was the only friend I had, the only one I was ever close to—but there was more, of course. Jeremiah had at last pieced it all together—all but Thor himself, naturally—and when I dropped by yesterday afternoon—I was curious as to why he should want my Latin edition of *Orderic Vitalis*, and afraid . . . Anyway," he said with a dismissive shake of his head, "I stopped by and—"

"You were on your way back from the airport."

"Yes," he said, looking down the long table at me in surprise. "That's right. I saw my family off at Kennedy Airport. They are going back to Europe." He looked puzzled. I said nothing more. Unconsciously he fingered the new wedding ring he wore on the third finger of his heretofore ringless left hand—the very hand on which Jennifer Pearsall's new husband, James Leigh, would be wearing a new, shiny gold band. It had glittered that afternoon in Uncle Jeremiah's parlour.

"He talked about the mooncalves that have been born. He talked about Edward Mordake, who was a janiceps mooncalf as you call it; of his daughter Forgiveness Basset and of their descent from Mauger and Adeliza. . . . He spoke of the creatures that have been born . . . and of teratogenerative lines . . . and of obsession and madness. . . ." Strangely, tears began to run down his fat cheeks as he spoke. "I tried to deflect his thinking," he said suddenly, looking at me down the length of the table with anguished eyes, "but he kept on and on—so kindly, so amiably, so close to the truth. . . .

"Thor heard it all, of course, and felt threatened, as well you may imagine. It—it took both of us quite by surprise, both Jeremiah Pearsall and myself. Thor never, never shows himself to anyone, ever—except at night in the van. He loves to drive, and of course I let him. He has so little to—"

"Tell me about Uncle Jeremiah," I whispered, trying to conceal the trembling of my hands on the table in front of me. It was not fear I felt but cold, implacable rage. His tears did not move me.

"I had come round his desk to see what he had written on those legal pads of his. That's when I saw his *Burke's Extinct Peerage* open to the Mordake entry. I saw the notes he had made in the margins. It was no purely academic interest. He had written Valdalene's name. I knew then that he knew too much. He swung the chair toward me a bit just then to block me, I suppose, and Thor—Thor was quite awake, you see. He usually sleeps. He has not much stamina . . . but this time he grew enraged at the danger to us. He thrust himself forward at Jeremiah Pearsall and you may imagine how shocked he was. He reeled back in his chair, quite stunned.

"When he had recovered—I was fearful for his heart, you understand—I tried to speak to him, to explain and tell him how it was. For a few moments I experienced the most liberating sense of release and hope." His eyes were glazed and he stared into space as he spoke.

"Hope," I exclaimed involuntarily.

"Yes," he said, blinking slightly and looking at me with sudden awareness. "I truly wanted to explain at last, to have him understand what I am, what it has been like for me all these years, all my life . . . but Thor would have none of it. He flew into a rage at what he sensed was my weakness, I suppose, and he snatched up the brass pen tray on the desk before either of us realized what he was about. He smote the old man, that good old man, a glancing blow on the side of the head. The temple, you see . . . ," he whispered. Huge tears rolled down his smooth round cheeks and dripped from his chin.

"It was all over in that one irreversible, awful second. There was no blood, nothing. I couldn't think at first. I was too stunned—utterly horrified, actually—at the momentousness of what had happened. It was Thor who brought me back to myself and made me see what I had to do. It was—Oh, dear God, Miranda," he pleaded, "it was a nightmare. I loved that dear old man. I loved him. It was not me," he repeated. "It was Thor, I tell you. He—"

"Don't blame that demented creature," I whispered down the length of the table. "He's a puppet—a thing, a pet, if you will. You must control him—"

"No, no, not always," Gilbert broke in, speaking hastily. "I can't always control him. He sleeps a great deal—his circulation is rather sluggish—but when he is very lively I must sometimes sedate him. It doesn't always work. And I rarely ever drink, of course, since I must always have control myself. . . ."

"If you can't control him, then you should damn well keep him in a cage," I snapped, "or have him committed and be done with it."

"You don't understand—"

"Oh, don't I? I understand that Uncle Jeremiah is dead well enough, and that whichever one of you did the actual killing, you are the sane one. You are the responsible one, and this brother of yours is mentally unfit, mad, and should be institutionalized."

He shook his head so sadly that, even in the bitterness of my own anger and loss, I could almost pity him. All the while Thor watched me, listening to my words, his malignant little eyes watchful and filled with quiet hate.

"You do not understand," Gilbert repeated, "but if only you could have. If only you could have understood. If ever there might have been an answer for me, if ever I might have found love and redemption in a woman's arms, it would have been with you. . . ."

"What about Jennifer? Doesn't she redeem you?"

Again he touched the new gold ring with an unconscious gesture. "She is a child, a frightened child who needs a father more than a lover."

"Yet you married her?"

"Yes, I married her. It made her very happy to think that I wanted her. She is carrying—"

"Your children," I interrupted bitterly.

He shook his head slowly. "No, she is carrying Thor's children actually, though of course she does not know it. She has never met Thor, though I hope one day she shall. She thinks the babies are mine, and she loves me—or at least she thinks she does, and that, my dear Miranda, is as close as I have ever come to being loved. For what it is worth, I shall take it."

"Thor's child?"

"His," he said simply, "but with you and me it would have been different. I'd never have let him touch you. For a few brief days I had such hopes." He paused for a moment to take hold of himself and collect his thoughts. "I thought that there was something between us, you see, something that had come down the ages to us from them. 'In our blood,' Jeremiah would say. 'From our earlier incarnations,' I believe. You and Adeliza and Mauger and I. Her love for him was the one grace in his life, a forbidden gift from a forgiving God. I had designs on you, of course, from the moment I met you, because of the bloodlines. I knew how strong they must be in you and I knew too that marriage would be the only possible approach to a respectable woman of your years. Jeremiah Pearsall's niece to boot. But then, during our visit to the Metropolitan, I began to sense that there was something between us, something that was undefinable and rare. What I felt and sensed in you at the Cloisters—the power I seemed able to exert over your passions and the feelings of love that you aroused in me—gave me hope, real hope, that I too in my poor life might find God's grace through you. I saw on your hand the little peridot and pearl ring that he had given to her and which she had placed on his little finger at the very edge of his grave—her lasting pledge of her love and of his redemption.

"I saw that ring as surely as I see you now, and my heart filled with such love and such hope and passion as I had never known in all my life. Even though I ran from it and from you, within hours I had come to realize what it was . . . and I was no longer afraid."

"And what was it?" I asked with a pained shake of my head. Thor, his brother, having eaten most of one sandwich piecemeal and lapped greedily from the tumbler of milk, had fallen asleep with his head against his brother's naked white chest.

"It was Mauger's soul reborn in me—and I have always known that he is within me and has been from the hour of my birth—discovering and recognizing her soul reborn in you. Oh, Miranda, what children we should have had, you and I. Our descendants would have gone on for another thousand years as theirs have done."

"Then why did I not feel it, too?" I asked softly.

"You did feel it," he declared firmly. "I know you did, but you have chosen to deny it," he said, his words hitting home. "You have refused to accept her reincarnated soul lodged deep within your own. Perhaps what Jeremiah Pearsall believed is true as well. Perhaps we are both right and it is in the blood and the soul together, this thing that calls us inexplicably across the gulf of time to a place or a person or even to a mode of living.

"There is so much of Mauger in me, so much of Thoret in my little brother here. Though you too are of our blood and of his, in you it is so polluted by other, weaker strains: by the mongrel lines of Dutchmen and Huguenots and English yeomen like the Bassets and Pearsalls and God knows who else in this mongrelized country of yours, that Adeliza has not the power over you that Mauger commands over me and Thoret over Thor. It is, Miranda, a measure of my love and compassion for you that I can forgive you the weakness of your blood and realize the hopelessness of ever convincing you of my beliefs. That is why I married the girl. She loves me—or at least believes she does—and she needs me. That is something anyway, isn't it? There is an Arab saying that 'to love is nothing, to be loved is something, but to love and be loved is everything.' So, my love for you, unrequited as it is, amounts to nothing. Jennifer Pearsall's love for me is something at least . . ."

He looked at me down the table, his eyes welling with tears, his voice deep and strong, nothing in it of the prissy, emasculate schoolboy that was his sometime guise. "But, oh, Miranda," he said at last, "if the soul of Adeliza had been stronger in you, or your determination weaker, we could have had everything, been everything to each other, to the end of time. . . ."

The anguish with which he spoke was almost unbearable to witness. He had convinced himself of what he said, of that wild, appealing, romantic notion. It might almost have convinced me as well, that romantic dream, if I had not remembered Valdalene, dead for days, her open belly teeming with maggots, and her aborted mooncalf, its distorted carcass a parody of a human child. If there were no Brenda Soldano and her monster offspring, or if I did not know young Jennifer, whose womb swelled with quickening life and whose heart was filled with pathetic, impossible hopes. I remembered too the pain of Pamela Howard, who had no sister anymore, and the lovely face of that sister, now smashed and rotting in a lonely grave over the sea in England.

Gilbert's dream might have convinced me if I had not remembered Guy in his Valpo cast, or the bony, snatching fingers that grazed my cheek in a deserted corridor of the darkened library. Or if I had not remembered Uncle Jeremiah, so decent, so worthy, so lovable a man, stiff in his chair in that elegant library across Dissoway Drive from the shabby room in which I now sat.

"The Baroness Derevenkov. Where does she come in?" I asked at last.

The suddenness of my query pulled him from his reverie.

"One of life's small, strange ironies. She was in the room in my father's hospital when I was born. Her father was my mother's physician and she acted as his midwife. Paris, it was. He delivered us, both of us. There were reasons why their silence and discretion were invaluable to my father—and to Mama, of course. It was a very small, private hospital, you see, and so there were no disclosures. . . ."

"Your father was the Dr. Augustin she spoke of with her dying breath. I thought then that 'Augustin' was a surname but I realize now that I misunderstood. Augustin St. Mauger. I saw the portrait over the desk in the library. Since you are the image of him she recognized you at once."

St. Mauger nodded solemnly. "I do not often speak of him, but yes, she worked for him before her marriage. Afterward, during the war, my father saved her and her sick husband from starvation. He was a Nazi collaborator. He did research that no more bears the light of day than does Thor here," he murmured, looking down on the deformed creature that he called brother, lying asleep against the quilted collar of his dressing gown, one hand against his big brother's bare chest. "He experimented for the Nazis with human monsters like—his own son." As he spoke his voice cracked. "Is it any wonder that I hated him, that I chose to revere a man like Jeremiah Pearsall rather than the man whose face was the image of my own—and yet I am so much like him. Haven't I experimented too, in my own way?"

Suddenly, the Baroness Derevenkov's last, raving words made sense. "She guessed that Valdalene was the subject of an experiment too, carrying a child that the baroness felt duty bound to help abort. She knew how urgent it was for Valdalene to abort that fetus. She had known the father; she had seen the son."

Gilbert St. Mauger winced and looked down at his brother. "I suppose so," he whispered. "Yes, I suppose so."

"You raped Brenda Soldano, didn't you?" I asked abruptly. He looked up at me with a jerk of his head. "Yes, I know her name. It didn't appear in the papers, but Uncle Jeremiah learned her identity. Guy witnessed the autopsy on the child. According to his blood

work, the same man who fathered Valdalene's child could have—
and did—father the Soldano monster."

"Thor."

"Thor," I repeated with an ironic smirk. "Of course, Thor."

"You knew more than I realized, you and Jeremiah Pearsall," he
murmured thoughtfully.

"Was it Thor who beat Samantha Bedell to death in her flat in
London?" I asked with sudden and deliberate force. He looked as
stunned as if I had slapped him. He closed his eyes momentarily.

"She woke up. The wine and the pills weren't enough. She was
used to drugs, it seems. She woke up and started screaming. . . ."
He passed a hand over his eyes as if to blot out the image. "That
was the first . . . I met her quite, quite by accident. The name
Bedell—I knew it was one of the Mordake lines that descended
from Ivy Basset in America. When it turned out that she was an
American and that one of her ancestors was indeed a Pearsall, it
didn't take me long to discover that we were, in fact, related.

"Then an idea took form. It might never have, but you see, she
was a bit loose. She was easy enough, willing after a few dates, a
few drinks, to have sex. She was perversely attracted to me, I could
tell. I was, I suppose, the proverbial older man. She liked my
polished manners, and I suppose too that I was rather a novelty
after the West End boys she knew. I seemed to know what to say
to keep her interested. I felt that if I got her pregnant, I could get
her to marry me or at least to give me the child. She had a wide
streak of the Puritan beneath that rebelliousness of hers that I
sensed I could appeal to. She was very lovely, really beautiful,
but—"

"She woke up."

He nodded. "But nothing was lost. It was she and her remote
but quite definite Mordake bloodlines that set us off on the quest
to beget another child. If only René had not died. After he was
gone, it began to seem like the only answer—a child who was as
much a descendent of Mauger de Rouen as it was possible to
conceive."

"René is—excuse me, was—Hillary's son? Your nephew."
St. Mauger looked at me in an odd way. "Hillary's son, yes. My
nephew, yes, and my son as well. It was my son Hillary bore
nineteen years ago—you do not seem surprised."

"After all that has happened in the past month, nothing surprises
me. As it happens, Uncle Jeremiah told me that there were rumors
to that effect at the time. I didn't credit them, and I doubt he did
either."

Again he winced. It evidently hurt to think that my uncle had
known all along. "Oh, I imagine he credited them, all right, but I
think he must have chosen not to hold it against me. How kind of
him and how like him. He had been proof against Hillary himself,
but I think he must have realized that I might not be. And I wasn't,
in the end, though I had resisted her for a very long time. I did give
in," he ended in a whisper, bowing his head toward Thor in shame.
"It was her obsession that started it all. She and Mama had believed
that I—that neither I nor Thor would be able to carry on the line
and that the St. Maugers would die with us as the Hilaires had died
with Mama's brother in nineteen forty-two and as the de Baineses
had died with Sebastian de Baines in eighteen thirteen. It was up to
Hillary to carry on the line for us. She herself wanted a son by
Jeremiah Pearsall—

"Hillary is obsessive, you see—not so much about sex or men,
but about youth and beauty—yet when she met Jeremiah Pearsall,
she became as completely obsessed with him as she was with
herself. She had always had anything and anyone she wanted and
she wanted him. She pursued him for years, and the more she
pursued, the more he resisted. I suppose that is why I let go so
quickly of the idea of you and me—I saw the fruitlessness of her
pursuit and the fierceness of his determination to resist. They were
two perverse and stubborn people, my sister and your uncle. If
they had had a child, all this might never have happened. . . ." He
reached for the tumbler and drank thirstily.

"Finally, twenty years or more ago, after having given up on
him, and after several failed, rather halfhearted attempts to conceive

by various lovers, she began on me. She insisted that as she was nearing forty it was imperative that she have a child soon."

"What did your mother say to all this?"

"Oh, she approved. She always let Hillary have her head in all things. She was the perfect one, you see. The beloved, beautiful daughter. And I think Hillary herself actually enjoyed it, enjoyed my agony and my shame before her. She is too perverse for words," he concluded with just a hint of that old petulance in his voice.

"She didn't want Thor, I take it."

"No, she didn't want Thor," he repeated softly. "Strangely, she conceived immediately. From our one incestuous coupling, René was born. I hated him. He was, however, innocent, the product of that shameful act of ours, and I couldn't bear the sight of him. For a long time I hated Hillary as well for having seduced me. And that is what it was—seduction." He pondered the word for a few seconds. "I was, you see, a virgin until that one act of ours, and it would have been better, kinder, had I remained so. I knew, you see, from that moment on, what it was that I had been missing, what it was that other men had that I had not. . . ." He looked down at Thor, asleep against him. "It awakened something in Thor as well. Neither of us has been quite the same since."

He sighed deeply and continued in a different, more conversational tone. "I never saw young René. Those who did—my mother, Hillary, friends, doctors—extolled his beauty of face and his brilliance. His mind was remarkable, they say, and he had the angelic beauty of all the St. Hilaires, but he was born blind and dwarfed, with terribly misshapen legs. Yet there seemed no reason to suppose he would not reach his majority or that he would be unable to beget children. From the age of sixteen he was encouraged to try. . . ."

"As Edward Mordake must have been encouraged to try with Ivy Basset, his servant's daughter," I murmured.

"Precisely. I have no doubt that if that child had been a son and hence able to carry on the line, there would have been a marriage and the name of Mordake would not have died with Edward in seventeen hundred and one. But René could have no children at all. It was discovered after his death that he was quite sterile."

"Nature protecting its own," I said with bitter irony.

Gilbert winced but did not reply. Instead, he continued the story of René St. Mauger. "Last November, nearly a year ago now, he died. Hillary was beside herself. She loved him, you see, as much as she was capable of loving anyone but herself. Mama called me from Paris to Vevey. Hillary was recovering from tissue injection treatments at the time. Rejuvenation," he explained with an ironic smile. "They told me that it was up to me now to carry on the line. At first I resisted the very idea. I had begun to think that with the birth of myself and Thor, that perhaps the cycle had come full circle from Mauger and his Thoret, and that with us, the line was destined to end. But, of course, that was just a rationalization on my part. What frightened me was the ordeal of being with a woman. It is so painful—the attempt at wooing, the rejection, the drugging of the ones who might be willing. . . ." He paused and then went on. "It was easiest with Valdalene Pearsall. She was a whore to begin with and money would make her consent to anything. Drugging her was just part of the game as far as she was concerned. Yes, she was the easiest. . . ." He bowed his head, covering his eyes with both his hands. Thor stirred on his lap but did not waken.

"But it began in London, as you guessed, so accidentally outside a West End theater. One night in the rain I met Samantha Bedell and offered her a lift in my car . . . and it all began.

"I felt impelled to leave London after she died. I came here at the end of January and began to research in earnest the other lines that descended from Ivy Basset and Edward Mordake through their daughter Forgiveness. I knew something of them already, having inherited the Mordake papers from the St. Hilaire side of the family. I knew far more than poor Jeremiah Pearsall. I had always wanted to tell him all about the connection between us and how closely we were related, all the way back down to Mauger himself, but then too, I lived in dread of his ever finding out about Thor."

"I should think if there was anyone who might understand about your obligations to a—a sibling," I said for want of a better, less kind word, "it would have been my Uncle Jeremiah."

He shook his head. "There were—there are—too many irregularities. I could not have borne his scorn, or even his pity." He sighed. "And what a shame too for the papers, volumes and volumes, folio after folio, are in a vault in a bank at Vevey. A thousand years of the history of five allied families, the bloodlines, sins and vices of which are as interlocked as the veins and arteries of a single human body. Jeremiah Pearsall would have given his soul to see—"

I felt the anger well up in me again at that callous rumination of his. "Instead, you have taken his soul to keep him from—"

"It was Thor. I couldn't have killed him. At least," and here he looked down the length of the table at me, his large eyes oddly reflective, "I don't think I could have killed him. . . ."

I thought I could read his mind at that moment. "You raped and sodomized Samantha Bedell and found yourself quite able to kill her. You were inspired to violate Brenda Soldano and Valdalene . . ." I egged him on dangerously.

"Brenda Soldano, as it happens, was the first whose line I was able to trace. I realized that, given her background, age, and upbringing, I could not approach her directly, but once she conceived, I knew that she'd be bound by her religion to carry the child to term."

"That was where the Kennedy Center came in, I take it, and Mr. and Mrs. Sidney. Or Dr. Kennedy and his nurse, as they sometimes claim to be."

"Sidney and India Swindon are my personal servants. They have been with my family since the war. They are among the few who know of Thor. . . .

"If that plan had failed, Thor and I would have kidnapped the infant. Not long after, while I was waiting to see if the attack had led to a conception, I discovered Valdalene Pearsall, and I realized in tracing her line that not only was she a direct male-line descendant of Forgiveness Basset, but that she was also, on her mother's side, a de Bains as well, through the bastard black son of Francoise de Bains, a Louisiana planter. I was particularly anxious to have her child. Black it might be, but it would also be more a descendant of Mauger than any child of Samantha Bedell or Brenda Soldano could ever be."

"And so you beat her up," I said with irony.

"Yes, to intimidate her, to keep her from aborting the baby. She was a fool. The pain wouldn't have mattered as long as the child was born. I even offered her more money, but I had overplayed my hand—she was terrified of me after the beating. I would have thought she'd have been used to rough treatment from the sort she knew, pimps and perverts, but she was afraid of me after that. . . . Well, you know the rest."

"Yes, I know the rest. For good measure you pursued Pamela Bedell, not knowing she had married and you also found Jennifer Pearsall. Jennifer, of course, is your greatest success."

"One out of five," he smiled sadly. "Not very great odds, but they'll have to do. I was proud of thinking up the Kennedy Center. So deliciously sardonic, don't you think? I still didn't know why I found no record of your birth until, in a moment of what he took to be idle chat, Jeremiah Pearsall mentioned that you'd been born in Caracas. If I had known, if I had met you first, how very different things might have been."

"Not so different, I imagine," I said dryly. "It was after you did meet me and realize that like Valda, I had a double descent from Mauger, that Guy Galveston's car was forced off the road."

"Thor wanted him dead," he said simply. "He knew that I wanted to marry you."

"Yes, it was Thor. That I believe. Guy saw the driver's face just before his car went off the road."

"It was Thor too who has made you a widow." And Thor,

hearing his name, roused drowsily from his nap and yawned, showing a repulsive, toothless pink maw.

"A widow," I breathed. True, there had been a welcome silence from Max for a while now. When I collected myself I was able to calculate that it was over a week since he had called.

He nodded slowly, and I could see the quiet, malicious satisfaction glittering in his large gray eyes. "He'll be found soon," he shrugged, "another body floating in the Hudson like so many others. It won't be long. Depends on the tides, I suppose."

"Oh, God," I bowed my head. "When?"

"Late last Sunday night, after we'd been to the Cloisters. Thor wanted to help me, and he loves to drive Sidney's van. . . . It wasn't hard to accost him. He keeps—kept—late hours."

"No," I murmured, close to the tears I dare not shed, close to losing the control that would, if I let go, cost me my life. "I never wanted that. I wanted to be free of him, but I never wanted that." I rose from the table nearly blinded by tears and groped my way to the door. Once in the hall, which lay in almost total darkness, I stopped and leaned against a table that stood in the center of the floor. I had to get my bearings.

Across the small entry hall to my left was the front door. In the dull bar of light that fell from a sconce in the upper hall I could not see if it was locked, though I could tell that the bolt above the old-fashioned box lock had been shot. That was one way out but not the best way. There was snow on the ground, a road to cross, servants to rouse, and the locked door of Uncle Jeremiah's house to negotiate. I did not think that Gilbert St. Mauger or his little brother Thor would let me get that far.

If I could get back past the dining-room doors and down the short hall to the library, I could take up the last of Uncle Jeremiah's books and papers from the desk and disappear through the panel. Still, to get out before he could collect himself might be the wisest course. The things left on the desk were not so vital as what I had already removed and hidden behind the panel. Gilbert didn't know about the panel or the tunnel so the things already there were safe for the time being.

I inched my way to the front door and shot back the bolt. The knob, however, would not turn. An old-fashioned brass key-cover hung down over the keyhole. The key itself, which should have been in the lock, was missing. The panel in the library and the tunnel behind it were my only escape after all.

I heard the dull rasp of a heavy chair on the worn carpeting in the dining room. In a moment, St. Mauger, moving with the slow deliberation of a complacent cat after a trapped mouse, loomed up, a dark figure against the dim light behind him.

"The key is in my pocket, Miranda," he said softly. As he came toward me, the creature he called Little Brother accompanied him, clinging to his chest like a monkey, his lower limbs lost in the folds of St. Mauger's dressing gown, his long, slender, muscular arms draped around his big brother's neck for support. The creature's scrawny, naked, slug-white chest and pale, lank hair made a vivid contrast to the rich burgundy of the robe, loosely belted at the waist by its silken cord.

As they approached, entering the one dim shaft of light that penetrated the darkened hall from above, the cord slowly began to work itself loose. With each step, the gown fell wider open until I, like a snake before a mongoose frozen with fascination by what it has most cause to fear, saw *all* . . . and in one nightmare instant, *knew* all.

St. Mauger saw my face and smiled, a smile at once as evil as Lucifer's and as sad as that of a compassionate Christ. All the while, his Little Brother, his Little Thor, chittered and gibbered in an ugly French patois that I could not understand, its dark eyes flitting between St. Mauger's face and my own, watching each of us in turn, its own countenance one of hideous malevolence and fear. If this was what St. Mauger had lived with all his life, it was a wonder he had not done long ago what my ancestor and his kinsman Edward Mordake had done to rid himself of his own devil twin: taken poison and died to escape.

Somewhere outside in the snow-muffled silence of the night there was a sharp, loud noise, a car backfiring down on Van Duzer Street at the foot of Dissoway Drive perhaps. Whatever it was, that sound saved my life, for it broke the spell of horrified fascination that had kept me for too many precious seconds in thrall to the hideous sight of Gilbert St. Mauger and his Little Brother and enabled me at last to think and to act.

I stepped away from the locked door, feeling my way toward the library, all the while keeping the hall table between us. Once at the mouth of the little passage, I backed down it toward the library doors, keeping my eyes fast on the grotesque figure moving slowly around the table toward me. Even in that low light, I could see that he was trembling with tension and had begun to sweat profusely. No wonder he kept himself so immaculately scrubbed—that choir-boy polish that I had so often noticed was to keep in check the sweat and potential stench of his terrible body.

He was completely naked beneath the dressing gown, and so was Thor, who still clung to his big brother's chest like a pet monkey, his arm around St. Mauger's neck for support. Even in the mercifully scant light that illuminated their two bodies, I had seen enough—could still see enough—to know why St. Mauger felt he could never lead a normal life, experience a normal man's love. I knew why his victims and his lovers as well had to be unconscious, drugged into insensibility before he could lie with them.

For one brief second I gave thought to Hillary St. Mauger, who had couched in incestuous passion with them. The depths of her depravity and perverseness must know no bounds. She had *not* been drugged . . .

The sight of them told me much that had been veiled in mystery. Rape and sodomy had been the pattern. In the one case where semen samples had been available, there had been the semen of two different men with two different blood types.

Brothers could have two different blood types. Twins can have different blood types. Even phantom twins, and parasitic twins . . .

St. Mauger and Thor *were* twins of a sort: fraternal twins, phantom twins, dizygotic twins in whom something in the process of twinning had gone mad, creating from itself a monster—for Thor was more than a mere twin of St. Mauger. He was his parasitic twin, quite legless, growing like a twisted, stunted limb from the perfectly normal body of his host-brother; Thor's loins and genitals growing from the loins of his brother at the pelvis, just above Gilbert St. Mauger's quite normal genitals.

From the hips down, one man; from the loins up, two men with two sets of urges, two sets of passions to sate.

Rape and sodomy. It would always have to be rape and sodomy. For them there was no other way.

"Lady Adeliza saw Mauger like this and still loved him, redeemed him with her love. I dared to hope that you could do as much, that you could love me. . . ."

I shook my head slowly from side to side. To that hopeless dream of his, born out of despair and lonely madness, I could make no answer. I was not Adeliza D'Arques. I was Miranda Fay and my soul was my own.

I stepped backward, feeling the woodwork of the door jamb, hoping against hope that I could get far enough across the room to make for the secret panel before Gilbert and Thor made their move. If I could close and lock the library door on them, they would find the room empty when they were finally able to break in. The panel, once shut and bolted, would betray no secrets and I could make my way safely through the tunnel to Uncle Jeremiah's library. After that, who knew . . .

As I backed into the room, still groping blindly with my right hand, my fingers touched the butt of one of the two medieval crossbows that hung among the arrangements of weapons mounted on the oak panels to either side of the door. I felt a surge of adrenaline and instantly began to think with clarity.

Once I had a solid grip on the stock, I took one more swift step
backward over the threshold and into the library, lifting the crossbow from its hook on the wall with surprising ease as I did. It was
short, compact, and lighter than I had expected. I held it before me
tentatively, trying my finger on the mechanism that fired the bolt
from the bow, praying that the menacing look of it would keep
them at bay just long enough for me to close the door and lock it
behind me.

By then, lumbering and slow though they had been, teasing in
their deliberateness, thinking that I was quite trapped, they were at
last upon me, the stench of their sweat overpowering—more the
musky scent of an animal in rut than that of a human being simply
perspiring.

Then I realized that before they killed me, they wanted me as
they had wanted Samantha and Jennifer and Valdalene.

Only I wouldn't have the mercy of being drugged.

Gilbert lunged and Little Brother grasped my left wrist with his
small, misshapen hand. The dark, ugly talons dug into my skin
painfully with a grip of iron, backed by the whipcord muscles in
those long, slender arms of his. St. Mauger, aroused with both
passion and fury, bent over me, intent on wresting the crossbow
from my hands.

As we struggled, I squeezed the trigger unwittingly and heard
the twang of the catgut cord, the soft thud of the bolt. It had not
much force behind it, the old cord breaking with the release of the
tension after who knows how many years unfired, but it had
enough, at such close quarters, to drive the dart through the breast
of Gilbert St. Mauger and kill him instantly. Only Thor, last of
the St. Maugers, remained alive. He squealed and chittered demo-
niacally as St. Mauger crumpled heavily to the floor at my feet.

I felt as cold as ice as I looked down on them. I knew that that
evil creature, Little Brother, however long he lasted, was ultimately
doomed. Archbishop Mauger's mooncalf twin had lasted a day or
two, terrifying all but Adeliza who knew the secret of Thoret and,
who in her love, had somehow conquered her revulsion. As I

looked down upon the hideous, pitiful being who had been Gilbert St. Hilaire St. Mauger, I could not help but think how sad it was that he had not been loved; that for him there had been no Adeliza D'Arques.

And then I remembered Jennifer. Perhaps somewhere there would have been love for Gilbert St. Mauger after all.

$\triangledown$

Epilogue

As Thor gibbered and pleaded, dread of his own mortality mirrored in his horrid little eyes, I did what I had come to do: I reopened the panel and took back almost but not quite all the papers and books that St. Mauger had stolen when he or Thor had killed Uncle Jeremiah. It would be nice, I reasoned, if the police found stolen items in that house, pointing to Uncle Jeremiah's murder. Finally, I went back down the hall and into the dining room, replaced my chair, wiped any surfaces that I might have touched there and in the front hall, at the door, and back along the walls leading to the library. I took up my flashlight, placed the crossbow artfully by St. Mauger's hands, where Thor obligingly grasped at it, covering it with his own fingerprints in the process, and withdrew behind the secret panel that led to my uncle's house.

My last sight of that dusty, grim room was of Thor, his little eyes red with rage and frustration, beating futilely on the dead body of his brother with what little remained of his own waning strength. His heart would go on pumping for a short while yet, I imagined, but in the end, without the life and strength of his host-brother, he would wither and die.

I came back through the tunnel only once, to rebolt the panel and wire it shut from the inside so that it could not, even by chance, be opened from the Fenton Gibbs house.

Back in Uncle Jeremiah's library, I set his briefcase where it belonged, reshelved the books that St. Mauger had taken, and replaced everything in the bookcase cupboard that hid the secret passage into the tunnel.

By then, the day had dawned, birds had begun to sing to the thin sun that rose over the pristine layer of freak autumn snow that blanketed everything, covering the gardens of the two houses, the walks, and the front steps of two old, near-twin mansions that faced each other across the untouched whiteness of Dissoway Drive.

At a quarter after seven, the caretaker couple, Mr. and Mrs. Swindon, Sidney and India to their few friends, shoveled their way from their quarters over the garage at the back of the Fenton Gibbs property directly to the back door of their master's house.

At seven thirty-five, the police and a paramedic unit in an EMS vehicle arrived at the top of the street and struggled through the unshoveled snow in the front garden and into the house.

At eight, a white-faced, rather shaky policeman walked through the spotless, untrampled snow to the door of my uncle's house to ask if any of us had heard anything unusual in the early morning hours. Of course, none of us had. Rogers slept in the back over the garage in his own quarters and the Lynches, who might have heard something, were, like his niece who had stayed over, in shocked grief and mourning for Mr. Fay, who had died the day before. All had taken sleeping pills and gone through the night in merciful slumber.

At eight-fifteen, the body of Gilbert St. Hilaire St. Mauger was removed from the Fenton Gibbs house by a group of paramedics, all of whom looked like they could use a good stiff drink, and taken to the same morgue that housed the body of his neighbor, Jeremiah Pearsall Fay.

No one who had seen him in death could doubt the fact of his suicide, especially when it was discovered that he most probably had been responsible for the single blow to the side of the head that had killed the elderly retired lawyer who had been his only friend.

It was a wonder, most thought, when the full story of his grotesque deformity came to light, that he had chosen to live so long in such a condition.

Learned papers, the texts of which never got beyond the groves of academe, were written by the score. Newspapers the world over made a nine days' wonder of Gilbert St. Mauger's tragic secret. None of those who wrote connected his story or even his impulsive murder of my uncle with the death of Valdalene Pearsall or the births of the mooncalves whom only we few knew he had fathered.

On the same day that Uncle Jeremiah was laid to rest in Moravian Cemetery in New Dorp, Staten Island, beside the graves of his long dead wife and infant son, his simple casket surrounded by banks of flowers and followed by nearly two hundred mourners, the friends and associates of a lifetime lived in goodness and kindness, Gilbert St. Hilaire St. Mauger and his twin brother Thor were cremated at Fresh Ponds Crematory in Middle Village, Queens, and their ashes released into the custody of Mrs. India Swindon. Neither his young widow nor his sister nor his aged mother were in attendance.

As for myself, I just wanted, as I walked down the long hill from my uncle's grave, to take Molly Brown and go home to Nyack: to Meta and Peter Polhemus and to the cozy comforts of the Hudson Street Tearoom, to the good browsing in the Ben Franklin Bookshop and the Collector's Corner, to long walks along the Hudson, watching the winter sun grow low in the sky—to rest and heal and hibernate till spring—home to Nyack.

THE NEW YORK TIMES, SUNDAY, JANUARY 23
SOCIAL ANNOUNCEMENTS
BIRTHS
St. Mauger
Born to Mrs. Jennifer St. Mauger, née Pearsall, and the late
Gilbert St. Hilaire St. Mauger of New York, Paris, and Vevey,
Switzerland, twin sons on January 18, at Vevey.

If you have enjoyed this book and would like to receive details of other Walker Mystery-Suspense Novels, please write for your free subscription to our:

Crime After Crime Newsletter
Walker and Company
720 Fifth Avenue
New York, NY 10019